Gay Panic in the Ozarks

Ed Bethune

ALSO BY ED BETHUNE
Jackhammered, A Life of Adventure
Anatomy of a Memoir

ISBN: 1497512530
ISBN 13: 9781497512535
Library of Congress Control Number: 2014906447
CreateSpace Independent Publishing Platform
North Charleston, South Carolina

COVER: The Randolph County Courthouse in Pocahontas, Arkansas, built in 1872, is still standing. The photograph is by John Gill of Little Rock. Note: Randolph County is the site of some action in this novel, but the main story is set in fictional Campbell County.

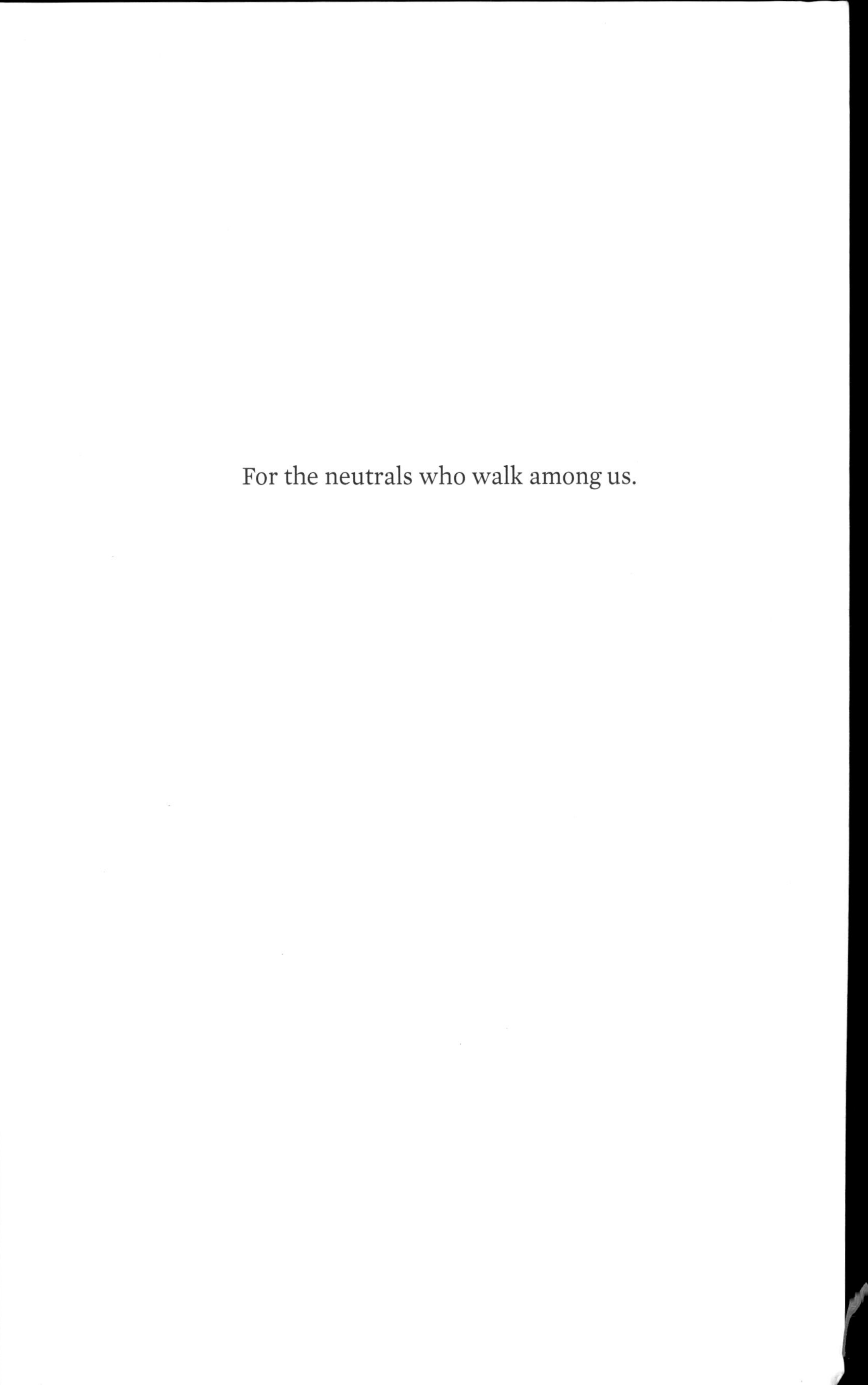

For the neutrals who walk among us.

ACKNOWLEDGMENTS

Writing is a lonely endeavor, but eventually you seek support from others, and this is the place to thank friends and family for their good counsel and encouraging words.

I have always wondered why authors give so much credit to their editors. The process of getting this book ready for publication has cleared that up for me. In 2013 Gene Foreman, who grew up in Arkansas, made a speech in Little Rock. My wife, who went to school with Gene's wife, Jody Baldwin, was in the audience, and afterward she handed him a copy of my manuscript. He read it, liked it, and offered to copyedit it for me. It was a breakthrough to have a man who served as a copy editor at *The New York Times* and, later, as the managing editor of *The Philadelphia Inquirer*, to clean up my work.

Another Arkansas journalist, Jimmy Barden, was a classmate at Pocahontas High School. He wound up as a writer and a national editor for *The New York Times*. Jimmy and his wife, Mel, read my first draft and gave me a boost of confidence,

Judge Robert Edwards, a former law partner and longtime circuit judge from Searcy, Arkansas, and Judge Morris "Buzz" Arnold, a retired judge from the United States Court of Appeals for the Eighth Circuit, graciously volunteered to read my manuscript. Their reviews were timely and insightful.

Several friends read early versions and gave me honest feedback. Janet Crain, Dr. Larry Killough and his wife Julie, and Dr. Porter Rodgers Jr. and his wife Carol, are all members of my Sunday school class. Marshall and Thom Hall are friends from my days in Congress.

Celia Rowe, Jim and Charlotte Gadberry, and Dr. Larry Lawson and his wife Nikki are friends from college days at the University of Arkansas. Steve Stephens is a Marine Corps brother in arms. *Semper Fidelis.*

My son, Navy Lieutenant Commander Sam Bethune, and his daughter, Nicole, an English and art major at Mary Washington University, gave me their unique perspectives at an important moment. I love them.

My wife, Lana, read what I wrote all along the way, and she read and reread the finished manuscript. She has been my constant advisor and encourager from the beginning. I love her.

Finally, I point out that there is no Campbell County or Hawkins County in Arkansas. I created these places and my characterization of the culture in North Arkansas solely to make a point about how we humans can and should deal with our differences.

Indifference may not wreck a man's life at any one turn, but it will destroy him with a kind of dry rot in the long run.

--Bliss Carmen, Canadian poet (1861-1929)

What is indifference? Etymologically, the word means "no difference." A strange and unnatural state in which the lines blur between light and darkness, dusk and dawn, crime and punishment, cruelty and compassion, good and evil. ... Indifference can be tempting—more than that, seductive.

--Elie Wiesel, Holocaust survivor, "The Perils of Indifference," Millennium Lecture Series, The White House, April 12, 1999

PART ONE

1968

ONE

Aubrey and Prissy finished their picnic and stretched out on a shady spot beside Sycamore Lake, wed to each other and to life in the hills of Arkansas.

They listened to the mockingbirds singing their different songs, copycat chords in harmony with the whisper of pine needles and the rustling of leaves. A gentle breeze made a cat's paw on the still water and then came ashore, a zephyr of cool air. The young couple snuggled and spoke warmly of living an unfussy life in the Ozarks. Their sweet talk added melody to the score. It was music, the music of the hills.

Their dream, a bond made as childhood sweethearts, was coming true. Prissy would teach kindergarten; Aubrey would run the family hardware store and work part-time as the deputy prosecuting attorney for their sleepy little county.

Life in the Ozark Mountains, for those who love it, is a magnetic blend of simplicity and hardship, grounded in faith and in an unshakeable belief in the pioneering spirit. It had been good for their parents and grandparents. Surely, it would be good for them.

Soon the afternoon shadows crept farther out onto the lake, darkening the water, warning of wounds and prejudices stemming from the Civil War, the Great Depression, the World Wars and other human tragedies. Such frailties run deep, and like the scab of a putrid wound, they will—from time to time—reopen and ooze pus. When that happens, a discordant note seeps into the music.

On this September afternoon in 1968, a day made for lovers, Aubrey and Prissy Hatfield heard only what they wanted to hear. This is our home. Life is good.

TWO

Nearby, a small boat chugged across the flat surface of the lake, weighed down to the gunwales. The three men in the boat had fished all day without doing a lot of catching. Now it was getting late; bulbous dark clouds gathering in the west explained the stillness and signaled the coming of a thunderstorm.

Their repartee, stoked by a day of beer drinking, turned from arguing about the best crappie holes to naming local heroes. The largest man, Doughboy, was working himself up to do an imitation of the notorious bigot, the Reverend Gerald L. K. Smith.

Junior saw that his friend was getting ready to perform, so he told about seeing the reverend at a tent revival in nearby Holly Springs. "I heard him when I was a kid. He let go with a stem-winder." Junior, a brawny man who had spent his life working on his daddy's hog farm, was eager to brag about having seen a genuine celebrity.

"He had 'em all stirred up about the Jews, and the niggers, and the perverts. He was something else." Junior reared up as if he had more to say, but being a man who used words sparingly, he was finished. He scooted back a little on his end of the boat and pushed his John Deere ball cap back over a disheveled shock of dirty-blond hair. He was ready for Doughboy to begin.

Cletus twisted halfway around to cut off the outboard motor, letting the sixteen-foot flat-bottom boat drift to a standstill. His end of the boat rode a little higher in the water, but otherwise the setting was perfect for the telling of Gerald L. K. Smith lore.

Cletus Bolton had often heard Doughboy mimic Gerald L. K. Smith. He loved to listen to his pasty-faced, roly-poly friend tell about the time the reverend went around the country campaigning for The Kingfish, Huey Long of Louisiana. That episode of politicking was a legend among the natives of North Arkansas, especially those living in the boondocks up near the Missouri border.

Doughboy sat in the middle of the boat, facing Cletus. He always took the center seat because he was so heavy that, if he sat on either end, it would have swamped the boat. His life was uncomplicated: He fished, read and ate, in no particular order.

Cletus' fat ass looked odd on his scrawny body, and Junior had a pooch-gut that hung over his belt, but Doughboy was fat all over. His third-grade classmates called him Doughboy because of his likeness to the Pillsbury logo, and the nickname stuck. That is all anyone ever called him, and it did not seem to bother him.

Doughboy had finagled his way onto the dole before he turned twenty-five by claiming he could not work due to low-back ailments, but his main problem was being fat and lazy. Even so, he had a strong memory. Most folks had heard about Gerald L. K. Smith's oratorical skills, but Doughboy was the one who could recite, word for word, speeches he had memorized from pamphlets saved by his daddy. His daddy, a wiry old coot, had gone to a Huey Long rally in the early 1930s and then had become an apostle for the man many people called The Great One.

Doughboy always took a few minutes to set the stage and get into character. It was his way of storytelling, and he was good at it.

He straightened up, took a deep breath, pitched his voice an octave lower and took on an air of seriousness befitting the memory of the iconic preacher. He started with what the esteemed journalist H.L. Mencken swore was "the best populist speech he ever heard." As his words rolled out across the lake, anyone hearing the recital would agree with Mencken, who also said, "Gerald L.K. Smith is the greatest orator of them all, not the greatest by an inch or a foot or a yard or a mile, but the greatest by at least two light years. He begins where the best leaves off."

"My friends, I am Gerald L. K. Smith." Doughboy's rendition was a thing of beauty. "Let's pull down these huge piles of gold until there shall be a real job, not a little old sow-belly, black-eyed-pea job, but a real spending money, beefsteak and gravy, Chevrolet, Ford in the garage, new suit, Thomas Jefferson, Jesus Christ, red, white and blue job for every man!"

Hill-country folks loved to hear Doughboy tell that one. It is a classic—a rack-up of the hardships and hopes of country people during the Great Depression that puts the worldview of North Arkansans into short verse.

After a pause, during which Junior and Cletus murmured approvingly, Doughboy went on to recite Smith's political war cry for Huey Long supporters: "Lift us out of this wretchedness, O Lord, out of this poverty, lift us who stand in slavery tonight. Rally us under this young man who came out of the woods of North Louisiana, who leads us like a Moses out of the land of bondage into the land of milk and honey where every man is a king, but no man wears a crown. Amen."

Doughboy could have gone on and on, for he had a storehouse of quotes from The Great One. Junior would have listened reverently, but Cletus interrupted.

He usually listened to Doughboy's performances without butting in, but this time the hot rhetoric set Cletus off. "Back then it was jobs and being hungry, but nowadays it's the hippies and the queers. They're fucking up our way of life, and we are just standing around watching it happen."

Railing about the country going to hell in a handbasket was Gerald L. K. Smith's specialty for getting people fired up. Doughboy and Junior may have been targets for such demagoguery, but they were good at heart and easygoing by nature. Cletus, on the other hand, had a mean streak in him that ran deep. He was not a mere target; he was the target's bullseye, and he was quick to explode when provoked about the queers.

Cletus was the only one of the three who had ever been outside of Arkansas. The Campbell County Draft Board called him up in late 1964 at the outset of the war in Vietnam, and he spent thirteen months in the Army at Fort Bliss near El Paso, Texas. Although he did well enough as a mechanic in the motor pool, Cletus was a misfit for military service. He got a General Discharge as a buck-private in 1965 and never told anyone why the Army sent him home early.

Cletus took his mustering-out pay and caught a bus back to the hills. He married twice to women who thought him handsome, but neither could stand him. The first marriage, to an underage girl, ended early by annulment. His second wife turned him in for brutality, a charge she dropped when Cletus agreed to give her the few sticks of furniture they had gathered up in the year they lived together. Now he made enough money to live on by working as what he called a shade-tree mechanic. He lived by himself in an old eighteen-foot trailer. The beat-up Airstream Globe Trotter was parked by his mother's clapboard house, a two-room shack that sat on an acre of weather-beaten land her daddy gave her when her third husband ran off.

Junior did not want to fuss with Cletus. He was in his fifth year of marriage to a girl he started dating in the ninth grade. She had given him two strapping boys, and he liked the way his life was going. Nevertheless, he answered Cletus' rant: "Well, it ain't got too bad around here yet, and I reckon it will be a spell before it will."

"That ain't so," Cletus said. "Just a couple of months ago that A-rab son-of-a-bitch Sirhan killed the other Kennedy boy, and Martin Luther King got shot just a hundred miles from here, over in Memphis. I'm saying the whole world is coming unglued, and the worst of it is coming here!"

"You never gave a tinker's damn for King or Kennedy." Doughboy laughed and then farted to make his point.

"That don't matter," Cletus said. "The niggers burned down Newark last year and then, after King got killed, they did it again. I'm telling you, this ain't like nothing before."

Doughboy said, "Well, that ain't exactly right—how about Lincoln getting shot, or some of the bad shit that happened during the Great

Depression? The stuff that's going on nowadays will pass, just like it has before."

Junior and Doughboy had sparred a lot with Cletus about what they called "the troubles." Their lines were the same every time they argued. Cletus would recite the most recent scuttlebutt about the communists, the One World plotters, the Bilderbergers, the perverts, the hippies, and the liberal Democrats. Junior and Doughboy would let him run on, saving their best line to the end of the argument. When Cletus wound down, one of them would say, "Folks 'round here ain't never gonna cave in to such bullshit." It was a winning point that usually brought a grump from Cletus, allowing them to go on to less controversial subjects, like girls or the latest news about the Arkansas Razorbacks or the St. Louis Cardinals.

This time, however, the customary wordplay took a different course. Cletus did not stop when Junior invoked the "never going to cave in to such bullshit" line.

Junior tried another approach. "Well, it may get worse, but there ain't much we can do about it, and anyway, Cletus, you better stay away from that jackleg preacher over at Draco. Him and that bunch he's put together ain't nothing but trouble."

This was the first time either of them had brought up the group started by Artus MacArthur, a timberman and part-time preacher who lived in nearby Draco. Artus was stirring up the locals and getting some of the ne'er-do-wells to join an outfit modeled after a radical group that The Great One started back in the 1940s.

"Bullshit, Artus is OK. We need more like him," Cletus said. "I'm telling you, it's coming. Look at that mess, them riots in Chicago where the Democrats just had their convention. And how about them perverts in San Francisco, pictures of faggots all over the TV. Fact is, it's already here, right here in these hills. There's a queer running that new grocery store in Woodville. He came in from Chicago, and they say he's sucking dicks all over town, including boys on the high school football team."

Cletus sulked for a while, and then he gathered steam. "This kind of shit's got to stop. Next thing you know, they'll be coming in here in droves."

Junior and Doughboy had listened to Cletus rail against the "perverts" many times, but this was different. Now he had a live target in Campbell County.

"Something's got to be done about that queer."

Doughboy and Junior stared at Cletus as if he were a stranger. He was not frothing at the mouth, but the diatribe about "that queer" bloated his jugulars and bugged his eyes.

Doughboy did not want to hear any more. He used a sure-fire technique to change the subject: "Hey, the Cardinals are about to clinch the National League pennant! Let's talk about that."

It did not work; Cletus restarted his rant.

Just then, Junior jumped into action and let out a whoop, "Hot damn! I got a good-un on the hook. This is that crappie hole we found last month. Where there's one, there'll be a mess. This ain't fishin', boys, this is catchin'!"

Cletus wheezed. He wanted to carry on about the queer—he needed to get it out of his craw—but getting into a mess of crappie took precedence. He picked up his fishing pole and got a line in the water. For the time being, his tirade was over.

THREE

Campbell County Sheriff Mark Odom was watching the second game of the 1968 World Series in his office on the afternoon of October 3. Six friends were crowded into the small room with him. The sheriff had a brand-new twenty-seven-inch RCA color TV, and his office was the only place that the men, county employees, could watch the game and arguably claim to be working.

Ducky Medwick, a Hall of Famer who played left field in 1934 for the Cardinals' Gashouse Gang, tossed out the first pitch. The Cards had won Game One, but they were behind in this one, and the sixth inning was starting. Norm Cash, the Detroit Tigers' first baseman, stepped into the batter's box, and as he did, a message blared on the VHF radio in the sheriff's office. It was the screechy voice of young Dillard Wayson, one of the sheriff's two full-time deputies: "Sheriff, we got a dead body out near Possum Knob, on the old Spradlin Mule Farm."

The sheriff asked his deputy for more details, but just as he did, Norm Cash hit a home run and brought loud groans and a chorus of "Oh, shit" from the sheriff's friends. When things quieted down, Sheriff Odom explained to his deputy that the Cards were now behind 3-0. He said, "I'm going to watch the last few minutes of the sixth inning and then I'll head out to Possum Knob. Has anyone identified the body?"

The deputy said, "No, and that ain't going to be easy."

"Ok, let's hold off on the radio chatter. We'll talk about it when I get there. I'll pick up Mutt and head out that way," the sheriff said.

Mutt was Aloysius Mutchler, the sixty-six-year-old county coroner whose parents had shown no mercy when they named him. He was not a doctor, but, as is commonplace in the hill counties, Mutt ran for the office of coroner uncontested because he was the local undertaker and nobody else wanted the job.

It was late afternoon when the sheriff turned onto Carmie Spradlin's place. There were no mules there anymore—they were long since obsolete—but in the old days, the Spradlins turned out the best line of work animals in North Arkansas.

Deputy Wayson met the sheriff and Mutt as the marked car rolled to a stop near an old breeding barn. He said, "The guy's face is a mess, but judging from what was done to him, I figure it's the new guy at Woodville, the one running that new grocery store."

The sheriff said, "You talking about the queer?"

"Yeah, I'm guessing it's him."

Possum Knob is about as remote from modern civilization as one can get. The closest city, Springfield, Missouri, is almost a hundred miles as the crow flies. But the knob is only twenty minutes from Woodville, a town of three thousand that serves as the county seat of Campbell County.

The three men walked east a hundred yards to Muleshoe Creek, which divides the Spradlin property and runs north to south. Carmie Spradlin found the body there when he was checking a stretch of dilapidated barbed-wire fence that dead-ends into the shallow creek.

The Spradlin place is a good bit east of Possum Knob, and Muleshoe Creek is a backwater tributary that drains into Sycamore Lake. The creek is bone dry during most of the summer, but it fills when the rains come. Sheriff Odom, now fifty-five and in his sixth term, had been all over this place when he was a boy because he grew up on a nearby farm, and the Spradlins allowed hunters to stomp around the place, so long as they did not shoot toward the house. The sheriff, like most boys in Campbell County, grew up hunting but he got his fill of it by the time he was in his forties. In the old days, he could have run full speed to the creek, but now he was thirty pounds overweight, and the short walk had him huffing and puffing. Mutt and the young deputy pulled ahead at first; then, without saying a word, they slowed down so that the three of them reached the creek at the same time.

Most folks in North Arkansas, especially these men who grew up on farms and worked in law enforcement, are accustomed to the rough edges of life. But the grizzly scene at Muleshoe Creek was like nothing they had seen before. This was more than murder. It was the worst kind of torture, the kind driven by hate—the kind that makes the victim scream, call out for mother, and then beg to die.

Sheriff Odom's upbringing included a strong belief that homosexuality is a sin, and there had been a lot of talk lately that the hippies and perverts in the anti-war movement were going to ruin the country. The local preachers inveighed almost every Sunday against the draft-dodgers, free love, and homosexuality. Sodom and Gomorrah got into most every sermon. It was hard to find anyone in Campbell County who disagreed with the preachers, and even harder to find someone willing to promote tolerance for the sinners.

"Man, I don't like faggots any better than the next guy, but this is hard to look at." The victim was hanging by the neck from a large oak tree. The face, grayish in color, was a mess, but there was enough of it left for Sheriff Odom to agree with his deputy. "It does look like the new guy at the grocery."

"It's hard to look at all right, but the smell is worse," Mutt said. He pointed to the mound of goo—excrement and vomit—that lay beneath what was left of the corpse. "There's blood mixed in with that, and I'm betting they busted something inside of him by sticking that hoe handle, over yonder, up his ass." Mutt pointed to a garden-hoe that lay between the body and the creek. The tip of the handle, covered with excrement, bore witness.

The young deputy headed over to the creek to throw up. When he finished, the sheriff told him to go back to the car to get the camera and the crime-scene kit. When he returned they began collecting evidence, marking it the way the sheriff had learned to do at the FBI National Academy in Washington. Sheriff Odom was proud to have graduated from the academy, one of the few sheriffs in North Arkansas to have done so. He always listed that accomplishment first on his reelection campaign cards.

The sheriff put a mint-scented paper mask over his nose and mouth and started collecting samples from the noxious pile of stuff that appeared to have come out of the victim. Mutt had volunteered to get the specimens, but the sheriff said he ought to do it so he could testify that he personally made the collection, thus establishing a direct chain of custody for the evidence.

Meanwhile, Mutt and the deputy made notes and took photographs of the scene from every angle, enough to fill several rolls of film.

The three men then cut the body down and pulled it away from the stink-pile. Mutt began an inspection of the remains, first counting and studying the knife holes that riddled the body. The sheriff and Deputy Wayson scoured the area looking for other clues. They took casts of a few footprints but otherwise found nothing of significance.

When Mutt finished poking around, he announced his working theory of the cause of death. "They beat him up first, and that accounts for his face being messed up. Then they cornholed the poor bastard with that hoe handle and hung him up here and stabbed him, twenty-five times by my count. It was the stabbing around the heart that killed him."

The sheriff thought to himself, *Mutt is never shy about making pronouncements based on the sketchiest proof.* "I expect you are right, Mutt, but as soon as I get back to the office, I'll call the prosecutor to see how he wants us to handle this. I expect he will say we need to send the body to the state medical examiner for an autopsy."

The sheriff told his deputy to stand by at the crime scene. Then he and Mutt got in the car and headed for town. As soon as they were rolling, Mutt said: "It took at least two to do all that, don't you think?"

The sheriff said, "Right, I think one man could have done it, but it looks more like the work of two or more people. There's a bunch of folks up here around the lake that have got no use for queers and perverts." After that, silence. Finally, when they turned onto the main road, the sheriff said: "It's not going to be easy to find out who did it unless someone turns them in, and that ain't likely. There's just not a lot of sympathy for queers around here."

When he got to the office, Sheriff Odom called his old friend, the prosecuting attorney for the Twenty-Ninth Judicial District, Fred Cooksey, who lived in a neighboring county. The sheriff had considered calling the new deputy prosecutor, Aubrey Hatfield, but had decided against it. Young Aubrey had just finished law school, and the sheriff was not sure how he felt about law-and-order issues. Cooksey, on the other hand, was his strongest political ally. The sheriff knew he could talk freely to Fred Cooksey about anything, especially a queer-killing. He knew such a thing as that could become a troublesome political issue, if handled poorly.

The sheriff had met the tall, gangly prosecutor fourteen years before, when he was a deputy sheriff serving as bailiff for an embezzlement trial. Cooksey was prosecuting a man who was so dumb-looking that his own lawyer, in his closing argument, pointed to his client and said, "Look at him. He's too stupid to have planned such a crime." Everyone in the courtroom thought it was a winning argument; the man was sure to get off.

When Cooksey rose to make his rebuttal, he pointed to the defendant and said in a loud voice, "His lawyer says he is too stupid." Then he paused, leaned into the jury box and said, in a crackly whisper, "But I tell you ... he's smart, he's criminally smart." The jury took less than fifteen minutes to return a finding of guilty on all counts.

Deputy Sheriff Mark Odom was impressed with the prosecutor, and Fred Cooksey was impressed with him. He saw the young lawman as a man with a future. They bonded, creating a political machine that had no rival. Cooksey was a great trial lawyer and a master politician. Mark Odom was the best-known, strongest politician in Campbell County.

"Hey, Mr. Prosecutor, it's Mark."

"Hi, Sheriff, what's up?"

"We got a killing up near Possum Knob. The dead man has only been in town for a few weeks. He was the manager at the new grocery store, Bracey's Market, and people have been saying he is—was—a queer."

"Do you know who did it?"

"No, but the body is a mess and, judging from the crime scene, it looks like the guy was killed because he was a queer."

"How do you figure that?" Cooksey asked.

"Well, we have heard it around town—that he was a queer. And, Mutt was up to the crime scene with me, and he thinks the guy was cornholed with a hoe handle."

Fred Cooksey said nothing in response, and the silence caused Sheriff Odom to think the phone had gone dead.

"Mr. Prosecutor?"

"I'm here, just thinking. Let's go slow and not do a lot of talking about what happened. People are mad as hell about everything that is going on in the country, especially all the riots and perversion they are seeing on TV every night. Let's get the facts together before we say too much about this publicly."

The sheriff said, "Right. People are not going to want to point fingers. We need to handle this carefully."

"I'm in a trial right now, but I'll be over in a couple of days and we can talk. Tell Aubrey Hatfield to give me a call and go ahead and send the body down to the medical examiner."

FOUR

"Fred, this is Aubrey Hatfield. The sheriff said you wanted me to call."

"Hey, Aubrey. Looks like we've got a sure-enough murder case for you to cut your teeth on, if we can figure out who did it."

Aubrey said, "The sheriff told me the body was a mess. He thinks the guy was killed because he was a homosexual, but I don't know much more about it. What do you want me to do first?"

"Well, the coroner was at the Spradlin Place with the sheriff, but we'll have to send the body to the state medical examiner for an autopsy. I'll come over there as soon as I finish the case I'm trying, but for openers you ought to go down to Little Rock and watch the autopsy. It'll be good training for you, and you can bring me a plain-English version of what the doctor says. Those damn autopsy reports read like Greek."

"OK, I'll go." Aubrey was amused when Fred pretended that the autopsy report might befuddle him. He knew better; Fred loved to play the fool, but he was one of the state's craftiest prosecutors.

There was a pause, then Fred Cooksey said, "I told the sheriff—and I'll tell you—we need to get the facts together before we start talking about this. The crazy stuff that is going on in the country has people all hot and bothered, and something like this can turn into a political nightmare overnight. Let's take it slow and easy. Get yourself down to the autopsy and then give me a call."

"OK," Aubrey said. He was new to the law-and-order business. This was his chance to learn.

FIVE

Folks in Campbell County seldom miss a chance to go to the big city. Springfield is closer, but a trip to Little Rock, the state capital, offers more to Arkansans. When Aubrey told Prissy he was going there to observe the autopsy, she jumped at the chance to go with him. There was shopping to do, and she wanted to visit her best friend from college who had just taken a teaching job in the big city. It would be a fun day for both of them. Watching the autopsy would be grim, but the two-and-a-half-hour drive would give them a chance to talk. Aubrey was eager to brag about his new responsibilities.

They got up early. The autopsy was set to begin at 10:30 a.m., and they needed to allow a safety margin for any unexpected trouble on the drive down from the hills. Aubrey put on his new blue suit, the one he bought to wear on the day he took the oath to be a lawyer. He was an even six feet tall with a lean athletic look that led most people to judge him handsome, in spite of a knobby nose that listed to starboard—the result of catching a baseball game without a catcher's mask when he was twelve. Prissy LeFever Hatfield, on the other hand, had no distracting features. She was the proverbial china doll—perfect features and a silky look that set her red hair and sapphire eyes ablaze. Aubrey and Prissy were the couple to watch in Campbell County, and they knew it, but it did not seem to affect them, especially Prissy. She never met a stranger, and people filled the pews at the Methodist Church when she was going to sing a solo.

They had barely reached the edge of town when Aubrey began telling how the killing of the homosexual was his opportunity to gain experience and make a name for himself.

"Cases like this come along once in a blue moon, Prissy. We've got to find the killer, but when we do, there will be a big trial, and I will be right in the middle of it."

Prissy started to say something, but she let him go on.

"If the man, Ike Swanson, was killed because he was a homosexual, it raises all kinds of questions that a jury will take into account. People are sick and tired of the assassinations, the riots, and the perverted scenes from San Francisco, but they cannot sanction murder, much less torture and lynching, to protect the way of life we have in the hills. Fred Cooksey says we need to go slow and not rush to judgment. He says the whole thing, if not handled right, could become a political nightmare." Aubrey paused to see how she would react to her husband being a key player in such high drama, but Prissy just stared out the window on her side of the car.

When Aubrey started to tell what he expected at the autopsy, Prissy interrupted. "I don't want to ruin the day talking about such things, Aubrey. Let's talk about good things. And just pray that the prosecutor and the sheriff will not turn a blind eye to finding the killer, and that they will do the right thing."

"They wouldn't turn a blind eye," Aubrey said. "I don't think that is what Fred meant when he said we need to go slow."

Prissy sighed a little and abruptly changed the subject. "This is my favorite part of the trip, from here to where we cross the Buffalo River. I'm so glad the river will be preserved forever."

It was a woman's way to expose flawed motives, and Prissy had the technique down pat. Aubrey got the message. Prissy did not want to hear any more about the murder, particularly what it might do for his career. She had discreetly put her finger on two sensitive issues: Aubrey's preoccupation with what the case might do for his career, and the possibility that the prosecutor and sheriff might let politics and prejudice get in the way of doing their duty. He decided to shut up.

Prissy tuned the radio to a country music station and turned the volume down. Then she started talking about something pleasant. She reeled off a long recitation of the great political victory that protected the free-flowing Buffalo River by designating it as a national river, the first in the nation. For as long as Aubrey had known her, Prissy had loved science, particularly biology and geology. Arkansas was The Land of Opportunity, and Prissy believed deeply that the state's strength lay in the natural beauty of the land. She could have gone on for hours, but once they crossed the Buffalo River, she shifted from things natural. "When we get there, why don't I let you off and then I'll take the car to the mall. I'll pick you up at one o'clock and we can have a late lunch."

"That sounds good to me," Aubrey said, but he was still thinking about her incisive critique of the murder case. For a small woman, Prissy packed a big punch. It was not the first time she had impressed Aubrey with deep thinking and the ability to sum up complex situations. She had been doing it ever since they found each other in the third grade.

She was his first love and, judging by the number of times she asked Aubrey to stop on the curvy road to Little Rock, Prissy was going to be a perfect mother for their firstborn child.

SIX

Prissy dropped Aubrey off at the State Hospital, the old building that housed the office of the State Medical Examiner. There was no receptionist or sign to welcome visitors, but an elderly janitor was mopping a poorly lit hallway. Aubrey asked the man where he might find Doctor Oliver Whitelock. The janitor rose up from his work, gave Aubrey the onceover, and pointed toward the end of the hall he was cleaning. Aubrey headed that way with some anxiety. He had heard stories about the forensic pathologist who had been the state's medical examiner for almost two years. By all accounts, Whitelock was a character of the first magnitude. Some of the tales had made it into the newspapers, and these reports, along with many yarns that remained unreported, supported the consensus of the law-enforcement community: Whitelock is a weirdo.

Aubrey decided to reserve judgment. In fairness, he would treat the rumors as pure scuttlebutt.

He came to a small office at the end of the hall that was next to a set of closed double doors marked "Autopsy." The door to the office was open, and Aubrey saw a man leaning back in an executive chair watching a soap opera on a tiny TV. He had his back to Aubrey.

"Doctor Whitelock?"

The man swiveled around. "Yes?"

Aubrey saw a gnomish little man with a face so busy that he forgot what he had planned to say for openers. The doctor's dark eyes, enlarged by thick glasses, were set overly close to a bulbous nose centered on an oversized head. A longish goatee, half-black and half-silver, grew straight down from the round of his chin, and a green surgical cap sat atop his head.

Whitelock seemed to understand Aubrey's surprise. He smiled, revealing yet another peculiarity—a gold eyetooth with a missing spot just behind it.

"So, my good fellow, you have come to see your first autopsy?" The doctor sounded like a highbred Brit. His speech had the tone and quality of perfect King's English.

"Yes, thanks for allowing me to observe." Aubrey said the words, but he was thinking something else: *This man is a puzzle. I have heard he is weird, but no one told me he looks weird and talks weird.*

Soon, however, Aubrey's genteel manner took over. He decided to push his odd feelings aside and give the doctor the benefit of the doubt. His resolve to be fair did not last long.

With no provocation, Whitelock reeled off a string of salty jokes about homosexuals, bisexuals, and transsexuals. Cackling, he mixed the jokes into a string of blunt opinions about what he expected to find in a body that had been "buggered" with a hoe handle.

Aubrey reversed course.

Good grief! Don't forensic pathologists have a code of conduct? Maybe they don't. Maybe they don't need a code—the dead do not know or care. Doctor Oliver Whitelock is truly weird, but if he is going to be a doctor, he is in the right place. Hmmm ... if there is such a code, I'm certain he is in violation of it.

"Shall we get on with it?" Whitelock led Aubrey through the double doors, into the autopsy room. Aubrey knew he needed to ignore the trash talk and Whitelock's strangeness. He needed to pay attention to the conduct of the autopsy. It was time to focus on the investigation.

When he walked into the laboratory, Aubrey got a shock. No amount of imagination could have prepared him for what he was about to experience. He noticed the chill, and as he absorbed that feeling, he began to process the strange sights, a range of odd but necessary items. A large stainless steel table was in the center of the room directly beneath a powerful light fixture. Strange tools, arranged around and suspended above the table, gave the scene a butchery look.

Large steel sinks and shelves overloaded with supplies were set against the stark white walls. In one corner where the shelving made a turn and ran to the double-door entrance, there were rows of glass containers similar to the Mason jars Aubrey's mother used for home canning. The jars contained assorted body parts from earlier autopsies, presumably kept for some educational purpose.

Doctor Whitelock pointed to one of the larger jars as they entered the room. He guffawed. "This, young laddie, is Henry—well, that is, this is Henry's doinker. It is the largest penis in captivity." Whitelock made a heehawing noise, and that ended the spectacle concerning poor Henry.

Aubrey gave an ambivalent nod and turned away. *How can someone in this line of work be so disrespectful of the dead?*

Whitelock went to the autopsy table. It was time to deal with the indispensable object in the room. The cold, scarred and bloody body of Ike Swanson was face up on the table. Two plastic bags lay between Ike's legs, and a garden hoe was propped against the end of the autopsy table. Clear plastic, held in place by yellow evidence tape, covered the handle of the hoe. The largest plastic bag contained Ike's clothes and the smaller bag contained various specimens collected by the sheriff at the crime scene.

Aubrey was struggling to adjust to all he had seen and heard in the last five minutes. Then, as he focused on Ike's body, it came to him that he was about to watch the weird little man use the gruesome tools to cut the body wide open.

Whitelock offered to put some smell-blocker under Aubrey's nose, but the young prosecutor took it as a challenge to his manhood. "No thanks, I'll be OK."

Whitelock shrugged and set to work on the corpse. He dictated every step of the procedure into a microphone that Aubrey had not noticed; it was above the table, hidden amongst the tools.

Aubrey quickly realized that, for all his faults, the doctor knew his business. In a precise, professional manner, he called out the medical names of each organ—assessing and weighing things, collecting specimens for further study, taking photographs, and moving around the table in a way that bespoke vast experience. Vulgarity had given way to professionalism.

Aubrey was impressed. He asked the obvious question: "How many autopsies have you done?"

"This makes one-thousand-fifty-five," Whitelock said as he pulled an electric saw down from the overhead rack and sawed off the top of Ike's skull. The sound was bad, but the smell of burning bone got to Aubrey, and it was obvious.

Whitelock pointed to the tube of smell-blocker and said, "Why don't you try a little of that? The burning bone is not so bad, but I am about to pull the top of the skull off to examine the brain. Then I will go into the stomach and bowels and that, my good young laddie, will be rather odorous." He guffawed, and Aubrey's pride gave way to common sense. He reached for the smelly stuff and put a good dose under his nose. Then he returned to his spot by Whitelock.

The work went on for another thirty minutes. Then Whitelock said, "Well, that's it for the noisy and smelly part of the autopsy."

Thank God, the gnome has finished sawing, cutting, probing and plundering around in half-digested food and feces.

"I can now opine that the victim was beaten and tortured, but a knife wound to the heart caused his death. There will be a detailed report explaining each wound that I found, but I can tell you now that the traumatic penetration of the anus and damage to the anal canal appears to have been done with the handle of the garden tool found at the scene and brought here for examination." Whitelock was still in professional mode, his proper English and choice of language in stark contrast to the ill-placed jokes and vernacular he used in the beginning.

"I must say, however, that the most interesting thing I found were the burns on the scrotum and the underside of the victim's penis. I have a pretty good idea what caused the burns, based on other work I have done, but I've never seen it during an autopsy," Whitelock said.

"What do you mean?"

"Here, let me show you." He lifted Ike's penis and pointed to several darkened spots. "See, these are burn marks. The killer used some sort of electrical device to shock the victim. It would be very painful."

"No kidding." Aubrey instinctively cupped his left hand over his balls.

Whitelock said, "These burns were most likely caused by something similar to the Tucker Telephone. Ever hear of it?"

Aubrey said, "Yes, guards used it for punishment at Tucker Prison Farm back in the time of Governor Orval Faubus."

"Right you are. Soldiers use similar techniques in wartime to torture prisoners and get information. In those cases, the military uses hand-cranked field phones to generate the electrical current. At Tucker Prison, they used an old-timey hand-cranked telephone."

Aubrey said, "When did you learn about all this?"

"I once moonlighted on a private case. A father sent his son to a clinic that claimed to have a cure for homosexuality. The boy tried to commit suicide, and the family hired me to give an opinion about what the clinic had done to the boy. I established that the people running the place had used a technique they called electroconvulsive therapy. They would send an electrical shock to the boy's genitals while showing him photos of men having homosexual sex. Then they would show the boy pictures of heterosexual acts featuring a man and woman without sending a shock to his genitals. The contrast was supposed to end his preference for men. It was pure quackery. I know of no patient that has ever been cured by it."

Aubrey said, "Are you suggesting they gave poor Ike electroconvulsive therapy before they killed him? Man, that's sick."

"Well, it's just a theory, but it tends to explain how and why the burns got on the victim's genitalia." The doctor was still in professional mode, and Aubrey was gaining considerable respect for the odd little man.

Whitelock then opened the plastic bags and began an examination of the clothes. He noted what appeared to be body-fluid stains, possibly semen, on the underwear the victim had been wearing. "All this—the hoe handle, the clothing, the specimens, all of it—needs to be sent to the FBI Laboratory in Washington, D. C. for further testing. I'll check for blood types, but the FBI has the capacity to check hairs and fibers and analyze these spots on the decedent's underwear that appear to be semen stains."

"What about the chain of custody, how do you typically handle that?" Aubrey felt the need to act like a lawyer.

Whitelock said, "Well, the state police brought the body and other items to me, so I will ask them to pick it up and send it to the FBI. That's what I usually do and that preserves the chain of custody, something you lawyers always worry about."

"You said those might be semen stains. Can the FBI tell us whose semen it is?"

"The semen samples will only reveal a blood type. The semen could be the victim's, or it could have come from another person. If the blood type of the semen is different from the victim's, then it obviously came from another male, and that might be of some help in the investigation, even though it will not conclusively tie a particular person to the collected sample."

Aubrey said, "I thought it might tell us more."

Whitelock paused. "The research scientists are working on a model they are calling DNA. They say it will be a foolproof way to establish that a particular person is the source of a particular sample of body fluid, but it will be several years before they perfect it. For the time being we are stuck with blood type."

The autopsy was over and Aubrey's first impression of Whitelock as a weirdo was almost gone, washed away by the doctor's professional demeanor and precise language. He shook Whitelock's hand and said he looked forward to talking again when the FBI finished its work.

Aubrey started out the door and Whitelock said, "Hey, young laddie, did you hear the one about the faggot confessing to the priest?" He was out of professional mode. Mister Hyde had returned.

"Doc, I've got to go. My wife's picking me up and we've got a date for lunch."

Whitelock reprised the heehaw noise he made when he was discussing Henry's doinker.

Aubrey hustled down the hall to the exit, shaking his head. *Whitelock may be weird, but he is also a pro.*

SEVEN

Aubrey and Prissy went to the historic Sam Peck Hotel in downtown Little Rock for a late lunch.

Aubrey whispered something to the hostess when they entered the restaurant, and she led them to a corner table overlooking a small swimming pool. It was where they had dined on their honeymoon in late May. Aubrey said, "I love this place." Then he winked at Prissy and added, "And I especially love the memory of our wedding night."

Prissy blushed and picked up her menu. She took one look at it and started giggling. "Look, Aubrey, the chef's special today is pasta primavera. What a coincidence. We had chicken cacciatore the last time we were here. And then we spent hours talking about going to Italy."

"We'll go to Italy someday, Prissy. We are off to a great start. I'm going to make my mark as a lawyer and then ..." He pointed upward, "The sky is the limit."

They ordered the primavera with insalata mista, and when the waiter left Prissy returned to her dream. "I love living in the hills and coming to Little Rock, but I really do want us to travel abroad. In Florence I want to see the statue of David and go to the Uffizi. And then we will go to Paris—to the Orsay and the Louvre."

Prissy was unleashed. Aubrey knew it, so he leaned back and relaxed, occasionally nodding agreement and grinning. She was in her dream world and loving every minute of it. This is what had attracted him to her when they were young teenagers. Once they started dating, they never broke up, not once. Aubrey mused, *I am a lucky man to have such a woman. She loves me. And, best of all, she loves life and wants to live it to the fullest.*

Their food came, but it did not slow Prissy down. Aubrey got in a few words, mostly to show his interest. Finally, she wound down and it was time to leave. She giggled again. "Sorry, I get carried away."

"I know. It is what I love most about you."

In mid-afternoon they drove north across the Arkansas River, heading for home. It was a beautiful Indian summer day, a perfect time to talk about Prissy having a baby.

"I have to pinch myself," Aubrey said. "We have talked about having a family since we first started dating, and now it is all coming true."

"Oh, it's real, all right. I'm beginning to show, and for the first time in my life I get carsick, especially on hilly roads."

"Well, there are many good stopping places on the way home. Let's relax and enjoy the trip, especially the views." Aubrey pointed to the trees bordering the highway. "There isn't much color down here yet, but when we get farther north, closer to home, we'll see plenty."

"That sounds good, particularly the part about stopping several times," Prissy said.

They laughed, and that gave Aubrey a chance to sneak a quick peek. Although Prissy said she was showing, he could not see it. The talk of pregnancy, carsickness, and showing was a new experience that made him anxious but not overly so.

Prissy is petite, but she is very strong physically and no one questions her emotional makeup—she is a woman of strong faith. When she sets her mind to something, it is best to get out of her way. Everyone knows that about Prissy.

It was getting dark when they parked in front of their apartment, one of eight in a small building near the center of Woodville. They had spent the entire drive home talking about getting a house, saving up enough money to make a down payment, decorating a nursery for their baby, and making ends meet, things like that.

The stops along the way gave Prissy a chance to breathe the crisp fall air and get her bearings, but they served a greater purpose. The Ozarks, as seen from a variety of overlooks along the road north to Campbell County, are stunning. Each panorama offered a fresh perspective to the young lovers. Sometimes, the valley caught their eye; sometimes, the hilltops. The ever-changing vistas took them beyond day-to-day practicalities. Inspired, they made sweet talk and created memories. Prissy said, "The valleys and hilltops are such a contrast. It's God's way of reminding us of the highs and lows in life."

They stopped four times in all. The colors were prettiest when they got higher in the hills, nearer to home. At each site, they held each other close and spoke of their love and the miracle of childbirth.

EIGHT

Aubrey woke up early the morning after they got back from Little Rock. Taking pains not to wake Prissy, he gave her a kiss on the cheek and left the house for the short walk to Hatfield's Hardware.

Before going into the store, Aubrey stopped at Gentry's Pharmacy to join the Saturday morning coffee klatch.

"All right, we'll get the straight skinny now—here's the new deputy prosecutor." The ruddy-faced man at the end of a large oblong table was Sonny Childs, the town loudmouth. His black cowboy hat was cocked back, a sure sign that he was holding court. He never missed the Saturday morning klatch.

Similar gatherings take place in every little town in the South. The klatch at Gentry's Pharmacy got started just as the Great Depression was winding down. Since then, at least eight full-throated participants have filled the table by 7:30 every morning except for Sundays and Christmas Day.

Sometimes as many as a dozen men showed up to gossip, sip coffee, and eat the homemade cinnamon rolls that Ernie Gentry baked fresh each morning.

There were only eight chairs around the table. Latecomers had to stand, lean against the wall, or sit on anything close to the table. One of the extras could take a seat in an old dentist's chair positioned between the klatch table and a wood-burning fireplace. It had been in that spot for so long that no one, not even Mr. Gentry, could remember how it got there.

The klatch table was full when Aubrey came in. He knew they were going to quiz him about the murder of "the queer," so he decided to show courage. He took a seat in the dentist's chair—a choice that made him look silly and guaranteed at least two minutes of ridicule.

"So what are you doing about the murder of that queer, Mr. Brand New Deputy Prosecuting Attorney?" Sonny was insufferable most of the time, but this question oozed sarcasm as well as prejudice. Aubrey decided the best course of action was to abandon the courage strategy. He ducked the question, hiding behind the fact that he was just the deputy.

"Well, it happened just four days ago, and we are in the early stages of investigation. I am meeting with Fred Cooksey next week—he's in trial over in Hawkins County. I can't talk about it much until after I meet with Fred."

"Bullshit. You all ain't got anything, and you know it. At least that's what the sheriff says." Sonny drew laughter from the usual sycophants, but a few did not seem to think it funny.

Aubrey did not take offense. He had been a regular at coffee klatch since he returned to Woodville earlier in the year, a brand-new graduate of the University of Arkansas School of Law. Rude questioning was standard procedure.

Aubrey ended Sonny's clumsy inquest. "Give us some time. These things are not solved overnight."

With that, the conversation turned to something that really mattered to the klatchers. It was what they had been arguing about when Aubrey came in: the shellacking that the lowly Woodville High School football team had taken the night before at the hands of the Brasstown Bengals.

The Friday night football game got a twenty-minute replay, down for down. The klatchers worked themselves to frenzy level, finally concluding that the Woodville team was the worst in twenty years—not, as Sonny contended, the worst ever.

Aubrey decided to take his leave before the klatchers returned to the murder. He worked his way out of the dentist's chair and slipped through a narrow opening in the wall that led from Gentry's Pharmacy directly into Hatfield's Hardware. Squire Gentry, the first Gentry to run the pharmacy, and Aubrey's grandfather were the best of friends. In 1918, they knocked an opening in the shared wall that separated the two businesses and called it "The Hole." It allowed customers to pass from one store to the other without going outside, but more important, the Gentrys and the Hatfields could visit and cover for one another when business was slow. Aubrey loved The Hole. To his way of thinking, it symbolized the best part of small-town life in the hills of Arkansas.

Aubrey unlocked the store's front door and turned the double-sided cardboard sign so that "Open" faced the street. Hatfield's Hardware first opened for business in 1910 as a combination dry-goods store and blacksmith shop. When the newfangled automobiles and auto-trucks showed up in Woodville, Aubrey's grandfather, "Mac" Hatfield, closed the blacksmith shop and converted from dry goods to hardware. It was a good move. The store—a true family business run by every member of the family—prospered until the Great Depression hit in 1929. The family took a beating financially, but they managed to keep the store open, and the business recovered during World War II. Grandfather Hatfield died the day the atomic bomb obliterated Hiroshima. Aubrey's father, Amos, took Grandfather Hatfield's place, and that put Aubrey next in the line of succession. He had worked in the store since he was a boy, sweeping out, dusting, stocking shelves, and making sales after he got old enough to handle money.

Now that his father was dead, Aubrey—the last of the Hatfields—was the sole owner of the store he loved. It was in a red-brick, one-story building on a corner near the courthouse. People approaching the store from any direction could not miss the stylish sign painted on the big glass window: HATFIELD'S HARDWARE. The letters were in black bordered in gold, and the paint was always fresh; Grandfather Hatfield believed people would judge a business by its signage, so he had the lettering repainted every three years whether it needed it or not.

A 1915 photograph on the wall behind the cash register showed Aubrey's father when he was a boy, standing alongside Grandfather Hatfield. Behind them were rows and rows of perfectly organized merchandise. Now, more than fifty years later, shelves loaded with goods of every description ran from the oiled wood floor to the ceiling. Kegs of nails and boxes of who-knows-what lined the aisles, all tactically placed. It was safe to say, as Grandfather Hatfield first proclaimed in 1920, that Hatfield's had "everything under the sun." The occasional customer would need help finding things, but the regulars, the plumbers and carpenters, usually knew right where to look. Occasional or regular customers who needed help could turn to a Hatfield, and if that did not work, they could ask Mabel.

Mabel Ostner was a fixture at Hatfield's Hardware. She began working there in 1918, shortly after Aubrey's grandfather changed from blacksmithing and selling dry goods to hardware. Mabel might have lived a different life, but she had been smitten at age twelve with a neighbor boy who was five years older. It was love at first sight, but the boy joined the Army to fight in World War I and died during a poison-gas attack in the fields of France. Devastated, Mabel could not bring herself to love another. Grandfather Hatfield gave the girl a job at the hardware store, and she outlasted him and his son Amos. Now, fifty years later, she was working for Aubrey, a third-generation Hatfield.

Mabel was a town favorite, particularly with the tradesmen. Everyone knew about her lost love, but she never showed the grief she felt. On the contrary, Mabel was flirtatious. When she was young, she used her blue eyes and provocative figure to enliven the place. Now sixty-eight years old, Mabel found other ways to keep the customers happy. She was still a flirt, but her voice had become raspy, coarsened from her incurable habit of chain-smoking ultra-strong Picayune cigarettes. Her sensual body had given way to deep wrinkles and the shriveling of old age. None of these changes bothered the customers. *Au contraire*, everyone loved Mabel.

She had opened and closed the store almost every day for forty years. The Hatfields were lucky to have her, and they knew it. She kept the books, paid the bills, ordered the merchandise, and supervised the boys who cleaned up, stocked the shelves, and made deliveries.

When Aubrey's father died in 1967, Mabel began to change. Aubrey noticed it when he was home for Christmas during his senior year of law school. He was working the cash register and Mabel was helping a new customer find a plumbing fitting. She called out, "Aubrey, can you come over here a minute?"

Aubrey finished checking out his customer and made his way from the cash register to the end of an aisle stuffed with goods. There he found Mabel and the young customer plundering through bins that held fittings of every size and shape.

Mabel said, "We are looking for a half-inch brass, ninety-degree barbed elbow, and I can't seem to find one. Can you help me?"

Aubrey knew something was wrong; she had never asked for help before. When he got close, he saw a Mabel he had never seen. A tear filled the corner of her eye, and she was struggling to make the best of a clumsy situation. Mabel was looking in the wrong place. When Aubrey was a boy, he and Mabel had moved all the brass fittings to the shelf behind where Mabel and her customer were looking.

Aubrey made a quick decision to take the blame. He said, "You know, Mabel, I moved those to the shelf behind us last month. Sorry, I should have told you." The three of them turned around and Aubrey pointed to the exact half-inch brass fitting they were looking for. "Here it is," he said.

Mabel led the customer to the cash register and checked him out. When he was gone, she turned and looked into Aubrey's eyes. Before she could say anything, he put his arms around her and pulled her close.

Mabel was his mentor. Aubrey followed his mother's counsel when it came to family and spiritual matters, but for advice about earthy things, he turned to Mabel. She had taught him a lot about the hardware store, but she had also taught him to understand and accept people for what they are. She always said, "There's good in everyone, Aubrey. Your job is to look for it." Most important, when Aubrey entered pubescence, he had felt free to ask her questions about women. He had hundreds of questions that Mabel tactfully answered, questions he would never have asked his mother.

Now Mabel was hurting, but with classic stoicism, she eased away from Aubrey's embrace. She squared her shoulders, looked him in the eye, and said, "Aubrey, I've got a memory problem." Then, before he could say a word, she said, "The doctor says it is dementia. He thinks it is the slow kind, but he is not sure about that. I'd like to keep working—this store is my life—but I don't want to be a problem for you."

"You could never be a problem for me, Mabel. You are family. I'm just getting my feet on the ground as deputy prosecutor and I'm opening a little law office across the street, but I'll be here in the store most of the time."

Aubrey could see that Mabel was uncomfortable with the prospect of living with limitations. He held her face in his hands and looked deep into her eyes. "I love you, Mabel. Don't you worry. We'll work this out, together." Mabel seemed relieved.

Aubrey did not know much about dementia. But he knew it would get worse, it would not get better.

NINE

Aubrey was looking forward to docket day at the Campbell County Courthouse. The old gray-stone building, one of the oldest courthouses in the state, was interesting if not charming. It was a perfect setting for Aubrey's first appearance in Circuit Court, and he was proud that he would have a role to play as the new deputy prosecuting attorney.

It was customary for Circuit Judge Homer Simpson to sit at one of the counsel tables when he called the civil docket. Lawyers for plaintiffs and defendants responded to the call of each case with a short statement about its status. Some cases were set for trial, some were dismissed, and some were passed to the next term of court. The relative importance of a case seemed to make no difference; the lawyers for the affected parties performed on cue. They preened themselves to curry favor with the judge, using styles that ranged from bombastic to silly. It was crude theater at best, and Judge Simpson, an ultraconservative who had his favorites, was always the star of the show.

Aubrey, being the newest member of the bar, had no civil cases, so he watched the first thirty minutes of the docket call to get the feel of it. Then he went into the empty jury room for a meeting with his boss, Prosecuting Attorney Fred Cooksey, who had just finished a four-day trial in Hawkins County. Sheriff Mark Odom had a stack of files concerning the dozen criminal defendants scheduled for arraignment that day. The sheriff had worked out plea bargains for all twelve cases before Aubrey took the job as deputy, so the docket call was going to be pro forma. The defendants would enter pleas of guilty, the judge would ask for the prosecutor's recommendations, and Judge Simpson would impose the agreed-upon sentences. It was the time-honored way to clear the criminal docket; Aubrey would learn later that the sheriff was all-powerful when it came to deciding what the sentences would be.

He listened and learned, but Aubrey was eager to give his report on the autopsy. Fred Cooksey finally turned to Aubrey and said, "OK, tell us what the medical examiner said about the body."

Aubrey led off with what he believed would be most interesting. "Doctor Whitelock—he's a real character—thinks Ike Swanson was tortured with a Tucker Telephone shocking device before he was killed. He saw some burns around the scrotum, and it reminded him of a case he worked on a few years ago that involved a homosexual."

They were attentive but oddly quiet, so Aubrey continued with what Whitelock said about the hoe handle and electroconvulsive therapy. He was well into the subject of aversion therapies when the prosecutor interrupted.

"That's all very interesting and it goes to motive, but what did Whitelock say about the cause of death? After all, the charge—if we ever find the killer—would be murder, not torture."

"He said a knife wound to the heart is what caused the death." Aubrey said.

Sheriff Odom said, "Well, old Mutt had it right. He's pretty good at these things. I don't know why we waste time and money on autopsies in cases like this."

Aubrey then told about the blood-type testing that Whitelock was going to do. "He took some samples that he will analyze, but said he was going to ask the state police to send the clothes, hoe handle, and other evidence to the FBI Laboratory to check for hairs and fibers, semen stains, and things like that."

The prosecutor pointed to Sheriff Odom and said, "Well, the sheriff here has asked the state police to follow along on our investigation. Isn't that so, Mark?

The sheriff nodded and said, "Yes, 'follow along' is right. They know I'm always going to take the lead. In this case, my deputies and I have already been asking around to see if anyone knows anything about the killing. The motive seems pretty clear. Somebody doesn't want queers in Campbell County."

Ted Cooksey said, "Well, you'll do a good job—you always do—but it won't be easy getting someone to tell who did the killing. But, for now we better get back in the courtroom. Judge Simpson is about ready to start calling the criminal docket. I'll do the first two or three cases so you can see how it is done, Aubrey. Then you can take over and finish up so I can get an early start back to Hawkins County. Let's keep each other posted on developments in this murder case, but let's continue to downplay it until we have all the facts."

The meeting was over. Aubrey left the jury room and headed into the courtroom. As he did, two words drifted through his mind. Prissy had used the words the day they drove to Little Rock for the autopsy: blind eye.

TEN

Once docket day had come and gone, the job of deputy prosecuting attorney did not take much time. Aubrey had to attend Municipal Court to oversee traffic tickets and misdemeanors, but that took only a couple of hours every Tuesday and sometimes Friday.

It had taken him less than half a day to furnish and decorate the small room he rented for his law office. He put a sign on the door telling prospective clients to walk across the street to Hatfield's Hardware if they wanted to see him.

It was the best he could do for the time being. The prosecutor's job paid only $175 a month. Prissy's teaching job paid a fair salary, but she was pregnant and wanted to be a stay-at-home mother after the baby was born. He thought about closing the store to give him more time to build a law practice, but he loved the store and needed the little bit of income it generated. Besides, he had to think about Mabel. It would kill her if Hatfield's Hardware were to shut its doors forever.

Aubrey also had to worry about his mother. She was sixty and her health took a nosedive after she lost Amos, Aubrey's father. The doctor told her she had an enlarged heart and gave her some medicine, but she needed someone to look after her. Aubrey was her only child and the last Hatfield, so he pledged himself to check on his mother, every day if possible.

Vera was living alone in Hatfield House, a slightly eccentric Victorian three-story that Grandfather Hatfield built in 1915. The bright-white, blue-trimmed house was downtown, now surrounded by businesses and a cluster of cheaply built duplexes. It was an impractical place to live, suitable only for someone with a spiritual bond to its oddities. Aubrey grew up there and had such a connection. So did his mother. Aubrey told Prissy it would take a stick of dynamite to get her out of the old place.

Prissy had brought Vera Hatfield to the courthouse to wish her son well on his first day as a lawyer. But he had not been to Hatfield House to see her for several days, and he felt bad that he had not. It was Thursday, Prissy's night to play bridge with girlfriends, so as soon as Aubrey closed the store, he walked to the homeplace. It was a short walk he had made thousands of times.

As soon as he stepped onto the porch and neared the screen door, his mother called out, "Is that you, son?" She knew it was Aubrey because her sitting spot in the kitchen gave her a clear view of anyone walking to or from the hardware store. Nevertheless, she always framed her greeting as a question, and he loved her for that. She was a soft-hearted woman from the Delta, reactive by nature. It was not her way to be pushy or declarative. She met and married Amos when she was eighteen years old, and he brought her to the hill country where the natives had a harder, more independent makeup. Vera fit right in, but she never surrendered a bit of her gentle nature. Eventually she became a role model for the churchgoing folks at First Methodist, where she was a fixture. People said "Vera Hatfield has a shine about her," meaning she acted the way a Christian ought to.

Her closest friends – the pastor and other churchgoers – figured Vera for a simple believer because she did not flout the depth of her knowledge about religion. She just smiled, gracious to all. Aubrey knew better. Vera was a complex woman, well read—a deep thinker. When she was not in her sitting spot in Hatfield House, she would go to her thinking spot, a small library to the left of the foyer.

Vera loved the Bible and knew it from cover to cover, but as she drilled into Aubrey, "You can't know about heaven if you don't know about hell."

So, to learn about hell, Vera turned to the poetry of Dante Alighieri. But to avoid sounding snooty when talking about such things, she downplayed her knowledge. "Oh, I just learned those things from Al, a friend I met at school."

Vera was more open about her study of the great poet when talking to her son. She would say, with a wink and grin, "The poet Virgil took Al on a tour of hell, and Al has been kind enough to tell me all about it in his *Divine Comedy.*" That was just one of the ways she encouraged Aubrey to study the classics. But, he found them boring and preferred to spend his spare time on the baseball diamond. Later, when he was a freshman at the University of Arkansas, Aubrey tried to read Dante, but he got confused, lost interest, and put it aside.

Aubrey's father, an independent cuss, professed Christianity but was not a churchgoing man. Although Vera could talk circles around most theologians, she never pushed Amos to religion. Instead, she took her son to church every Sunday and encouraged him to be an usher when he turned fifteen. That, she said, was a job he could and should keep for the rest of his life.

Aubrey liked to think he had inherited his mother's gentle, God-fearing nature and his father's rugged independence. He loved them both, but one had a soft heart and the other a hard head.

"Hi, Mother. What's for dinner?" Aubrey knew she loved him to stay for a sit-down meal. He also knew that she would have spent the afternoon making cornbread and cooking a pot of greens, his favorites.

They sat at the kitchen table, she in her usual spot and he across from her, sitting on a stool he used as a young boy. When he finished off the greens and sopped up the last of the pot liquor, Vera handed him a clipping from the weekly newspaper. It was a short story reporting that Aubrey had passed the bar examination. It also mentioned that Fred Cooksey had selected him to be the deputy prosecuting attorney for Campbell County. She said, "I'm so proud of you, Aubrey, and your father is proud too." She always spoke of dead Christians as if they were still alive.

They talked about the store and his new job as deputy prosecutor, but Vera was more excited about the fact that Prissy was going to give her a grandchild. As it neared the time for Aubrey to leave, he felt he had to tell her about Mabel having dementia. Though Mabel and Vera were polar opposites, they loved each other like sisters.

Aubrey was a little surprised when his mother took the bad news in stride. “I know. She told me some time ago that she was having trouble remembering things, but she thought it would pass. I told her she ought to go see the doctor, but she kept putting it off.”

Aubrey said, “She told me she wants to stay on at the store as long as she can, and I told her we could work something out. She doesn’t want to be a problem—isn’t that just like her?”

They talked for a while about how Mabel chose to live the life of an old maid after her true love was killed in World War I, and they agreed that she had done it out of loyalty, her strongest character trait.

Aubrey said, “It’s that sense of loyalty that has kept her at Hatfield’s for fifty years, and that’s why we have to help her in every way we can.”

“You always do the right thing, son. I pray every day for you and Prissy, and Mabel.”

ELEVEN

Deputy Prosecuting Attorney Aubrey Hatfield made his fourth official appearance in the Woodville Municipal Court three weeks after the murder of Ike Swanson. Unlike on docket day in circuit court, he was the only lawyer in attendance except for the judge, George Stanhill, a one-eyed octogenarian who had the job mainly because he was the only other licensed lawyer in Campbell County.

The court was meeting upstairs in a buff-brick two-story building that the WPA put up in 1939. City offices took up most of the first floor.

It was a slow day at court. Only a few poor souls had come to answer for traffic tickets and minor criminal offenses. Three arresting officers, present to testify if necessary, sat to the right of the old judge on a pew salvaged from the rubble of the One Way Church after a tornado leveled it in 1950.

One of the officers was Deputy Sheriff Dillard Wayson. Aubrey heard him joking and bragging, in stage whispers, to the other officers about his role as the first officer to arrive at the scene where "the queer" was murdered. His crude talk about the murder concerned Aubrey, because he had not heard from Sheriff Odom or Fred Cooksey since docket day, and he thought the strategy was to keep the matter low key until they had all the facts.

When Judge Stanhill adjourned court, Aubrey got Deputy Wayson off to the side, and said, "I heard you talking about the murder case. I haven't heard anything, but then I've been busy at the hardware store. Anything going on that I need to know about?"

Wayson said, "No, we have been asking around, but so far we don't know any more than we did. The sheriff himself has been busy with politics and other stuff, and he says Cooksey told him to go slow until we get a final report on the autopsy and the stuff that was sent off to the FBI."

"Well, keep me up on what you are doing." Aubrey did not like the sound of what he heard from the deputy sheriff. He headed back to the hardware store, stopping first at Gentry's Pharmacy to get a cup of coffee. When he started through The Hole, he heard Mabel entertaining two young tradesmen with one of her bawdy stories. It was good to hear her laugh. She was in top form, thoroughly enjoying herself. Aubrey grinned and quietly backed out of The Hole into the pharmacy. He waved to the counter-girl and headed across the street to his law office to call the medical examiner.

Doctor Whitelock answered Aubrey's phone call on the fourth ring. When Aubrey identified himself, Whitelock said, "Hello, laddie. I was about to ring you up, but I'm busy just now. I'll ring you back in a few minutes." He hung up, but not before Aubrey heard the voices and music of Whitelock's favorite soap opera in the background.

At the top of the hour, Aubrey's phone rang. "Aubrey, Whitelock here. I have just received the lab reports from the FBI, and I am about to write my final report. You will be receiving all this from the state police, but I now have an opinion about what took place at the crime scene."

Aubrey thanked him for calling back, but he skipped the customary chitchat that most Arkansans use before getting to the heart of things. "Go ahead, Doc. I'm eager to hear what you think."

"First, my report will say that the cause of death was a penetrating stab wound to the right ventricle of the heart. It went through the cartilages of the seventh and eighth ribs, severed them, and then passed through the pericardial sac and through the heart. The fatal wound was one and one-half inches end to end, and the depth of the wound was approximately three and one-half inches. The other knife wounds, twenty-four of them, were similar in width, but none was deeper than the fatal thrust. The killing instrument was probably a common hunting knife, not a big Bowie knife, but I cannot be sure about the length of the blade."

Aubrey started to ask about the blows that struck the victim, but Whitelock did not give him a chance. "By the way, the laboratory report says they found no hairs or fibers of interest, but they did find several semen stains, and this is where the report may help you with the investigation."

Whitelock paused. Aubrey assumed the doctor wanted to see if he had learned anything when he attended the autopsy. He remembered Whitelock's dissertation about semen and blood typing, so he said, "When I was in Little Rock you said it is possible to determine the blood type of a person from their semen. Is that what you mean?"

Whitelock, sounding pleased with his student, said, "Exactly, young laddie, but the laboratory found three different blood types among the semen samples. One was type AB, a relatively unusual type that matches the victim. Another was type O, the most common blood type. And, the third was type A, the second most common blood type."

"Does that mean there were two assailants?"

"Well, you are skipping a more important question. Why were the stains on the victim's undergarments, and were they there due to some previous sexual encounter with men who had nothing to do with the killing?" Whitelock paused again, giving Aubrey time to realize that he still had much to learn.

"Good point, Doctor. What do you think it means?"

"I will not put this in my formal report because I should not speculate based on assumptions that can be disproved rather easily. Nevertheless, I think it is plausible for investigative purposes to assume that the semen came from the assailants—two assailants."

"But that doesn't answer the question of how or why the stains were on the undergarments," Aubrey said.

"Laddie, you are new to this business, so let me put it in the vernacular. My educated guess is that the killers first tortured the victim with the Tucker Telephone. Then they beat him half to death, and buggered him with that hoe handle. That got them excited, so they had a circle-jerk and shot their loads onto his undergarments. By then they realized they had no alternative but to kill the poor devil, so they strung him up on the tree and went to work with the knife. Is that plain enough for you?"

"It's more than plain, but I got it, Doc." Aubrey realized that he had been unfairly judging Whitelock. A split personality like Whitelock's is a good, perhaps essential qualification for a forensic pathologist. It takes Doctor Jekyll to probe with medical precision, but it takes Mister Hyde to visualize the evils that haunt the criminal mind.

Aubrey thanked Whitelock and promised to keep him up to date. He left his law office and headed straight to the sheriff's office. It was time to have a talk with Sheriff Odom, and then he would call Fred Cooksey.

TWELVE

Aubrey was eleven years old when Mark Odom won a hotly contested race for sheriff. He had served less than a year as a deputy sheriff, but his lack of experience made no difference to the voters. The Odom family came to Campbell County before the Civil War. Mark's father and grandfather each served two terms as county judge, and his mother served ten years as county clerk. All the Odoms knew a lot about county-level politicking, but Mark was born to be their star. He had the lean, lanky look of a young Abe Lincoln with the face of a cherub, but he also had a knack for schmoozing with bankers one minute and truck drivers the next. He was a natural-born politician and proved it by defeating his boss, a twenty-year incumbent. Mark Odom was forty-three years old when he took the oath of office; he was now in his mid-fifties.

Aubrey was eager to tell the sheriff what he had just learned from the medical examiner. It was the first time he had anything of real significance to report in his role as the deputy prosecutor, and he hoped it would give him a chance to learn more about the investigation. He knew it would be pure luck to catch the sheriff in his office. Mark Odom was not a desk jockey; his style was to travel around the county taking care of politics.

When Aubrey stepped into the sheriff's office, he was surprised to see a strange face at the reception desk. A shapely middle-aged woman with her hair done up in a bun said, "You're Aubrey Hatfield, right? I'm Lois Langford."

Aubrey said, "Yes, hello." He looked around the office and then turned back to the woman. "Sorry, I was expecting to see Shirley Barden."

"Oh, you mean Sweet Pea?"

"Well, yes." Aubrey knew that most everyone called Shirley Barden "Sweet Pea," but he could not. He worried that his mother might hear about it if he did, and Vera Hatfield got very fussy when men called women anything she considered suggestive.

The woman at the desk said, "Sweet Pea quit about six weeks ago, so now I'm the sheriff's secretary."

"OK, nice to meet you. Would you tell the sheriff I have just talked to the medical examiner? I need to tell him what I learned."

"He was over at the jail, but I think he's out running around in the car. Let me see if I can raise him on the radio." It took two tries, but she managed to get through to him.

Five minutes later Mark Odom, middle-aged and showing it, walked through the door. "Yo, Aubrey. What's up?"

They went into the sheriff's small office, and Aubrey gave the sheriff a cleaned-up version of Doctor Whitelock's theory of the case. Then he asked what, if anything, the state police had learned.

The sheriff said, "Well, they aren't working any new leads around here, but they did learn more about Ike Swanson. He was born in Red Clay. His mother still lives there, but as soon as he graduated from high school he hightailed it to Chicago and got arrested for giving a blowjob to a minor in a public restroom. He got out of that somehow and came home to live with mommy."

"How did he wind up here, in Woodville?"

"He had worked in grocery stores since high school, so when Bracey's Market advertised for a manager he sent in an application, and they gave him the job." Mark Odom shook his head. "For the life of me I can't figure out why a certified, fulltime queer would think he could fit in around here and not be noticed. He was just asking for it, if you ask me."

Aubrey frowned and looked straight at the sheriff. "Well, maybe so, but that doesn't take anyone—including us—off the hook. Can we push the state police to put more men on it and do more now that we have the medical examiner's working theory of the case? Shouldn't they be talking to some of those hotheads up around the lake?"

The sheriff glared at him and stood up. "They've done a little of that." He hesitated, and then pointed his finger at Aubrey. "But let's get something straight, Aubrey. I run this county. My boys and I are taking the lead on this one, and if I need the state police to do more, I will call them and tell them what to do. Besides, Fred Cooksey says we ought to take it slow and easy, and I agree with him one-hundred percent."

Aubrey nodded and said nothing, mainly because he could not think of a sensible way to deal with the sheriff's arrogance. He knew it would be useless to tangle with him, so he proceeded diplomatically. "I understand."

The sheriff smiled, but the smile that had always seemed genuine now seemed phony.

"Leave it to me, Aubrey. I plan to talk to some more of the boys up around the lake. I saw Artus MacArthur the other day, and he flat-out denied having anything to do with it, said they don't like queers, but killing and torture ain't their way. He's a preacher, you know. He got pretty riled up and cussed me out for even thinking such a thing. That's why I think Fred was right when he said we need to be careful with this. You can't just go around singling people out if you don't have something solid to go on."

Aubrey thought the sheriff was finished when he made the point about "singling people out," but he was not done. "The girl at the Black Cat Café told me about a guy who called Ike Swanson a queer to his face, so I found out who that was and talked to him. It was Cletus Bolton. He lives in a trailer up near Draco on his mother's place and does mechanic work. He admitted harassing the queer, but said that was the only time he ever saw him. Then he told me, 'Sheriff, if you are going to suspect everyone around here who mouths off at queers, you are fixing to be real busy.' Cletus is a piece of shit, but he had a point."

Aubrey started to say more. He knew he needed to, but he did not. "Is there anything you need me to do, sheriff? I've been real busy at the store. You know Mabel is getting old, and she can't do as much as she used to."

"Just let me know if you hear anything, and say hello to Mabel for me."

THIRTEEN

Aubrey went directly to his law office and called Fred Cooksey. The prosecutor was not in his office, but his secretary took Aubrey's message and said she would make sure Fred called him back.

The prosecutor did not return Aubrey's call that afternoon, but he did call late the next day.

Aubrey summarized his conversation with Doctor Whitelock and said he had reported all that to the sheriff. Then, being as delicate as he could, Aubrey said, "It looks to me like the sheriff is pushing the state police out of the case at a time when we need more manpower. When I told him we ought to ask them to interview some of the hotheads up around the lake, he got huffy and told me he runs this county."

Cooksey interrupted him. "Well, Mark called me yesterday and told me you had been in to see him. Look, Aubrey, let the sheriff handle this the way he wants to. He's a good sheriff, and he says we need to take our time and wait for good leads. I agree with him. We can't go off halfcocked."

Aubrey was itching to say more—his gut told him he ought to—but he said nothing.

Cooksey continued his praise of the sheriff. Aubrey listened, but his mind was churning.

I'm Fred Cooksey's deputy, but he is taking the sheriff's side of things. They talked yesterday about my meeting with the sheriff, but Fred waited until today to call me back.

This call is to put me in my place; that's the main message....

FOURTEEN

Aubrey left his law office and walked across the street. He entered the hardware store, still puzzling over Fred Cooksey's blunt rejection of his suggestion that the sheriff ought to ask the state police for help.

He wanted to talk to Mabel, but she was busy with a customer explaining the workings of a newfangled plumbing gadget.

Aubrey nodded to her. Then he walked down the dusky aisle that separated the hand tools from the power tools, his favorite place from the time he worked as a stock boy. He brushed the back of his hand against a row of long-nosed pliers, wishing there were a tool to fix the mess in his head.

He thought to himself: *There is certainty in hardware and tools. Everything has a purpose. Yes, our displays in the store are jumbled-up and overcrowded. That has gotten worse over the years, but you can still find what you need, and you can always straighten things out.*

Aubrey put a fallen tool back where it belonged. But his mind was grinding, rummaging through wisps of memory and the jumbled-up uncertainties of law and politics. Something inside him was judging and sorting, but Aubrey was not listening to that voice. He shied away from the painful work of unjumbling right from wrong. He was looking for a hiding place, and he found one.

I need to lighten up. The work of doing justice depends on people, and people are not perfect. It is always messy. I should not judge Cooksey or the sheriff, because I do not know their hearts, their motivations. That is why I did not press my point with Fred. What happened to Ike should not happen to anyone, homosexual or not, but the case is only three weeks old. Maybe it will all work out. I will focus on other things. I will work here in the hardware, and I will do the minor cases at Municipal Court—that is what I will do. I will let the sheriff control the Ike Swanson case—that is what they want. There is no need to bother Prissy with all this. It is complicated. I will just keep it to myself. It is hard enough for me to understand how the justice system works, and I am a lawyer.

—~—

By the time Aubrey got to the end of the aisle, his head hung low. He felt better, but he was tired and did not want to think anymore about what had been going on in his mind. He headed to the front of the store, where the outside light shone through on the cash register. The first words he spoke to Mabel were these:

"I may not be cut out for this prosecuting attorney business, Mabel. I'm going to focus more on my private life. I'm new to the law. The prosecutor and sheriff have their way of doing things, and I have to accept that. It's not like running a hardware store. I'm just the deputy."

Mabel said, "Don't worry about it, Aubrey. You are a good man."

—~—

For the next four months, Aubrey did busywork at the store and in his law office. He prosecuted mundane offenses at Municipal Court. And he stayed out of the Ike Swanson investigation, such as it was.

Other distractions helped Aubrey stay in his hiding place. On November 5, 1968—one week after Cooksey told him to butt out, and one month after Ike Swanson's murder—the world turned its attention to Election Day. Richard Nixon won the White House, but Arkansans created a big political story too. The voters proved how independent, how contrary they could be by giving majorities on the same ballot to a reform Republican governor, Winthrop Rockefeller; a progressive, anti-war Democratic senator, J. William Fulbright; and, a conservative, pro-war, anti-integration, independent presidential candidate, George Wallace. The talk of that anomaly lasted a full week.

Thanksgiving and Christmas soon followed. Prissy's performance at the church cantata was her best ever. All this allowed Aubrey's mind to stay where he wanted it to be.

Occasionally, someone would say something about the Ike Swanson case, forcing Aubrey to think about it. In late January 1969, he learned at coffee klatch that Sheriff Odom had interviewed the father of a teenage boy whom Ike Swanson had supposedly accosted. The sheriff said the father might have killed Ike out of revenge, but his inquiry came to naught when the man came up with an airtight alibi. When Aubrey asked the sheriff about that, he said, "I feel bad that I singled him out as a suspect. I mean, Ike was going after several young boys in town."

More time passed. On March 3, 1969, the news reported that Sirhan Sirhan had admitted to killing presidential candidate Robert Kennedy. No one in Campbell County thought to say a word about the unsolved killing of Ike Swanson.

Fred Cooksey and Sheriff Odom had long since begun to call Ike's lynching a cold case.

FIFTEEN

On a bitter, rainy day in early March 1969, Aubrey took Prissy to the doctor for a prenatal examination. The baby Aubrey had struggled to see when Prissy started to show had gotten bigger and bigger. Now that Prissy was great with child, Aubrey loved to put his hand on her belly to feel for movement. When the child kicked, they made a game of it. Sometimes he was going to be an All Star baseball pitcher or field-goal kicker. At other times they guessed she was going to be a great conductor or an Olympic high jumper. It was fun. Their dreams were coming true; they would soon be a family.

Doctor Miles Randolph, who delivered most of the babies in Campbell County, gave them a good report and predicted the baby would arrive in the middle of March, perhaps on St. Patrick's Day. Aubrey's pride was easy to see, but inside he had the helpless feeling known only to expectant fathers, a feeling that magnified his admiration for Prissy. She was the one bearing the burden; he was just a bystander. The miracle of childbirth was a new and exciting moment in their life, and with it came the special kind of love known only to parents.

Aubrey, in good spirits, took Prissy home and returned to his law office.

He had just started the examination of an abstract of title, a $25 piece of business, when a strange man walked in.

SIXTEEN

Blacky Blackburn was a legend all across North Arkansas. Aubrey had never seen the man, but he had heard stories about him. Fred Cooksey called Blacky "a crackpot, but a damn tough trial lawyer." He even confessed, reluctantly, to underestimating Blacky on more than one occasion.

When the gangly old man opened the door to the law office and stepped in out of the rain, Aubrey thought: *This has to be Blacky.* He wore an ink-black topcoat and a wide-brimmed black fedora. When he took them off and tossed them on a chair, he said, in a voice too loud for the little room, "Man, it's cold as a witch's tit out there." Then, shivering theatrically, he made a *woo-eee* sound and extended his bony hand in Aubrey's direction.

"Hello, my good young man. I am Benjamin Blackstone Blackburn, but you can call me Blacky, if you like."

He was in full regalia. The double-breasted black suit with large, high-cut lapels was from another era, but it looked smart, rather dapper on a man who had a full head of gray hair even as he was about to celebrate his eightieth birthday. A red handkerchief, carefully arranged in the breast pocket of his suit, matched a tie that had an old-style forehand knot in it at the point where it disappeared under a high, white collar.

The out-of-sync clothing was enough to identify Blacky, but indisputable proof came when Aubrey looked at his footwear. The shoes were black, of course, but the high-cut trousers revealed Blacky's trademark:

a pair of white spats, each fastened snugly over the shoe by a string of black buttons running from top to bottom on the outer side.

Aubrey wondered why this strange man had come to see him, but he knew it would take a while to find out. Blacky was a traditionalist, so there would be a period of idle conversation before he got to the main subject. They talked about Blacky's knowing Aubrey's grandfather and father. They talked about Prissy's family, the LeFevers, and they talked about having children—Blacky had six children, twelve grandchildren, and eighteen great-grandchildren.

The man mesmerized Aubrey. He could see why Fred Cooksey called him a crackpot, but the leathery face and pale blue eyes were captivating. Blacky was easy to like. Aubrey could have listened to his stories for the rest of the afternoon, but Blacky suddenly got to the point.

"I represent Martha Swanson, the mother of the boy who was killed up by Possum Knob almost six months ago. My client says the case has not been properly investigated, mainly because Ike was a homosexual and people here—especially the authorities—don't give a rat's ass that he was tortured and killed."

Aubrey needed some time to deal with Blacky's blunt accusation, so he said, "Well, you know Sheriff Odom and Fred Cooksey. Surely you don't believe that about them."

Blacky said, "It's not what I believe that matters; it is what she believes. And I must tell you that she thinks you are part of the problem."

"That's not true. The state police and the sheriff have been on the case from the beginning, and if they can prove who did it, I will be all for prosecuting the case to the fullest extent of the law."

"The boy's mother simply doesn't believe that, and that is why she hired me. In the old days—when families feuded and somebody got killed—it was common practice for kinfolks to hire their own lawyer to do the prosecuting if they felt like the state's attorney was too close to the family of the one who did the killing. My client wants you and Fred Cooksey to step aside and let me be appointed to prosecute the case."

Aubrey had never heard of such a thing, but he wanted to end the painful meeting. He said, "I'll call Fred and tell him what you want, but I think it is something you ought to say to him, face to face."

Blacky said, "Fred doesn't like me. I've taken his britches off in the courtroom too many times, and it drives him crazy when I do."

"Well, I'll pass along what you have said and get back to you."

Blacky slipped on his coat, carefully positioned his fedora and left. Aubrey did not like him as much as he had at first.

When Blacky was gone, Aubrey got his boss on the line. "Fred, you'll never guess who was just in my office." Aubrey paused, then said, "Blacky Blackburn."

"He's a crackpot. He actually picks juries using some half-baked numerology theory to figure out the 'life path' for each prospective juror. What did the old fart want?"

"He said he represents Ike Swanson's mother, and she thinks we are not doing our job. She wants you to let Blacky take over and prosecute the case. I never heard of such a thing, but I told him I would tell you what he said and get back to him."

"That old private-prosecutor shit went out with the dark ages, and Blacky knows it. He's just earning a fee. He probably took the Swanson lady for at least a thousand dollars. Call him back and tell him I told him to go piss up a rope. He'll tell his client that he put the pressure on us, and that there is nothing more he can do. That will be the end of it. Anything else?"

Aubrey thought, *Blacky seems to bring out the worst in Fred.* Then he said, "OK, I'll tell him what you said, but it bothers me to be accused of not caring whether we find the killer."

"It goes with the territory, Aubrey. Anyway, it's the sheriff's job to investigate, and we need to leave that to him." Fred seemed especially curt. But before he hung up, he said, "I'll see you in a few weeks for docket day. We can talk some more then."

SEVENTEEN

Aubrey waited two days before he dialed the number Blacky had given him. When the old lawyer came on the line, Aubrey gave him a sanitized version of what Fred had said. He thought that would be the end of it, but Blacky gave him an earful.

"You're new to this business, Aubrey, but Fred knows better and he ought to be ashamed. I asked around when I was there the other day, and it's pretty plain that the sheriff isn't trying to find the killer. There's a bunch of legitimate suspects in those hills up around the lake, in Campbell County as well as across the line in Missouri. There's at least four or five groups that rail against commies, queers, and perverts. The sheriff or the state police ought to be talking to them, one by one, but people I trust are telling me the sheriff hasn't done much—that he's not about to stir up a bunch of political trouble for himself over the death of a queer. Now if that is true—and that's exactly what I'm going to tell my client—then anybody that is letting the sheriff get away with it is just as wrong as he is."

Aubrey said, "Well, I promised I would call you back, and I did."

Blacky said, "You seem like a nice young man, Aubrey. You come from good Hatfield stock and your life path number is a good one. You ought to get out of that job before it ruins your reputation."

EIGHTEEN

Aubrey was in low spirits when he left the law office that afternoon. Blacky had hit a nerve. Ike Swanson's mother had a point. The sheriff had talked to a few people of interest, enough to cover his ass, but if the victim had been a well-known heterosexual male, he would have turned the county upside down looking for the killers.

He planned to tell Prissy about Blacky's visit and the accusation Ike's mother was making about him not caring, not doing his duty. He needed her words of comfort, but when he got home, Prissy was at the kitchen table poring over their collection of baby names.

"We have got to cut this list down, Aubrey. What if the baby comes early? Let's cut it to three boy names and three girl names. And let's do it now, tonight."

Aubrey gave her a kiss on the cheek. "There's no time like the present. Let's get started."

He sat down next to Prissy, and they began to whittle. Fifty or so names that had made the list on a whim were easy to scratch, and in short order they got their list down to one page. Then the whittling slowed. Most of the serious contenders were rooted in family history, the Bible, or nature—the seasons, flowers, gemstones—but a few competed well simply because they were cute. Prissy enjoyed the name game, and she got misty-eyed when the naming project gave way to talk of buying a house and having more kids.

Aubrey's personal concerns would have to wait. He craved empathy, but it was a bad time to bother Prissy with talk of murder and sloppy police work.

NINETEEN

Aubrey struggled through a sleepless night, but by morning he knew what he was going to do.

He got up early and headed for the coffee klatch. The first part of his plan was to probe, as subtly as he could, for the latest street talk about the Ike Swanson murder case. He wanted to validate what Blacky had found, and he would do it by talking to the people who would give a straight answer.

He got to Gentry's in time to get the last seat at the klatch table, and the counter-girl brought him a cup of coffee and one of Ernie Gentry's hot cinnamon rolls. The usual group was present. The topic of conversation was Cardinal baseball; spring training was not yet underway, but trade talks were running hot and heavy.

When the table talk changed to politics and the general incompetence of politicians—a favorite topic—Aubrey took the occasion to ask, "Have you all heard any talk lately about the murder of the queer?"

"Why ask us? You're the deputy prosecutor." Loudmouth Sonny Childs meant to cast suspicion when he turned the question back, but Aubrey was ready for him.

"No particular reason. It's just that the sheriff and the state police have been working on it for almost six months, and they need all the help they can get."

Sonny said, "They ain't been working all that hard, but I don't blame them. Nobody knew that queer, and nobody gives a shit."

"Well, sometimes people get to bragging or feeling guilty, and they will say something that helps the cops." Aubrey fished for other opinions.

One of the longtime regulars said, "Well, a lot of time has gone by, Aubrey. I don't think they are ever going figure out who did it."

Another klatcher said, "I think they gave up on it a while back. The sheriff's a good politician, and his antennas tell him what Sonny said: 'Nobody gives a shit.'" Sonny Childs ended Aubrey's foray with his customary rudeness. "Looks like you won't be strutting your stuff in a big murder trial after all." The loudmouth chortled, but Aubrey let the insult go by. He had accomplished his purpose, but the truth was hard to accept.

I have been part of this indifference. And it makes me feel rotten.

TWENTY

Aubrey got up from the klatch table and headed through The Hole into the hardware store. Mabel was already there, clearing the register and making ready for the day's business. If he had not known about her dementia, Aubrey would have thought she was just getting old. She was not moving as fast, and her voice was a little shaky. But otherwise she was the same old Mabel.

"I'm having a pretty good day, Aubrey. If there is something else you need to be doing, I can take care of things here."

Aubrey said, "Thanks, Mabel. I'm going to do some work at the law office, but I'll be back later this morning."

He went across the street to his office and called Dwane Pollard to see if he could come by. Talking to Dwane was the second part of Aubrey's plan.

Prissy and Aubrey first met Dwane when they were teenagers. They were on a bus headed to Mount Sequoyah for an overnight retreat of the Methodist Youth Fellowship. Dwane and his wife, Mary, chaperoned the trip. The curious youngsters would have a chance to see for themselves why so many people referred to Dwane as the smartest man in Campbell County.

Dwane was very talkative on the trip, and it was not long before Prissy asked, "Where did you go to college, Dwane?"

"I didn't go to college, Prissy. In fact, I never finished the third grade."

Prissy and Aubrey said nothing.

"It's OK, I don't mind talking about it," Dwane said. "You see, I was born in 1919 on a poor dirt farm in Hawkins County. I was one of thirteen kids, and we had to work on the farm from the time we were big enough to help. I might have gone further in school, but the Great Depression came along, and our hard times got harder. We—"

Prissy interrupted. "People say you are the smartest man in the county."

Dwane laughed. "I don't know about that, but I'm glad they aren't saying I'm the dumbest man in the county, and that is what they would be saying if I hadn't gone into the CCC when I was seventeen. President Roosevelt set up the Civilian Conservation Corps to give young boys like me a chance to work. They gave us brand new workclothes and a fine pair of shoes. We earned $25 a month and sent most of it home to the family. But the most important thing that happened to me at the CCC camp was that I learned to read and write. It was hard at first, but I got the hang of it, and by the time I was twenty I felt pretty good about myself."

Aubrey had just celebrated his fifteenth birthday; the idea of not knowing how to read and write was foreign to him. He wanted to say something nice, so he said, "You have every reason to be proud."

Dwane said, "This is a church trip, so let me remind you. Pride goeth before destruction and a haughty spirit before a fall. Proverbs 16:18." He laughed and gave Aubrey a friendly poke on the shoulder. "That's one of my favorites. The CCC man who taught me to read started me off in Proverbs."

Dwane Pollard spent two years in the CCC. And he joined the Marines in 1941 three days after the Japanese attacked Pearl Harbor. He fought in the Pacific theater for two years and received three medals for valor. In 1944, during the invasion of Kwajalein Atoll, shrapnel from enemy mortar fire shattered his left shoulder and tore a chunk of flesh from his face between his left eye and ear. His face healed, leaving a conspicuous scar, but Dwane could not do much with his left arm, which hung limp at his side. He spent six months at the Navy Hospital near Sydney, Australia, and that is where he met Mary. She was nineteen at the time, working as a volunteer nurse's aide. Dwane, lovestruck, soon proposed marriage. Since Mary was an Australian citizen, he had to get permission from the Marine Corps to marry her, which he did. He came home in 1945, and Mary joined him a few months later.

They settled in Woodville and Dwane took a job selling used cars for Trice Motor Company. He made enough to live comfortably, but making money was never his goal. Dwane loved to learn. He read extensively. Literary fiction, history, and philosophy were his favorites, but he never quit reading and studying the Bible. It was his touchstone, his connection to the days when he could not read or write.

Dwane Pollard had come a long way, but he had aged well. The rawboned face of his youth had given way to a refined look in spite of the squiggly mass of scar tissue on his cheekbone. Friends drawn to his handsomeness and the badge of honor on his face soon learned the best part of Dwane. His rich experience and the knowledge gained from a lifetime of reading had transformed the gentle, illiterate farm boy into a fount of wisdom.

The smartest man in the county was now sitting across from Aubrey in his law office.

"Thanks for coming, Dwane. I need to talk about something, and I can't bother Prissy with it—she's about ready to deliver."

"I know, Mary and I have been praying for you all."

Aubrey and Prissy trusted Dwane Pollard implicitly. They had grown very close to Dwane and Mary in the ten years after the church retreat to Mount Sequoyah. They were like family, and it was no surprise to anyone when Aubrey asked Dwane to be the best man in his wedding.

Aubrey did not have to mince words with Dwane, so he got right to the point.

"Dwane, this is about the Ike Swanson murder. Blacky Blackburn, the flamboyant lawyer from Hawkins County, came here to see me a few days ago because he represents Swanson's mother. Blacky believes the killer came from one of those groups up by the lake that preaches against commies and perversion. He claims there has been no arrest because the sheriff does not want to stir up a bunch of political trouble for himself over the death of a homosexual. The victim's mother—to make matters worse—believes Fred Cooksey and I have been part of the problem. That last part bothers me. It forces me to think hard about the case and my role in it."

Dwane said, "Well, I have to agree with Blacky's assessment, but I don't think anyone around here feels that way about you. Fred Cooksey, on the other hand, is a politician, pure and simple. If the sheriff wants to look the other way and let a lynch mob run free, Fred will not stand in his way."

Aubrey said, "I got the same feedback at coffee klatch this morning, and it makes me sick to my stomach to think that I have not stood up to Fred and the sheriff. In the beginning, I thought they were going to dig in and find the killer, and there would be a big trial. I was eaten up with self-interest—thinking way too much about what the case would mean for my career. Now, looking back, I should have known better. I can think of several times when I should have spoken out and pushed them to do more."

"I agree, but I doubt you could have changed anything, Aubrey. You are Fred's deputy and you serve at his pleasure. He and the sheriff are safe, politically—strong as an acre of garlic, some would say. They can do as they please. The question for you is not what you could or should have done. It is what you can and should do, now that you see things clearly."

"Blacky said I ought to get out of the job before it ruins my reputation. Is that what you are saying?"

"Blacky may be an oddball, but he has a point. You are a good man, Aubrey, and you have a good name. I would hate for people to think that you shirked your duty as a man of the law."

Aubrey said, "I started to talk to Prissy about all this last night but decided not to. She doesn't need that right now."

"That is for certain," Dwane said. "But Prissy reads you like a book. I bet she knows that something has you worried. Why don't you tell her we talked about all the things you are trying to do—the store, the law office, the prosecutor's job—and I said it was too much for any one man. Tell her I think the deputy prosecutor job is not a good fit for you.

She deserves to know you are thinking about quitting, but she does not need to hear about murder and lawmen violating their oath of office. Not right now."

As Dwane was leaving, Aubrey said, "There's an irony here that proves the value of a woman's intuition. Early on, when the case was brand new, I told Prissy that Fred Cooksey said, 'We need to go slow and not rush to judgment; the whole thing, if not handled right, could become a political nightmare.' When Prissy heard that, she told me: 'Well, I hope they are not going to turn a blind eye to finding the killer.'"

"You are blessed, Aubrey. Your wife is a very smart woman."

TWENTY-ONE

"I could tell something was bothering you," Prissy said.

Aubrey had waited for the right time to tell her about his meeting with Dwane. It came at the kitchen table, shortly after they decided to name a baby boy Amos, in honor of Aubrey's father; if Prissy had a girl she would be Bridgette, in honor of Prissy's Irish grandmother.

Aubrey took Dwane's good advice. He downplayed the whole thing as nothing more than a general discussion about giving up the job as deputy prosecutor. Telling Prissy that much made him feel better; she deserved to know that he was thinking about quitting. The details could come later, after the birth of their baby.

"I'm glad you told me. I figured it had something to do with the prosecutor job, and I'm glad you talked to Dwane about it. He's a good sounding board, especially on political stuff."

Aubrey felt better. He gave her a hug. "Let's put all that aside for now. We've got a baby coming."

TWENTY-TWO

"Three more days," Prissy said, as she marked another red X on the wall calendar. "There goes Thursday, March 14." She put her hand on her belly and turned to face Aubrey. With a mischievous look, she said, "St. Patrick's Day is March 17. Does Irish green trump the usual baby colors—blue for boys and pink for girls?"

They had a good laugh, but Aubrey thought to himself: *Prissy can find the fun side of anything, even when she is miserable.* At first, Aubrey did not see the pain she was in because Prissy believed in staying busy every minute of the day. It was her nature to work, not rest. The pregnancy had seemed to speed her up, not slow her down; her projects—sewing, writing, cooking, painting—filled every room of the apartment. Lately, however, Prissy was spending more time on the couch and less time on her feet. Aubrey even caught her catnapping, something she regarded as sloth. It was a sure sign she was not feeling well.

Aubrey decided to spend as much time with her as he could, leaving her only to check on Mabel and his mother. He wanted to do something, but Prissy would not let him help her. She just kept saying, "I'm close to delivery; such things are to be expected."

Shortly after noon on March 15, Prissy asked him to lie beside her on their bed. "I haven't felt the baby since early this morning. Not a single jab, punch, twist or turn. And I am worried because this is the time of day when I usually feel a lot of movement."

Aubrey said, "Let me feel." He moved his hand back and forth and put his ear to Prissy's belly. He did not feel or hear anything, so Prissy got up, walked around the apartment for a few minutes, and drank a glass of sweet tea. It was something the doctor told her to try if the baby was quiet.

Aubrey tried again, listening and feeling for movement. He said, "Have you talked to Doctor Randolph about this?"

"I saw him about ten days ago, and he said the baby and I are doing fine. I told him I was having headaches and some discomfort, but he said that was to be expected. He did tell me to watch out for bleeding and to keep track of the baby's movements."

Aubrey started to ask about bleeding, but Prissy beat him to it. "I've been a little sore, but I haven't had any bleeding."

"I'm still not hearing or feeling anything. I think we ought to call Doctor Randolph," Aubrey said.

Prissy placed the call, and Aubrey heard her tell the doctor's nurse, "The baby hasn't moved since very early this morning. I had some hard pain in my abdomen this morning as well as a strange kind of back pain." There was a pause, then Prissy added, "Doctor Randolph knows I've been having headaches, but this afternoon I've got a doozy."

Aubrey was hearing the specifics of her pain for the first time, and it made him think. *Isn't that just like her? She didn't tell me because she didn't want me to worry, but I am worried.*

The nurse told Prissy they should head to the hospital. They did not waste any time. Prissy's "hospital bag" was sitting by the front door where it had been for the last two weeks. Aubrey grabbed the bag, helped Prissy into the car, and drove as gently as he could to the town's small hospital, five minutes from their apartment.

Doctor Randolph met them at the hospital, and the attendants helped Prissy onto a gurney. The doctor listened for a heartbeat, moving his stethoscope from place to place. He said he needed to examine Prissy, and a nurse rolled the gurney into a nearby room. When the door closed behind them, Aubrey used a pay-telephone to call Dwane. He told him what Doctor Randolph had said, and asked Dwane to tell his mother and Mabel that they were at the hospital.

A couple of minutes later, the nurse asked Aubrey to come into the examination room. Doctor Randolph said, "Aubrey, I have told Prissy that I can't hear a heartbeat. I'm as sorry as I can be, but I believe the baby will be stillborn."

Prissy turned her head first one way and then the other. Aubrey leaned over the bed and consoled her as best he could. He laid his hand on her cheek and slid it back, smoothing her hair. He kissed her and whispered, "I love you."

Prissy was ashen, and in a tired voice said to Aubrey, "It's my fault. I waited too long to call."

Doctor Randolph heard her. "No, Prissy, it is not your fault. You were bleeding, but you did not know it. The placenta broke loose and trapped the blood inside you. That's very rare, but it does happen." With that, the doctor turned to leave the room. On the way out, he signaled for Aubrey to follow him.

The nurse began to wash Prissy's face with a cool towel, and Aubrey went into the hall to see what Doctor Randolph wanted. He had the feeling there was more bad news on the way. He was right.

"Aubrey, Prissy's in trouble. She has had a placental abruption. A large amount of placenta separated from her uterus, and that led to the death of the baby. Now I am concerned that she may have an infection, so we need to remove the stillborn as quickly as we can. I need to get her into the operating room right away."

First, it was the baby, and now the doctor was telling him that Prissy might be in danger. Aubrey could not think straight. He stared at a misshapen ceiling tile, and then found himself calculating the number of tiles that were soiled. "Doc, we trust you to do what's best," Aubrey heard himself say the words even as his bizarre interest in the tiles faded in and out. "But let me have a moment with her before you take her."

Aubrey went back to Prissy's side. For the first time in his life, he was thinking what it might be like to lose her. It shook him to the core, but he pushed the thought aside. He needed to be brave, but it did not matter; Prissy was unconscious.

He kissed her lips and said, "I love you." Then he left Prissy with the doctor and nurses and headed toward the waiting area. Dwane, Mabel, and Aubrey's mother had just arrived. They were crying, and he did his best to explain things. Dwane said a prayer for Prissy and the baby.

It was nearly an hour later when Doctor Randolph came to where they were. As he got close, he looked Aubrey in the eye and shook his head. Aubrey knew from the expression on the doctor's face that the worst had come. He sank down on the couch by his mother, and she held him to her breast as she had done so many times when he was a little boy.

Doctor Randolph told Dwane and Mabel that Prissy died when he was removing the baby and treating her for the placenta abruption that caused the stillbirth. He said, "She had an amniotic fluid embolism. It is rare, but it does happen when amniotic fluid or fetal material gets into the maternal bloodstream through tears in the fetal membranes. That causes clotting in the mother's lungs and blood vessels. Prissy was unconscious from loss of blood, and the embolism caused a stroke. She died suddenly, before we could do anything to save her."

TWENTY-THREE

Aubrey did not want to leave the hospital. He clung to his mother, perplexed by the sudden loss of Prissy and their baby girl, Bridgette. The hopes, dreams, and wishes he shared with Prissy, so real just hours ago, were gone. He wanted to hold Prissy and hear her laugh just one more time, but that could never be. Prissy, the love of his life, was dead. Aubrey felt helpless, confused. A sense of bitterness crept in, but he cast it out. *Prissy would not like that.*

Doctor Randolph returned to pay his respects to Aubrey and the family. He offered to stay as long as they wanted, but Aubrey could see no sense in that. The doctor said he would be at the hospital for another hour, but suggested to Aubrey that he ought to go home and get some rest.

Dwane said, "That's good advice, Aubrey. Let's all go to Hatfield House. I'll come back here and take care of whatever needs to be done."

Aubrey agreed, but his drive to the house was short and miserable. He was all alone—no family, no Prissy, no baby.

When Aubrey got to Hatfield House, he went directly to his room on the second floor. His mother had not changed it. Filled with photographs and memorabilia, the room told the story of his life and his romance with Prissy. He sat on the bed and thought of the years to come, years without Prissy. He was alone, but it came to him that being alone is not the same as loneliness.

His love for Prissy and the dreams they dreamed would never fade. Loneliness was going to be his greatest challenge.

TWENTY-FOUR

On the day after St. Patrick's Day, hundreds of people gathered at First United Methodist Church for the funeral of Prissy and Bridgette. A young girl, Prissy's protégé, sang the hymn that Prissy loved, "How Great Thou Art." It was more than Aubrey could bear, but he was not alone. The townspeople who filled the pews were also crying. Later they said they could not remember a sadder time.

They buried Prissy and Bridgette together in the Hatfield plot and left a space where Aubrey one day would lie. The preacher suggested that they should bury the loving mother and her stillborn child in the same grave, and Aubrey agreed. Prissy would like that—she and Bridgette together, forever, body and soul.

It was warm and sunny at the graveside. The preacher spoke of Prissy and Bridgette, and said comforting things. Aubrey listened, but the words were a blur. Then the children from Prissy's kindergarten class sang, "Jesus loves me." It was a vision he would treasure for the rest of his life.

TWENTY-FIVE

Aubrey did not leave the house for a week. Mabel and Dwane were taking care of the hardware store, and Mary hired a young man to move everything out of the apartment and into a large room on the second floor of Hatfield House.

Vera Hatfield did what mothers do best. She listened and encouraged her only son to be patient. She let him cry, saying it is natural to suffer. Most important, she gave him hope and told him of her own experience with grief.

Mary and Dwane offered to help Aubrey go through some of Prissy's things, but he said he was not ready for that.

On March 25, Aubrey left the house early, went to his law office and typed a letter of resignation. It was to be effective immediately. He did not mention the real reason he was quitting as deputy prosecuting attorney for Campbell County, Arkansas. He simply wrote that he needed to spend more time running Hatfield's Hardware and taking care of his new civil law practice.

Aubrey then called Fred Cooksey and told him that he had put his official letter of resignation in the mail.

Cooksey told Aubrey he was sorry to hear of Prissy's death, and he "reluctantly" accepted the resignation. Aubrey thanked him and hung up.

TWENTY-SIX

Aubrey did not do much work for several days after he resigned. He made a trip or two to the store, but for the most part, he spent the days rummaging through Prissy's things. He tried as best he could to take his mother's advice: Be patient and keep hope alive. He felt better after resigning. He knew that Prissy would have said, "Good for you. You have washed your hands of that mess." But something was still gnawing at him, deep inside.

Vera Hatfield encouraged Aubrey to go to church with her on Palm Sunday, two weeks after Prissy and the baby died. He knew it would be hard because Prissy loved Palm Sunday, so much so that she volunteered each year to be in charge of the children's processional. It was a sight to see the children marching down the aisle waving the big palm fronds. Prissy said her main responsibility was to teach the kids that they could not swing the fronds too far to the right or left—a rule installed soon after a mischievous boy knocked a big bonnet completely off the head of an elderly widow-woman. To make matters worse, the widow-woman's wig stayed with the bonnet. Prissy loved to tell that story, complete with theatrics and her special bellylaugh.

On this Palm Sunday when the kids walked down the aisle waving their palm fronds, Prissy was there for Aubrey, and he whispered: *God, how I miss you.*

The following Sunday was Easter, April 6, three weeks from the day Prissy died. To her, Easter was the greatest of all celebrations. The choir performed the middle part of Handel's *Messiah*—the libretto presenting the death and resurrection of Jesus. Prissy was there again for Aubrey, singing the Hallelujah Chorus at the top of her soprano voice.

TWENTY-SEVEN

The nights were hardest for Aubrey. He tried reading, listening to music, and strolling through the neighborhood, but he could not get his mind off Prissy and Bridgette. In the daytime, he fought loneliness with work. It helped that there was plenty to do at the hardware store, and he also had a few pieces of legal work to keep him busy. But for the long hours of evening, he needed a distraction. The numbing effect of television appealed to him.

He had offered to connect his television set shortly after he moved into Hatfield House, but his mother would have no part of it. Most of her friends had been watching TV for ten years or more, but Vera Hatfield held out for the old ways: reading, and listening to the radio. Aubrey knew it would take a goodly measure of diplomacy to change her mind.

His opening came on Mother's Day 1969 as they were leaving church. The preacher had spoken of Apollo 11 and the coming attempt to put a man on the moon. Vera said some people were saying it was a hoax and would never happen. She babbled about her lifelong fear that sleeping in the light of the moon would make you crazy, saying the Romans called the moon "Luna" and telling how they discovered that lunacy came from sleeping in the moonlight. She obsessed about the moon at lunch that day, and again when they sat down to dinner.

Aubrey made his move. "The whole thing is going to be on television—the launch, the orbit, and the moon landing."

Amazingly, the gambit worked. Vera's curiosity dissolved her resistance. Gone were the doubts; gone were the arguments about lunacy and about TV being the work of the devil.

"I never thought I would say it, Aubrey, but let's hook up your TV."

Thus ensued several weeks of watching everything they could find about Apollo 11. For Aubrey it was a good diversion when he was not working. But for his mother it was a blessing, especially the all-day coverage of the run-up to launch.

There now was a limit to what she could do with her time. Doctor Randolph had made that clear when he said she was losing her battle with heart disease.

On June 28, Aubrey and Vera were watching moon-news when the commentator switched to a story about the New York City police raiding the Stonewall Inn, a place in Greenwich Village that catered to homosexuals. He did not get very far into the story when Vera said, "Aubrey, turn to something else. I don't like to hear about people like that. They're the people Al encountered when he and Virgil got to the seventh circle of hell. You know, the place of confinement for lost souls who will be punished for violence against God."

Aubrey gave her a quizzical look, but he knew it was unwise to argue about heaven and hell with Vera. He turned the television to a channel that was not carrying the story, and Vera said, "See. That is why I never wanted to get television in the first place. It is better to study the classics."

Aubrey said, "Well, TV may be the work of the devil, but just think: You are going to watch America put a man on the moon."

—෴—

On July 16, 1969, Aubrey and his mother were spellbound as Jack King, the voice of Apollo 11, said, "... Ignition sequence start, 6, 5, 4, 3, 2 ... all engines running, commit, liftoff."

The Saturn V rocket roared, slowly lifting man from the face of the Earth to the face of the moon. As it raced toward the heavens, Aubrey heard his mother say, "Oh, my."

When he turned to see the joy on her face, he knew right away: His mother was dead.

Vera Hatfield, the Christian woman with a shine about her, had gone to heaven right along with Apollo 11.

Aubrey sank back into his chair. He wanted to cry, but his heart and mind would not cooperate. Random thoughts and feelings were on the loose.

Mother was my last blood relative. Wait, I should turn off the TV; it is not right for me to see more of the Apollo 11 launch than Mother did. Thank God for Dwane and Mary, and Mabel, but they are much older than I am. Prissy, I—. Mother felt like she was a part of the Apollo 11 mission. What has happened to the dreams I had? I ought to say a prayer for Mother...

Aubrey picked up the telephone and dialed. "Dwane, Mother just passed away. Can you come over and help me with this?"

—∞—

Two days later, *Columbia*, the command module of Apollo 11 neared the moon, and an inescapable deluge of positive, patriotic news reports filled the newspapers and airways. Even so, the people of Woodville turned out *en masse* for yet another Hatfield funeral. Prissy and Bridgette had been gone just four months and three days.

The sky was dark and hung low over the gravesite when Aubrey eulogized Vera. Everyone wept when he told how his mother went to heaven, right along with the astronauts.

When the service was over Aubrey lingered with Dwane, Mary, and Mabel. The townspeople paid their respects and scattered; all were eager to get home in time to watch the journey of *Columbia*. Aubrey understood their feelings because the moon story also had him in its grasp. He tried to push it aside to think solely about Vera, but the moon story kept intruding, and that gave him a sense of guilt: *This is not right*. He shut off the TV. *I can't let Mother's passing take a back seat to the moon story.*

For a day and night, Hatfield House was quiet, eerily quiet, way too quiet for a lonesome man. Aubrey tried to clear his mind but could not.

On Sunday afternoon, July 20, Aubrey got out of his chair in the living room and turned on the TV. Then he walked across the foyer and opened the French doors leading into the small library. It was a round room fourteen feet in diameter with a high, conical ceiling—a turret on the northeast corner of the Victorian house when viewed from the street outside. The room, lighted by three long windows and an ornate chandelier, had walls of solid pecan paneling. Decorated with period furniture to match Vera's rocking chair, the cozy room reeked of antiquity. This had been Vera's domain—the place where she studied, and where she read to him when he was a little boy.

Aubrey stood for a moment at the threshold, thinking.

And he changed his mind. He would watch the moon news and regard the journey of Apollo 11 as an allegory for the good life Vera had lived, her good heart and her journey to heaven. The journey to the moon could also stand for man's quest to find and obey God, and this would lead Aubrey to happy thoughts of Prissy and their dreams, his childhood, baseball, and working as a stockboy at the hardware store under his father's tutelage.

The allegory seemed right to Aubrey, but he knew his mother would expect more of him if he were going to think deeply about good things and heaven. He could hear her saying, "What about hell, Aubrey? Satan is tricky. He lures men through the gates of hell and makes them think they are on the doorstep of heaven. That's why you can't understand heaven if you don't understand hell."

Aubrey walked across the room and pulled a large leather-bound volume from its place on shelving that filled a chord of the circular room. Vera's favorite classic, Dante Alighieri's three-part *Divine Comedy,* was in a featured spot next to a half-dozen Bibles and an early edition of Milton's *Paradise Lost.*

Aubrey remembered how he had found Dante difficult when he tried to read his masterpiece as a college freshman. Now he would take his mother's advice; he would read "Al's" poem and think about the other side of things: hell.

He took the book into the living room and settled into his easychair just in time to see Neil Armstrong jump from the last step of the landing craft, Eagle, to the moon's surface and say, "That's one small step for a man, one giant leap for mankind."

Then, for hours, he watched the astronauts bounce around, collecting rock samples and hitting golf balls. Aubrey, enraptured by man's great achievement, soon returned to his allegory.

What about hell? Where do I stand on the scale of good and bad?

He opened Dante's book, grimacing—wondering how long it would take to find passages that would apply to his life and the sense of despair he felt. It did not take long. The Third Canto of the first poem, *Inferno,* hit him right between the eyes.

Dante's verse took Aubrey through the gate of hell with its foreboding inscription, "Abandon every hope, ye who enter." The poet told of hearing the cries and torment of the neutrals, those indecisive cowards who were so weak-minded in life that they were relegated to the vestibule of hell. So pathetic were they—the miscreants who maintained their neutrality in time of moral crisis—that they did not deserve a place in hell proper.

Aubrey squirmed as he read about the lost souls in the vestibule. He put the book down and sorted through the memories of what he had done and not done about the lynching. He knew he could not deny the strength of Dante's argument.

He had resigned as deputy prosecutor to assuage the guilt he felt for making a mistake that hurt *others,* particularly Ike's mother. But his encounter with the neutrals brought shame, a deeper, more painful feeling about *himself* personally, a feeling that *he* was the mistake.

The next verses told how the neutrals faced an eternity of chasing a blank banner with swarms of insects stinging them mercilessly. Tears streamed down their bodies, gathering in putrid puddles swirling with worms.

Aubrey nodded, *Yes, that is exactly how the shame of cowardly indifference feels. The punishment fits the crime.*

His heart ached. He had found his place in Dante's hell.

In the wee hours of Monday morning, Aubrey finished *Inferno* and closed the book.

I should have done more, but I didn't.

—∾—

On Wednesday, July 23, one week after Vera died, Aubrey stayed up late to watch *Columbia's* return to earth. The splashdown was expected to occur somewhere near Johnston Atoll in the Pacific Ocean.

Thank goodness, something upbeat to watch.

The U. S. Navy recovered the astronauts after the splashdown and took them to safety aboard the aircraft carrier *Hornet*. Aubrey turned off the TV and returned *Divine Comedy* to its place in the library.

That night, when he was all alone at Hatfield House, Aubrey opened a bottle of Jack Daniel's and took his first drink since he was a freshman at college.

TWENTY-EIGHT

On the day *Columbia* returned from the moon, a scrawny man with an odd-looking fat ass approached the service manager at the Crawford Ford Dealership in Somerset, Kentucky. He was applying for a job.

"I'm Cletus—Cletus Dacus. I'm an Army-trained truck mechanic, and I can fix anything with wheels and a motor."

"Where are you from, Cletus?"

"I spent right much time down around El Paso, Texas, when I was in the Army, but I'm living here now. I like the hill country."

PART TWO

THIRTY-SIX YEARS LATER

TWENTY-NINE

"The ushers may bring the collection to the altar."

The congregation of First United Methodist Church stood as one, singing the doxology with gusto, "Praise God, from whom all blessings flow..."

Aubrey started down the aisle, carrying a half-full offering plate. He stared at the large circular stained-glass window high above and behind the altar and choir. The beautiful piece—Jesus offering himself to adoring supplicants while two angels circled above—was the constant in his church life. Sunshiny days played with the colors, changing the imagery, but Aubrey's thoughts about his faith were unchanged.

I used to believe, like a child, but—. Prissy, Bridgette, Mother, Mabel—the women in my life—are all gone, lost forever. The window, the art, is all that is left of my faith. It is what I tie to...

Aubrey plodded toward the altar counting his steps, never looking down, right or left, eyes locked on the window. He placed the collection on the altar, turned around, took exactly seventeen steps, and sat down in the Hatfield pew. The longest-serving usher in church memory had done his duty for one more Sunday.

The preacher's sermon that morning, August 28, 2005, was about Hurricane Katrina wreaking havoc all across the Gulf Coast. The hurricane had just turned into a Category 5 storm, killing hundreds of people and destroying property. Aubrey heard the preacher say, "I don't know why bad things happen to good people, but we need to hold onto what we know about God—His love, His plan to give us a life of hope..." Aubrey tuned out, wondering for the millionth time about the women he loved and lost.

I am still with Dante's neutrals. Worse, I am now with the hypocrites in the eighth circle. I go through the motions every Sunday, and I drink too often and I...

—ᴍ—

Dwane Pollard, now eighty-six years old, watched Aubrey as he had every Sunday for the last thirty-six years. The handsome young groom was now sixty years old. His blue suit had a well-worn look, and his hair, receding as it whitened at the edges, was a quarter gone. His athletic frame was buckling a little, and a paunch was beginning to form. But overall, Aubrey looked like a man who could still catch nine innings of minor-league baseball.

Dwane did not see the changes as signs of aging. To him, the few wrinkles and the rest of it were more a reminder of all that Aubrey had lost—his father, Prissy and the baby girl, and his mother. All had died before Aubrey turned twenty-five.

Dwane thought of a painful time years ago, a memory that returned all too often. He had gone to the hardware store to pick up a bag of charcoal. Aubrey was talking to a customer about a car wreck that had killed a young mother and her daughter that day. When the customer left, Aubrey turned to Dwane and shook his head. "This is St. Patrick's Day, the first anniversary of Prissy's death." His voice cracked and he surprised Dwane by opening up, in an uncharacteristic way. "We expect our parents to die before we do, but I can't get over the loss of Prissy and the baby. It is so wrong, so unfair. It eats at me like a cancer." He broke down, and he turned away to hide his face.

Dwane vowed to pray every Sunday for Aubrey to find another woman and make a new dream. He kept his vow, but God did not answer his prayers. Aubrey did not find another woman, nor did he find a new dream. Instead, he turned to work, endless work.

Aubrey devoted himself to keeping Hatfield's Hardware open. It was his link to the past, to his family, and to the community. It seemed to help him, but in 1971, Aubrey lost his best connection to the past.

His helpmate and lifelong mentor, Mabel, gave in to the scourge of dementia. Aubrey moved her to Hatfield House to take care of her. She was the last of the women who had touched his life, and he could not bear to send her to a nursing home. He found a kind woman who agreed to help when Aubrey had to be at the store, and together they took care of Mabel. It was excruciating work, but they did the best they could. The disease, after slowly destroying Mabel's mind and bodily functions, finally killed her in the summer of 1973.

The store that had been good to Aubrey began to consume him. He was there, all alone, from sunup to sundown and beyond. He practiced a little law on the side—just odds and ends—but his main concern was the store.

In 1986, the inevitable occurred. A big national chain opened a hardware store just outside Woodville on the road to Brasstown. Aubrey fought it as hard as he could, but with every passing year, he lost money. In 1992, he came to grips with the hard realities of running a small business in the modern world. He could keep going and face bankruptcy. Or he could close the store and walk away with just enough money to pay his suppliers and other creditors. That is what he did, and it was painful, especially on the last day of business when all his regular customers came by to sympathize and tell their favorite stories about the old days at Hatfield's Hardware. The store, along with Gentry's Pharmacy, had been on the square for so long that it was part of Woodville's culture. Now it would be vacant, and The Hole that led to Gentry's would be cemented shut. It was the end of an era for Aubrey and for Campbell County.

After the store closed, Aubrey took to hiking the trails that crisscrossed the forests near Woodville. He was only forty-seven years old. Hiking kept him in shape and offered solitude, something he cherished.

He worked just hard enough practicing law to pay the taxes on Hatfield House and to keep body and soul together. But when he was not at the law office or hiking, he, like his mother, found comfort in the library at Hatfield House, reading and trying to write.

In 1996, Aubrey was hiking along the White River. As he stopped to rest near a sandbar, he noticed an odd-shaped stone half-buried in a cluster of smooth river rocks. He dug around it carefully and soon unearthed an arrowhead. He took it to a friend at the Campbell County Historical Society, who told him it was commonplace to find artifacts in that particular spot because it was near the Benge Route of the Trail of Tears.

The Indian Removal Act of 1830 forced Native Americans in the Southeast to relocate to lands west of Arkansas. Aubrey had learned about it when he was a child, but now the story had new meaning. His tussle with the national chain store that forced him to close Hatfield's Hardware had taught him how it feels to be "removed" from a place you love.

Aubrey read everything he could find on the Trail of Tears and wrote an article for the Historical Society. It was about the 1,100 people, mostly Cherokees, who were forced to walk from their homes in Alabama to a strange land in Oklahoma. Led by their halfbreed wagonmaster, John Benge, they traveled through Tennessee, Kentucky, and Missouri. In 1838 they entered Arkansas in Randolph County, crossed Eleven Point River, and meandered in a northwesterly direction through North Arkansas in the dead of winter. As many as 300 Cherokees died along the way.

Aubrey's article dealt exclusively with how the Cherokees must have felt. It was a good piece of writing, but key members of the Historical Society thought it was too one-sided. They urged Aubrey to insert an explanation justifying why the government did what it did. They wanted the article to be more like a travelogue, focusing on the route and reciting facts that might justify the placement of yet another historical marker. Aubrey retrieved his draft and quietly abandoned the project. He felt the society members were trying to downplay the great wrong done to the Cherokees, and he wanted no part of that.

Throughout this long period, Dwane watched Aubrey closely. He knew that his friend was drinking too often, and that he had hit rock bottom. But to everyone else he was the same old Aubrey: A good man and a faithful Methodist.

—~—

When the preacher finished his sermon about Hurricane Katrina, he moved quickly to give the benediction, and the Sunday service ended. Aubrey said a polite hello to those around him, then took a few steps to the small area set aside for those in wheelchairs. Dwane was there alone. He smiled at Aubrey and made a favorite wisecrack in a voice loud enough for others to hear, "Good job, but you have got to be a more reliable usher. Everyone knows you have missed six services in the last forty years." Aubrey smiled, as always, and then rolled the wheelchair and Dwane through the narthex, out the door, and into the parking lot. He lifted Dwane into his old Ford Taurus and put the wheelchair in the trunk. They would go to lunch at Ma Phipps's Cafeteria, then on to Hatfield House to watch the Baltimore Orioles on television.

Just as they finished off the last bite of Ma Phipps's comfort food, Dwane said, "Aubrey, I am going to move into an assisted-living place. I am a mess. I cannot walk and my left arm is dead as a doornail—it has been that way ever since I was hit by mortar fire. Mary has been gone for months, and I am all alone. It's the best thing."

"No, Dwane. You are not going there. You are going to come live with me at Hatfield House. I've got lots of room, and it will be good to have you as company."

Taking care of the elderly would not be a new experience for Aubrey. He had taken Mabel in when dementia finally got the best of her. Helping Dwane would not be a burden. He might be a mess physically, but his mind was as good as ever.

"I don't want to be a bother," Dwane said.

"It will be an honor, not a bother. After all, how many people get a chance to live with the smartest man in the county?"

Dwane smiled, then turned his head and faked a cough.

Five days later, Aubrey moved Dwane into Hatfield House. It was the beginning of an interesting time for both of them.

THIRTY

Aubrey locked the door to his law office and started the short walk to Hatfield House. Just as he did, his brand-new cellphone rang. Aubrey fumbled to find it and answer before the caller gave up and left a voicemail. He had figured out how to receive calls, but voicemail was still a mystery.

"Aubrey, I know it's late, but can you write a deed for me this afternoon?" The realtor had a closing at five o'clock. Her regular attorney had left town that morning, and she was in a bind. It was typical for Aubrey's law practice; he got the leftovers. People liked Aubrey and trusted him, but he gave off an air of not wanting to build his law practice. He was still renting the small one-room office across from where Hatfield's Hardware used to be, and he had never hired an assistant or a secretary.

"Well, I just locked up early, but come on over." Aubrey closed the flap on his cellphone and sighed. *Ten bucks is ten bucks.*

As he fiddled with the door lock that had given him trouble for several years, he heard a familiar voice shouting, "Uncle Aubrey?"

The boy was half a block away. Aubrey waved and shouted to him, "Hey, Zach." Aubrey liked the towhead. He was in church every Sunday, and it was hard to miss him because he seemed to be in everything. When he was little, he had a prominent role in the youth programs. Then he became the pastor's favorite acolyte, a job he seemed to love. When he got bigger, he served as a greeter. Zach Barrett excelled in that role; he was a natural-born greeter with the scrubbed look of the All-American boy—six feet tall, muscled and sleek.

His mother, Tolece Barrett, was a washerwoman and part-time house cleaner. She and Zach lived alone in a small rent house on the edge of town. Prissy's sister, now dead, married a Barrett back in the early sixties, and they had a boy who got Tolece pregnant and then ran off.

Zach never had a father figure. When he was twelve years old, he walked right up to Aubrey in church and said, "Is it OK if I call you Uncle Aubrey?" It caught Aubrey by surprise because the family connection was distant. But he instinctively said, "Yes, of course."

Aubrey was still trying to get the door to his office open when Zach got over to where he was. They shook hands, and Zack motioned toward two boys who were with him. "These are my buddies, Hank and Harry Ball. They look alike, but actually they are fraternal twins."

Hank Ball grinned and gave what seemed to be his standard line. "My mom had six kids before she had us. I came first, so they call me Seven Ball. And they call my brother Eight Ball."

Aubrey and the boys laughed. Zach gave Seven Ball a teenager's punch on the shoulder, and then came right to the point. "Uncle Aubrey, everybody in town says you have forgotten more about baseball than most people know and that you used to be a great player."

"Well, I do love the game..."

Eight Ball, a boy who could not stand still, blurted out, "People say a scout for the Detroit Tigers came all the way to Woodville to see you play. Everyone thought you were on the way to the big leagues, but you went to college instead."

"It is true that I got scouted. I even went to a tryout, but the Tigers found out right away that I couldn't hit the curveball, and that was that." Aubrey laughed when he said it, but it was a sore spot for him.

Zach said, "Well, we've been talking with the other boys who will be on next year's American Legion team, and we want you to be our coach." Seven Ball and Eight Ball high-fived Zach and nodded in support.

Aubrey was dumbfounded and looked the part. "I'm flattered, but you all have caught me by surprise. Let me think about it."

Zach said, “Sure, Uncle Aubrey, just let us know—but we hope you will say yes.”

Aubrey, sensing impatience and disappointment, said, “Who are you all pulling for in the World Series? It starts this weekend.”

Zach said, “We are Cardinal fans—disappointed that they didn’t make it in—so we have decided to pull for the National League team, the Astros. How about you?”

Aubrey said, “I’ve been a Baltimore Oriole fan ever since Brooks Robinson brought honor to Arkansas with his play at third base. I’m going to hold my nose and pull for the American League team, the White Sox.”

Eight Ball said, “Yuk.”

They all had a good laugh, and Aubrey saw it as an opportune time to change the subject. “You all are juniors this year. What are your plans after high school?”

The Ball boys said, “We are going to the University of Arkansas. Our parents went there.”

Zach said, “I’m going to enlist in the Marine Corps. I’m following in Mr. Dwane’s footsteps. It is something I have thought about for a long time, and it’s right for me. I can help my mom, and after three years the GI Bill will pay my way through college.”

“Well, boys, let’s keep in touch. I’ll let you know pretty soon about coaching the Legion team.” The meeting broke up, and Aubrey went back to fiddling with the door lock to his office, vowing to get it fixed.

He finally got the door open and went into the office, but he was not thinking about the deed that he was going to write for the realtor. He was enjoying the thrill he felt when the boys asked him to coach their team, and he was thinking about something not so pleasant: Iraq.

THIRTY-ONE

"The White Sox have not won a World Series since 1917—two years before the infamous Black Sox scandal when Shoeless Joe Jackson and other Chicago players conspired to throw the 1919 World Series." The TV announcer waxed nostalgic, talking too loud.

The color man for the broadcast chimed in with a sedate prediction. "If the Sox win today they will be the 2005 World Series Champions, and this will be remembered forever as the year of redemption in the Windy City."

Aubrey and Dwane watched every pitch, pulling for the White Sox to break the curse. Dwane said, "The curse has lasted as long as I have—eighty-six years."

During the game, Aubrey told Dwane that Zach and the Ball boys had asked him to coach next year's American Legion baseball team. Dwane said, "I think you ought to do it."

"I'd like to, but it might not be the best thing. I haven't done anything like that since Prissy died."

Dwane knew what was bothering him. "Aubrey, you can beat your drinking problem. I'm the only one who knows about it, and you are just a binge drinker—you don't drink all the time."

"I drink when I get real low, which is pretty often, and I've had a lot of binges over the last thirty-six years. I hate to say it, but it helps to get smashed for a couple of days."

The World Series announcer, louder than ever and ecstatic, broke into their conversation. "The White Sox win, 8 to 5. The curse is broken. This is the year of redemption for the Windy City."

Dwane looked Aubrey in the eye, "If the city of Chicago can be redeemed after the Black Sox scandal, so can you. Don't you agree?"

"In theory, yes, I'd like to. But I've been down in the dumps for a long time."

"It's time to put all that behind you. You lost all the women that mattered to you, and you lost the family store when the big chain stores moved in, but none of that was your fault." Dwane had said these things many times, but for the first time Aubrey seemed willing to listen.

"When Zach and his friends asked me to coach, it took me back to when I was a kid—to boys and baseball. It might be good for me. But I'm not going to do it unless it will be good for the boys."

"Why wouldn't it be?"

"I might screw up, go off the wagon, or just lose interest. I can think of a thousand reasons to worry about it. I get spells of melancholy—times when I beat myself to a pulp. I bury bad memories, but they will not stay buried. They keep coming back to haunt me, regular as clockwork. I have the sorriest law practice in North Arkansas, and I live hand to mouth—"

Dwane interrupted, "Stop focusing on the negatives. The White Sox would have lost today if they had done that. Now they have redeemed the entire city of Chicago. You can find redemption too."

Aubrey got up and walked to the front door. He stared outside.

Neither man spoke for a while.

"I agree that coaching would be good for me, and it could be good for the boys, but the thing I want most is to help Zach. Tolece works her fingers to the bone and has for years, but they don't have a pot to piss in. The boy says he wants to join the Marines so that he can help his mother and get the GI Bill. He says he wants to follow in your footsteps."

Dwane pointed to the big scar on his face and then to his limp left arm. "Look what that did for me."

"That's my point. Just today, the news people are reporting that the U. S. military death toll in Iraq has reached 2,000. I'd like to help Zach through college so he wouldn't have to go into the Marines, but I'm broke. Hatfield House is run down and worth very little, and my income from the law practice is barely enough to cover expenses."

Dwane said, "Let's talk about it tomorrow. I've got an idea I have been working on for quite a while."

THIRTY-TWO

Aubrey cooked country ham and eggs for breakfast, Dwane's favorite. It was a once-a-week thing, a break from cereal or toast, the usual fare for two men living alone. When the food was gone, Aubrey poured two cups of coffee and sat across from Dwane. It was time for their morning talk, a ritual.

Dwane, cocked and primed, said, "Yesterday, you said you wished you had enough money to help Zach go to college. Now hear me out before you say my idea is crazy."

Aubrey sniggered. "Are we going to rob a bank?"

"Just the opposite. I believe you can win the upcoming election for prosecuting attorney of this judicial district. The pay is good and so are the benefits."

Aubrey was speechless, and then he scoffed. "I established years ago that I am a lousy prosecutor. I did not stand up when Cooksey and the sheriff turned a blind eye to the lynching of Ike Swanson, and that still bugs me. Who would vote for me, a lawyer who can barely get by?"

"You should hear me out before you shoot from the lip." Dwane seldom raised his voice, but Aubrey's tone bothered him.

"Go ahead, I'm sorry."

"First, I know you still feel bad about the lynching of Ike Swanson, but it was Fred Cooksey and that bucko-sheriff who turned their backs and failed to investigate the case. It was shameful all right, but the shame is theirs, not yours. You resigned when you saw what they were doing."

"I don't mean to be contentious, but I need to make one more point. Then I will keep my mouth shut."

"OK, what is your point?"

"I did resign. That is true, but I did not have the courage to tell Cooksey why I was resigning. I just quit. I ran away."

Dwane stiffened as if he were going to climb out of his wheelchair. He groaned and started to say something. Then he settled back and flashed a puckish smile.

"Well, Moses got scared and ran away from Pharaoh. He stayed away for forty years, and then God called him to go into Egypt to free the slaves. Guess what, Moses turned God down five times. He kept saying, 'Why me, Lord?' You see, Moses doubted himself. He didn't think he was up to the job of leading the Israelites out of Egypt."

Dwane let his point sink in. Aubrey gave him a bewildered look and then laughed out loud. "That's the first time I've been compared to Moses."

"You are the right man for this job, Aubrey. Stop doubting yourself. Now let me tell you how you can win the election.

"There are only two counties in this judicial district. This county has forty-five percent of the votes in the district. People here like you, and they will vote for you because you are a hometown boy. Provincialism is one of the strongest forces in politics.

"That brings me to Hawkins County, which has fifty-five percent of the votes. Only two lawyers have shown an interest in the job, and both of them live in Hawkins County. They are bitter rivals, and the hatred goes back generations. One is a political descendant of Fred Cooksey, and the other is a blood descendant of Blacky Blackburn. Both men are Democrats, and they will split the vote in the Democratic primary. The primary election will be in May, and the loser's voters will be mad as hell. If you file for the Republican nomination, you will be unopposed, and that will put you on the ballot for the November general election. As the Republican nominee, you would face off against the winner of the Democratic primary. The pissed-off voters in Hawkins County will vote for you in November. It is simple math. You will win."

Aubrey said, "Wait a second. You said provincialism is a strong force. Would that not apply to the loser's voters in Hawkins County? Wouldn't they vote for their hometown boy even though he beat their favorite candidate?"

"Hatred trumps provincialism. The loser's voters will vote for you. Count on it."

THIRTY-THREE

Aubrey struggled with Dwane's idea for several months. He tried to give up whiskey by switching to wine, but that did not work. Twice he got drunk and told his old friend that he could not run for prosecuting attorney. Dwane was patient. He did not browbeat Aubrey, but their discussions always centered on Aubrey's misplaced sense that he did not deserve to be prosecuting attorney. Aubrey had managed, over time, to convince himself that if he had shown courage in 1968, Sheriff Odom and Fred Cooksey would have identified the thugs who lynched Ike Swanson.

Dwane empathized, but diplomatically turned the argument around. "You should seek the office to set new and better standards. Law enforcement should be about seeking the truth and rendering fair and honest punishment to wrongdoers. You know that better than anyone."

Dwane also believed, but never mentioned, that running for the office would be good for Aubrey personally. To his way of thinking, it would give Aubrey a chance to purge the demons of shame, drinking, and loneliness that had haunted him for thirty-six years.

In early March of 2006, on the last day allowed by law to file as a candidate for prosecuting attorney, Aubrey and Dwane drove to the State Capitol in Little Rock. Aubrey had not had a drink in six weeks and he was in an upbeat mood. They went into the Capitol rotunda, and Aubrey signed the papers and paid the filing fee to be a Republican candidate for prosecuting attorney.

No other Republican candidate filed, and when the ticket closed at noon, Aubrey became the nominee of the Republican Party.

The Democratic ticket closed at the same time, and, as Dwane predicted, there were only two candidates for the nomination: Claude "Red" Carper, the Cooksey protégé, and Jacob "Jake" Blackburn, the grandson of Blacky Blackburn. The stage was set.

When they left the Capitol, they did not talk until they got across the Arkansas River. Then Aubrey said, "OK, coach. What do I do now?"

"Get some cards printed and be nice to everyone."

"That's easy enough, but I still have reservations about the whole thing. I respect everything you have said to get me in this race, but the main reason I am doing it is to make a good salary so that I can help Zach."

"Well, that's noble. But I think you know you have come to a crossroads in your life. This will be a good way for you to change the downhill slide you have been on."

Aubrey thought for a minute. "OK, I admit to a measure of self-interest, but Zach is the nearest thing I have to blood kin. I like him a lot, and if I win, I can do something to help him and Tolece. I would never forgive myself if he got killed in Iraq."

"Don't say 'If I win.' From now on, it is 'When I win.'"

Aubrey smiled. "OK, coach."

THIRTY-FOUR

The coffee klatch table at Gentry's was full when Aubrey walked in the morning after he filed the papers to be a candidate for prosecuting attorney. The old loudmouth, Sonny Childs, who had dominated the group for almost thirty years, was long gone. Loudmouth Horace Zang was the new bell-cow. Everything else was as it had been since the Great Depression.

Zang mooed, "Well, look who's here—our brand-new politician. Who'd have thunk it?"

Aubrey settled into the dentist chair to take his licks, and the klatchers poured it on for a good fifteen minutes. "What were you thinking? ... I never thought of you as a pol ... Why did you do it? ... You're going to get your butt beat ..."

Zang soon tired of it and changed the subject to potholes, a topic guaranteed to last for a good while. Late freezing had caused an extraordinary number of potholes on county roads, and the klatchers were giving the county judge hell.

Aubrey slipped out of the meeting wondering if he had made the right decision. But over the next few days, friends and acquaintances all across town wished him well. They gave him hope, something that had not figured into his life for a long time.

THIRTY-FIVE

Aubrey shook his head and pushed his half-empty coffee cup to the center of the kitchen table. "I can't do that, Dwane, not today. I've been campaigning for almost two weeks and I'm tired of putting on phony smiles and making small talk."

Dwane said, "You need to go. I guarantee you the two Democrat candidates will be there. This particular auction at the sale barn is a big deal. People from all around will be there to buy and sell cattle."

"I'll look silly, like a turd in a punchbowl. I've never gone to the cattle sales and everyone there will know it."

"Maybe so, but they expect to see you. It's the way politicking is done."

Once Aubrey had become an official candidate, Dwane pushed him to attend weddings, funerals, meetings at City Hall, school events. When nothing was going on, Dwane sent him to the little towns in both counties to meet shopkeepers, local officials, anybody willing to shake his hand.

"It may be the way it is done, Dwane, but I'm not a natural-born politician. This is hard for me."

"Well, you've been telling people how you want to improve the criminal justice system. None of that will happen if you don't get out there and campaign."

Aubrey grumbled, and then said. "All right, I'll go to the dadgummed sale, but Monday is the first day of spring and I'm going to start working out with Zach and the Legion baseball team. We are going to practice every afternoon after school. Coaching those boys will help me keep my sanity."

Dwane scoffed, but agreed. Aubrey was one hundred percent right. He wanted to win the election and he loved the supportive comments he was getting out on the hustings. But he needed something to offset the part of politics that was foreign to him. His time with the boys would take him off the campaign trail and clear his mind. Baseball was in his blood; it would be the perfect antidote to politics, a magic elixir.

On Monday, March 20, Aubrey parked behind the stands at Military Park and walked toward the field. The boys were already there. He could hear the rattle of bats and the popping sound of balls landing in freshly oiled gloves. The boys were playing catch and beginning the chatter that took Aubrey back to his time as a player. Baseball does that for boys, no matter how old they get to be. The field, the uniforms, balls, strikes, outs, home runs, and bunt singles—stealing bases, pop-ups, and outs at the plate. All of that, and more, raced through Aubrey's mind even though he had not been on the field as a player or coach for years. He yearned for the good feeling of being in the dugout, the storytelling, the joking and all that goes with it.

The boys waved to him as soon as they saw him, and he suddenly felt very young. They circled around him, giving each other high-fives and chanting "Doughboys—Doughboys—Doughboys." Aubrey gave them a pep talk. They clapped their hands and took the field.

Zach was the catcher, Seven Ball the shortstop, and Eight Ball the second baseman. The three of them had done a good job of building Aubrey up to their teammates. The first practice went very well, and the boys were excited that Aubrey was running for political office. Their new coach was more than a coach; he was a celebrity.

The team's best pitcher was Jody Tucker, Zach's best friend. They favored each other in looks and build, but Jody had a mild case of acne and a thick crop of dirty-blond hair. The two boys were a formidable team, having been battery mates through Little League and Pony League.

When the practice was over, Aubrey and Zach offered to give Jody a ride home, but he said his grandfather was already there, waiting to pick him up. As he said it, he waved to an elderly, heavyset man standing beside a white GMC truck.

Aubrey said, "I'd like to meet him." It was foreign to Aubrey to hustle votes, but Dwane had given him strict instructions to give a campaign card to everyone he did not know, and ask for their vote.

When they got near the truck Jody said, "Grandpa, this is Mr. Hatfield. He's our new coach."

Aubrey reached to shake hands. "Hi, I'm Aubrey Hatfield."

Jody's grandfather said, "Hey, I'm Joe Tucker Jr., but most folks just call me Junior."

They talked about the coming baseball season for a minute. Then, as they were parting, Aubrey handed Junior a campaign card. "By the way, I'm running for prosecuting attorney and I would appreciate your vote."

"OK, but I'm not much into politics and law-and-order stuff."

Aubrey felt coolness he had not felt when he shook Junior's hand or when they were talking about baseball, but he did not think it odd. He had learned since filing for office that some people are uncomfortable when a politician asks for their vote. He supposed Junior Tucker was like that.

As he turned to leave, Aubrey said, "That's all right. I hope you will come to our games. Your grandson is quite a pitcher."

When he got home to Hatfield House, Dwane asked him how the day had gone.

"I had a good day. The political business is unnatural for me, but I feel better than I've felt in years, thanks to no booze, baseball, and boys. I jogged around the field with the boys during practice, and I am determined to lose this gut before the season is over."

Dwane said, "Good, you will be in shape for the final months of the campaign. By the way, primary election day is coming up soon, and my friends tell me the Democratic race for prosecuting attorney has really heated up. They say it is going to be a dead heat between Red Carper and Jake Blackburn. If that's the way it turns out, it will be perfect for you."

THIRTY-SIX

On primary day, Red Carper defeated Jake Blackburn, fifty-one percent to forty-nine percent. Close, but not close enough to warrant a recount. Red Carper would be the Democratic nominee for prosecuting attorney, and all eyes turned to November. Many people were realizing for the first time that Aubrey was in the race as the Republican nominee.

Two days later, Jake Blackburn walked into Aubrey's law office. He bore no resemblance to his notorious grandfather, Blacky, who had lived to be ninety-six years old. Aubrey had met Jake in early June when he debated Red Carper at the courthouse in Campbell County, but he did not know him well.

"Aubrey, I cannot stand Red Carper. He is a Cooksey protégé. My grandfather, Blacky, told me to stay away from the Cookseys and everyone associated with them, and I have tried to do that. I wish I had won the Democratic primary just for the sheer pleasure of beating Red. I came close, but in politics close doesn't count."

Aubrey said, "I'm new at this, but I hope to beat him in the November election."

"My people and I have been feuding with the Cooksey clan for years. It goes back to Grandpa Blacky. He said Cooksey was a crook, and he told me about the time he came to see you about that gay guy who got lynched. He said several times, 'Aubrey Hatfield is a good man—he has good life path numbers.'"

"I remember. He told me that to my face," Aubrey said.

"He was big into the numerology thing. I'm not, but hey, it worked for Grandpa Blacky. He used to skin Fred Cooksey every time they tried a case."

Jake laughed in a way that reminded Aubrey of Blacky. Then he got a warlike look on his face, and aimed a forefinger at Aubrey. "Aubrey, my people will be there for you in November. I'll see to it."

THIRTY-SEVEN

The last baseball game of the year for Woodville was an away game against the league-leading Brasstown Bengals. The boys boarded the team bus at 10 a.m., and the chatter started as soon as the driver closed the door. Most of the talk was about the pitcher they expected to face. He had a good curveball and a so-so changeup, but his main pitch was a fastball in the low nineties. Then they talked about the Bengal hitters and how best to defend against them.

At the halfway mark of the trip, the newest member of the team, a fine right fielder who had moved to town in mid-season, began raising questions about the team's name. "How did we get the name Doughboys? Has anyone ever thought about changing it to something else? What the hell is a Doughboy anyway?"

Zach said, "We used to be called the Bobcats, but someone changed the name a long time ago. Older folks in town say it comes from World War I, when everyone called our troops Doughboys."

Jody Tucker said, "My dad played for the Doughboys in the mid-eighties. He said my grandpa had something to do with changing the name. He had a friend who pulled a four-year-old girl out of a house fire, and then dropped dead due to a massive heart attack. He was big and fat, and everyone called him Doughboy."

Seven Ball said, "I'm for keeping Doughboys. If it honors the troops, then that's a good thing."

The right fielder said, "OK. I'm OK with that."

The game was a humdinger. Eight Ball stole home in the third, and Zach hit a double and a triple. Jody pitched well, but the Brasstown Bengals beat the Woodville Doughboys 8-7 with a walk-off home run. The boys were low sick, but by the time the team bus rolled into Woodville, they were talking politics, figuring out ways to help Coach Aubrey beat Red Carper on November 7.

School was in its third week when Zach got the boys together to plan a trip to Hawkins County to campaign with Aubrey. Every member of the team, except for the boys who had gone on to college, came to the meeting.

"Uncle Aubrey says the guy who lost to Red Carper wants to go around the county with us. He hates Carper and says his supporters feel the same way. He says they will vote for an outsider if they think he is OK."

"Can we bring our girlfriends?" Eight Ball asked the question, and most of the boys nodded in agreement.

"Of course," Zach said. "The more the merrier."

On Friday, October 13, a caravan of twenty cars and pickup trucks carrying fifty students from Woodville drove into Hawkins County, and followed Aubrey and Jake Blackburn through the main parts of the county. Upon entering a town, Zach and Jody would unfurl a homemade banner, AUBREY HATFIELD FOR PROSECUTING ATTORNEY, and the youngsters would fall in behind them, marching in step as Eight Ball beat his bass drum and Seven Ball hammered a snappy cadence on his snare drum. The girls led cheers imploring people to vote for Aubrey, who waved and smiled as he walked alongside Jake Blackburn.

Three weeks later Aubrey defeated Claude "Red" Carper by a good margin. He carried his home county, Campbell, with seventy-nine percent of the vote. In Hawkins County, the vote was nearly identical to the vote in the Democratic primary. Aubrey got forty-nine percent, and Red Carper got fifty-one percent. Jake Blackburn's voters stayed in harness, just as Jake had promised. When Aubrey made his victory speech, he gave full credit to Jake and his grandfather, Blacky Blackburn. Aubrey called them true believers who always fought for fair play and honesty in the administration of justice.

When the cheering was over, Aubrey and Dwane returned to Hatfield House. Dwane said, "I am very proud of you."

"Thanks, but I feel a little like the dog that caught the streetcar."

Dwane said, "There's a lot to think about, but you have a couple of months before you take the oath of office. That's plenty of time to get organized and make a plan for what you hope to accomplish."

THIRTY-EIGHT

On Tuesday, January 2, 2007, Aubrey took the oath of office and became the prosecuting attorney for the Twenty-Ninth Judicial District of Arkansas. Dwane was there, and so was Jake Blackburn. Zach, the nearest thing Aubrey had for kinfolks, was on the front row, and—to Aubrey's surprise—the coffee klatch bell-cow, Horace Zang, was there along with several of his sycophants. The courtroom of the Campbell County Courthouse was filled. Every player on the 2006 Doughboy team came and sat near Zach, all wearing their Doughboy jerseys. Their girlfriends came too, and they held the campaign banner up for all to see. Members of the First United Methodist Church, many of whom Aubrey did not recognize, were in the crowd.

Aubrey thanked them for coming and said he would try his best to do a good job. Then he sat down, having made the shortest political speech in Campbell County history.

The circuit judge gave the oath to several lesser officials, and when the ceremony ended, Jake Blackburn pulled Aubrey aside. "I've been thinking about who you might pick to be your deputy prosecuting attorney. We talked a little about it before the election, but I have a late entry to suggest."

Aubrey said, "I haven't named anyone yet. I got the resumes you sent, but the job is still wide open."

Jake said, "You'd be smart to interview Stephanie Brooks. You know the Brooks family—they own White Oak Stables, that big quarterhorse ranch off to the right just as you cross the county line on your way into Hawkins County."

"I know the place, it's beautiful." Aubrey paused, and then said, "I thought I knew every lawyer in these parts. Why haven't I heard about her?"

"She's been away for years. We grew up together and graduated from Brasstown High in 1985. I went to the University of Arkansas, but she went to Arkansas State and then she got an L.L.B. from the University of Virginia."

"That's a great school, she must be smart," Aubrey said.

"She was valedictorian of our class. Sometimes that doesn't mean much, but in her case it did. I think she graduated from UVA with honors."

"So, now she has come home?"

"Yeah, she was in D.C., working for Congressman Hastings, but her mother had a stroke last summer and Stephanie came home to take care of her."

"That speaks well of her," Aubrey said.

"She is a good woman, Aubrey. Her mother was bad off and living alone. She died right after Thanksgiving, and I thought Stephanie might go back East, but she has decided to stay here. She is a hill-country girl at heart. She loves horses, and she loves White Oak Stables. It is where she grew up. Now that the ranch is hers, she cannot bring herself to sell it, so she is planning to improve it. She is going to open the stables and the riding arena to the public. She's got it all planned out."

"And, she wants to be my deputy prosecutor?"

"Yes, she wants to stay busy, try some cases, keep up her legal skills—that sort of thing."

"She sounds overqualified, but tell her to give me a call. If our noses fit, I will hire her."

A week later Aubrey headed to his new office in the courthouse. It was a cold, wet January day, and he was eager to get inside and lower his umbrella. As he approached the revolving door, a chirpy voice called his name. "Mr. Hatfield?" He turned around and saw a woman who made him think of Prissy. She was not an exact match, but the resemblance was close enough to make him catch his breath.

Aubrey waved for her to follow. They made a clumsy entrance through the revolving door, and laughed about it when they were safely inside.

"Hi, I'm Aubrey Hatfield."

She pulled back the hood of her coat, and shook her long jet-black hair free. "I'm Stephanie Brooks, a friend of Jake Blackburn. He told me to call you about the deputy position, but I decided to drive over and meet you in person."

Aubrey was busy comparing her to Prissy, trying to understand what made him think of Prissy when he first saw her. Stephanie's hair was dark black, not red like Prissy's. Her eyes were green, not sapphire, but they were ablaze and her voice was electric, full of energy. That is it, he decided. *That is why she reminds me of Prissy.*

"I hope I'm not intruding. I should have called and made an appointment."

"No, that's OK. Sorry, I had my mind on something else. I'm glad you are here. Let's go into my brand-new office and talk about the deputy position."

Aubrey took her coat and invited Stephanie to sit in a Queen Anne chair next to his desk. As he sat down, he said, "Jake tells me you worked for Congressman Hastings."

Stephanie nodded. "Well, sort of. I moved from Atlanta to Washington after my divorce two years ago, and the congressman got me a job on the House Interior Committee. I spent the next eighteen months researching and drafting legislation. Sounds boring, but I enjoyed it because I have loved the conservation issues since I was a little girl. But then my mom died."

"I know how much that hurts. I lost my mother the day of the Apollo 11 launch."

They talked about other things, but Aubrey had no experience at hiring. It took him less than fifteen minutes to offer her the job. Stephanie's academic record was impressive, but she exuded common sense and honesty. That is what Aubrey liked the most, and she seemed pleased when he said she would have to serve as his deputy in both counties because he had already concluded that he would not need a fulltime deputy in his home county.

"I accept," she said.

They shook hands and decided that she would start the following Monday.

Stephanie's quick wit and big smile fascinated Aubrey; she was, indeed, very much like Prissy.

Aubrey hurried home to tell Dwane and get his advice on how to handle the attraction he felt for his new deputy.

THIRTY-NINE

Aubrey was set to attend his first docket day in Campbell County as prosecuting attorney at 10 a.m. Tuesday, January 23, 2007. He had been in office exactly three weeks.

He asked Stephanie to drive over from Hawkins County to help out, but the main reason he wanted her to come was to discuss his plan for running the office. He was determined to set guidelines for working with the county sheriffs and the state police.

Aubrey stopped at Ma Phipps's Cafeteria to pick up coffee and breakfast sandwiches, and got to the office just before 7 o'clock. Dwane was with him, and when they turned into the hall that led to his office, they saw Stephanie, dressed in a smart blue suit, looking very professional. She was waiting in front of a glass door that had fresh lettering, gold with black trim: AUBREY HATFIELD, PROSECUTING ATTORNEY.

Dwane said, "Aha, this must be Stephanie."

"And you must be Dwane Pollard, the smartest man in the county." Dwane smiled, they shook hands, and Aubrey unlocked the door. Stephanie stepped in, and when Aubrey rolled Dwane to a stop, she took the cafeteria tray off his lap. Soon they were deep into a discussion of how best to deal with the county sheriffs.

At first, Stephanie just listened.

Aubrey began. "We have two strong-minded sheriffs to work with. Jack Odom here in Campbell County is the grandson of Mark Odom, who was sheriff when I first started practicing law. He is personable, but he is full of himself, and his family has always been in cahoots with the Cooksey machine. When a crime is committed, he needs to understand that this office will control the investigation and prosecution of the case."

Dwane said, "Jim Sterling, the sheriff of Hawkins County, is part of the old Cooksey clan too. He's also a bucko-sheriff type, too big for his britches. It comes from years of doing it the way it has always been done."

Aubrey said, "Exactly. I do not want our sheriffs cutting deals with defense attorneys or telling the state police back off of an investigation."

Stephanie put her sandwich down and got into the conversation. "I agree one-hundred percent, but shouldn't we be careful in the way we do that? I mean, don't we have to show respect for history and tradition? County sheriffs have always been strong, particularly here in the hills."

Aubrey said, "That's a good point." He was about to say more, but Dwane and Stephanie took over the conversation, and Aubrey became a bystander.

Dwane, a man who did not finish the third grade and taught himself to read and write, and Stephanie, an honors graduate of the University of Virginia law school, dug into the history of county sheriffs. They started with sheriffs in the South, but soon they were deep into Winston Churchill's tome, *A History of the English-Speaking Peoples*; Will Durant's masterpiece, *The Story of Civilization*; and the *Federalist Papers*. It was a thorough vetting of the role of sheriffs throughout English and American history, tracing back to the Magna Carta. At first, it seemed to Aubrey that they were testing each other, but soon he saw nothing but mutual respect. The thirty-minute exercise ended with Stephanie making an interesting point.

She said, "In the beginning a sheriff was called the 'Reeve.' He was the chief law enforcement officer of the 'Shire,' the British name for counties—Yorkshire and Cheshire are examples. In time, he became the 'Shire Reeve' and soon that name morphed into 'Sheriff.' It is an interesting bit of trivia that reminds us to respect history and tradition."

Dwane said, "Stephanie, we must talk more. I love to learn."

FORTY

On Monday, February 5, Aubrey called a meeting of the Doughboys to talk about the coming season. He had considered quitting as coach after he won the election, but decided against it when Horace Zang, the coffee klatch bell-cow, volunteered to be his assistant coach. Horace was perfect for the job. In the early 1960s he played shortstop for the Arkansas Travelers, a Double A team.

As the meeting was winding down, Sheriff Jack Odom appeared outside the door and motioned for Aubrey to come out. Aubrey turned the meeting over to Horace, who began by growling off a set of do's and don'ts. Eight Ball and Jody Tucker broke down laughing, and so did Horace when he finally realized that the boys were laughing at him. The boys on the team had learned, as Aubrey had, that Horace's bark was worse than his bite.

When Aubrey was out of the room, the sheriff said, "Randy Trice has been killed. Someone whacked him on the head several times and left him to die at the Cherokee Access, right by the lake."

"Uh-oh, this is going to shake up the whole county."

Randy Trice was the third-generation owner and operator of Trice Motors. The company was the county's oldest car dealership, having been in existence since the 1920s. Dwane sold used cars for Trice Motors when he came home from World War II in 1945. The Trices were well known and respected throughout Arkansas; candidates for office, from governor on down, never campaigned in Campbell County without first paying homage to them.

Randy was thirty-eight years old. He married young, as soon as he got out of college, but it did not last. He dedicated himself to becoming an expert in the car dealership business. He served on the boards of several civic organizations, and he once filled a vacancy on the city council, but he did not like politics. He attended the First Baptist Church in Woodville and did some lay preaching in small churches that could not afford a full-time pastor.

Sheriff Odom said, "I can't think of a better-known person in this part of the country. Randy was popular; everybody liked him. I'll get right on this. My boys are already asking questions and working their sources to see what they can learn. We need to find the killer and give him some Campbell County justice."

Aubrey said, "Well, let's get the facts first. Notify the state police right now. We need them to send their best team of investigators up here, pronto. I want them to take the lead on this. If they need a nudge to treat this as a priority case, tell them to give me a call. I will call the governor if necessary. And, sheriff, tell the state police to keep me posted as to how their investigation is going, step by step."

"OK, Aubrey, if that's the way you want to play it." He wheeled and left without saying more.

FORTY-ONE

Two days later, Aubrey received a call from Lieutenant John Smothers of the Arkansas State Police. He wanted to have a private visit with Aubrey to report what his investigators were learning.

Aubrey said, "Fine. It is 10:30 now, so let's meet first thing after lunch. I will call my deputy, Stephanie Brooks. I want her to be in the meeting."

The lieutenant hesitated. "I had hoped we could visit privately, just me and you."

Aubrey said, "I want her in the meeting; she needs to know what I know. Can you be here at 1:30?"

The lieutenant agreed, and at 1:30 p.m. sharp, he and Sheriff Odom walked into Aubrey's office. Aubrey invited them to step into a small conference room where Stephanie was sitting with a yellow legal pad on the table in front of her.

Aubrey introduced Stephanie and looked straight at the lieutenant, "So, catch us up on your investigation."

The lieutenant, a statuesque man with graying temples, cleared his throat. "We did the usual work at the crime scene. The coroner looked at the body, and he believes the killer used something blunt to cause the head wounds, but we found no such instrument in the area. We did collect possible hair and fiber specimens from Randy's Cadillac Escalade. Those are at our laboratory in Little Rock, and we have sent the body to the state medical examiner. She is planning to do an autopsy tomorrow."

"Do we have any leads, any theories about who might have killed Randy?"

"That is what I wanted to talk about. We don't have any suspects identified as yet, but we do have an investigative theory."

Aubrey said, "Let's hear it."

"When my investigators looked into Randy's background to learn about his employees, his friends and other associations, we kept getting strong signals that Randy Trice was a homosexual. A few people said it was just a rumor, but we interviewed a twenty-five-year-old man in Morrilton who admitted to having a sexual relationship with Randy. He gave us the names of others who could back that up, and we are in the process of interviewing them."

Aubrey said, "That surprises me, I wasn't close to Randy, but I remember when he came back to town after college. He was married to a very attractive woman from Fayetteville, but come to think of it, the marriage didn't last very long."

Aubrey pondered the new information, and then asked, "So, what is your investigative theory?"

The lieutenant said, "There is no indication of robbery. It could have been an irate customer or someone who just didn't like Randy. But I think the most likely scenario is that he was killed by a jealous boyfriend or someone he was trying to have sex with, someone who did not want to do homosexual sex."

"How do you plan to proceed?" Aubrey was thinking of his first days as a deputy prosecutor, in 1968, when Ike Swanson was tortured and murdered—a lynching that, he reminded himself, was still unsolved.

"We are going to continue our interviews and wait for the laboratory results and the autopsy report. With luck, we will identify a suspect. That's about all we can do at the moment."

Aubrey said, "All right. Let's stay on top of this."

When the meeting broke up, Aubrey followed the lieutenant and the sheriff into the hall. Stephanie stayed in the office. The sheriff, who had said nothing during the meeting, said, "Hard to believe all this about Randy Trice. He was a smart guy. You'd think he would have known not to hit on someone around here. Queers get what they deserve when they do that."

Aubrey said, "Don't rush to judgment, Sheriff. Let's wait for the facts."

The sheriff got a cellphone call and headed down the hall to take it.

Aubrey got in the lieutenant's face. "Lieutenant, it is fine for you and your people to keep the sheriff and his people apprised of your investigation, but in the future I want you to report directly to me or Stephanie when you have new information. I do not want to be the last one to learn what is going on. This is an important case. Are we understood?"

FORTY-TWO

On Monday, February 12, Aubrey and Stephanie met in his office at 9 a.m. to go over their active criminal cases in preparation for the next docket day. She had received several inquiries from defense attorneys who were trying to work out plea agreements for their clients, and she wanted to know Aubrey's thoughts about each case.

They were about to start the review when Stephanie heard someone tapping on the outer door of the office. She opened the door and invited a middle-aged man in overalls to come in.

"Is Mr. Hatfield here?"

Aubrey heard them and came into the anteroom. "Yes, I'm Aubrey Hatfield."

"I'm Charles Blodgett. Can I talk to you in private?"

Aubrey said, "Miss Brooks is my deputy. She needs to hear what I hear if you intend to speak to me in my official capacity."

The man shuffled around. "Well, all right, I guess."

They went into the small conference room and sat down.

"Mr. Hatfield, ma'am, I'm right sure my nephew killed Randy Trice, and it is driving my sister Lillian crazy. She is bad broke up, and the boy ain't been to school since that day they found Randy up at the lake."

Aubrey said, "What is your sister's name?"

"She was Lillian Blodgett, but she married Carl Ransom, and they have two kids. One of them is Cody Ransom."

"Is that the same boy who plays on the high school football team?"

"Yes sir, he's the one. He's already got two scholarship offers to play college ball."

"What makes you think Cody killed Randy Trice?"

"They ain't said anything particular, but I can read my sister pretty good. I think she wants to work all this out, but her husband is a mean son-of-a-bitch, and he won't let her."

Stephanie said, "Maybe we should ask Lieutenant Smothers to take it from here."

Aubrey said, "You are exactly right."

"Mr. Blodgett, I am bound by duty to pass this information to the state police, but you can rest assured I will urge them to do what they can within the law to protect you as the source, and I will tell them of your concern for your sister's safety. That's about all I can do until we know more about what happened."

Blodgett said, "I feel like a snitch, but I am worried about Lillian and the boy. I'm pretty sure this is what my sister wants to do."

Stephanie gave him her card. Blodgett nodded a couple of times and left.

As soon as he was gone, Aubrey called Lieutenant John Smothers.

FORTY-THREE

The next day, Tuesday, February 13, Aubrey and Stephanie were talking about how they might proceed if Cody Ransom, an eighteen-year-old boy, became the target of their investigation into the killing of Randy Trice. The phone rang; it was Lieutenant John Smothers.

"Mr. Prosecutor, we have the boy. Sergeant Nestor is taking him in and I am following them to the sheriff's office to do a video of his confession. Do you want to meet us there?"

"You say he has already confessed? Catch me up on what you did, how you approached the boy, and all that."

"We went to the home and the boy's mother came to the door. We told her we were interviewing a number of people believed to have known Randy Trice in one way or another, and that we wanted to talk to Cody. She was very nervous, but she called the boy in. We told her and him that we wanted to talk to him, but that he didn't have to talk to us. Sergeant Nestor gave him the Miranda warning."

"What did they say to that?"

"The mother broke down, big time, and the boy just blurted out, 'I didn't mean to do it. I just panicked when he made a move on me.' At that point the mother said she needed to call the boy's father."

"Where was he?"

"He was working at Tommy's Sawmill, which is right close to the house. It took him about five minutes to get there, and he was mad as hell when he came in."

Aubrey said, "Were you able to calm him down?"

"We told him we needed to take the boy to the sheriff's office for further questioning, but he pitched a fit, mainly cussing at the mother."

"They say he is a mean son-of-a-bitch," Aubrey said.

"The boy blew up and told his old man to leave her alone. Then he said he would come with us, and he did."

"Was that it?"

"Pretty much. We took the boy, and the father followed us out to Nestor's car. He was losing it, waving his arms and screaming that he was going to sue us. Anyway, I am right now about ten minutes from the sheriff's office. Our ETA is 3:55."

Aubrey said, "Stephanie and I think it would be best for us to stay where we are. If you need me for any reason, call me here. You know what to do; just be sure to do it right so we won't have any problems when we get to court."

FORTY-FOUR

Lieutenant Smothers called Aubrey again at 4:45 p.m.

"We got the confession on video, but when we were ten minutes into the interview we got a call from Tom "Spike" Spivey, a big-time lawyer from Little Rock. He told us he had been engaged by Carl Ransom to represent the boy, and he told us to stop the interview, so we did."

"You say it is on video?"

"Yes, we got him saying he did the killing with a five-pound dumbbell. He said he was out jogging on Sawmill Road near the Cherokee Access when Randy Trice drove up in his Escalade. He said he wanted to talk to the boy about the football scholarship that Calico University was offering. The boy recognized Trice, so he got in and they went into the access area. Trice was telling the boy that he graduated from Calico, and that he would be very supportive if Cody took the offer to play football there."

Aubrey said, "Cody is a really good running back, fast and strong. They say he has offers from a number of Division I schools."

"Yeah, anyway, the boy said Trice slid his hand over and put it on his leg near the crotch and asked Cody if he had ever had a blowjob. The boy said it took him by surprise, and he slugged Trice with one of the dumbbells. He kept on slugging until Trice was unconscious."

"Did he say anything to Trice before he hit him?"

"Don't know, because that's when we got the call from the lawyer. We stopped the interview, but we have the video here if you want to see it."

"I'll come over."

FORTY-FIVE

Aubrey and Stephanie got to the sheriff's office just in time to see Carl Ransom giving Sheriff Odom and Lieutenant Smothers an earful.

"Let my boy go. The queer had it coming. You people are going to ruin his life. I got a lawyer coming. Let him go."

Aubrey walked closer to the father. "I'm Aubrey Hatfield. I'm the prosecuting attorney here. Nothing will happen until I talk to your lawyer, but if you will calm down and give us a half-hour, I will come back and talk to you."

Carl Ransom made a guttural noise. His eyes had gone beady, and he smelled of Copenhagen snuff, some of which was seeping from the corner of his mouth. "I want to see my boy," he said.

Aubrey turned to the officers. "Let him go in and see his son in private."

Ransom cooled off a bit and when the sheriff led him away, Lieutenant Smothers took Aubrey and Stephanie to a nearby room and started the video.

Cody Ransom filled the screen, reminding Aubrey of Michelangelo's David—athletic, interesting—but the first voice they heard was that of Lieutenant Smothers stating the basics: time, date, place, persons present, and the purpose of the interview. He then read the Miranda warning, and Cody agreed on screen that no one had pressured him, that he was giving the statement of his own free will.

Aubrey noticed right away that Cody was sitting up tall. He was looking directly into the camera, his voice clear and staccato; the image was that of a proud and confident kid. It struck Aubrey as odd, given the circumstances.

Cody did not flinch when the lieutenant went to the crux of the matter.

VOICE: "Cody, I'm Lieutenant John Smothers. You told me when we were at your house that you were jogging on Sawmill Road on Monday, February 5, when Randy Trice came alongside you in his Cadillac Escalade. If that is so, please tell us in your own words what happened after that."

CODY: "I was out jogging on Sawmill Road, and he drove up by me in a black Escalade and said he wanted to talk about me going to Calico U to play football—said he went there. I knew him as the guy who owned Trice Motors, so I got in the car with him and he pulled into that spot by the lake and started telling me he would help me out if I decided to go there. I thought that was pretty cool, if it was OK and everything. Then he reached over and went for my package, and asked me if I had ever had a blowjob. That's when I hit him with the dumbbell. I hit him a couple of times, and he was knocked out. I got out of the car and ran home. I didn't know he was a queer."

The lieutenant then asked Cody to give his birth date and other background information, such as where he went to school. They talked about what Cody planned to study in college. Then they talked about football and family. It was a remarkably casual conversation.

Aubrey admired the lieutenant's technique. He had gotten an admission; now he was putting the boy at ease, and then he was going to go into the details—searching for contradictions and contentions that could be proven or disproven.

Suddenly the video paused for a few seconds, and then it came back on:

VOICE: "This is Lieutenant John Smothers. We have just received a call from Tom 'Spike' Spivey, an attorney who has been engaged to represent Cody Ransom. I am terminating this interview at his request. The time is 4:42 p.m."

FORTY-SIX

"What do you want us to do with him? Are you going to charge him or what?"

Aubrey said, "Not now, Lieutenant. Let him go home. I could charge him, but I think you ought to check his story out, and I will talk with his lawyer to see what he has to say. The boy is not going anywhere, and we need to get this right."

Aubrey then called Spike Spivey and told him it would be a few days before he decided what he was going to do. Stephanie listened in on the speakerphone.

Spivey said, "Go ahead and file your papers, Hoss. I'm going to walk him out no matter what you charge him with."

"The state police have a video of him admitting that he hit Randy Trice with a dumbbell. Did you know that?"

"What I know is this: The queer was trying to go down on the boy, and the boy hit him. That may sound like a confession to you, but to me it sounds like a good defense."

Aubrey wrapped up the conversation. "I'll call you in a few days to let you know how I am going to proceed. Meanwhile, I need your word that the boy will not run off, and that you will bring him in if I do charge him."

"OK, it's a done deal, no problem."

Aubrey hung up and said to Stephanie, "Well, the fat's in the fire."

Stephanie said, "Where did he get the name Spike?"

"The lieutenant said he was a tight end in high school, and when he finally caught a touchdown pass in his senior year, he tried to spike the ball and threw his shoulder out."

Aubrey chuckled, but Stephanie did not.

"He is itching for you to charge Cody. He sees a big trial with lots of publicity. An acquittal would be a big victory for him personally. What a gadfly."

"I am probably going to charge the boy. I think we have got to, but it won't hurt to think about it over the weekend."

"I've already started doing some research. I'll have some ideas for you to consider before you make the charging decision."

"Thanks, Stephanie." Aubrey paused and then said, "Listen, I've had it for the day, and Dwane and I have something important to do in the morning. I'll be back in the office by noon, but call me if you need me."

FORTY-SEVEN

At 8:30 in the morning, Tolece Barrett came to Hatfield House. Aubrey and Dwane were just finishing breakfast.

"You all wanted to see me this morning?" Tolece looked worn out; she always looked worn out. Her brown hair had not been to a beauty parlor in a long time, and her eyes sagged a little at the edges. However, she was clean and neat, as always, and she stood ramrod straight. She was medium-tall and a little chunky, but anyone could see that she was proud of her son, and proud she was making it on her own. Tolece Barrett was a hard-working woman.

Dwane said, "Thanks for coming over, Tolece. Aubrey and I want to make you an offer we hope you will accept. We need someone to take care of this big house and the two of us. Aubrey is busy as all get-out, and I need somebody to help me now and then. We'll pay you for full time, but you should have enough free time to make a little extra by taking care of some of the people you have been working for. Are you interested? Will you come help us?"

Tolece lit up. "You betcha, Mr. Dwane. I've been praying for something like this. Zach keeps talking about going into the Marine Corps so he can send me money. He's going to graduate in June. Maybe this'll help me change his mind. I can't sleep thinking about him going to Iraq."

Aubrey got up, pulled a chair out, and asked Tolece to sit down with them. "You are now part of the family, Tolece, so let's talk about Zach. He's got a good heart and loves you more than life. The Marines would give him a way to help you and go to college later, but I want to help him go to college now. He's the nearest thing I have to kinfolks, and I've got this new job that pays pretty good. Do you think he would let me do that?"

Tolece slumped, put her hands over her eyes, and laid her head on the table. No one said a word; it was not a time for talking.

Dwane knew how to end the golden moment. After a few minutes, he said a little prayer. Tolece said amen and hurried out to find Zach.

Later that morning Zach came to Hatfield House and hugged Aubrey and Dwane. He said, "My mother has never been so happy. I can't thank you enough."

Then he turned to Aubrey. "Uncle Aubrey, you are the best. I never had a father, so I picked you out to be my father figure when I was twelve. I couldn't have made a better choice, and now with your help I'm going to college this fall. Thank you, thank you."

"You're a good kid, Zach. I'm happy to help."

When Zach left, Aubrey said, "This was a good morning, Dwane. My new job is going to be harder than I thought, but we got a boost out of this, didn't we?"

Dwane lifted his good right arm, reached across his body, and touched the scar on his left cheek. "This scar and my dead left arm and dead legs remind me every day that the best part of us is inside. Praise God."

FORTY-EIGHT

The killing of Randy Trice, a prominent and well-liked businessman, was widely reported by the media after his body was found on February 5. But the coverage dwindled to a trickle and disappeared completely on February 8, when the TV newsreaders, national and local, found a hotter trail to chase.

The anchors were giving breathless reports each evening about the mysterious death of Anna Nicole Smith, a buxom blonde who was *Playboy* magazine's 1993 Playmate of the Year. Her celebrity status had quadrupled shortly thereafter, when she married an eighty-year-old oilman worth more than a billion dollars. Anna Nicole was only twenty-six when the oilman died in 1995. She was filthy rich.

On February 15, the Arkansas media returned to the death of Randy Trice. A teenage high school football star was under suspicion for killing a gay man who had attempted to perform a homosexual act on him. The bygone story of a dead car dealer took off; the national media had the ingredients for yet another morality play, a cultural struggle in "the backward hill country of North Arkansas."

When Aubrey saw the story in the morning paper, he called Lieutenant Smothers. "Do you know who leaked the story about Randy being a homosexual?"

"No, none of my people have a history of doing that. If I had to guess, I would say Spike Spivey leaked it. He's a newshound."

"Could it have been the sheriff? He seems ticked off that I told him to take a backseat to you."

"I just don't know, Mr. Prosecutor. I hope that is not the case."

"Well, remind your people to avoid all contact with reporters. And if you figure out who is leaking, let me know."

FORTY-NINE

The news leak became a gusher, and Aubrey reconciled himself to the fact that he was in the midst of a media circus. Reporters were looking for fresh angles—salacious stories to boost circulation and increase ratings.

On Sunday, February 18, a small newspaper in Southern Missouri carried a story recalling the 1968 torture and murder of Ike Swanson in Campbell County, Arkansas. Headline: GAY MAN LYNCHED. Subhead: 1968 CASE STILL UNSOLVED.

Stephanie saw the story first. She called Aubrey right away. "The story suggests local authorities did not make a serious effort to find the killers. It says you were the deputy prosecutor at the time."

"I was wondering when someone would go there. Can you meet with Dwane and me tomorrow afternoon? We need to talk."

"I'll be there at 1 o'clock sharp."

Aubrey slowly closed the flap on his cellphone and sank into his chair at the breakfast table. "Dwane, can you go with me to meet Stephanie tomorrow afternoon?"

"Of course. What's up?"

"The ghost of Ike Swanson is back."

FIFTY

When Stephanie got to the office Monday afternoon, Aubrey and Dwane were still trying to figure out who had leaked sensitive information about the case to the media. Stephanie listened politely for a few minutes, and then blurted out her razor-sharp opinion.

"I think the gadfly did it for publicity. Spike Spivey is a creep."

"Well, I guess that settles that issue," Dwane said.

"Not entirely," Stephanie said.

Aubrey could see that Stephanie was uneasy about the Missouri newspaper story, because it made him look bad. She deserved to know more about the 1968 lynching case, particularly his role in it. He looked straight at her. "Let me tell you about the 1968 case."

"Please do. It happened the year I was born, but it sounds like we are going to have to explain it, because you were the deputy prosecutor at the time."

Aubrey said, "Ike Swanson came to Woodville in 1968 to be the manager of a grocery store. He was a homosexual, and shortly after he got to town, he was tortured and murdered. I was the deputy prosecuting attorney for Campbell County, young and inexperienced. I thought the sheriff and state police would work hard to find the killers, but after a while, I realized that Sheriff Mark Odom was a control-freak. He was not trying very hard to solve the case. I told him we ought to get more help from the state police, but he did not want their help. I told the prosecutor, Fred Cooksey, but he took the sheriff's side and said we ought to let him handle the investigation. Almost six months passed, and I became ashamed that I had not done more to push for a better investigation. I talked to Dwane about it, and he said I should resign. At about the same time, my young wife, Prissy, died as she was trying to deliver our stillborn child. I was a mess emotionally, but I did resign two weeks after she died. That's it in a nutshell."

Stephanie said, "Now I understand why you are so determined to keep the county sheriffs in their place."

Dwane said, "Aubrey has told it straight. I wish he had never agreed to be Fred Cooksey's deputy. The Odom-Cooksey machine had too much power, and they cared more about a bunch of hate-mongers up around the lake than they did about bringing justice to the thugs who murdered Ike Swanson. Aubrey's wife, Prissy, told him she thought Cooksey and Odom were turning a blind eye to the whole thing, and she was right. He did the right thing by resigning."

"The sheriff back then was related to Jack Odom, our current sheriff ... Right?" Stephanie said.

"Yes, our very own Sheriff Jack Odom is Sheriff Mark Odom's grandson," Aubrey said.

Stephanie looked at Aubrey and sighed. "I appreciate you telling me all this. It must be a painful memory for you."

Aubrey looked down. He opened the Cody Ransom file and began shuffling papers.

Dwane broke the silence. "It took a while for Aubrey to sort it all out, but now he is in a position to make sure that things are done right."

Stephanie turned her legal pad to a fresh page and sat bolt upright. "And that we must do. Speaking of which: If we are going to charge Cody, what will the charge be?"

Aubrey closed the file. "That is exactly what we need to talk about. Lieutenant Smothers told me this morning that he has confirmed Cody's story, and developed other information that we may want to consider. He said he would be here at 1:30."

FIFTY-ONE

Lieutenant Smothers was on time for the meeting with Aubrey, but Sergeant Jim Nestor, who had done most of the fieldwork, was not with him.

"Hi, Lieutenant, I halfway expected Nestor to be with you."

"He's still collecting information, but I have his interim report. Besides, I wanted to visit about a few other things."

"Does Cody's story check out?"

"Yes, we have confirmed the basics. He was out jogging at the time of the killing. Witnesses have seen him running that road a lot, and they say he always carries dumbbells, to build upper-body strength. We have also identified several men, in addition to the one I told you about earlier, who have had homosexual sex with Randy. And, for what it is worth, Randy is a graduate of Calico U, but the NCAA says he has never been mentioned in connection with any recruiting violations. It appears he just used that line as a come-on to get Cody in the car with him."

"What about Cody personally, what did you learn about him?"

"He is an above-average student, well-liked by his classmates. Several Division I schools, including Calico, have offered him a full ride to play football. He has had several girlfriends and all of them, even the ones he jilted, say nice things about him. His buddies at school, on the team and off, say he is not a hothead, and they find it hard to believe that he would hit anyone with a dumbbell. That's about it. I think Cody was telling me the truth when we did the video."

"And the parents?"

The lieutenant pulled a sheet of paper from his file. "We heard nothing unusual about his mother; everyone seems to think she is salt of the earth. The boy's father is a different story. Many people we talked to said he has the reputation of being a mean son-of-a-bitch. He hangs out with some of the boys in Mysterion—that's Artus MacArthur's outfit—and we are working to nail that down. Before he married, he got into a few brawls and was arrested twice for assault and battery. Neither case amounted to much. One was dismissed, and he paid a hundred-dollar fine in the other for disturbing the peace."

Aubrey said, "That's about what I expected."

"Do you want us to dig deeper into the father's background?"

"Not right now, but we may need to do that later."

"Just let us know." The lieutenant put his papers away and pushed his chair back as if to leave. But then he said, "Aubrey, can I have a word with you privately?"

"Sure." Aubrey nodded to Stephanie, and she rolled Dwane out of the room and closed the door.

The lieutenant said, "Are you going to charge the boy?"

Aubrey said, "Yes, but I haven't decided what I am going to charge."

"Well, I personally believe you need to charge him, but you are going to run into a buzzsaw no matter what you do."

"What do you mean?"

"Sheriff Odom doesn't like you, and won't like what you are about to do. He could be a problem. I don't know how it will play out, but I wanted to give you a heads up."

"Thanks, Lieutenant. I suspected as much."

They shook hands, and the lieutenant started toward the door. Then he turned toward Aubrey. "Look, I know he also has deep connections with Artus MacArthur and the boys in Mysterion, and they are planning to raise money on the QT to help pay Cody's lawyer. The boy's daddy is pushing for that, and the sheriff is sympathetic. I don't think Jack Odom would do anything real stupid, and I don't know what he might do to hurt your case, but I thought you ought to know where he is coming from."

"I appreciate you leveling with me. I know you have to keep good relations with all the sheriffs, so I will not let on that you have given me this tip."

"Thanks, Mr. Prosecutor. By the way, my grandfather was born over in Hawkins County, but he hightailed it to Little Rock as soon as he got old enough to run off. He didn't see much future in the hills for a black man."

They shook hands again, but this time their grip morphed into an African handshake. They studied each other for a second but said nothing. Then the lieutenant left.

FIFTY-TWO

Dwane watched and listened as the two lawyers sat across from each other in the small conference room, haggling over the distinct offenses of second-degree murder and manslaughter. As they parsed each crime into countless fragments of legal gibberish, they barely mentioned Cody Ransom or Randy Trice.

Dwane sat quietly for half an hour and then said, "What am I doing here? You all are talking a foreign language."

Stephanie said, "We're done. We were just kicking around the options. We are going to charge second-degree murder, with manslaughter as a fallback."

Aubrey said, "This is where you come in, Dwane. You have served on lots of juries. Would you vote to convict Cody?"

"Damned if I know. It's a hard case."

At 4 o'clock that afternoon, Aubrey signed a felony information charging Cody Ransom with second-degree murder. Stephanie filed it at the courthouse.

The television newscasters led with the story at 6 o'clock. Tom "Spike" Spivey was on all channels, attacking Aubrey and crying crocodile tears for poor Cody Ransom. A subdued Carl Ransom was at his side.

Spike, dark and paunchy, wore a gray gabardine suit a size too big. His open-collared shirt revealed a crop of black chest hair resembling Velcro, but these oddities did not lessen the power of his talking points.

"This fine boy, an outstanding student and all-star athlete, is being persecuted. He did what most red-blooded teenagers would do if attacked by a homosexual. He resisted; he defended himself, and I aim to bring him clear. Aubrey Hatfield was deputy prosecuting attorney in 1968 and never charged anyone when a lynch mob tortured and killed a homosexual up by Possum Knob. Now he picks on a boy who is not guilty of anything."

Stephanie winced as she watched the third and last interview. "The gadfly is in rare form, but you have to give the devil his due. Those are tough talking points, as good as any I ever heard in the eighteen months I worked on Capitol Hill."

Neither Aubrey nor Dwane contested what she said.

When the news was over, Aubrey picked up the remote and turned off the TV.

"He's just doing his job. He is supposed to fight for his client, but our job is not to convict or acquit; our job is to do justice. We are duty bound to present the case based on the law and the facts. A jury will have to decide it. That's the way the system works."

"True enough," Dwayne said. "But it's going to be a rough ride."

FIFTY-THREE

Six days after he charged Cody Ransom, Aubrey greeted arrivals at the rear of the sanctuary, handed out programs, and ushered people to their seats for the Sunday service at First United Methodist. He was keeping the promise he made to his mother. He intended to usher for the rest of his life, even though he had lost the Holy Spirit when God took Prissy.

Aubrey still honored Jesus and the church, but his fellow worshipers had become people to seat—nothing more. Scripture readings were prose, poetry—nothing more. Aubrey heard the sermons but thought of other things. His favorite art, the stained-glass window behind the choir, was the focal point of his religion, such as it was. Artwork and reverie appealed to him more than the story of the cross.

The congregants did not know Aubrey's heart, and that suited him. He had lived in a shell for a long time.

But when he ran for office and won, things began to change. Thanks to politics, the protective shell was cracking. People were eager to shake his hand or say hello, because he might have the power to help them now or in the future.

When he charged the boy, the gentle touches gave way to feverish opinion.

"Aubrey, I know you will do the right thing about poor Randy Trice. It's such a shame," said one. "Aubrey, that young boy only wanted to go to college and play ball, and that queer ruined his life," said another.

Everyone had an opinion for the usher-man; he no longer seemed distant.

There were only two opinions: A large majority wanted to let the boy go, period. The others said they felt sorry for Randy Trice, "even if he was a homosexual." Aubrey studied the people when they spoke to him about the case, wondering about their inner thoughts and thinking that might tell him more than their words. He soon reconciled himself to the inevitable: *I asked for this job. This is part of the deal. Time will tell whether I have made the right decision.*

When the church was near capacity, Aubrey saw Sheriff Jack Odom and his family slip into the sanctuary through the side door. They made quite a sight. The sheriff's wife had long blond hair brushed straight, and two mid-sized girls and a little boy followed her into a front-row pew. The sheriff, an infrequent church visitor, brought up the rear, looking more like a banker than a sheriff. Tall and rail-thin, Jack Odom had the Lincolnesque look of his grandfather. All heads turned to watch his grand entrance.

Aubrey sighed. *Such is the life of a local celebrity. I am one whether I like it or not.*

The sermon ended, and so did church. Aubrey rose from his pew and pushed Dwane's wheelchair into the narthex. As he did, the sheriff tapped him on the shoulder. "Aubrey, can I talk to you outside?"

Dwane overheard the sheriff. "Go ahead, Aubrey, I'll sit right here and visit with folks."

When they got outside, away from the crowd, Jack Odom went from churchgoing family man to pissed-off sheriff in record time. "Aubrey, you should have talked to me before you charged that boy. No jury is going to say he is guilty for hitting a queer that was trying to blow him. This thing would have cooled off and blown over, but now it is turning into a circus."

Aubrey's first thought was to say nothing, but he could tell the sheriff was itching for a cuss fight. He decided to provoke him, just to see what he could learn. "Well, sheriff, I think things will work better if I do my job and you do yours."

That did it. The sheriff's face went from near handsome to downright ugly, and he revealed what was eating on him. "You don't know shit about law enforcement. We Odoms have been sheriffin' in this county for a long time, and you are the first prosecutor who has been too dumb to take our advice about things. You have treated us like dogshit. My granddad felt that way about you, and so do I."

"Are you done?" Aubrey liked the way he was feeling. He had not lost his cool, and he felt a sense of superiority.

"No, I'm not. You, and that little twit that works for you, have been going around saying my granddad and Fred Cooksey did not do enough to catch whoever killed that queer back in 1968. You need to knock it off. If you had a set of balls, you would own up to the fact that you were the deputy back then. It was just as much your fault as theirs."

Aubrey knew he looked cool on the outside—and that was good—but he was boiling inside. He stood up as tall as he could. "Sheriff, I am doing my duty as I see it, and I better not find out that you are working against me. Are we clear on that?"

Odom pivoted and stomped into the parking lot, heading to where his wife and children were waiting. Suddenly he slowed down to work the people who were leaving the church. He shook every hand, patted some on the back, and put on his best big smile. When he got to his car, he gave a conspicuous hug to each child and waved to everyone in sight. Then he slipped behind the wheel and drove away.

When Aubrey got back to where Dwane was sitting, Dwane said, "Looks like you all were getting after it. I can't wait to hear about it."

"It's as we expected. The sheriff is going to make a bad situation worse."

FIFTY-FOUR

Aubrey called Lieutenant Smothers early Monday morning to tell him about his encounter with Sheriff Jack Odom. At 11 o'clock, the lieutenant arrived to talk about "the sheriff problem." Aubrey opened the meeting with a blow-by-blow retelling of the skirmish at the First United Methodist Church. Dwane said, "I didn't hear what was said, but I could tell the sheriff was red hot." The lieutenant turned his head first one way and then the other.

Aubrey said, "We need to talk about this and figure out how to handle it. But let's stay on the high ground."

Stephanie said, "That probably means I should keep my mouth shut."

Everyone sniggered, and in that moment Aubrey got the same warm feeling he felt the day he first met Stephanie. *She is Prissy, made over.*

Aubrey looked at Lieutenant Smothers. "When Sheriff Odom interrupted a meeting I was having with the Doughboys to tell me that Randy Trice had been killed, he said, 'We need to find the killer and give him some Campbell County justice.' Then, the day you and the sheriff came here to tell us that Randy was a homosexual, he changed his tune. He was saying, 'You'd think he would have known not to hit on someone around here—queers get what they deserve when they do that.'"

"He hates homosexuals, but I think there is more to the sheriff problem than that," Dwane said.

The lieutenant said, "I agree. It's an oversimplification to think the issue of homosexuality is the only thing driving the sheriff. The things he said to you after church tell us he does not like you, and his granddaddy did not like you. The entire Odom-Cooksey machine thinks you are incompetent as a law-enforcement official."

"Hey, don't forget me. He called me a little twit for telling people it was his granddaddy and Fred Cooksey that let the lynch mob get off scot-free in 1968."

Aubrey got the warm feeling again. He smiled at Stephanie. "Thanks. Misery loves company."

Dwane said, "Well, let's talk about what Stephanie said, because it shows the sheriff is concerned about the Odom reputation He wants to squelch any talk that puts him or his granddaddy in a bad light. Really, it all comes down to politics and power. The Odoms and the Cookseys have controlled things for way too long. They decide everything based on the political impact it may have on their reputation with the voters; the turnaround Jack Odom made after finding out about Randy's homosexuality is a good example."

Aubrey said, "That's fair enough, but there's an elephant in the room: The Odoms, when it comes to homosexuality, are reflecting the views of most folks in Campbell County."

"And, they always want to be on the right side of public opinion," Dwayne said. "That's why the sheriff switched horses as soon as he learned that Randy was a homosexual."

Stephanie said, "I agree that most people in the county are where you say they are on the issue of homosexuality, but the young people tend to be more tolerant. I can say that because, at thirty-nine, I'm easily the youngest person in this room."

That drew a round of catcalls, with Dwane's the loudest. Stephanie pointed at them, using both hands, and said, "Gotcha!"

When they had finished teasing each other about their ages, Aubrey said, "There are other things to consider, especially when it comes to understanding how and why people think the way they do. But let's get to the heart of why we are meeting today—the sheriff problem."

Stephanie said, "Before we get to that, there is something we need for you to check out, Lieutenant. We are getting killed with news stories and street talk about the 1968 lynching. Spike Spivey never misses a chance to say how unjust it is for Aubrey to prosecute Cody Ransom when he did nothing to find the 1968 lynch mob. An outright lie, but it hurts. Can you get us a copy of the state police file for the 1968 case?"

The lieutenant was about to answer, but Aubrey said, "Can you get it to us on the QT? I do not want to trigger a series of stories saying we are reopening the case. We just want to review the investigation to see what was done and who did it."

"I'll get you a copy of everything we have on it, and I'll do it personally."

Aubrey thanked him and said, "Now, back to the sheriff thing. I intend to keep him at arm's length from here on out. I do not trust him, and he does not like me or trust me. I know you have to maintain relations with local law enforcement, but I'd appreciate it if you will do everything you can to help me work through this."

"I'll do the best I can, Mr. Prosecutor. For your information, I have taken Sergeant Nestor out of the loop on anything that does not directly involve the work he has already done on the Cody Ransom case. I have to trust him, but he is very close to Sheriff Odom, and it would be hard for him to clam up if the sheriff pumped him for information about what is going on in your office. He said he understands and agrees with my decision."

Stephanie said, "So Sergeant Nestor will not know that I have asked for the 1968 lynching file?"

"That's right, ma'am."

FIFTY-FIVE

On March 17, the 2007 Woodville Doughboys went to Hatfield House for a pre-season cookout and team meeting. Zach borrowed three long folding tables from the church and set them up in the backyard. Tolece laid out the buns and other fixings, and Aubrey, wearing a Razorback apron and chef's hat, grilled three dozen hamburgers under the all-too-close supervision of Dwane. It was going to be a good night—lots of baseball talk and laughter, and no talk of Cody Ransom or Randy Trice.

Just as they were sitting down to eat, Stephanie arrived dressed in fitted blue jeans, sneakers, and an emerald green sweater. Aubrey stood up, intending to introduce her to the boys. But when Stephanie turned her head, he saw the big green ribbon that held her ponytail. That is when it hit him: *This is St. Patrick's Day, the day Prissy thought the baby would come. The baby she joked about dressing in green, not blue or pink.*

"Aubrey ... Aubrey, are you going to introduce Stephanie or just stand there gawking?" Dwane roared, and so did all the boys.

Aubrey mumbled something and then laughed along with the others. "Boys, this is Stephanie Brooks, the best deputy prosecuting attorney in Arkansas."

The team gave a cheer, and one of the boys said, "And the best-looking too."

Almost immediately, the talk returned to baseball: the coming major league season and the Doughboys' important first game against the Brasstown Bengals.

Aubrey was in the midst of another warm feeling about Stephanie when she made her apologies. "Aubrey, I'd like to stay, but I've got to drive back to Hawkins County. I've got a date, the first I've had in months."

Aubrey tried to look calm but did not do a very good job of it. "Oh, anybody I know?"

"Steve Rankin. You probably know him. He is a family-practice doctor. His wife died a long time ago. I've known him for years."

"Yes, I have met him. Have a good time, and I'll see you Monday."

Aubrey's emotions cycled from the valley to the hilltop once he calculated Rankin's age.

The man has to be in his mid-fifties. I'm only sixty-two. Hope springs eternal.

The boys left around 9 o'clock, but the evening did not go by without a mention of the Cody Ransom trial. The boys resolved the case in less than five minutes. Eight Ball summed it up, "Cody was wrong to hit Randy. He should have just gotten out of the car and gone on with his run."

FIFTY-SIX

On May 1, 2007, Dwane and Aubrey went to Ma Phipps's Cafeteria for lunch. Aubrey rolled Dwane to an open table, shaking a few hands and making small talk along the way. When he got Dwane situated, he asked him what he wanted to eat. Dwane said, "Get me some greens, black-eyed peas, and a slice of country ham."

Aubrey said, "You sure? That stuff is like Miracle Grow for the plaque that's clogging your arteries."

Dwane scowled. "Lay off. I'm eighty-seven years old. Get me what I want, and bring me some of Ma Phipps's homemade rolls—two of them."

Aubrey gave up and headed to the line to get his salad and Dwane's comfort food.

When he returned to the table, Dwane gave him the onceover. "I see you have lost some of that belly. Does that mean you are going to quit moping around and ask Stephanie out?"

"I don't know. It's not that I'm afraid she will say no."

"Then why not ask her out?"

"I've been out with women a few times since Prissy died—dates for dinner or a movie, that sort of thing. But it didn't work out, and those women were closer to my age."

"So what? Stephanie is thirty-nine. She seems to like you. And compared to me, you are a spring chicken."

Aubrey shrugged his shoulders and tied into his salad.

"Ask her out, Aubrey. Women like Stephanie don't come along every day."

Aubrey did not look up, so Dwane buttered one of Ma's rolls and laid his knife across the top of his plate. He motioned toward the lunch crowd. "By the way, have you noticed anything since we came in here almost an hour ago?"

"No. What?"

"We have seen a bunch of people that we know well. They shake hands, nod a greeting, and pass the time of day. But ninety-nine percent of them have said nothing to you about the Cody Ransom case."

"So?"

"Silence is a bad sign. I think it means your case is in the ditch. Most people in Campbell County do not like homosexuality, and they are looking for a way to help Cody get out of a mess. Meanwhile, the media keeps repeating the crap put out by Spike Spivey, doing their best to whip this into a morality play. It has made for a bad scene, and now the demagogues are showing up, making things worse."

"You're talking about Kress and Fremont?"

"Yes ... who else?"

Jamie Kress, a transplant from New Jersey, came to Arkansas to work as a field man for the Al Gore presidential campaign in 2000. He met a young man from Malvern at the Gore headquarters, and they shared an apartment. When the campaign was over, they bought a house on South Gaines Street in Little Rock and announced that they were gay. Kress set up an organization, raised money, and began a fulltime effort pushing the gay rights agenda. He soon demonstrated a talent for getting his message out to the public. He followed the TV cameras to trials, protests, marches, and sit-ins. He wrote letters to the editor for the newspapers and columns for the magazines, and he stalked the halls of the legislature when it was in session. He never missed an opportunity, and if one did not exist, he would create it by outing a closet homosexual or endearing himself to people who were hurting, such as the parents of Randy Trice. He insinuated himself into their lives shortly after Aubrey charged Cody Ransom with murder in the second degree. For Jamie Kress, a big trial in Campbell County was a bird's nest on the ground. He convinced the Trice family that his activities would help Aubrey get a conviction, but Jamie Kress did not care about that—he only wanted publicity for himself and for his cause. The Trice family donated money to his group, and Jamie launched a full assault on "the small-minded people of Campbell County who looked the other way when a homosexual was tortured and murdered in 1968."

His counterpart was George Fremont, a hardcore conservative who had made a good living for ten years using the same tactics as Jamie Kress. They showed up at the same events, said their usual lines, and accomplished little beyond stoking up their financial supporters. Occasionally, they would show up at legislative hearings to comment about state or federal legislation, each knowing precisely what the other was going to say. Fremont catered to the fundamental churches and far-right groups, one being Mysterion. He was singing their song, and they liked it. Fremont played them for all they were worth. But, like Jamie Kress, he was promoting himself, generating income, and getting headlines.

Aubrey said, "They don't care about Cody or the people who live in this county."

Dwane said, "Right, but this case is a way to sell their special point of view, just like the old medicine men who sold secret formulas and magic cures. They want to make this case as big as the Scopes Monkey Trial, and with the media's help they may succeed."

Aubrey said, "Some people think I am to blame for the bad publicity."

"That's because your nemesis, Sheriff Jack Odom, is telling everyone that you are the one who is bringing embarrassment and shame to the county. He never misses a chance to say that you don't know what you are doing, and that he told you from the start not to charge the boy."

Aubrey said, "So, what do you think I should do? The case is set for trial on July 30, some three months from today. Are you saying I ought to back off?"

"No, you are doing the right thing, mainly because the old lynching case is being paraded around for the whole world to see. I'm sure you could work out something with Spike to put this to bed, but I think the people of Campbell County need to deal with this mess—out in the open, once and for all."

"Well, if I am not going to back off, then what should I do? You seem to be saying I need to do something to change public opinion."

"Well, in the Marine Corps we used to get on the radio and call 'mayday' when we needed help. This morning, when I heard the radio talk-show people talking about this being May Day, it got me to thinking about your predicament. I don't think you ought to back off, and I don't think you ought to holler 'mayday'—that would show weakness, and people can smell fear and weakness quicker than anything else. But you do need a game-changing break. Something needs to happen."

"No kidding. Got any ideas?"

"Could you ask the judge for a gag order? You know, to shut down the demagogues and zip up Spike's lip. It would give you a chance to say it is Spike and the headline-hunters who are bringing embarrassment and shame to the county."

"Stephanie and I talked about that, but I don't think it is the way to go."

"Why not?"

"There was a time when the courts did a pretty good job of balancing the right to a fair trial with the right to a free press, but those days are long gone. Today's social media and cable news outlets have made it difficult to stop the demagogues and the talking heads on TV. When they latch onto something as spicy as this case, they are like a dog with a bone. They'll keep going until the bone is gone and they have licked up the last drop of drama."

"Good point. I agree." Dwane gave Aubrey a wink. He poured a swirl of honey onto his second roll, making it his dessert.

Aubrey said, "We do need to catch a break to change public opinion before we go to trial, but I'm not counting on it."

FIFTY-SEVEN

Aubrey got up early on June 6. Judge Harry Oglethorpe wanted the lawyers in the Cody Ransom case to come in at 8:30 a.m. for an informal conference. Stephanie planned to go along, saying she wanted a first-hand look at "the gadfly."

Dwane was already out of bed. He had rolled his wheelchair close to the TV to watch the annual D-Day memorials. "I'm reminiscing, Aubrey. I was in the Navy Hospital near Sydney in 1944 when news of the Normandy invasion came over the radio."

Aubrey noticed he was slumping a little in his chair. He looked tired, but his voice was an odd mix of pride and sadness. Aubrey was at first concerned about his health, and then he realized that, for Dwane, the memories of D-Day were true to life.

Dwane said, "You all have a meeting with the judge today, so I'm going to stay right here to think about the old days, the war, my buddies, meeting Mary—stuff like that. It's an old man's right, you know."

Aubrey patted him on the back, said nothing, and headed for the courthouse.

Stephanie was waiting for him at the revolving door. "I thought we might relive our clumsy attempt to go through this door at the same time. The maneuver we tried the first day we met."

She gave Aubrey a devilish smile, and they spun their way through at the same time. When they got inside, they agreed that their technique had improved.

"See, it's easier when you are thinner."

"I didn't know you were paying attention to my appearance," Aubrey said.

"I wish you paid more attention to mine," Stephanie said.

"I do."

"Well, then. Isn't it about time for you to ask me to go out?"

Aubrey hesitated, but the warm feeling was back, and Stephanie was giving him a very serious look. "Yes, I'd like that. Let's work on it as soon as we get out of this meeting with the judge."

They climbed the stairs, and went into the anteroom adjoining Judge Oglethorpe's personal office. Spike Spivey was waiting for them. "What say, Hoss?" Then he looked at Stephanie. "I take it this is the brains of the outfit?"

"Hello, Spike." Aubrey had never been one to respond to indignities. Best to let them slide by.

"Yes, this is my deputy prosecutor, Stephanie Brooks, and she is indeed a very bright lawyer."

"Good, you are going to need all the help you can get."

Aubrey could tell that Stephanie was about to go after the insufferable Mr. Spivey, so he said, "Is the judge ready for us?"

Spivey said he was ready, so they entered, shook hands with the judge, and sat down to talk about the way he hoped to handle the case.

Judge Harry Oglethorpe was an old-school judge, very conservative and prosecution-minded. He was nearing retirement, and he liked to schmooze with the lawyers and tell jokes when they were in chambers, out of the public eye. His repertoire included gags about ethnics, homosexuals, sexy women, Poles, and Aggies. Lawyers practicing in his court had to make a choice. They could play along and laugh at his jokes, or they could signal their discomfort, in which case the judge would get right to business.

Stephanie's presence handcuffed the judge. He skipped the jokes. "Thanks for coming, gentlemen and Miss Brooks. The media have blown this case out of proportion, and we are less than two months from trial. Let me start by telling my thoughts, and then we can talk about areas of agreement and disagreement.

"I've read the motions you have filed, Spike. The so-called 'gay panic' defense is interesting, and my initial thought, Aubrey, is to let the defense have wide latitude to show how the boy may have panicked because he has been influenced by a culture that rejects homosexuality. I think all that would go to his state of mind at the time he hit Randy with the dumbbell. I'm not sure whether I should give an instruction telling the jurors that they can acquit based on that theory, and that's why I want you all to file briefs on this point."

Aubrey said, "Your Honor, the defense of 'gay panic' has been rejected in most jurisdictions where it has been litigated. Miss Brooks has done extensive research on the subject, and we filed a memo brief about it a few weeks ago. Even so, we will rework our brief in light of your comments and get it to you right away."

Spike did not say anything. He did not need to; the judge was leaning his way.

"Another thing, gentlemen and Miss Brooks, I am not going to allow a blow-by-blow description of what happened in 1968. This case is about what happened on February 5, 2007. It may be appropriate for Spike to mention the 1968 lynching in his effort to define the culture that influenced the defendant—everybody has heard about it anyway—but we are not going to spend a lot of time on it."

Again, Spike said nothing. He just sat there, nodding approval and grinning mischievously.

The meeting lasted a while longer, but it dealt mostly with technicalities.

When they got outside, Stephanie said, "Dwane's right, we need a break. The judge is leaning in favor of the defense. It is going to be hard to get a conviction."

Aubrey said, "Remember, our job is not to convict; it is to do justice."

"That's honorable, but if we lose this case, the media is going to say the people of this county are a bunch of bigots. It's not true, but that's how they'll play it; that's how it will come out. We need to get a verdict that says it was wrong for Cody to kill Randy Trice. As the Doughboys have said, 'Cody should have gotten out of the car and gone on with his run.'"

"I agree, but how can we get the break that Dwane says we need? Any new thoughts about that?"

"Yes, as a matter of fact I've been scouring over the 1968 lynching file, and I keep coming back to this conundrum: It is not reasonable to believe that Sheriff Odom and Prosecutor Cooksey took a dive simply because they were against homosexuality, or because they thought it would hurt them politically to prosecute the case. They were super-strong politically."

"Dwane said they were strong as an acre of garlic, and he's right about that," Aubrey said.

"So, if we are right about that, then there must have been some other reason for them to look the other way." Stephanie stamped her foot and said, "They let a lynch mob get away with torturing and murdering a homosexual. Why did they do that?"

"I buy your logic, but what's the solution?"

"I know you are leery about reopening the case, but Dwane says we ought to talk to people who worked for Sheriff Mark Odom in 1968 to see if anyone knows why the case was dropped like a hot potato."

"Who would you talk to? It's been thirty-eight years."

"Do you remember Sweet Pea?"

FIFTY-EIGHT

"They called her Sweet Pea in high school, too." Stephanie shoved the 1961 Woodville High School Yearbook across the table to Dwane and Aubrey. "Check out the pageboy hairstyle and the love notes on the pages I have marked. She was very pretty—active in everything—and her classmates chose her as the girl with the best personality."

Dwane said, "I've known her a long time. She volunteered every year to work with my wife at the County Fair. Mary loved her. She always said, 'Sweet Pea fits her to a T.'"

Aubrey pulled the book closer, turning it so that he could see Shirley Cosgrove's official class photograph. "This is pretty good, but it doesn't show the twinkle in her eye. That's why everyone calls her Sweet Pea—there's a glow about her."

Stephanie said, "I know it's a long shot to talk to her, but she did work for the sheriff for almost five years."

"She was there in 1968, but I haven't seen her in years," Aubrey said.

Dwane looked at Aubrey. "I have. She is living at The Garden Spot, that assisted-living place I was going to before you lassoed me, and drug me kicking and screaming to Hatfield House ... I saw her there when I was checking it out. She's sixty-three now, but she still has the twinkle, and everyone still calls her Sweet Pea."

"I always called her Shirley because my mother would have skinned me if she had heard that I was calling a woman by a name like that. Mother was old-school."

Dwane said, "I called her yesterday afternoon, and she invited me to come see her this morning. I think Stephanie and I can go visit her, and no one will think anything about it. If you go, Aubrey, everyone will wonder why the prosecuting attorney is talking to Sweet Pea."

"I agree. I'll stay here."

Just before they left the office, Dwane pulled Aubrey aside, "How did it go last night? Didn't you and Stephanie go out?"

"Yes, we went out for dinner. It was nothing big, but it did give us a chance to talk about something other than the Cody Ransom case. We got along fine. She reminds me of Prissy."

"I'm not an expert on such things, Aubrey, but can I say something personal?"

Aubrey scowled. "You'll do it anyway, so go ahead."

"She is not Prissy, she is Stephanie—a fine woman. If she thinks you are interested in her because she reminds you of Prissy, it will not work."

"I know. I'm wrestling with that, and the age thing. Cut me some slack."

It was a short trip to The Garden Spot. Stephanie rolled Dwane into the building, and the two of them blended in with other visitors as they headed to Sweet Pea's little apartment.

Dwane wrinkled his nose. "I guess you get used to it, but all these places smell the same. It's indescribable and ever-present."

Sweet Pea opened her door, smiled, and said, "My goodness, Dwane, aren't you a sight? Is this pretty thing your latest girlfriend?"

She looked like the picture in the yearbook, adjusted for the normal wear and tear of aging. The pageboy hairdo had yielded to a bluish-gray bouffant that was on the verge of collapsing, but the twinkle was there, in full force.

"Sweet Pea, you are as radiant as ever, but I regret to say this beautiful lady is not my girlfriend. If Aubrey Hatfield plays his cards right, he may have a chance with her, but alas, I am too far gone."

Stephanie blushed, and Sweet Pea changed the subject by showing her the best place to park Dwane's wheelchair. She offered them a glass of sweet tea. Then she eased into a remembrance of Mary and the many seasons they worked a booth at the County Fair.

"She loved the fair," Dwane said. He swallowed and lowered his head, and when he did, Sweet Pea leaned over and put her hand on his shoulder. The quiet moment, filled by the ticking of an old-timey windup clock, led to talk about mutual friends and shared condolences for those who were gone.

Dwane soon found a chance to ask Sweet Pea about her recent activities.

Sweet Pea said, "My life has been pretty much the same. I worked until I was thirty, and then I just settled down on my own. I've been living on my Frank's Army pension." She sighed and looked to Stephanie, "My Frank was one of the first Americans killed in Vietnam." Stephanie said she was sorry to hear that, but Sweet Pea let no time go by. "It's OK, he is still my only love. I think of him all the time."

Dwane said, "War is hell. I've studied it for over sixty years, ever since I got hit on Kwajalein. We were right to fight in World War II and Korea, but these other wars have troubled me."

Sweet Pea said, "You are right, Dwane, but I'll always be proud that Frank answered the call and did not run off."

"Frank Barden was a good man," Dwane said.

"You mentioned Aubrey, Dwane. How is he these days?" It was Sweet Pea's way—the way of the South—to suggest there had been enough warm talk. She was ready to learn what they had come for.

Dwane knew the signal. "Aubrey wanted us to visit with you about your time at the sheriff's office, particularly back in 1968, when that homosexual boy was lynched. Aubrey was deputy prosecutor when it happened, but he resigned a few months later, after Prissy died. Now, he is trying to figure out why the sheriff and state police seemed to lose interest in the lynching case. Do you remember that case?"

"I think everybody remembers that one—it was a terrible thing—but I wasn't working there when it happened. I quit my job at the sheriff's office about a month before they found that boy."

Dwane noticed that Sweet Pea was tense and fidgety when he asked about her days at the sheriff's office, but as soon as he said Aubrey was digging into the 1968 lynching, she relaxed. The twinkle returned and the fidgeting stopped.

Stephanie noticed it too, so she took another tack. "Was there something else going on in the office that bothered you?"

Sweet Pea hesitated and then winked at Dwane. "Oh, there are always things that bother us, but that's just part of life, isn't that so, Dwane? Can I offer you all some more sweet tea?"

Stephanie said, "Mrs. Barden, if there was something that bothered you almost forty years ago, you can talk freely about it now if you want to. The sheriff you worked for, Mark Odom, is dead, and the statute of limitations has run out on everything except murder cases. There's no way anything you say about your time in the sheriff's office could ever be a problem for you."

Sweet Pea looked at Dwane. "What should I do, Dwane? I don't want to be thought of as an old gossip or someone who is spiteful."

"The truth is never gossip, or spiteful. It's the perfect tonic for curing things that bother us."

"Amen to that." Sweet Pea sat forward in her chair and lowered her voice a notch. "Well, the year after I started working there, the sheriff asked me to take over the job of paying the grocery man for the food we bought for prisoners in the county jail. He had a deal with Gerald—the owner of Gerald's Grocery—to get a cash bonus for food bought at the store. The sheriff told me he got the idea from sheriffs in other states that he met when he went to the FBI National Academy in Washington, D. C."

Stephanie said, "That was a pretty common kickback scheme back in the 1950s and 1960s."

Sweet Pea said, "Well, I was young and naïve. He was an experienced sheriff, so I figured he knew what he was doing. He put the grocery money in a moneybag along with cash he took from bond deposits or found on people that he arrested, particularly those arrested for drug violations. It was a lot of money, but he didn't try to hide any of it from me. He just always said the money was needed to pay informants and give rewards, and that we needed to keep quiet about it, so as to keep such records away from prying eyes, mainly defense lawyers."

"Is that what he used the money for?"

"No. He used it however he wanted to, mostly for himself. He did give me cash Christmas bonuses, always $200, and in 1968 I came to my senses. I admitted to myself that I was part of a bad thing. I just wanted to get away from it. I felt guilty, ashamed. I needed to talk to someone about it, so I told my pastor."

Stephanie said, "Did you consider telling the prosecutor, Fred Cooksey, about it?"

"Oh, honey, Fred Cooksey did not care. He let Sheriff Odom run the county. He would have done nothing, and the sheriff would have fired me on the spot. The Cookseys and Odoms were powerful politicians back then, and they had a cozy arrangement. When Cooksey came to town, the sheriff always picked up the tab for lunch and dinner."

"The Odom-Cooksey machine is still a powerful force in this district," Dwane said.

Stephanie said, "You said you told all this to your pastor."

"Yes, I was scared to death. I did not know what they would do to me if I just quit. I needed to talk to someone about the mess I was in. My pastor told me I ought to quit and get out of there, but to protect myself, I should give him a statement telling what the sheriff was doing. He said he would keep my statement and the copies of my diary in his safe, and if the sheriff or prosecutor ever threatened me, he would shut them up real quick."

Dwane said, "Sweet Pea, you did the right thing. That was almost forty years ago, and you need to forget it, wipe it from your mind. By the way, who was your preacher back then, the one you told?"

"Artus MacArthur."

Dwane glanced toward Stephanie, then looked straight at Sweet Pea. "He's still preaching, isn't he?"

"He is, Dwane, but I don't go to his church anymore. I grew up out in the sticks, up by the lake, and my family went to a primitive church. That is how I got started with Artus. He was young, but the old pastor of the church let him preach and make prophecies, and after a few years he took over the church. Nowadays most people seem to think he is a little off the wall, but he helped me when I needed it."

As Dwane and Stephanie were leaving, Sweet Pea gave them a hug. "I'm glad you all came. I don't know whether I've helped you, but my burden is much lighter."

FIFTY-NINE

Dwane and Stephanie got back to the office shortly after noon. Aubrey had picked up an assortment of heartburn specials from the serving line at Ma Phipps's, and the three of them sat around the conference table having lunch and going over what Sweet Pea said about the time she worked for Sheriff Mark Odom.

Dwane said, "I have heard people say, for years, that Mark Odom was crooked. Well, today we confirmed it from a most unlikely source—Sweet Pea."

"I was hoping she would remember something about the lynching, and that she might know why Odom and Fred Cooksey cooled off on the case. But you all are telling me she left the sheriff's office before the lynching," Aubrey said.

Stephanie said, "What she told us is more important. Her preacher—the man she went to for advice—was Artus MacArthur. The 1968 state police report says Sheriff Odom talked to him and another guy from up around the lake about the lynching, but they denied it. That's it; the investigation seems to have ended right then and there."

"So why is Sweet Pea's statement about Odom skimming money so important?"

Stephanie said, "Lieutenant Smothers says Artus has, for more than forty years, been the leader of a group that appeals to hotheads, a cast of characters that might do a lynching if sufficiently provoked."

Aubrey said, “I made that very point to Sheriff Odom during my short tenure as deputy prosecuting attorney. I told him we ought to ask the state police to put more men on the case to follow up on that. He told me—bluntly—‘I run this county, Aubrey.’ Fred Cooksey backed him up, and I backed off. So how does Sweet Pea’s revelation change anything?”

“Think about the game of Monopoly. Once Sweet Pea told Artus MacArthur about the sheriff being a crook, he had the equivalent of a GET OUT OF JAIL FREE card.”

Stephanie was talking faster, weaving a net around the preacher, but Aubrey slowed her down. “Wait a second. We have no proof that Artus or any member of his group did the killing, even though Sweet Pea has given us a piece of information that may explain why the sheriff and Fred Cooksey let the investigation grow cold and die.”

Aubrey looked to Dwane to see what he thought of Stephanie’s theory, but Dwane did not respond. He was stretching back and holding his good right arm over his heart. “Aubrey, I feel lousy. It may be Ma Phipps’s spaghetti and meatballs, but it could be my ticker. Can you all take me to the hospital?”

In record time, they loaded Dwane into Stephanie’s car and raced to the county hospital, only a few minutes away. Dwane was still having chest pains when they rolled him into the emergency room. He kept stretching and rubbing his heart, and when the doctor moved him to an examination room, Aubrey and Stephanie took seats in the patient’s lounge. Aubrey had waited the same room the day Prissy died.

They stayed all afternoon. The doctor came out several times, and at the end of the day he told them he was going to keep Dwane overnight for observation. He said he felt good about Dwane’s condition, but he did not want to take chances with an eighty-seven-year-old man.

At 7 o’clock the nurse told them that Dwane was resting comfortably. The doctor had gone home, and there was nothing more for them to do. Aubrey looked tired, so much so that the nurse asked if he felt all right. He told her he was fine, and when she was gone, he asked Stephanie for a ride home.

When they drove into the yard at Hatfield House, Aubrey said, "Don't worry about me. I'm just depressed. Dwane is like a father to me, and this makes me realize that he won't be around forever."

Stephanie said, "Why don't I come in and find something for us to eat? I'm starving."

"Good. Maybe that will pick me up."

Aubrey sat at the kitchen table, and Stephanie found sandwich makings in the refrigerator. "I'm surprised that the kitchen is so spick and span. Not bad for a couple of men living alone."

"You should have seen this place before we hired Tolece to take care of us. It was always a mess."

Stephanie was spreading mayonnaise on the bread, but she stopped long enough to look at Aubrey. "Zach is such a good boy. I think it is great that you are going to help him go to college. It would be a shame if he had to go into the Marines right now."

Aubrey was listening, but he was also admiring the easy way Stephanie moved about the kitchen, cleaning up as she worked. When she finally sat down, they talked about Dwane and the way he had touched Aubrey's life. Then they talked about her return to Hawkins County after years in the East. Stephanie bubbled as she told Aubrey of her plan to improve White Oak Stables, the quarterhorse ranch and riding arena she had inherited. She had all the figures in her head and began telling him why it would be a financial success, but she stopped in mid-sentence. "I'm going on too long about horses, sorry. I didn't realize how much I missed horses and the ranch until I got back home."

Aubrey grinned and confessed that he did not know much about horses. "I spent most of my youth playing baseball and working in the hardware store."

When they finished talking, Stephanie began clearing the table, and Aubrey stayed in his chair, sipping a cup of coffee. He had enjoyed their talk, but he was still feeling low, worn out. He closed his eyes, leaned back, and rolled his neck around, trying to relax. It was then that he felt her soft hands, rubbing first his shoulders, then the back of his neck. She said nothing, but Aubrey felt her warm breath.

"Oh ... that's good ... I'm just downhearted. I get this way every now and again. Dwane says we all spend time in the valley."

Stephanie whispered to him. "I have a sure cure for that."

She took his hand and pulled him gently toward the bedroom, her green eyes afire, locked on his. Halfway there, they stopped and looked at each other to make sure, and then they came together. Aubrey smoothed back a wisp of jet-black hair that had fallen to her forehead and began to kiss her, tenderly at first, then with a passion that matched hers.

SIXTY

The doctor released Dwane at 10 o'clock the morning after his one-night stay in the hospital. Aubrey was there to pick him up. The doctor said his heart seemed to be fine, and he found no other reason to keep him. Dwane said, "False alarm, Aubrey. Doc says it was probably a gas pain or a pinched nerve."

When they got to Hatfield House, Tolece was putting fresh linens on Dwane's bed, and Stephanie was at the kitchen stove, in the midst of preparing brunch—Eggs Benedict, coffee, crispy bacon, and oatmeal. Stephanie said, "I wasn't sure what you could eat, so that explains the oatmeal."

Dwane said, "Give the oatmeal to the prosecutor. I'm having the real stuff."

Aubrey stepped next to Stephanie and put his hand on her shoulder. They smiled at each other, and she bumped her hip against his. "OK, so you want the oatmeal, Mr. Prosecutor?"

"No, he doesn't speak for me. I want the Eggs Benedict too."

When they were finished with breakfast, Stephanie gave Dwane a kiss on the cheek and headed toward the door, saying she needed to drive back to her ranch in Hawkins County to freshen up. As she left, she gave a little wave and a wink to Aubrey and said she would meet him at the office around 1:30 that afternoon. He smiled and waved back.

When she drove off, Dwane said, “When you get to be my age, there is very little that slips by unnoticed. Figuring people out is one of the things old folks can still do.”

“What do you mean by that, you old codger?”

“I’m seeing goo-goo eyes. Am I right?”

Aubrey grinned, a wide grin. “We’ll see. Time will tell, but for the first time I am seeing Stephanie as Stephanie, and I am not worried about the age thing anymore.”

Dwane laughed aloud, whacked his good hand down on the table and shouted. “All right!”

Aubrey smiled and shook a teasing forefinger at Dwane. “You old lecher.”

Dwane said, “Hey, knock off the wisecracks. I’m in love with her too.”

SIXTY-ONE

Stephanie got to the office just before 1:30. Aubrey was already there, standing by the conference table sizing up the work they had to do. The Cody Ransom file covered almost half of the table. A six-inch-deep, neat stack of papers marked "1968 Lynching" sat on the opposite end of the table.

When she entered the room they embraced, and then she pushed Aubrey back. "OK, here's the deal. We need to make a new rule and follow it religiously."

"What's the rule?"

"When we are working on the case, we've got to be all professional, all the time—no fooling around. Otherwise we will never get anything done. Agreed?"

Aubrey said, "Reluctantly, I agree, so let's get started." They grinned and bumped fists.

Stephanie said, "I've been rethinking what Sweet Pea told us. Why would the sheriff do such a dumb thing? I mean, the cover story that he was using ill-gotten cash to pay informants and give rewards is ludicrous."

Aubrey said, "I believe every word of Sweet Pea's story. The sheriff stole money because he was greedy and thought he was above the law. It is a classic case proving the arrogance of power. I saw his arrogance when he told me to back off the lynching case, saying 'I run this county.'

I regret that I did not do more to force his hand, but I can see now that there was not much I could have said or done that would have mattered.

The shame I have felt all these years is beginning to go away, thanks to what Sweet Pea told us, but I am still embarrassed by the fact that sworn law officers would stoop so low. We need to get to the bottom of this, if we can."

Stephanie said, "OK, then." She pointed to the stack of papers at the end of the table. "There are two good leads in that 1968 file that need further investigation."

"Only two?"

"Yes. The first lead is Artus MacArthur and the group he started. There is very little in the file beyond what Lieutenant Smothers told us, but I have been searching the internet, and I have come up with quite a lot of information. We'll need to verify it, but if the group is as far out as its website suggests, then I think you should consider reopening the 1968 case."

"We have to be careful about reopening the case. We have suspicions, but the lynching took place thirty-eight years ago, and the trail is cold. If we fail, we will look like fools, and that would damage our credibility and hurt our chance to win the Cody Ransom case. I can hear Spike Spivey spinning it now. It would not be pretty."

"I agree, but we can't just slog along from now to the trial date. It is set to begin three weeks from today, and Spike Spivey and the rabble-rousers, Fremont and Kress, are not going to slow down no matter what we do. They are going to keep the lynching case front and center, each for their own reasons. A constant barrage of bad publicity is a bigger threat than reopening the lynching case."

Aubrey could not keep his eyes off Stephanie. He was listening to her, but he was also reliving the tender moments of their night together at Hatfield House. Her incisive comment about trial strategy forced him to think of her in a new way.

She is the whole package—a beautiful, fun-loving, passionate woman who happens to have an extraordinary legal mind. She is bright and good with technicalities, but she does not get lost in the weeds of legal minutiae. Lawyers who get hung up on fine points of law often discover, too late, that a backwoods lawyer like Blacky has cleaned their clock by talking to jurors about things that matter. Stephanie has what it takes to hold her own against crafty lawyers like Blacky, but she also has a keen knowledge of the law and an intuitive eye for strategy. She is a rare woman, and she cares about me...

"Aubrey, quit daydreaming. Do you agree with my take on the strategy or not?"

"Sorry, I was on the verge of breaking your new rule. Yes, I agree with your strategy, but what about the group—Artus' group. What have you learned about Mysterion?"

"It comes from the Old Testament word for 'mystery.' Mysterion disciples believe mortal man cannot know the total truth of Christianity through intellect and reason."

Aubrey said, "Well, you can't argue with that. That's why we are told to accept Christ on faith."

"True enough, but this bunch of loonies believes they have been specially chosen to decipher the Christian mystery for the rest of us."

"Like Alchemists?"

"Sort of, but Mysterion makes the Alchemists look good."

"How so?"

"Artus MacArthur started this outfit a long time ago. He grew up in the North Carolina Appalachians in a backwoods church that sang in the primitive way, using shape-note songbooks. He started calling himself 'Apostle' when he was fourteen years old, about the time his folks moved to North Arkansas. Artus says he is one of the chosen few who can interpret the real meaning of the Christian mystery. It's all on his website, and there is some other information about Mysterion that has been gathered by various civil rights organizations that keep track of such activities. Artus started Mysterion when he was nineteen years old, and he has managed to keep it going by appealing to folks who like the drivel he puts out."

"I like the old-timey do-re-mi singing," Aubrey said.

"I do too, but stay on point, Aubrey. Singing those good old songs did not do much for Artus. He does not preach the high ground of Christianity. He gives his disciples what they are looking for:

explanations to justify their prejudices, their hatred for Jews, blacks, and homosexuals."

Aubrey said, "Dwane says Artus is a bigoted know-it-all."

"Yep." Stephanie closed the file and tapped on it with her fist. "It vexes me that people buy the crap he puts out. He has no special insight; he pulls his proclamations right out of thin air. Prejudice is a powerful magnet, and he uses it to a fare-thee-well."

"You said there are two leads. What is the other one?"

"Cletus Bolton. We need to know more about Cletus."

PART THREE

THE FOURTH OF JULY 2007

SIXTY-TWO

At 10 a.m. on Independence Day 2007, Stephanie carried a seat cushion and mini-cooler up to the fifth row of the bleachers behind the home team's dugout at Military Park. She was dressed for the day—blue short-shorts with a red-and-white-striped top. When she got to a good spot, she brushed away a chunk of dried bird-doo, positioned the seat cushion, and sat down. Then she looked toward the field of play, wondering why Aubrey and the boys called the busy place just beyond the chain-link fence a "dugout." *It is above ground, not dug out of anything; it is just a long bench beneath a corrugated sheet-metal roof. Oh, well.*

She stretched her legs to get an even tan, pondering how long it had been since she had been to a baseball game at Military Park.

Was it my senior year in high school? 1985? No, I think it was the summer after my junior year. Whatever, nothing has changed. The old ballpark is the same, but today it is alive, vibrant, festooned in red, white, and blue.

The ball game, an annual affair, was the first big event of the day. The stands filled first with family members and girlfriends, but soon others came. As cars and trucks vied for spots in the parking lot, grown-ups and kids marched back and forth like ants, hauling coolers and colorful banners into the stands. The place hummed, afire with the spirit of Old Glory.

The Doughboys, jumping up and down, circled around Aubrey, broke their huddle with a handclap, and took the field. They were going to play a team of young men who had grown too old for American Legion baseball. The crowd roared its approval, and the game was on.

Stephanie saw Dwane, the Doughboys' mascot, in his wheelchair, sitting in the shade of the dugout exactly where she had parked him before she headed to the bleachers. He was wearing a Doughboy jersey that matched his blue American Legion cap. When she picked him up that morning, Stephanie had noticed a small medal pinned to the right side of his cap. She asked him what the medal was for, and he ducked her question. He just pointed to his cap with his good right arm and said the medal was something he was supposed to wear on his "pisscutter" cap. Later, Stephanie asked Aubrey about the medal, and he told her, "Dwane won't talk about it, but it is the Silver Star he won for bravery at Kwajalein Atoll in 1944. He's like most other World War II veterans. He won't talk about such things because he thinks it is disrespectful to those who were left behind."

Stephanie's eyes kept coming back to Aubrey. When his team was in the field, he moved from one end of the dugout to the other, talking to his substitute players but always spending a few minutes with Dwane. And, when the Doughboys were at bat, Aubrey would stand near third base giving mysterious signs and shouting words of encouragement. He was trim and tanned, having a good time. She was happy for him.

He is in his element—baseball, boys, and a perfect day in the hills. He has lost all the women in his life, the family hardware store, and he has failed as a lawyer, but now he is back on his feet and looking to the future and a new life, perhaps with me...

Stephanie had not felt this way about a man in a long time. Her marriage at age twenty-five failed after eleven years when she realized her husband was never going to grow up. He did not want children, and he was in constant pursuit of the next fun thing to do. She told Aubrey about her unhappy marriage when they talked about the age thing, an issue that bothered him more than her. Now, the age thing was behind them, and they were beginning to talk about their chance for a life together, an unfussy life in the hills.

In the midst of her reverie, Eight Ball connected with a fastball and sent it over the fence in dead centerfield, making it 3-0 in favor of the Doughboys. That boy has a future, she thought. When she sat back down, a handsome man about her age was in the space next to her. He reminded her of the husband she divorced two years ago, slightly built but muscular rather than frail. His blond hair was too long for that part of the country, but it was neatly coiffed.

"You are Stephanie Brooks, aren't you?" His voice had a singsong quality to it.

She did not know him, but his eyes were kind, and he seemed eager to talk. "Yes. I'm sorry, do I know you?"

"I am Timmy ... Timmy Harper ... Randy Trice was my lover."

Stephanie's first thought was about the coming trial. She wondered why Timmy was seeking her out and telling her of his love for the victim. Soon she understood; he had not come to talk about his homosexual relationship with the victim of a murder. He had come to talk about what Spike Spivey was saying to the media—that his client, Cody Ransom, was innocent, and that he was going to assert the defense of "gay panic."

"Spike goes around saying there is no jury in this part of the world that will convict Cody Ransom for hitting a gay man who made an unwanted sexual overture."

Stephanie said, "Well, it is going to be a hard case. People around here are not sympathetic to homosexuality in any way, shape, or form. You do know that, don't you?"

"Yes, of course. I know it will be hard, and I appreciate the fact that Aubrey Hatfield has charged Cody with second-degree murder. Many prosecutors would not be so bold."

"Aubrey would be quick to tell you it is not about courage. He charged second-degree murder because he thinks, as I do, that the law requires it. If a jury wants to find a lesser offense, or let the boy go free, that is its prerogative."

"I understand, but I came here today to tell you that I know a lot about the 'gay panic' defense. I wrote a law review article on it when I was a senior at law school, and I have kept up with the cases ever since. It is a fascinating subject, especially for me."

Stephanie said, "Yes, it is an interesting legal question. But what can you tell me that I haven't already learned in my research?"

"What I have to say is not so much about the legalities of the defense. I have watched several trials, and in every case the defense lawyers—particularly unscrupulous lawyers like Spike Spivey—do damage by weaving prejudice into the way they present their case. They insinuate. They make sly, not-so-subtle comments; it's all done with a wink here and a nod there."

"We are expecting that. Aubrey thinks the best way to handle it is to be open about it. He thinks it would be dumb to act as if the case doesn't involve deep-set prejudice."

"Spike Spivey is going to turn Randy Trice into a monster."

"We can see that coming," Stephanie said.

Timmy dropped his head and sighed, and then he looked directly at Stephanie, his eyes glazed and hurt. "I loved Randy Trice. He was a good and kind man. All we wanted was to live life, and love. Now, a scumbag like Spike Spivey is going to destroy his good name and tarnish what we had. It's not right."

At that point, Zach threw a runner out at second base to end the game, and the crowd jumped up and started a chant: "Doughboys ... Doughboys ... Doughboys..."

When Stephanie turned back to answer Timmy, he was gone. She looked down to the lowest row of seats and saw him step onto the ground and head for the parking lot. It bothered her to see him slumping, inching his way along, but her high spirits—the happy, Fourth of July, upbeat, can-do spirits—came back when she looked at Aubrey. He was beaming and giving high-fives to Zach and the other players as they mobbed one another at home plate.

Stephanie worked her way down to the dugout to join Aubrey, Dwane, and the Doughboys for a post-game celebration. When the cheering and loud talk died down, she said to Aubrey, "You'll never guess who sat by me during the game."

"Who?"

"Randy Trice's lover."

SIXTY-THREE

On the first Monday after the Fourth of July, Lieutenant Smothers and Sergeant Roy Albright walked into the prosecuting attorney's office. It was early; Aubrey and Stephanie had just opened the office, and they were standing by the coffee pot, waiting for it to brew.

After the usual niceties and a few sips of fresh-perked coffee, the lieutenant lowered his voice and put a serious look on his face. "Can we have a few minutes with you all to talk in confidence about a sensitive matter?"

Aubrey nodded his agreement and motioned them toward the conference room.

When they were all seated, Lieutenant Smothers said, "I'm going to ask Sergeant Albright to report some worrisome information he developed over the weekend."

"Yes sir, Lieutenant. Well, Mr. Prosecutor—ma'am—I work the area around Little Rock, where Spike Spivey is from, and I have a confidential source who is telling me that Cody Ransom's father is working as hard as he can to undermine the case you are building against his son."

"That's to be expected," Stephanie said.

"Yes ma'am, but my source tells me he is offering cash money to anyone who will testify that Randy Trice propositioned them to have homosexual sex. He knows Randy had a good reputation around here, so he wants to make him look like a predator."

Stephanie said, "If we confronted Cody's father with that allegation, wouldn't he just deny it? In other words, we can't do much with this if we don't have some hardcore proof that he is doing what you say."

"Yes ma'am. I agree. If we plan to catch them in the act of manufacturing evidence, we would have to set it up legal-like, so as not to entrap anyone."

Aubrey said, "Do you all have any ideas along that line?"

The lieutenant intervened. "Yes, and we can talk about that, but this problem has another dimension to it." He gave Aubrey a knowing look.

"Uh-oh. My antennas are sky high. I think I know where this is going," Aubrey said.

The lieutenant nodded. "Right. You and I talked about this once before, but we now believe Cody's father is actively working with Sheriff Jack Odom to screw up your case. It is hard to believe a sworn law officer would do such a thing, but he despises you and wants to destroy you politically."

Stephanie looked directly at Sergeant Albright. "Would your source testify to any of this?"

"No ma'am."

The lieutenant said, "We are not here to say we can prove these allegations, and we are not certain we can catch the sheriff and these guys in the act. It would be a hard thing to prove, and failure is not an option in such cases."

Aubrey looked at Stephanie and then turned to the lieutenant, "What are you suggesting?"

"I'm saying Sergeant Albright and I will do everything we can to support you as you prosecute this case. We have to respect the office of sheriff because he is an elected official, but from this moment forward, I am operating on the assumption that Sheriff Jack Odom is a member of Spike Spivey's defense team."

"Lieutenant, I appreciate your support." Aubrey straightened up and took a deep breath. "Now, I don't want to complicate an already complicated matter, but I need to know more about the lynching of Ike Swanson in 1968. I need your help, and I want you to report your findings directly to me. I do not want Sheriff Jack Odom to know what we are doing."

"It will be hard to keep it from him; he is the chief law-enforcement officer of the county. If we start nosing around, asking questions about the 1968 case, he will hear about it, and so will the media."

Stephanie said, "For openers, we need to locate and preserve the exhibits and laboratory specimens that were collected at the crime scene or at the office of the state medical examiner in 1968. Can't you do that without creating a stir?"

"We can do that," Lieutenant Smother said.

"And we will want those items processed for DNA."

"Our lab guys can handle that."

Aubrey said, "That's all we want you to do right now. Can you all work with us in this way?"

"We can, and we will," the lieutenant said.

Aubrey stood up, signaling the end of the meeting. "I have no illusions about this. Once we start poking around, the media is sure to hear about it, and so will the sheriff and the others who want us to fail."

The lieutenant said, "I agree, but we'll do our best to keep this quiet. But if it gets out that you are actively investigating the 1968 case, all hell will break loose."

SIXTY-FOUR

One week after their meeting to talk about Sheriff Jack Odom helping Spike Spivey, Lieutenant Smothers called Aubrey. "Mr. Prosecutor, we have located the slides that were examined by the state medical examiner back in 1968, and we have sent them off for DNA testing. We have not found the items of clothing and other pieces of evidence that were collected at the crime scene, but we are still looking."

"When do you expect to hear back about the DNA?"

"It takes longer than we like for the analysis to come back, but I'll let you know as soon as they tell me something."

"OK, keep me posted."

The lieutenant said, "It looks like the media are cranking up their coverage of the Cody Ransom trial. I guess that has to be expected. Right now they seem to be stuck on the line that Spike Spivey gave them: You didn't do anything about the lynching in 1968 and now you are persecuting a young boy who was just defending himself against a monster."

"That's their favorite line, all right."

"I know you want us to work on the QT, and we are trying to do that, but one of the big, liberal papers in the East is about to report that you have reopened the 1968 case. We had a call late yesterday from a stringer, George Maxwell, asking us to confirm or deny that you have reopened the case. We told him we had no comment. "

Aubrey said, "I got the same call, and gave the same answer. We'll know soon enough what he intends to say."

—∞—

On Sunday morning, July 22, eight days before the trial, Stephanie called Aubrey at 7 o'clock. She was worried, and it showed in her voice. "Have you seen the paper?"

"Is it good or bad?"

"It's bad. George Maxwell has put a story on the wire that is going to be a big headache for us."

"He's a curmudgeon, a troublemaker. He will write anything if he can sell it to the big boys. What does it say?"

"Maxwell takes a new approach. The headline says you are now working on two tracks, that you have reopened the 1968 lynching case."

"I'd rather not have the story, but that's not so bad."

"That's not all of it. He couples the two cases and writes that people around here are insensitive to the rights of gay people, that we are a bunch of church-going, Bible-thumping bigots. He goes on to say you did not do anything about the lynching in 1968, and you are just going through the motions now. It's rough."

"So is it in our local papers?"

"Yes, but it is bigger than that, much bigger. It is an international story. I have checked the internet. It is everywhere—blogs, papers, websites, wires, and it is creeping into new sites like Facebook. The genie is out of the bottle, Aubrey."

—∞—

By 8 o'clock, the telephone at Hatfield House was ringing continuously, so Aubrey disconnected it. He had read Maxwell's story and searched the internet to see how other outlets were dealing with it. As he expected, every story repeated the bigotry theme, often in detail. *Why do they circulate such crap? Do they care that they are slandering the good people of this county?*

As he studied the coverage, he was surprised to see that the headlines fairly summarized the truth. *Isn't it usually the other way around? Isn't it usually the headline that is out of whack?*

He wrote down a few of the better ones:

PROSECUTOR WORKING ON TWO TRACKS ... INVESTIGATES OLD AND NEW KILLINGS OF GAY MEN ... INVITES COMPARISON OF CULTURE, THEN AND NOW ... 1968 LYNCHING AND 2007 KILLING OF GAY MAN GET CLOSE LOOK....

Aubrey felt better. He was still mad at Maxwell, but he chalked it off as the work of an ill-informed stringer trying to make a buck. He turned off his computer and hollered to Dwane. "It's time to get ready for church."

SIXTY-FIVE

Aubrey pushed Dwane into the sanctuary and down the aisle to the place set aside for wheelchairs. As soon as he stopped, several men gathered around him, each ready with a comment about the news stories. "I know you are trying to do the right thing, Aubrey, but the whole world is looking down its nose at us," one said. Another was more direct: "I wish you had not charged that boy with murder; that's what got it started." There were more comments, all similar. Aubrey squirmed as he took the barrage, but he had to stand his ground. He told them he could not control the media, that he hoped there would be better stories later on. They listened, but George Maxwell's accusation that they were bigots had them in an uproar.

Aubrey thought to himself: *Who wouldn't be upset? I'm upset too, but what can I do about it? I can do nothing—not right now.*

Soon the sanctuary began to fill, the cluster around Aubrey dispersed, and the complainers stalked back to their pews. Dwane winked at Aubrey, "Comes with the territory, Bub. Hang in there."

When he ushered people to their seats that morning Aubrey got the message, loud and clear. Even though they were in a house of worship, the eyes—most of them—were hot with anger.

The service qualified as a good one in Aubrey's mind. It was shorter than usual, and the preacher spoke of love being the most important thing, or something along those lines. When it was over, he started toward Dwane, and someone tapped him on the shoulder. It was Zach.

"Hi, Uncle Aubrey. I saw those men giving you a hard time, but I'm proud of you for what you are doing. Most of my friends think Cody overreacted."

"Thanks, Zach. Maybe when this is all over, people will see it in a different way. I hope so, anyway."

—

On Monday morning, the news was just as bad. Aubrey headed to the coffee klatch at Gentry's to take temperatures. He climbed into the dentist chair and braced himself. The feedback was the same he got at church the day before. It was one thing for the media and Spike Spivey to contend Aubrey was being unfair to Cody Ransom after failing to prosecute the 1968 lynch mob. That was OK. It was another for them to call the people of Campbell County a bunch of bigots. That was inexcusable.

He left Gentry's and headed for the courthouse. The first call he made when he got to his office was to Lieutenant Smothers. "I was mistaken to think we could keep the lid on any of this. I am going to issue a news release this morning confirming that I am looking into the 1968 lynching case, and I am going to say that I am confident that the people of this county want to resolve both cases, and that they will do the right thing when the facts are put before a jury."

"I think that is a good move, Mr. Prosecutor. It won't stop the provocateurs like Spike, George Fremont, and Jamie Kress, but it will be well received by folks in Campbell County."

"I don't actually know the reporter George Maxwell, do you?"

"Yes, I have met him."

"Would you mind calling him to see if he would drive up here and meet with me? From all I have heard about him, I doubt I can change his mind, but I ought to try."

"It's worth a try, Mr. Prosecutor. I'll see if I can reach him."

SIXTY-SIX

On Wednesday, July 25, five days before the trial, Aubrey stopped by Military Park to encourage the Doughboys. Assistant Coach Horace Zang was working with the outfielders, hitting balls in the gap. The other players were taking a break, sipping water and sitting in the shade of the dugout. Jody Tucker was on the grass near the left-field foul line, throwing practice pitches to Zach. Aubrey said hello to everyone, then walked over to watch Jody. He was working on his changeup, a pitch he was trying to learn to broaden his repertoire.

Aubrey watched him pitch a few, then said, "Good job, Jody. Nothing fools a batter more than changing the speed of your pitches. It's like everything else in life."

"Thanks, Coach." Jody motioned to Zach that he wanted to take a break, and the two huddled around Aubrey to talk baseball.

After a few minutes, Aubrey told the boys he had to get back to the office to get ready for the Cody Ransom trial. He said, "You know the trial starts Monday."

In unison the boys said, "Everyone in the country knows that, Coach."

Aubrey grinned, waved to the other boys, and headed toward his car.

He had taken only a couple of steps when he heard Jody say, "Coach?"

Aubrey looked back. "I almost forgot, my granddad asked me to tell you he would like to talk to you about something." He pointed to a white GMC pickup in the parking lot. "He's out there sitting in his truck. He watches me from there; it's too hot to do anything else."

"Sure, Jody, I'll go over and say hello to him."

Jody tipped his cap, and Aubrey walked toward the pickup. When he got close, Junior Tucker motioned for him to get in on the passenger side of the cab. As Aubrey climbed in, Junior clicked off the radio just as Loretta Lynn was finishing "You Ain't Woman Enough (To Take My Man)."

Junior said, "It's too doggone hot today."

"Boy, you can say that again," Aubrey said.

The two men talked first about the Doughboys, and then they went over the latest major league baseball standings. They talked about the National League and the American League, and in particular, they talked about Junior's favorite team, the St. Louis Cardinals, and Aubrey's favorite team, the Baltimore Orioles. Then they got to Zach and Jody and spent several minutes on them, each telling the other how proud he was of the boys. Aubrey used this sizing-up time to notice things. Junior was laid-back, more inclined to react than provoke, a trait that meshed well with a voice that was closer to tenor than bass. He had the ruddy-faced look of a man who had spent his life doing farm work. He was brawny and way too fat, and his belly rubbed against the steering wheel when he laughed.

Soon they were done with the ritualistic chitchat—a necessary prologue to any serious conversation between two men of the South.

"They been beatin' up on you pretty good, ain't they, Aubrey?"

"Oh, it comes with the territory..."

"It ain't right, what they're saying about folks around here."

"I know, but it's how they sell newspapers and get their ratings up."

"The radio said this morning that you're fixing to look into the killing that took place in 1968."

"I am. I put a statement out yesterday saying that I am reopening the case. I don't know if I can prove who did it, but I've got to try."

Junior looked out the side window, away from Aubrey, cleared his throat and spoke in a cracked voice. "I know something about that mess, but I ain't ever talked about it."

Both men sat still. Aubrey tried to be nonchalant, but he did not do a good job of it. Finally, Junior turned and looked at Aubrey, and then he lowered his eyes and his voice. "I reckon I should have said something, but nobody ever asked me to."

Aubrey thought of his own shame. He should have done more to force a full investigation into the lynching of Ike Swanson, but he had not. "I know how you feel, Junior. I was the deputy prosecutor at that time and could have done more than I did."

"You have been right good to Jody, and he tells me the boys all think you are doing the right thing. They think the Ransom boy should not have hit Randy Trice with that dumbbell. They say he should have just walked away."

Aubrey said, "Those boys—the Doughboys—have given me a new lease on life. To be honest, I had lost my way, and it took baseball and boys to get me back on track."

"You know, I got the team to change its name to the Doughboys back when my son, Jody's father, was playing. I did it because I had a friend whose nickname was Doughboy. He was my fishing buddy back when I was young, and that's a good place to start telling you about the 1968 mess."

Aubrey said, "You tell it however you want to, Junior."

Junior swung his belly to the right and pulled his right knee up so that he could look at Aubrey without twisting his neck, and Aubrey did the same from the opposite direction. The moves signaled trust and a willingness to talk things through from beginning to end.

"When I was seventeen I was searching for something. Some friends told me about a group that was fighting against all the bad stuff that was going on in the 1960s. That sounded good to me, so I went to a couple of meetings. A young preacher, Artus MacArthur, had started the group. It was called Mysterion."

"I've heard of it," Aubrey said.

"Yeah, it has been around for more than forty years, and Artus is still running it."

"Did the group have something to do with the lynching of Ike Swanson?"

"I don't know that—firsthand, that is. I quit going after two meetings. I was a pissed-off kind of kid, but Mysterion was not my kind of thing."

"Well, how does the group fit into what you know about the killing in 1968?"

"I mentioned my friend, Doughboy. We used to go fishing all the time with a guy named Cletus. He was fun to fish with, but he was totally freaked out about commies and queers. My grandson says I'm supposed to say 'gays,' but I ain't got used to that yet."

Aubrey said, "I've seen the name Cletus Bolton in the old case file. Is that who you are talking about?"

"That was Cletus' last name, all right."

"Was he in Mysterion?"

"Yeah, he bought into that stuff hook, line, and sinker."

"Did Cletus have something to do with the killing?"

"I don't know firsthand what he did or didn't do. All I know is what he told me and Doughboy when we were fishing."

"Was Doughboy in Mysterion?"

"Shoot no, Doughboy was way too smart for anything like that."

Aubrey said, "I keep getting us off track. Just tell it like you want to."

"You ain't getting us off track, because it all fits together. A little while before the killing, Cletus was at a Mysterion meeting, and there was talk about a queer that had moved to town to run that grocery store, Bracey's Market. They got all het-up about it, and a few days later Cletus saw the queer at what used to be the Black Cat Café. He chewed him out and accused him of giving blowjobs to high school boys."

"That's why his name is in the state police file," Aubrey said.

"Me and Doughboy told him he ought to stay away from that jackleg preacher and Mysterion, but Cletus never heard anything when he was pissed off. He just kept going to the meetings."

"Did he say anything to you all after the killing?"

"Yep, we went fishing once after the killing, and Cletus told us he was there, but he said he only went for the curing part."

"What did he mean by that?"

"Cletus said Artus had come up with a way to cure queers, and that is why they caught that boy, Ike, and took him into the woods up by the old Spradlin Mule Farm. He said Artus and two other members of Mysterion tied the boy up and then hooked up wires to an old-timey crank telephone. They would show him pictures of queers doing their thing and crank the handle to send an electrical shock to the boy's balls."

Junior squirmed around a little. "Then they would show him pictures of regular-screwing between a man and a woman, and when they did that, they did not crank up the phone. Ain't that something?" He squirmed some more.

Aubrey said, "The doctor at the autopsy suspected that. He said it was like the Tucker Telephone they used down at the Arkansas prison back in the old days of Orval Faubus."

"Cletus said he and two other guys left after the curing. I don't know if any of this is true, it's just what Cletus told us."

Aubrey said, "You said you got out of Mysterion after a couple of meetings because it was not your kind of thing. What did you mean by that?"

"Artus used that group to round up all the local boys who talked against commies, Jews, and perverts. Once they were in, he could get them to do just about anything to protect the group. It is a mind-control kind of thing."

"Is that why you got out?"

"Well, I had some help in seeing the light. I was just seventeen when I went to those meetings. I was just plain stupid."

"Who helped you?"

"Jo Belle and Jesus! Jo Belle is my wife. I started going with her way back when we were kids, and we got married as soon as I turned twenty. We've been married now for forty-four years. I kept telling her about Artus MacArthur and Mysterion, and she told me how the cow ate the cabbage. She said I could stay with Artus and Mysterion, or I could have her and Jesus."

Aubrey said, "Sounds like your wife is a good Christian."

"She puts it real simple. She says Artus and people like him are always searching for a way to live life. She says there ain't no need to search because the Bible already lays out the best way to live." Junior grinned. "Jo Belle knows more about the Bible than anyone. I ain't near as good at witnessing as she is."

"Well, you just did a pretty good job of saying you are a believer."

Junior laughed and took on a serious air. "It's hard for me to witness straight out—I don't know why, it just is. I've had to come up with a different way to do it."

Aubrey could see that Junior wanted to say more about his faith. "What's your way?"

"I tell about the guitar player who was strumming the same chord over and over. A man came up and asked him why he was playing the same chord, and he said, 'Them other fellers are searching for it, but I've flat got it.'" Junior broke up laughing at his own story, and he punched Aubrey on the shoulder.

Aubrey laughed too. "Jesus would approve. He used parables too."

"Amen, brother."

Aubrey said, "What would we do without women? I fell in love with a beautiful woman when I was a teenager and we got married, but she died young. Now there is another woman—my first in thirty-eight years—and she is changing my life."

"Praise God."

Junior bowed his head and closed his eyes. Aubrey figured he was praying for the two of them and their women, but he did not join in Junior's prayer. He was thinking:

This is a good man—I like him—and he is trying to do the right thing.

Aubrey sat perfectly still until Junior was finished. Then he said, "Junior, do you know where Cletus is?"

"No, I ain't seen hide nor hair of him in years. He lit out of here right after he told us about the killing. He came back once when Doughboy was still alive and said he was living in a little spot in Pulaski County, Kentucky. Funny, ain't it—same county name as we got down where Little Rock is—but I ain't heard from him since then."

"Junior, I'll need to get a statement from you in writing, so I'll have my deputy, Stephanie Brooks, to get in touch with you to do that. Is that OK?"

"I've seen her talking to you and the boys at the games. You bet it's all right. I like her."

Aubrey shook Junior's hand and stepped out of the pickup. As soon as he got to the office, he told Stephanie about Junior and asked her to set up a meeting with Lieutenant Smothers.

SIXTY-SEVEN

Lieutenant Smothers arrived in mid-afternoon. Aubrey and Stephanie were waiting for him in the conference room. Stephanie said, "Thanks for getting here as fast as you did. You will see why I said ASAP when you hear what Aubrey has learned."

Aubrey said, "I went to the ballpark today to check on the Doughboys, and Jody Tucker told me his granddad wanted to see me. I thought it was about the team, but he was upset about the media portraying all of us as a bunch of bigots."

"That puts him with a long list of folks," Lieutenant Smothers said. "It's a bad rap, but it has everyone up in arms."

"I agree, but the bad publicity has given us our first break in the 1968 lynching."

"How so?"

"Junior Tucker told me that his old fishing buddy, Cletus Bolton, was at the crime scene the night Ike Swanson was tortured and killed. He says Cletus told him that he left before Ike was killed, but he named Artus MacArthur as the one who probably did the killing."

"Artus? Yes, that figures. What was Cletus doing there?"

"Apparently, Artus told him and some other Mysterion boys that he was going to cure Ike's homosexuality by using the old Tucker Telephone technique—shock his genitals while showing him photos of homosexuals in action, and not shocking him while showing photos of heterosexual activity."

The lieutenant looked at Stephanie, "Sorry."

Stephanie laughed and shook her head. "Don't worry about my sensibilities, Lieutenant. I'm full-grown. Besides, I have read the Ike Swanson autopsy report, and Aubrey told me what Junior said about the Tucker Telephone before you got here."

Aubrey smiled and changed the subject. "Junior said he will give us a written statement, and I would like for you and Stephanie to handle that as soon as you can."

"Of course. And, I guess your next assignment will be for me to find Cletus, the sooner the better?"

"Right. Junior said Cletus left here and settled in Pulaski County, Kentucky, but that was years ago. We can't charge Artus based on what Junior heard Cletus say—that would be pure hearsay. We need to find Cletus and get him to testify against Artus, and we need to find corroborating evidence to back up what Cletus says about Artus."

The lieutenant said, "We'll get on this right away. I'll contact the Kentucky State Police."

"Thanks, Lieutenant. The Cody Ransom trial starts Monday, and I would really like to find Cletus as soon as possible. It would help, in every way, if we could make an arrest in the 1968 case."

The lieutenant said, "Speaking of moving things along, I heard back from the laboratory. They need you to request expedite treatment of our DNA request. There is a long waiting list for DNA analyses, but you can move up on the list if you show that the case is about terroristic, gang-related activity."

"I'll do that as soon as we get through here," Aubrey said.

Stephanie said, "Before we break up, can we talk some more about Mysterion? We have learned a lot, but we need to know more." She then told the lieutenant what she had learned about the group from internet research. "There is one particular issue that we need to know more about. Junior told Aubrey that Artus has managed to convince those who are part of Mysterion that they must always protect the group—do anything and everything to protect it. I believe—and this is just a theory—that Artus tells his disciples that God chose Mysterion to interpret the mysteries of the Bible, and that the group must live on, at all costs. Can you dig into this without tipping off Artus? Perhaps you could interview former members of the group?"

"Let me give that some thought, Stephanie, but I see your point. If members of Mysterion buy into that, then any one of them might be willing to help Artus get rid of a witness like Cletus."

"Exactly."

SIXTY-EIGHT

Cletus pinched the burned-out cigarette stub between his thumb and forefinger and unstuck it from his lower lip. He coughed—two easy hackers and one deep rattler—to clear things out. Then he tossed the butt over the side and turned his attention to the jiggling red-and-white float. It was moving one way and then the other, making a semi-circle, a sure sign that he was about to get a strong bite, a catching bite.

Bet it's a channel cat ... nibbles like it ... that's what I'm hoping ... go ahead ... take that chicken liver, you son-of-a-bitch ...it's too damn hot out here ...

Wham!

Cletus coaxed the two-pounder up from the bottom of the river and into the boat. Then he headed for his tie-up spot, a small opening on the west bank of the Eleven Point River. When he got close to shore, he turned off the motor, let the boat drift to a standstill, and looped a line around a young sycamore that leaned his way. Cletus rubbed the sweat from his forehead with his shirtsleeve and sat still, enjoying the cool of the shade. He sat there for a few minutes arranging his gear, and then he took the catfish from the bottom of the boat and stepped out onto a low-lying rocky ledge. He checked his tie-up and headed up the narrow path that led to Josie's cabin.

—∾—

Cletus had come back to Arkansas in February when it was freezing cold. Now it was July and blazing hot. He smiled a little as he thought about it.

Man, oh man, it goes from ice-cold to boiling-hot—that's Arkansas. But I'm safe here. This is a good hiding place. Josie has never let me down.

Josie McBride was Cletus' second cousin. She was two years older, but they got started with each other when Cletus was thirteen. The McBride family was burying an old aunt, and they were having the funeral at her house, which was the way they did it back then. Family and friends listened to the preacher and stood around looking at the corpse in an open casket, but Josie did not. She lured Cletus out of the house and into a dimly lit storm shelter, where she announced, "I'll let you see mine if you'll let me see yours." One thing led to another, and Cletus lost his virginity, right there in the storm cellar.

That led to a summer of sex with Josie, a relationship that would continue for years. In 1967, when Cletus' second marriage failed, he turned to Josie for relief. She would always take him in and let him have his way with her, even after she married Jimmy Belford when she was nineteen. Jimmy was almost forty years old when they wed, but he was a perfect husband for Josie. He had inherited a large parcel of land along the Eleven Point River and made a fair income as a rural mail carrier. Jimmy was crazy about Josie and never kicked her out of the house, even though she had a habit of going off with other men, sometimes for as long as a week.

When Jimmy was fifty-five, a drunk driver ran into his truck head-on, killing Jimmy outright. Josie wound up with their house, the land, an old one-room cabin on the Eleven Point, and a lump-sum settlement from the drunk's insurance company. She never remarried, but she did not lack for men friends. She told everyone the men who stayed at her place—sometimes for as long as a month—had come just to fish the river. Few people believed that, particularly those who knew her well.

—∞—

On February 15, 2007, Josie was watching the news about Anna Nicole Smith, the Playboy centerfold celebrity who married a man three times her age and turned up dead in a Florida hotel. The story captivated Josie. She identified with Anna Nicole because she herself had married a man twice her age, and people judged her poorly for it. She never missed the evening news, eager to hear the latest reports from Florida, and she was furious when the local station broke into the Anna Nicole Smith story to report the killing of a homosexual man in Woodville, Arkansas. Josie flipped to another channel, but the story of the Woodville killing was on it too.

She fumed.

So he was a big-shot car dealer. Who cares if a queer gets himself slugged with a dumbbell? Why don't they get back to Anna Nicole?

Five days later Josie was still camped in front of her TV watching the Anna Nicole news when her telephone rang. She hesitated, and then something told her to answer.

"Josie, it's Cletus."

"Good God, it's been years. How're you doing, cousin?"

"I'm OK. Can I come stay with you for a spell?"

"Where are you, Cletus? Are you still in Kentucky?"

"I'm on my way to Arkansas. Some boys from Campbell County came to my trailer last night, aiming to kill me or beat the hell out of me. Some queer got killed in Woodville the other day, and that set the news people off. Now they've started talking about the 1968 lynching case again. I heard it on the radio, way up here. You know I didn't have nothing to do with that killing, but them that did the killing—Artus and that bunch—is after me. Scared I'll talk is what I figure."

Josie said, "I heard about the queer getting killed in Woodville, but I haven't heard anything about the lynching in years. Come on down. You can stay at the cabin if you want to. No one will know you are there if you stay put and let me bring eats to you ever so often."

"I'll be there tomorrow evening, just after dark. See what you can find out about the killing of the queer and the 1968 thing without letting on that I'm coming."

"I'll call Ruby Lou. She's living over that way. She'll know what's going on, and she won't say anything."

"All right, but don't say my name. Just say you wanted to know."

Cletus spent a cold and nervous night in the cab of his old Ford truck at a roadside park just east of Bowling Green, Kentucky, waking up every time a car or truck stopped close to him. When day broke, he eased his way back onto the highway and took the back roads to Cairo, Illinois, where he crossed the Mississippi River into Missouri. From there he drove west to the little border town of Thayer, timing his trip to arrive there after dark. When he crossed into Arkansas, a dry snow began to fall. He was only twenty miles from Josie's place, and the last half-mile to her house was over an isolated dirt road. Josie aimed to keep her place secluded; she owned the property on both sides of the dirt road.

Cletus rolled his truck to a stop in front of her place, turned off the engine and grabbed his duffel bag. When he got out of the truck, he knew he had done the right thing by coming to Josie's. It was ghostly quiet, the only sound being the slight clicking of his truck engine as it quickly began to cool.

The old place was the same as he remembered: a low-lying, redbrick ranch house with an odd-looking covered porch that Josie added after she buried her husband. Josie was on the porch waving to him. When he got to where she was, she gave him a hug and pulled him inside, out of the cold.

"You're a sight for sore eyes," she said.

"You're looking pretty good yourself." Cletus put his duffel down and patted her on the bottom.

Josie said, "We can get to that later. First, catch me up on what's going on."

They sat down by the fireplace, and Josie poured Cletus a drink of whiskey.

"It's like I said, the killing of the queer car dealer in Woodville has started talk about the lynching thing—I heard about it over in Kentucky. I got worried that Artus would sic his Mysterion boys on me, so I started keeping most of my necessaries in the truck in case I had to leave out real quick."

"That was pretty smart, Cletus." Josie poked him in the ribs and scooted a little closer to him on the sofa.

"I didn't fall off no turnip wagon." Cletus winked and puffed up, then his shoulders slumped and he got serious. "Josie, they was going to dry-gulch me in my own place. I was coming home early from a job I was working and saw a strange truck with Arkansas plates parked in front of my trailer, and somebody was inside looking around. I eased down to the end of the trailer park so I could see what they were up to. And pretty soon these two guys came out and one of them got in the truck and moved it to the other end of the park. And then he walked back to my trailer. He went inside with the other guy and they turned off the lights. And that's when I knew that they was up to no good."

Josie interrupted him. "Hell, that lynching was almost forty years ago. Why would they want to kill you now?"

"Like I told you before, I was there the night that Artus and two others killed that boy. I wanted to tell the cops back then that I left before the killing, that I was only there for the curing part, but Artus told me I was crazy. He said they would put me away, because I would bring him and Mysterion down if I did that. He was mad as hell and told me to skedaddle, get out of the state and not come back. So that's when I went to Kentucky. And I been there solid except for the times when I've been back here to see you, and once when I went back to see a couple of old fishing buddies, Junior and Doughboy."

"You've been back five or six times by my count," Josie said. "Why hasn't Artus got you before now?"

"Because I did what he said. I left out of there and went to Kentucky, and he didn't see no need to get rid of me. Besides, Artus said he had it fixed with the sheriff, so long as none of us opened our mouths."

Josie said, "OK, that's it, then. After you called me, I talked to Ruby Lou and she said they had a big political shakeup in Campbell County. There's a new prosecuting attorney there, and he's the one that just filed charges against the boy that killed the queer. Now the papers are saying he had something to do with not solving the lynching case back in 1968. Ruby Lou says it's a mess; the whole county is up in arms."

Cletus put his arm around Josie and pulled her close. "Well, it blew over once before. Maybe it will blow over again."

"Spend tonight here with me in my bed, and then tomorrow we'll move you down to the cabin and hide your truck in the woods."

"I just need to lay low for a while."

"You can lay low with me anytime, Cletus."

Cletus gave her a kiss and thought to himself: *She still looks pretty damn good—she's gray-haired now, mostly lean but plump in just the right places. I'll stay right here until this is over. I'll either be free, or I'll go to jail, or Artus will kill me. No matter how it turns out, Josie is the woman who taught me how to screw, so it's only right if she winds up being my last piece of pussy.*

SIXTY-NINE

Aubrey stayed at Hatfield House as long as he could. Cody Ransom's trial was set to begin at 9 a.m., and the judge wanted the lawyers to be there thirty minutes early to hash out a few procedural matters. He left the house at 8:25, ambling toward the courthouse. The cool of night was fading away, and it was going to be scorching hot before the day was over—in many ways. Then it hit him.

What's going on? My familiar walk is oddly unfamiliar. What is it that is different? That's it—it's the cars and trucks. There is no place to park; the spots are full. People, some dressed up and some in overalls, are drifting toward the square. There's a peculiar silence, but it's broken up by mysterious noises coming from the square. Something is humming, but I'll see what is causing that when I round the corner. There, now I can see. Oh, man. The whole world is watching our little town.

Aubrey made his way through the crowd, past the TV trucks with their generators and satellite dishes, all tied together with huge yellow, gray, and black cables.

That word—LIVE—is everywhere. It's on everything, the panel-trucks, the strange pieces of TV equipment. Busybodies are scribbling in notebooks—are they reporters? Well-wishers are calling my name, but the ones hurling insults are drowning them out. Thank God I am nearing the door. A nod to the guard. Now, I'm in.

The judge was in his robe when Aubrey, Stephanie, and Spike entered his chambers, an upstairs office overlooking the courthouse lawn and the backside of a Confederate memorial. On the street beyond the statue, in line with the general's drawn sword, George Freemont and Jamie Kress stood with small huddles of supporters, presumably to issue marching orders for the day.

Judge Harry Oglethorpe seemed fidgety to Aubrey, but Spike—no stranger to high profile lawyering—was in his element. "What say, Hoss? Stephanie. Your Honor. It's a fine day in the Ozarks."

The judge said, "Let's talk about jury selection. I hope neither of you intends to turn this into an ordeal."

Spike said, "Your Honor, I'm almost ready to say I'll take the first twelve that are drawn from the wheel."

Aubrey smirked at Spike's theatrics. "I'm not willing to go that far, but I do agree that we should seat a jury as soon as possible."

"Good, that's what I wanted to hear. Now let's talk about the media. I've seen the comments attributed to each of you, and I have given some thought to a gag order, but these days those orders seem to be more honored in the breach than the observance. It is virtually impossible to control the coverage, so I am going to ask each of you to help me: You can talk to the press, but don't throw gasoline on the fire just to get your name in the paper or to get a headline calculated to prejudice the jury. Can I have your word on that?"

The lawyers agreed, but Aubrey had no illusions. Spike was famous for doing exactly what he had just agreed not to do.

The judge said, "We have already discussed a number of pretrial issues, and I have read the briefs each of you submitted on the issue of 'gay panic,' which I prefer to call 'homosexual panic.' Spike, you contend you can offer proof and argument on that subject. Is that right?"

"Yes, Judge, but given the weakness of Aubrey's case, I probably won't have to put on a defense." Spike snickered, and when nobody laughed, he said, "If I do put on a defense, I will definitely show that the boy, Cody, did what any red-blooded American boy would do if attacked by a homosexual." Spike leaned back in his chair with a satisfied look on his face. His ploy was crass, but Aubrey knew Spike had just delivered a summary of his trial strategy.

The judge said, "Does that mean you are going to raise 'homosexual panic' as a defense?"

"At the appropriate time, Judge, I will proffer a jury instruction that will define 'gay panic.' It will say that the jury can acquit if they find that my client was in such a state at the time he struck Randy Trice."

"Aubrey, what do you say to that?"

"That is not the law in Arkansas, and it is not, to my knowledge, the law in any jurisdiction. The state will object to such an instruction."

The judge said, "I'm certain Aubrey is right about that. I will refuse any instruction to the jury along those lines, Spike."

Spike started to say something, but Aubrey beat him to it. "Your Honor, 'gay panic' is more a trial strategy than a legal defense. From the start Spike has been making statements about 'gay panic' to the media, and I expect he will take every opportunity to let the jurors know that Randy Trice tried to perform an unwanted homosexual act on Cody Ransom, which caused him to panic and hit Randy with the dumbbell. He will do it during jury selection, and he will do it throughout the trial of the case."

"Are you saying I should rule now that Spike cannot offer proof to that effect, or make statements and arguments to that effect in the presence of the jury?"

"In a perfect world we would try this case without prejudice, but I am not naïve. Defense counsel is a clever lawyer, and the jury is not stupid. Spike has said he will raise the defenses of insanity, provocation, and self-defense, and that will give him many opportunities to deploy his 'gay panic' strategy. He will do it through innuendo or oblique reference if he cannot do it directly. For these reasons, I have decided that I will not object to Spike's effort to raise the concept of 'gay panic' during the trial of this case; however, it is not a legal defense, and he is not entitled to a jury instruction saying that it is a legitimate defense."

The judge said, "Well, Spike, that's it. I will not instruct the jury that they can acquit if they find 'gay panic,' but you will be able to mention it, offer proof on it, and argue it, especially as part of your provocation defense.

"One final point. I know there are likely to be veiled references to the unfortunate events of 1968. The media continue to report details about the lynching of Ike Swanson right alongside their reports about the case we are trying today. But I am telling you now that we are not going to try the Ike Swanson case in this court at this time. If and when someone is charged with the killing of Ike Swanson, we will deal with it, but until then I expect you lawyers to respect the suggestion I am making right now."

In unison, Aubrey, Stephanie, and Spike said, "Yes, Your Honor."

The judge stood up. "All right, let's get started."

As they headed into the courtroom, Spike got between Aubrey and Stephanie and the door. "You think that was pretty clever, don't you, Aubrey—agreeing to let me do what I was going to do anyway. Well, hitch 'em up tight, Hoss. I'm fixing to clean your clock."

Aubrey winked at Stephanie and then leaned toward Spike. "Let's just lay it all out and let the jury decide."

When they were seated, Stephanie whispered to Aubrey. "Spike's ticked off. He was hoping you would resist all mention of 'gay panic.' In that way he could slip it in and get the benefit of it, and you would be left sputtering and objecting, looking like a fool. Like you were trying to keep something from the jury."

"I would probably be in that position if it had not been for the good research you did on 'gay panic.'"

Jury selection, ordinarily a time when lawyers plant suggestions that might be out of order if offered in the course of a trial, was remarkably smooth. Spike did not accept the first twelve, and he used all his peremptory challenges. So did Aubrey. Spike's questions to the jurors were indeed suggestive, all calculated to support his trial strategy, but Aubrey did not object. Having decided to meet Spike's "gay panic" strategy head on, it suited him to talk openly about it from the beginning. Objecting to every mention of "gay panic" would have done nothing but highlight the point Spike was trying to make.

When the judge gaveled the session to an end late Tuesday afternoon, the jury was in the box—seven men and five women, with one man and one woman as alternates. The judge gave them the oath and the usual instruction to avoid media reports and discussions about the case. Then he said, "Ladies and gentlemen, we will resume tomorrow morning at 9 a.m., at which time the prosecution and defense will give their opening statements."

SEVENTY

At 8:45 a.m., the custodian of the Campbell County Courthouse opened the heavy double doors to the courtroom, and a swarm of people from every occupation and lifestyle scrambled to get seats. The large room filled quickly, but the front row did not. Cordoned off and marked "Reserved," it designated seats saved for the families of Cody Ransom and Randy Trice. Latecomers made way for the families to enter, and then they pushed their way into the room to stand in a small space behind the last row of seats. When the standing room was full, the custodian herded the frustrated overflow back into the hall and closed the double doors. The old courtroom was jam-packed, a record crowd.

Lawyers, clerks, and other officials dribbled into the courtroom through a door to the right of the judge's bench—a majestic perch designed to suggest apotheosis for the one sitting there. The first lawyers to come through the door were not involved in the case. They wandered around like popinjays, feigning importance. They would soon disappear, slipping out before their irrelevance became obvious. The clerks and other court officials took their places, and the jurors, arriving in ones and twos, took their seats in the jury box.

The prosecution and defense attorneys came in all at once, taking seats at separate counsel tables—a sure sign that the action was about to begin. Aubrey and Stephanie sat at the table closest to the jury box. Spike sat at the other counsel table, dressed in his favorite trial garb, a greenish suit of neon iridescence set off by a yellow tie. Aubrey wore his blue suit and Stephanie had on a tan, tailored dress highlighted by a royal-blue scarf.

Spike and Aubrey looked busy, overly so. They shuffled stacks of paper and rearranged books, constantly fidgeting with one or the other. Stephanie was at ease. She had no books or papers in front of her, just a laptop computer that was open and plugged into an outlet on the table. She presented a vivid contrast of sex, youth, and modernity.

Randy Trice's parents and Randy's sister sat on the first row, directly behind Aubrey and Stephanie. Dressed formally, they looked stiff, depressed. Timmy Harper, Randy's lover, was seated on the same row several places away from the Trice family. Neither gave signs of recognition to the other.

Cody Ransom was at the counsel table with Spike. He looked casual, younger than his eighteen years. Spike had him dressed to look more like an adolescent than a young man. Cody's mother, Lillian Ransom, sat behind him on the first row. She wore her hair in a bun, a style that exaggerated the puffy look of her face. Lillian was only thirty-six years old, but she had the full-bodied, tired look of an older woman. She sat still and looked down most of the time, a habit that hid a once-pretty face. Her choice of a dress, a faded, loose-fitting smock, took away her only chance to show an upbeat spirit. Carl Ransom, a burly man, tall and trim, sat next to his wife. His eyes, hot and squinty, scanned the room but always came to rest on Aubrey. He looked like the woodsman he was, wearing khaki trousers, work boots, and an open-collared work shirt.

Wes Caldwell, the bailiff, moved easily from one end of the courtroom to the other resolving seating disputes and keeping order. Wes was almost eighty years old and had been bailiff for as long as anyone could remember. Blessed with a friendly countenance and deferential manner, Wes had long since mastered the job of bailiff. He also knew how to make a buck, an interest not missed by the savvy provocateur George Freemont. At the last minute, Wes led him to a choice seat on the front row near Spike. Jamie Kress, not knowing Wes as well as his counterpart, sat near the back of the courtroom.

Soon everyone was in place, and Wes disappeared though the door to the left of the judge's bench. Moments later, he reappeared to sing his song. "Oh yez, oh yez, the Circuit Court of Campbell County, Arkansas, is now in session, the honorable Judge Harry Oglethorpe presiding. God save this honorable court."

Judge Oglethorpe, black robe flowing, made a grand entrance. He stepped up onto the judge's bench, and at the height of his ascension—apotheosis within reach—he sat down and told his audience, "Please be seated."

He announced the case and looked at Aubrey. "Mr. Prosecutor, you may make your opening statement."

"Your Honor, as I indicated to the court earlier, my deputy prosecuting attorney, Stephanie Brooks, will open for the state."

"You are recognized, Ms. Brooks."

Stephanie rose. She had no papers or notes in her hands, and she took pains to look each juror in the eye as she approached the lectern. Then she spoke.

"May it please the court, ladies and gentlemen of the jury, I am Stephanie Brooks, and I am honored to serve as deputy to Mr. Aubrey Hatfield, your prosecuting attorney. This is, in many ways, a simple case." Stephanie then outlined the state's proof dispassionately, saying the case would boil down to the issue of provocation. She said there would be no proof that the defendant was insane as defined in the law, or that he was in danger of physical harm. She talked about the anticipated defense of "gay panic" and said the state would deal with the issue of homosexuality openly throughout the trial. "Quite simply, if Randy Trice made a homosexual overture to Cody Ransom, Cody should have said, 'No.' He did not have to hit Randy. He should have gotten out of the car and continued his run. If he had done that, Randy Trice would be alive today, and Cody would not be on trial. It was wrong for Cody to hit Randy. He killed a good man."

Stephanie was finished. She took her seat and the judge recognized Spike. He paraded to the lectern, one hand in his pocket, the other bumping against his head as if to clear it of misinformation. "Well, ladies and gentlemen, where should I begin? My client is innocent. He is a fine boy who wants to go to college and play football. He will testify that he was out running, and Randy Trice pulled up alongside and lured him into his

Cadillac with a lie. He said he wanted to talk to Cody about a scholarship offer to play football at Calico University, a Division I school. What boy wouldn't want to hear more about that? Then, when they were alone in the car, Randy reached over and grabbed his privates, saying he wanted to have homosexual sex with Cody. Cody was totally surprised, and he panicked. Bear in mind, and our proof will show this: Cody and most young boys around here are taught from childhood to despise homosexuality, that it is wrong biblically, morally, and legally. Cody did what most Campbell County boys would do; he hit Randy and ran off. This is what the proof will show, and that is why you must let this boy go."

Spike turned away from the jury and headed back to his table. Sheriff Jack Odom was leaning against the wall by the door to the right of the judge's bench. Spike looked directly at him and winked. The sheriff grinned and gave Spike a slight nod.

Judge Oglethorpe said, "All right. We are ready to proceed. Mr. Prosecutor, you may call your first witness."

Aubrey first called the camper who reported finding Randy Trice in his Cadillac at the Cherokee access to the lake. Then he called the deputy sheriff who was first on the scene, and other witnesses who told of seeing Randy Trice at work on the day of his death.

The rest of Wednesday and all day Thursday dealt with medical and scientific proof. Aubrey called to the stand the state medical examiner who did the autopsy on the body of Randy Trice. She testified that she found ten lacerations on Randy's head and face, internal head trauma, and numerous skull fractures caused by hits to the head with a dumbbell or other heavy object. She also said there were wounds on his right hand and the inside of his left forearm that were consistent with defensive wounds. She concluded that the cause of death was blunt head trauma resulting from five, probably six, blows to the head.

Aubrey also called the expert who matched the bloodstains on the dumbbells with the blood of Randy Trice. The state spent the best part of two days on this, and the introduction of other evidence establishing the elements of second-degree murder.

Spike and Aubrey argued several times in court as well as in chambers over the issue of implied malice, an essential element of the crime of second-degree murder. Aubrey said Cody's use of the dumbbells constituted the use of a "deadly weapon," and he offered case law from several jurisdictions to support his contention. He conceded that his argument to imply malice would be weak if Cody had only hit Randy once, but the medical examiner proved that he hit Randy in the head five, probably six times. That, Aubrey said, was conduct sufficient to imply malice.

SEVENTY-ONE

At the end of the day on Thursday, Aubrey gathered his files from the counsel table and pushed through the gate on the railing that separates the media and spectators from the officers of the court. He was worn out and looking forward to getting to Hatfield House for some rest and a good night's sleep.

Lieutenant Smothers was waiting for him at the double door leading to the hallway and stairs. "Mr. Prosecutor, I just had a call from the Kentucky State Police. The town of Burnside, Kentucky, is very small, really just a crossroads outside of Somerset, up near the Appalachian Mountains. The police talked to the sheriff in that county, Pulaski County, to see if anyone had heard of a sixty-year-old mechanic named Cletus Bolton. No one knew that name, but several people knew a 'Cletus Dacus.' The KSP checked public records and determined that Cletus Dacus is Cletus Bolton, born in Arkansas on May 22, 1945. He registered for the draft in Campbell County, Arkansas, on June 10, 1963.

"Good. Is he still there? Did they make contact?"

"No, he's gone. Cletus was in Burnside, but he cut out in February."

"Where did he go? Do they know?"

"No. They talked to an elderly woman who ran the trailer park where he was renting a small trailer. She said he lived there for ten years and was a loner who made money doing mechanic work. She said he just disappeared in February—took part of his stuff and left. He said nothing to her and left no forwarding address."

"Is that it?"

"No, there's one more thing."

"The KSP talked to a couple of people who lived in nearby trailers, and they said two men in a white Dodge truck with Arkansas plates came looking for Cletus a few days before he disappeared. That would have been right after all the publicity about the arrest of Cody Ransom and the early stories about the 1968 lynching."

"Who were they? Do we know?"

"No. The witnesses told the sheriff they were big old boys, not dressed up, just wearing work clothes. The men told the neighbors they were old friends from down-home, that they went to the same church with Cletus, and they were going to wait for him to come home. They said Cletus told them it was OK to wait for him in his trailer."

"Mysterion boys?"

"Sounds like it. The next day the men were gone, and so was Cletus. The old lady waited for a month and then rented the trailer to someone else. Nobody could remember anything else, but in fairness to the neighbors, that was almost five months ago."

Aubrey said, "He's either running or dead. If he's alive, we better find him before Artus and the Mysterion boys get to him. If we can't get him to tell what he knows about the murder of Ike Swanson, we will never make a case on Artus."

"I want to put out an all-points bulletin to locate Cletus Bolton for questioning in connection with the 1968 murder of Ike Swanson. I have it ready to go, but I wanted to get your approval to send it out."

Aubrey said, "Yes, do it. Do it right now."

SEVENTY-TWO

The Campbell County sheriff's department moved to a new county office building in 2002, and memorabilia commemorating the glory days of Sheriff Mark Odom in the 1960s and 1970s adorned every room. Sheriff Jack Odom was determined to keep his grandfather's legacy alive. He loved to brag that the Odom lineage and loyal protégés of the Odom-Cooksey political machine had controlled the sheriff's office for the last fifty years.

The sheriff, like his grandfather, was not a desk jockey. He spent most of his time roaming the county, strutting and schmoozing. It was the Odom way, a proven style.

On the rare occasions when he was in the office, he sat behind the huge mahogany desk that his grandfather had used throughout his tenure as sheriff. A garish desk lamp, its massive base made of light-colored pine, consumed one-fourth of the desktop. Sheriff Mark Odom's badge and the pearl grips from his Smith & Wesson nickel-plated revolver were imbedded in the pine. Jack Odom made the lamp himself to honor his grandfather's service. He had the best of intentions, but the weird lamp quickly became the object of mockery when the sheriff was beyond earshot.

At 5:30 p.m. on Thursday, Lieutenant Smothers posted the all-points bulletin identifying Cletus Bolton as a person wanted for questioning in connection with the 1968 lynching. Minutes later, just as Sheriff Jack Odom was about to back out of his parking spot at the sheriff's office, a new deputy came outside waving the bulletin. The sheriff lowered the car window. "What's up?"

"This just came in," the deputy said.

Sheriff Odom read the first words of the bulletin, looked at the deputy, and shook his head. He said nothing, but his eyes were scorching hot. He jerked the gearshift into the "park" position, got out, and slammed the car door so hard that the blue lights flickered.

The deputy followed him into the building. As soon as they got through the main entrance, the sheriff said, "Get ahold of Sergeant Jim Nestor and tell him I need to see him here, right now. I've had all this shit I'm going to take."

He went into his office, closed the door, and sat down behind the old desk. He read the entire bulletin, slowly, and it said exactly what he expected. The Arkansas State Police were seeking Cletus Bolton for questioning in connection with the 1968 lynching of Ike Swanson in Campbell County. As soon as he finished reading, he wadded the bulletin, squeezing it into a tiny ball. Then he stood up, turned and threw it as hard as he could at the wastebasket. When it missed, he kicked the wastebasket against the wall and a string of obscenities raced through his head.

Those sorry sons-a-bitches have been cutting me out of the Cody Ransom case, and now they are trying to bring in Cletus Bolton without giving me a heads-up. It's Aubrey Hatfield, he's behind this. He's been catching hell, so he is trying to cover his ass, making it look like he is going to solve the old case. He is setting this up to blame my granddaddy. What a prick.

Within the hour, Sergeant Nestor arrived at the sheriff's office. The place was empty except for the operator who monitored the radio and handled 911 calls, and she was at the other end of the building.

Sheriff Odom motioned for Nestor to come into his office and sit down. Nestor did, but before he settled into place the sheriff said, "Did you know about this APB?"

"What APB?"

"Don't mess with me, Nestor. I'm talking about the one for Cletus Bolton and the 1968 lynching case. It just went out, this afternoon, a little over an hour ago."

"They took me off that case."

"Why?"

Nestor hesitated. "I'm not supposed to say."

Sheriff Odom glowered. "I thought we were friends."

"We are, and that means a lot to me." Nestor hesitated again, "Look, I think what they are doing to you is shitty. If I had a lot of time left to serve, I would have to say I don't know anything. But I've only got two months before retirement. There is nothing they can do to me for telling you the truth."

"So what is the truth?"

"Aubrey Hatfield and Lieutenant Smothers think you are working against them. That's why they are keeping things to themselves. There are only a handful of people who know what they are up to, and I'm not one of them. They know you and I are good friends, so that is why they took me off the case."

The sheriff slapped his hand to his head and swiveled completely around in his desk chair. "Holy shit. Who do they think they are?" He leaned toward the big pine lamp and pointed his finger at his grandfather's badge and pistol grips. "We Odoms have been sheriffin' in this county for fifty years, and the people trust us to protect them. Aubrey Hatfield doesn't know shit about law enforcement, and I don't think Smothers knows much more."

Nestor held back a grin when the sheriff pointed at the lamp, but he bristled when the sheriff brought Lieutenant Smothers into the conversation. "I was in line to get that lieutenancy, but they passed me over so they could give the job to a nigger. It's the main reason I'm going to retire early. You aren't the only one who is tired of the way they do things."

Sheriff Odom said, "What do you know about Cletus Bolton? Do they have a line on where he is? What do they want him for?"

SEVENTY-THREE

Aubrey looked over Stephanie's shoulder as she scrolled through news stories on her laptop. It was only 8 o'clock on Friday morning, but the websites and blogs featured headlines screaming the news about Cletus Bolton, a sixty-two-year-old man wanted for questioning in connection with the 1968 lynching of Ike Swanson: ARKANSAS MAN SOUGHT IN 1968 LYNCHING ... POLICE PURSUING WITNESS TO GAY LYNCHING ... WITNESS SOUGHT IN LYNCHING CASE ... PROSECUTOR SEEKS MAN IN LYNCHING CASE.

Stephanie said, "I didn't think the case could get hotter, but the APB on Cletus has quadrupled the coverage. Our media frenzy has gone from intense to extreme. The national wire services can't seem to get enough of it, and the radio talk shows are covering it and nothing else."

"And this is not helping." Aubrey pointed out the window of his office to a score of protesters gathered around Jamie Kress as he gave a television interview. "Would you look at that? They have set him up so that the Confederate memorial is in the background of the picture that will be seen on television. When we find out what he is saying, I'm betting it will have nothing to do with the merits of our case. I bet he is ridiculing the ultra-conservative, insensitive people of Campbell County and pushing his agenda of gay marriage, repeal of 'don't ask, don't tell,' and all of that. Want to bet?"

Stephanie said, "No, but I will bet you that George Freemont is down there somewhere doing the same thing from the other end of the spectrum."

"It's what they do. It's the way of the world these days." Aubrey scowled and stuffed a stack of loose papers into his briefcase. "Let's get to court; the judge wants us in his office at 8:45. Apparently, Spike is pissed off. He is saying the news coverage about Cletus hurts his case. He might make a motion for a mistrial. My guess is he will not go that far, but we'll know soon enough."

Judge Harry Oglethorpe welcomed Aubrey and Stephanie to his chambers, and they were chitchatting about other famous trials in North Arkansas when Spike barged into the room. He said good morning to the judge, then unleashed a diatribe accusing Aubrey of trying to prejudice the jury by issuing an APB for Cletus. As he spoke, Spike poked the air with a jumbled-up batch of papers, referring to it as "copies of news stories designed to shame the jury into voting for a conviction." Then, with his right hand, he made a grandiose wave to describe the phalanx of TV trucks and reporters encircling the courthouse. Aubrey was tempted to respond, but Spike was putting on a show that was worth watching.

Judge Oglethorpe had finally had enough. "What do you want, Spike? Do you want to move for a mistrial? Or do you just want to bitch?"

Spike said, "I'm entitled to a mistrial, but I'm going to win this case because my client, Cody Ransom, needs to get his life back and go to college. Let's go on with the trial, Judge, but I want you to remind the jury that we are not here to try the 1968 case."

The judge turned to Aubrey, "Mr. Prosecutor, what do you say to that?"

Aubrey glanced at Spike and grinned. Then he looked at the judge and opened his palms in a quizzical way. "I'm fine with that, Your Honor, but if I'm not mistaken, it was Spike who said we need to talk about the 1968 case. He said the lynching is part of the anti-homosexual culture that influenced Cody Ransom and caused him to panic."

The judge said, "You did say that, Spike."

"It is one thing to mention it as a tragic part of the county's history to show how it might have affected the culture, but the showboating Aubrey is doing is wrong. He could have waited until this trial was over before he got everybody all worked up over an old case that he may or may not be able to solve."

Aubrey said, "I have to act on information when I receive it, Your Honor. It is my duty to investigate and prosecute. I cannot manipulate events to suit Spike, or any other defense counsel for that matter."

The judge looked at Spike, who glowered but said nothing. Pointing in the direction of the courtroom, the judge said, "Let's get in there. This is Friday. The jury is tired and so am I. I would like to finish today's work by mid-afternoon."

Thus, Friday became a relatively peaceful day in the courtroom. For Aubrey, it was a day to fill in the blanks, to be certain that the state had offered proof sufficient to support every element of the charge. Stephanie handled the witnesses, carefully verifying the authentication of all documents, objects, and photographs submitted since the beginning of the trial. Aubrey admired the thoroughness and professionalism of her work. She was a good choice for deputy prosecuting attorney, and he was thankful that she had come his way, for that reason as well as others.

At 3:45 p.m., the judge adjourned court, gaveling the day to a close.

SEVENTY-FOUR

When the historic area around Hatfield House began to change from residential to commercial in the late 1980s, Aubrey planted two rows of evergreen trees to shield the grassy spot directly behind the house from the view of passersby. Now, a quarter-century later, the backyard was shady and private, a perfect place to relax and enjoy a Saturday night cookout. The first week of the Cody Ransom trial was over. On Monday, Aubrey and Stephanie would call Lieutenant Smothers to the witness stand to testify about the day he went to Cody's home, the day the boy gave a video statement telling how and why he hit Randy Trice. Then, if all went well, the state would rest its case.

It was just beginning to turn dark, and Stephanie had set three places at the big picnic table. Aubrey was hovering over the charcoal grill, cooking hamburgers. He was busy tapping the top of each burger and squirting water to control the flare-ups of fire when Stephanie pushed Dwane's wheelchair to a spot close by the grill. Dwane said, "Turn the burgers over, Aubrey. You're cooking them to death."

Aubrey accepted Dwane's challenge to debate the proper way to cook hamburger meat on a charcoal grill. Stephanie mused as the two old friends fussed, mainly about the virtues of dry versus moist burgers. She could see what they chose not to see: Their debate was fated to end quickly, because the burgers could not take much more. Under either theory of burger-cooking, they were done.

When dinner was over, Stephanie and Aubrey rearranged their chairs close to Dwane's wheelchair, and the talk turned from food, baseball, and weather to national politics—anything to avoid a rehash of the Cody Ransom trial, or the 1968 lynching, or the slightest mention of the intense, often hostile media coverage of the last week. Dwane recited parts of a foreign policy speech given by the new presidential candidate, Senator Barrack Obama, on Wednesday, August 1, at the Woodrow Wilson International Center. He predicted Obama would get the Democratic nomination, but Stephanie took issue with him. She said it was impressive that a black man could make a serious challenge for the White House, but she did not see how he could overtake Senator Hillary Clinton, the first serious female candidate for the presidency. Aubrey said he had not been keeping up with the race. He doubted either could win if the Republicans nominated Senator John McCain, a genuine war hero.

Dwane, a war hero himself, said McCain's military record would not be enough to win. But before Aubrey could get into it with Dwane, they heard the sound of a vehicle pulling onto the chat-covered driveway next to the backyard. Seconds later, they heard the last of the engine noise and the sound of a car door slamming, then footsteps crunching on the chat.

"Aubrey?" Junior Tucker said, as he stepped through the opening in the evergreens. He took his ball cap off and nodded. "I hope I'm not busting up something private."

Aubrey stood up and went over to Junior. "Not at all, Junior. Pull up a chair and sit down with us. We weren't talking about anything important."

"I just need to tell you something—private like—then I'll be on my way."

Aubrey led Junior back toward his truck. They stopped close enough to it that Aubrey could feel the heat of the engine. "Is this OK, Junior, or do you want to go inside?"

"Naw, this is good."

Both men shuffled around to get comfortable, and then Aubrey said, "What's up?"

"Cletus called me. Said he heard the state police is looking for him."

Aubrey caught his breath at the news of what could be a big break. "When did he call?"

"About two hours ago. I couldn't believe it. I ain't heard from him in ages, but he said I was the only one around here he knew to call."

"Where is he?"

"He wouldn't say. Said he was calling because Artus and the Mysterion boys are after him. He hates the law and don't trust government people like you, but leastwise you ain't trying to kill him. That's the way he sees it."

"Why did he call?"

"Don't know, but I figure he is thinking about coming in. I told him that I know you on account of Jody's ball playing, and I told him I told you about him being there the night Artus was going to cure the queer. He said he figured I must have told that, and that's why the state police were after him."

"Was he mad at you for telling?"

"Naw, he said Artus and the Mysterion boys had been after him for a long time, long before I told you about the curing. He said they came looking for him at his trailer in Kentucky back in February right after all the publicity about Randy Trice and the 1968 lynching. He saw them and figured they were after him, so he cut out. Then he started talking about the good times we had back when we fished with Doughboy on the lake. I think he is plumb tired out and looking to put this behind him if he can."

"Did he give you a way to contact him?"

"No, he said he was calling from a payphone. Said he needed to think on this for a day or two, then he would call me back."

"Junior, give me your telephone number. I'm going to see if we can find out where he was when he called you."

Junior gave Aubrey his number, and then he climbed into his truck, started the engine and rolled down the window. "I feel like a tattletale, Aubrey."

"It's OK, Junior. You are doing the right thing, but let me ask you to do one more thing that is important to me, but it is also important to Cletus." Aubrey put his hand on Junior's shoulder and squeezed it firmly. "Don't tell anyone about the call from Cletus, and stay by the phone for the next few days, and let me know the minute you get another call."

"What should I tell Cletus if he does call?"

"Tell him he ought to come in. Tell him we talked, and that I will be fair with him—that I understand he was at the scene of Ike's killing, but only to see the curing."

"I done told him all that."

SEVENTY-FIVE

On Sunday afternoon, Lieutenant Smothers came to Hatfield House. He pulled a folded document from his hip pocket and handed it to Aubrey. "The call to Junior Tucker's home phone came from a pay phone in Thayer, Missouri. It started at 6:10 p.m. Saturday and lasted eleven minutes. There was another call from that pay phone at 6:05 p.m. and it was to directory assistance, we have confirmed that it was to find a number for Joe Tucker Jr. in Campbell County."

"Where is Thayer?" Stephanie said.

"It is just over the border, a couple of miles north of Mammoth Spring, Arkansas. That's where the Spring River begins, then it flows south to Hardy, Arkansas, and then on south to merge with the Black River."

Aubrey said, "That fits. I bet Cletus is back in Arkansas."

The lieutenant said, "Do you want us to find him and pick him up?"

"Let's find out where he is, but let's not make contact with him. I think we need to give Cletus a chance to call Junior again. Junior says he does not trust us, or any authority, so we do not want to scare him off or set him against us—you know how folks like Cletus can clam up. We need him, and he will be a better witness if he comes in on his own. When you get right down to it, he's our best—our only—way to prove what happened in 1968."

Stephanie said, "Can we talk about that? I mean the decision to just watch and wait?"

"Sure," Aubrey said. They all sat down at the kitchen table.

"Right now we are operating on the assumption that Artus killed Ike Swanson," Stephanie began. "We need Cletus to make that case. We know that Artus tried to get to Cletus in Kentucky, and he probably is still looking for him, most likely to kill him. Cletus called Junior yesterday, and Junior thinks he may be thinking about coming in.

"We need to keep him alive and in the mood to cooperate as a witness, but we also need to gather corroborating evidence to support what he says about Artus. As I see it, there are several possible outcomes: First, Cletus could run, disappear, and never be heard from again. Second, he could decide to come in voluntarily, in which case he might use Junior as an intermediary. Third, we could find him and bring him in as a material witness. And, fourth, Artus could find him and kill him. After all, Artus has been looking for him longer than we have, and our sheriff is probably helping him. I bet Odom has already heard that Cletus is somewhere near Mammoth Spring."

Aubrey said, "That's a good analysis of where we stand. What are you suggesting?"

"What if we created a diversionary tactic?

"Such as?" The lieutenant scooted his chair back and focused on Stephanie.

"Why not feed a false address to Artus? If he takes the bait and goes to that address, it would prove that he is actively looking for Cletus. It would also steer him away from where Cletus is now, and we could be at the address to greet Artus or his boys."

The lieutenant said, "That's inventive and borderline devious. You should have been a detective."

They all laughed, but Aubrey said, "I'd like to do that, especially if we fed the phony address to Sheriff Odom. If he passed it along to Artus, it would show his willingness to obstruct justice."

Lieutenant Smothers said, "We have a very reliable confidential source who is telling us that the sheriff is helping Spike, and that he is sympathetic to the Mysterion and Artus. But I'm not sure we could get Sheriff Odom to fall for it. He would be suspicious, wondering why we just didn't go to the phony address and get Cletus. Why tell him?"

Aubrey said, "You are probably right about that. He doesn't know what we know: that Cletus is talking to Junior, who is talking to us. I think you are right; he would be suspicious, and he might not take the bait."

"Anyway, I doubt my superiors would let me run a trick play on a duly elected law-enforcement official," Lieutenant Smothers said.

Aubrey said, "I'd like to catch Sheriff Odom red-handed, but I don't want to do anything that might blow up in our face, or get back to Cletus and scare him off. Junior says he is pretty edgy about people in authority, and it wouldn't take much for him to just run away."

Stephanie stiffened and cut her eyes toward Aubrey. "I did not say we ought to use the sheriff to give the false address to Artus—you did. We could use someone like Junior to funnel it to Artus, to misdirect him and thus help protect Cletus. Anyway, it is just something to think about. It seems to me our main concern has to be to keep Cletus alive. If Artus kills him, we will have blood on our hands and we will lose our only witness and never prove that Artus did the lynching. We are taking a chance by leaving him out there unprotected."

Lieutenant Smothers said, "Using someone who is not in law enforcement and faking out Artus is a better idea, because the Arkansas State Police would not want to be part of any plan to trick the sheriff. But I doubt you could keep any of that from Sheriff Odom. What if he found out that somebody had given Artus an address, wouldn't he smell a rat?"

Aubrey looked at Stephanie. "Your main concern is that we need to do more than just watch and wait?"

"Yes."

Lieutenant Smothers said, "If Cletus is back in Arkansas over around Mammoth Spring, I'm sure we can find him." He turned to Aubrey, "Do you want us to go get him?"

Aubrey hesitated and nodded to Stephanie. "I'm glad you pushed me on this. I have been too optimistic. It is simply too risky to assume Cletus will come in on his own, or that Artus will not get to him before we do."

Stephanie said, "So are you telling the lieutenant to go get him?"

"Yes. Find Cletus Bolton and pick him up."

The lieutenant said, "I'll send the order out right now."

SEVENTY-SIX

Sergeant Jim Nestor walked into the sheriff's office at 7 a.m. Monday, in time to catch Sheriff Odom having coffee with his deputies. Nestor pulled him aside. "You didn't hear it from me, but they think Cletus is back in Arkansas, somewhere around Mammoth Spring or Hardy. They are treating him as a witness, and that is why they wrote the APB like they did. I don't know any more than that. They first thought he was over in Kentucky, but he left out of there early this year."

The sheriff said, "I'll be damned. You know, Jim, I told Aubrey not to file those charges against Cody. Nobody around here gives a shit, and it just stirs up trouble. The boy had every right to protect himself from a queer that was trying to go down on him. I think Aubrey is a hard-headed queer-lover, and he is doing this just to spite me. He knows he is not going to get a conviction, so he is trying to make himself look good by going back to the 1968 case. Something is sticking in his craw from the time he was the deputy prosecutor and my grandfather was sheriff. They did not get along, and now he's trying to take it out on me, and hurt me politically. I can't take care of the good people of this county if I'm not in office—that's why I'm fighting the son-of-a-bitch."

"I'll try to find out more, but it's not going to be easy," Nestor said.

When Nestor was gone, the sheriff dialed the number of Sheriff Charlie Roberts in Sharp County. When he answered, Sheriff Odom said, "Hey, Charlie, everything all right over your way?" The two sheriffs were longtime friends and political soulmates, each holding office thanks to the Odom-Cooksey political machine that reached well beyond Campbell County and Hawkins County.

Sheriff Roberts said, "Yep, but I was just getting ready to call you. The state police just called me. I first thought it was about the big trial you've got going on, but they were asking if I knew the guy they named in the all-points bulletin—that Cletus Bolton guy. They said he was believed to be over here somewhere."

Sheriff Odom collected himself; no need to let his friend know that he was out of the loop. "Yeah, that APB is being pushed by Aubrey Hatfield; he's a pain in the ass. If our candidates hadn't split the vote in Hawkins County, we would have beaten him like a yarddog and none of this would be going on."

"I agree, but what's the Cletus Bolton thing about?"

"Well, it starts with the case they're trying right now. I told Aubrey not to charge the Cody Ransom boy for killing that queer, but he didn't listen. The jury is not going to find the boy guilty, so Aubrey's now in a mess of trouble, and this search for Cletus Bolton is bullshit. He's trying to make himself look good, but it ain't going to work."

Sheriff Roberts said, "Well, I don't think the Bolton guy is in my county. I steered the state police over to Randolph County. There's a little town there called Dalton. It ain't too far from Mammoth Spring, and there's a few Boltons around there. Maybe he's related to them or they know something of him—that's what I told them, anyway."

"Thanks, Charlie. You are a good friend. Keep me posted on what you hear, will you?"

"Sure thing, Jack. Us sheriffs have got to stick together."

As soon as the call was over, Sheriff Odom's jaw stiffened and he clenched his fists. After a moment, he leaned back and rubbed his temples, pondering what to do.

Aubrey and the state police are doing all this behind my back; now they are poking around in Randolph County. They don't give a shit about my reputation with my fellow sheriffs. I could call Randolph County, but it would look like I don't know what's going on. I'll wait. Maybe they will call me, or I'll learn more from Nestor.

He pulled an old file from a desk drawer. His grandfather had scrawled the name "Ike Swanson" on the folder almost forty years ago. Sheriff Jack Odom was a little boy when the lynching took place in 1968, but he knew about it; everyone in the county had heard about "the lynching of the queer." It was common knowledge. People spoke of it as a tragedy, but there was an unstated sense that Ike's killers went free because the community and the authorities looked the other way.

Sheriff Jack Odom had not looked at the file since he put it in the desk drawer on his first day as sheriff in 2001. Now, as he opened it, he began to think about what his grandfather told him before he died; that the case caused him to have a falling out with Aubrey Hatfield. He remembered his exact words, "Aubrey's too big for his britches. He can't be trusted."

Maybe I can find something that will help me put Aubrey in his place. Granddaddy was right: He's too big for his britches. I need to know more about Cletus Bolton. Granddaddy interviewed him in 1968.

The sheriff opened an envelope containing the crime-scene photographs taken by his grandfather. He caught his breath and winced when he saw pictures of the corpse and the hoe handle the killers had shoved up Ike's rear end. Then the sheriff's foul heart took his mind down a wicked trail.

Goddamn queers, fucking faggots, they're a scourge on the earth. When Grandaddy was sheriff, things were different. No politically correct bullshit, and no outsiders telling us what to think. They're going berserk over Randy Trice getting hit in the head. I'd hate to think what they would be saying if Randy had got what Ike Swanson got. This shit has to stop. It is ruining the country.

The sheriff put the photographs away and turned to the short, handwritten note his grandfather made after he interviewed Cletus Bolton in 1968, "Talked to Cletus Bolton, mechanic who lives in Draco—says he had nothing to do with the killing, but admits he called him a queer to his face a few days before." Jack Odom read it three times, parsing and pausing to think, but he could see no reason why Aubrey Hatfield had issued an APB for Cletus. He closed the file and put it back in the drawer.

Aubrey has something new on Cletus, but damned if I know what it is—and Nestor does not know, either. He is either trying to muddy the water with all the publicity, or he is on to something that might help him win the case against Cody Ransom. Artus and Spike need to know this, but I had better not call them direct.

The sheriff picked up the phone and dialed a number. "Carl? Can you meet me in ten minutes out by your house, at the old Draco post office?"

SEVENTY-SEVEN

Aubrey and Stephanie got to the office at 8:30 a.m. Monday to meet Lieutenant Smothers and prepare for the final day of the prosecution's case. There were a few legal issues to resolve in chambers, but the lieutenant would be the last and most important prosecution witness. He would testify about the video statement he took from Cody Ransom. Aubrey intended to play the video for the jury and then rest his case.

The lieutenant was an old hand at giving testimony, but Aubrey was a belt-and-suspenders kind of lawyer. Better to be overprepared than underprepared.

He stood up and approached the lieutenant, playing as if they were in the courtroom. "Let's start with everything that happened the day you contacted Cody Ransom at his house, the day he admitted on video that he hit Randy Trice. By the way, I'm still impressed that you got an admission on video in the short time you had before Spike called and shut down the interview."

Lieutenant Smothers grinned. "I learned that from an old FBI agent who told me to always go directly to the bottom line when interviewing a suspect. If you mess around, gathering details, they may decide to stop talking or an attorney may intervene before you get a confession. He said the first order of business is always to get the suspect to say, 'I done it.' If he stops talking, you might not have a lot of detail, but you will have an admissible confession."

"That's good advice, and it leads us to the testimony you will give today. I will call you to the stand as soon as the judge is ready to start, and we will lay the foundation to introduce the video statement you got from Cody. You are an experienced witness, so you know that Spike will try his best to minimize the damage you have done to his client. He will say Cody's statement is not a confession, that it is merely an honest account of what happened. If we call it a confession, Spike will make us back off of that, and the judge will support him."

"I'll be careful not to call it a confession. I'll just stick with what he told me and not characterize it."

"Right. Just let Spike huff and puff about 'gay panic' or whatever he wants to say. If he gets too far out of line, I will intervene, but the jury is going to watch the video of Cody's statement. They will put more emphasis on that than they will on what we say, you say, or what Spike says."

Stephanie said, "We better get in there. The judge said he wants to get started right on time."

—~—

At 9:30 a.m., the familiar entry of lawyers, clerks, and attendants began. When the key people were in place, the judge made his grandiose entry. The bailiff sang the off-key rendition of his song and the judge said, "Call your first witness, Mr. Prosecutor."

Aubrey called Lieutenant Smothers to the witness stand. He stuck closely to the guidelines rehearsed with Aubrey, and his direct examination concluded with the showing of the video. When Cody's image appeared, the jurors leaned forward in unison, as if on cue. They watched and listened, intently, until the voice of Lieutenant Smothers announced that he was discontinuing the video interview at the request of Cody's lawyer.

The judge recessed for lunch, but the jury was back, ready to go, at 1:30. Spike hitched his pants and sashayed to the lectern, entreating the jurors to focus on him. He cleared his voice and began a vigorous cross-examination of Lieutenant Smothers.

Spike spent the rest of the afternoon trying to get the lieutenant to agree that Randy's words and deeds amounted to sufficient cause to justify or excuse what Cody did. The lieutenant did not help him. He stuck to the facts and kept coming back to the exact words Cody used when he told what happened.

At 4:30 p.m., Spike gave up, and the lieutenant was finished. The judge asked the prosecutor to call his next witness. Aubrey stood and said with emphasis, "Your Honor, the state rests."

There was a rumbling amongst the spectators, quieted by the sound of Judge Oglethorpe's voice. "Ladies and gentlemen of the jury, you are excused for the day. I will see the attorneys in my chambers." When the judge pounded his gavel and left the bench, the rumble returned.

—∾—

When they were in chambers, Spike said, "Your Honor, I have motions to make."

"Yes, Spike. We will do that here. The court reporter is here, so you can begin whenever you are ready."

Spike offered the customary motions that the law requires in order to preserve a record for appeal. He was most persuasive and determined in his claim that there was insufficient proof to support the charge of murder in second degree. The judge denied all his motions, but did say that the state's proof of second-degree murder was "pretty thin."

The lawyers then began an esoteric debate about the complicated elements of second-degree murder, but their skirmish did not last long. They stopped talking when Judge Oglethorpe started tapping his finger on his desktop. After a moment of silence, the judge said, "Well, that does it for today. Tomorrow, Spike, you can start your defense. Do you have an idea how long it will take for you to put on your case?"

"One week is my best estimate, Your Honor, but it could go quicker depending on how much time the state takes on cross-examination."

SEVENTY-EIGHT

Spike did a workmanlike job of presenting the defense of Cody Ransom. It took three full days for his team of sociologists, psychiatrists, and a county historian to explain the culture of Campbell County—how it developed and how it passed from generation to generation. There was considerable talk about the 1968 lynching, but the witnesses were quick to assert that Campbell County is not the only place where cultural and religious hostility to homosexuality has resulted in murder and torture. The lead sociologist claimed to have taught a college course on the subject of homosexual lynching. He said there were horror stories from virtually every state in the Union—North and South, East and West.

Spike carefully managed the testimony of the experts to support his assertion of legal insanity, self-defense, and provocation. But his real purpose was to suggest that Cody's conduct was the product of "gay panic."

Throughout the testimony and Aubrey's cross-examination, the jurors were attentive when the experts gave examples and spoke in simple language. When they used ten-dollar words and the mysterious utterances of their professions, the jurors tuned out. They stared at the ceiling, doodled on note pads, and examined and picked their fingernails. One juror dozed off. The lawyers noticed, but they persisted with what they were doing.

In Spike's effort to show how the local culture influenced Cody to react as he did, the capstone came from the testimony of a longtime

Campbell County preacher, Elmer Blankenship. He said, "The culture throughout North Arkansas, and the South in general, is based on biblical scripture that, among other things, abhors the practice of homosexuality."

Spike then asked the preacher. "Do you have an opinion of how the local culture and religious beliefs might have caused this eighteen-year-old boy to panic when Randy Trice grabbed his privates, and tried to force him into having homosexual relations?"

Stephanie nudged Aubrey and whispered. "He's going way too far. You should object."

Aubrey stood up and interrupted before the preacher could answer. "Your Honor, the state has repeatedly made the point that we have no objection to an open discussion of our culture, and how it may or may not be relevant to the issues in this case. We think such a discussion is healthy, and the jury will surely consider such things, but I object to counsel's attempt to characterize what actually happened that day. He goes too far. The jury saw the video statement made by Cody Ransom. They will decide what took place that day and what to do about it."

The judge said, "Sustained. Counsel can—in the context of developing the insanity, provocation, or self-defense issues—ask about the culture and its general influence on the way people behave. But do not ask the witness to tell us what was in the mind of Cody Ransom on that fateful day. That is for the jury to decide."

"I'll reframe the question, Your Honor." Spike cleared his throat and rearranged his suit coat. Then he turned to the witness. "Preacher Blankenship, in your opinion, is there a deep-set, justifiable repugnance to homosexuality in the local culture that might cause a young man to react the way Cody reacted to Randy Trice's homosexual overtures?"

"Yes sir, the repugnance is justifiable, and it is deep-set ... thank God."

Spike continued with the preacher for another hour, skirting and probing the edge of Aubrey's objection, making the same point repeatedly. Aubrey, in keeping with his threshold decision to engage in an open discussion of everything relevant to "gay panic," gave Spike plenty of latitude. He had made his point about jury prerogatives, and did not want to look like "a jumping jack," the local slur for lawyers who object too often.

When Spike finished, Aubrey began his cross-examination. "Pastor Blankenship, I have heard you preach about this subject on the radio. Is it true, with respect to homosexuality, that your faith instructs you to hate the sin but love the sinner?"

The pastor squirmed. "I have preached that, yes sir."

Aubrey said, "Your Honor, I have no further questions for this witness."

The judge excused the preacher and adjourned for the day. Aubrey gathered his papers, and Stephanie went into the seating area to get Dwane who was posing like Rodin's sculpture, *Le Penseur*. She said, "So, you are in full thinking mode—is that it?"

Dwane laughed and sat upright. "I was hoping you would recognize my histrionics, and you did."

"You are something, Dwane." Stephanie said, as she wheeled him out of the courtroom. They met Aubrey downstairs and headed across the street to Ma Phipps's for an early dinner. When they were seated, Stephanie said to Aubrey, "You should have seen Dwane's imitation of *The Thinker*. I bet we are in for a lecture on something, most probably culture and religion."

Dwane raised an eyebrow and rubbed his chin in a devilish way. "I do have some thoughts about today's proceedings."

"Fire away," Aubrey said.

"I've got two points. The first is that all this complicated talk about insanity, self-defense, and provocation is lawyer talk. I have served on juries when insanity was an issue. The lawyers and expert witnesses use highfalutin words, but jurors ignore such gibberish when they get in the privacy of the jury room. In this case, they will ask simple questions. Do you think he was crazy? Do you think Cody panicked, and even if he did, was it right for him to hit Randy? Should he have just gotten out of the car and gone on with his run? That's how the jurors will see it."

Aubrey said, "Spike understands that. You have to give the devil his due. He is doing a good job with his 'gay panic' strategy. I'm glad we decided to meet it head-on."

Stephanie nodded in agreement. "I don't like the gadfly, but he is effective. He stays on message, just like the politicians I watched when I worked in D.C. He makes his point; then he repeats it over and over."

Dwane said, "My second point is a larger one. The media are portraying people around here as unenlightened bigots, and that is not fair. They know our deep faith in God informs our beliefs, our culture, and they will grudgingly concede, in private, that we are entitled to believe as we do. But that does not sell newspapers or drive up TV ratings. They do not seem to care that they are besmirching good, God-fearing people. If I thought they were all secularists—non-believers—I would cut them some slack, but most of them do not think beyond the end of their nose. They have no base, no worldview, Christian or otherwise. They are just making it up as they go along. They flit from one viewpoint to another, embracing the latest notion of political correctness."

Aubrey patted his old friend on the shoulder. "Are you trying to tell me I'm going to lose this case?"

"I don't know how it will come out, Aubrey, but I worry about a rudderless nation. If people forsake God's plan and worship a worldview constructed by man, through politics, how then shall we live?"

SEVENTY-NINE

When court convened Friday morning, Spike called Louie Jenkins, a twenty-two-year-old Little Rock resident, to the witness stand. Spike had given notice to the prosecution that he would call the man as a witness, but when the state police attempted to interview Jenkins, a week before the trial, he would not talk to them. Spike said Jenkins was going to testify that Randy Trice tried to force him to have homosexual sex, but he would not say precisely what he expected the man to say. Aubrey and Stephanie assumed Louie Jenkins was the paid witness Sergeant Albright heard about from a confidential source. If so, then he would try to turn Randy Trice into a monster.

When Jenkins, a smallish man wearing jeans and a blazer, stepped onto the witness stand, Stephanie stood up and asked the judge for permission to approach the bench for a sidebar conference. Judge Oglethorpe started to say something, but instead signaled his approval with a wave of his hand.

When the lawyers were all in place at the bench, Stephanie spoke in hushed tones. "Your Honor, we believe this witness may have been paid to give perjured testimony, and we want to take him on *voir dire*."

"I'm not a big fan of the Latin terminology, Counselor. If you want to examine the witness out of the presence of the jury before he takes the stand, why don't you just say that?"

"OK, Your Honor, that is what I want to do."

Spike squealed, "This is ridiculous. Are you suggesting I had something to do with paying a witness to testify?"

"No, but on information and belief we are stating that this witness is corrupt and should not testify."

The judge said, "Let's go in chambers." He recessed court to give the jury a break and told the bailiff to stay with the witness.

When they were all in the judge's chambers, he said, "Now, what is this all about?"

Stephanie repeated what she said at sidebar, then added, "Before this witness is allowed to say a word to the jury, I want to ask him if he has been paid, or if anyone has offered to pay him to testify for the defense."

Judge Oglethorpe said, "If he denies it, you will be stuck with his answer. You cannot impeach him with extrinsic evidence; you know that, don't you?"

"Yes, Your Honor, but if he lies under oath and we can prove it, we will prosecute him and those who put him up to it."

The judge looked at Spike. "You still want to call this guy, Spike?"

"I don't know anything about this, Judge, but he's my witness. Can I have a few minutes with him?"

"No, Spike. He may be your witness, but he's in my court. I'm going to bring him in here and see what he says under oath." The judge asked the reporter to tell the bailiff to bring the witness into his chambers.

Louie Jenkins shuffled into the room with his hands in his pockets. He looked nervously around the room, but came to attention when the judge swore him in.

When the witness sat down, Judge Oglethorpe looked at Stephanie. "You may inquire, Counselor."

Stephanie wasted no words. "Mr. Jenkins, has anyone paid you or promised to pay you or given you anything—money or property of any sort—to come here and testify?"

The witness hem-hawed around, and then said, "Judge ... Your Honor ... Sir ... I ain't going to say anything that might incriminate me ... I don't have to, do I? ... I want to take the Fifth."

"Bailiff, get this man out of here."

When Jenkins was gone, Judge Oglethorpe told Aubrey to investigate the matter. "I want to know if someone bribed or attempted to bribe this witness. Report your findings to me." Then, he turned to Spike. "I hope you had nothing to do with this, Spike. If you did, it could cost you your license."

"Your Honor, this is all news to me." Then, in an attempt to get back on offense, Spike said, "In any event, I don't have to prove what Jenkins was going to say to get an acquittal."

The judge said, "Let's get back in the courtroom. We will start in ten minutes. Who is your next witness, Spike?"

"Carl Ransom."

EIGHTY

Spike huddled with Carl Ransom in the hallway outside the courtroom, going over what happened in the judge's chambers. Carl shuffled his feet and pounded his hands against his hips as if he was getting ready to swing at Spike. "Are you saying they scared Jenkins off, and we won't have anyone to tell how that queer forced himself on other people?"

"Yes, but we can live without the testimony of Jenkins. We don't have to prove that Randy Trice was a monster—I'll argue it, and several of the jurors are likely to think that on their own. Besides, we can make that point when you testify how you raised Cody to protect himself, especially from queers."

"Artus ain't going to like this one bit. He's put a bunch of money into getting Cody off."

"We'll be OK, but don't blame me for the Jenkins thing. Blame Aubrey and his pretty deputy. She is the brains of that outfit."

—w—

In spite of Spike's confidence, Carl Ransom sensed that the case had taken a turn for the worse. When the bailiff told him it was time to take the witness stand, he entered the courtroom with a swagger, determined to make up for lost ground.

He scowled at Aubrey as he came down the aisle, wishing he could call him a queer-lover. Then he looked toward the other counsel table and nodded to Cody and Spike. Cody's mother, Lillian, was in the first row of seats behind her son. She had a troubled look on her face, but Carl did not look at her when he pushed through the swinging gate and marched to the witness chair.

Spike began his direct examination of Carl by developing the history of the Ransom family members, proving they had deep roots throughout North Arkansas, particularly in Campbell County. At first, Carl was tentative, but soon he got into the swing of things.

He told of his work, explaining that he got out of the Army and took the menial job at Tommy's Sawmill so he could be close to his family and raise his boy in the hills of Campbell County.

Carl felt especially good when Spike asked him to tell about Cody's success on the football field. Full of pride, he told how he spent hours teaching his boy how to throw and catch a football, and how to hunt and fish. As he spoke, he thought to himself: *This is not so hard after all. My boy is top-drawer; he's going places—places I never got a chance to.*

Suddenly a terrible mood settled on Carl. He felt his lip quivering, and he rubbed a tear from his eye. In a shaky voice he said, "Now, all this has happened."

Carl was embarrassed. He told himself to snap out of it. *I've got to tell it like it is. Enough of this crybaby bullshit.*

He blurted out, "My boy shouldn't even be here. All he did was protect himself from a queer that was trying to go down on him. He did what any red-blooded American boy would do."

The courtroom was quiet as a tomb, but it did not stay that way for long. The judge told Carl it was improper to use derogatory language to describe homosexuals, and that set him off again. "Why do they get to call us 'straight' and call themselves 'gay,' as if they are a bunch of harmless fairies dancing around a maypole? Randy Trice was a monster."

Carl saw that he had stunned the judge with his answer, so he jumped up and pointed at Aubrey. "If you cared half as much about my boy as you do about that dead son-of-a-bitching-queer, you would never have brought this case to court."

The judge was now standing up, calling for order. He banged his gavel so hard the handle broke, but Carl was not done. His insides were boiling hot. "My boy would never have gotten into a car with a faggot. The queer tricked him—made him think it was about his football scholarship. This whole thing is a dirty rotten shame."

Spike and the bailiff got to Carl at the same time. They managed to get him off the witness stand and out of the courtroom.

The judge recessed court and told the lawyers to come directly to his chambers. He told the jurors he would speak to them about the outburst when they came back to the jury box after the recess.

—∞—

Judge Oglethorpe was standing behind his desk when the lawyers came into his chambers. He said, "That was the worst outburst I have seen in twenty-five years on the bench. Pure vitriol. I got so wound up trying to get Carl Ransom to shut up that I broke my damn gavel, the one the Bar Association gave me when I took office." He almost smiled. Then he said, "Aubrey, what do you want to do about this?"

"Your Honor, we have talked it over. The state might be entitled to a mistrial, but that is not what we want to do. We believe the jurors will understand that Carl Ransom is high-strung and that he lost control because his son is on trial for killing a man. If you will calm them down with a curative instruction, I think everything will be OK."

The judge did not respond to Aubrey. Instead, he turned to Spike. "If you can't control your witness, do not put him back on the stand. Another outburst like the one we just witnessed, and I'll cite Carl Ransom for contempt, and I'll make sure he stays in the county jail for a good while."

Spike said, "I understand, Your Honor."

The judge said, "Now, how do I handle this with the jury?"

Spike said, "Carl was absolutely wrong to go off like he did, but in fairness he raised a valid question. How should we refer to homosexuals—what is the correct terminology? The antonym of 'straight' is 'crooked,' which is closer in meaning to 'queer' than it is to 'gay.' I don't know when homosexuals started calling themselves 'gay,' but I expect it was done to make them seem harmless and to get away from the notion that there is something wrong with them."

"So what are you suggesting?" The judge did not attempt to quarrel with Spike's point, nor did Aubrey or Stephanie.

Spike said, "Perhaps you could, in your curative instruction, tell the jurors that in this court the proper terminology is homosexual. If the witnesses or lawyers use words such as 'queer' or 'gay,' the jurors can decide on their own if the usage is derogatory or misleading. I think we can all agree that the words 'faggot' and 'fairy' should not be used."

There was conspicuous silence when Spike shut up. The judge rubbed his chin for a full minute, then said to Aubrey, "What do you think about that, Mr. Prosecutor?"

Aubrey said, "We could argue for hours about this and come to no resolution. For that reason, the state is willing to go along with Spike's suggestion. Let's move on."

When court resumed, the judge addressed the jury in a very calm manner. He repeated almost verbatim what the lawyers had agreed to in chambers, and he made no mention of "faggots" or "fairies."

Spike then got the judge's permission to ask the clerk some questions about documents introduced in the course of the trial, and he pretended to be surprised that the state had introduced several photographs taken at Cody's home the day he gave his video statement. He fooled around for a good five minutes, asking one innocuous question after another, and then told the judge in a voice loud enough to be heard by everyone in the courtroom that he simply wanted to be sure that the exhibits were in good order. But his main purpose was to change the subject.

Judge Oglethorpe said, "Call your next witness."

Spike slinked around the space between the lectern and his counsel table, making it appear that he was about to call a witness. Then he hesitated and leaned over to say something to Cody Ransom.

The judge repeated his order, "Call your next witness."

Spike struck a commanding pose. He fiddled with his tie, looked at the jury, and said in his strongest voice, "Your Honor, we think the jury has heard enough. The defense rests."

—∾—

Judge Oglethorpe asked Aubrey, "Does the prosecution have rebuttal?"

Aubrey said, "No, Your Honor. The state has no further witnesses."

"Ladies and gentlemen of the jury: We have now completed all the testimony in this case, and the court will stand in adjournment until Monday morning at 9 o'clock, at which time I will give you your instructions and we will hear the closing arguments of counsel."

EIGHTY-ONE

Late Friday, after the jury was gone and the courtroom was empty, Judge Oglethorpe met with the lawyers in chambers to hear motions and go over the instructions he planned to give to the jury. Spike half-heartedly made several motions. The judge denied all of them.

The judge then handed half-inch-thick stacks of papers to Aubrey, Stephanie, and Spike. "These are the instructions I plan to read to the jury before you make your closing arguments. Let's go through them. You can make your objections and offer your own proposals for consideration."

Spike spoke first. "Judge, I don't have a problem with the standard instructions that you give in every trial, so can we skip over to the instructions you will give on insanity, provocation, and self-defense?"

"What says the prosecution?" Judge Oglethorpe looked at Aubrey and Stephanie.

"We agree, Your Honor." Stephanie said, as Aubrey nodded his approval.

Spike gave the others a sheepish grin. "I'm not going to make a big deal out of the insanity defense instruction. It is OK as far as I am concerned. I only raised insanity and let the state's shrinks examine Cody so I could get into the issue of how the boy's mind was working at the time of the killing."

"The state has no objection, Your Honor. I never thought Spike was serious about the insanity defense in the first place," Aubrey said.

"The damned insanity defense hardly ever works. And when it does, your client is branded as a kook and winds up going to the funny factory instead of going free." Spike was in rare form.

The judge said, "All right, let's go on to the self-defense instruction. What do you have to say about that one?"

All of a sudden, Spike got very serious. "I know you all don't think much of my self-defense argument, but what if Cody Ransom had been an eighteen-year-old girl, and a thirty-eight-year-old man lied to get her in the car, grabbed her crotch, and said, 'Have you ever had intercourse?' If she hit him with a dumbbell, we would be calling it self-defense and giving her a medal. There should not be a double standard, particularly nowadays, when everyone is saying there should be equality between men and women."

Aubrey said, "Your Honor, Spike is inventive if nothing else, but I have no objection to you giving the self-defense instruction. My reasons for that will become clear as we go on."

Spike gave Aubrey a funny look as the judge said, "All right, then. Let's move on to Spike's claim that there was sufficient provocation to excuse the killing of Randy Trice."

"Judge, I definitely want this instruction because it says the jury can reduce Aubrey's second-degree murder charge to manslaughter if they think Cody Ransom was under the influence of extreme emotional disturbance for which there was a reasonable excuse. And I especially like the part where they are told to figure that out from the viewpoint of a person in Cody's situation—under the circumstances as he believed them to be."

Aubrey grinned. "Spike, you sound worried. I thought you were going to walk Cody right out of here, not guilty of anything."

"I am going to walk him out, Hoss. I'm just being thorough."

"We have no objection to the provocation language, Your Honor. It is part and parcel of the standard manslaughter instruction," Aubrey said.

Judge Oglethorpe said, "OK, what's left?"

Spike said, "I'm not going to offer an instruction on 'gay panic,' or 'homosexual panic,' as you correctly call it, Your Honor. Aubrey has made it clear that I can argue 'gay panic' to the jury, and that is good enough for me. However, I am going to ask for another instruction that we have not previously discussed."

"Why am I not surprised?" Judge Oglethorpe rolled his eyes and lifted his palms toward the ceiling.

"Your Honor, I want the jury to be told that they do not have to follow the instructions that you give them. I want you to tell them that they have the power, as juries have had for hundreds of years, to do whatever they think is right."

Aubrey said, "The jury has that power, that is true, but the Arkansas Supreme Court has said on several occasions that a criminal defendant is not entitled to the so-called 'jury nullification' instruction."

"If they have the power, why not tell them they have it?" Spike feigned astonishment.

"The appellate courts have said it would undercut the other instructions." Stephanie had some heat in her voice, "What's the point in telling the jurors what the law is, if you are going to turn right around and tell them they don't have to follow it?"

Judge Oglethorpe said, "I agree with Stephanie. I will not give the jury nullification instruction."

Aubrey said, "Judge, I do believe Spike has the right to make a jury nullification argument to the jury in his closing. We have assumed all along that he would wind up saying that the law is irrelevant—that the jurors can let Cody go free if that is what they want to do. He believes the jury will pay more attention to the local culture than they will to the law."

"You got it, Hoss."

"All right, counselors. Save your fisticuffs for the jury." The judge closed his file and stood up. "We're finished here. Let's enjoy the weekend."

EIGHTY-TWO

Late Saturday afternoon, Lieutenant Smothers turned off the main highway and onto a pea-gravel drive that passed beneath an entry-arch bearing the name White Oak Stables. As he did, his wife, Annie, pointed to a rider on a tall chestnut quarterhorse. "Look, it's Stephanie. She's waving for us to follow her."

"Her family has owned this ranch for years, long before I was born," the lieutenant said. "It's easy to see why she wants to be here."

Stephanie galloped the chestnut over a slight hill and out of sight. The lieutenant followed the narrow road, circling around the hill in time to see Stephanie dismount and hand the reins to a young man who led the horse into the stable.

When they pulled to a stop, Stephanie—wearing a smart Levi's outfit and cowboy boots—opened the car door and gave Annie a hug. "Welcome to White Oak."

"It is so beautiful here." Annie pointed to the ranch house, a low-lying rustic made of native stone and white oak logs. "It's nice of you to invite us."

Stephanie said, "I thought it would do us good to get out of Woodville for a night. And, to be honest about it, I wanted to show off the place I love. Come on. Aubrey and Dwane are out back."

When they rounded the corner of the house, Aubrey waved. He was standing by a smoking barbecue grill, and Dwane was holding forth about something that had him agitated, waving his good arm from right to left. The instant he saw the lieutenant, he said, "Here's John Smothers. Let's ask him."

All eyes turned to the lieutenant. He pulled his wife to his side and pretended to be nervous. "Uh-oh. Am I in trouble, or something?"

Aubrey gave Annie a hug and laughed. "No, you are not in trouble, but football season is coming up, and Dwane is upset because neither of us can remember the name of the player who ran the trick play that helped Arkansas beat Auburn last year. Auburn was ranked number two in the nation at the time."

The lieutenant said, "It was Reggie Fish. He was a little guy. The quarterback backhanded the ball to him. He hid behind the big linemen, and then he scampered around left end and made a big first down. The sportswriters called the trick play a 'fumblerooski,' but don't ask me where they got that name."

Stephanie said, "Thank you, Lieutenant John Smothers. You have put these two macho-men out of their misery. They have been so busy replaying that game that they are ignoring the chicken that is cooking on the grill."

Aubrey quickly raised the top of the grill, and a cloud of smoke backed him away. When it cleared, Stephanie took a close look and said, "Actually, it looks just right. Let's eat."

They got all the way through the meal and halfway through dessert before anyone mentioned the trial or the search for Cletus Bolton. Then Aubrey said, "Speaking of trick plays, I wonder if Spike has a fumblerooski up his sleeve—something we haven't thought about? So far, thanks to your good work and Stephanie's good research, we have kept Spike on defense. I'd like to keep it that way."

Lieutenant Smothers said, "I haven't heard anything about tricks that Spike might pull, but on another front—my investigators are still looking for Cletus. They have not found him yet, but we will get him if he is still in the area. We are pretty sure he is holed up somewhere in Randolph County, but there's still a lot of wild country over there."

Aubrey said, "If we could clear up the 1968 lynching, it would give me some options I don't have right now."

Dwane said, "Amen. It would be poetic justice to take down Artus and the Mysterion for the poison they have been spreading for the last forty years."

Stephanie agreed with them, but then she looked at Aubrey. "I know the lynching case has bothered you for a long time, but right now we have got our hands full with the trial of Cody Ransom. Spike is no fool. He called one expert after another to prove that the local culture is strongly opposed to homosexuality. He is going to use that to explain and justify why Cody Ransom panicked and hit Randy Trice. Moreover, he is going to tell the jury they do not have to follow the law. He's going to tell them that they can and should do what they think is right." Stephanie paused for effect. "That is Spike's trick play, that's his fumblerooski. Are we ready for it?"

Aubrey pushed back from the table and wrinkled his brow. "Stephanie's dead right. The 1968 lynching has tormented me for a long time. But I need to stay focused on the case we are trying. Monday is going to be a big day."

Dwane said, "Have you all decided what you are going to say in your closing arguments?"

Stephanie said, "I have. I will speak first. I will go through the proof we offered, and then I will go over the proof Spike offered. My job is to make sure the jury understands the facts and the law. I will explain that 'gay panic' is not a legal defense to murder or manslaughter, and I will spend some time showing how we have met our burden to prove Cody's guilt beyond a reasonable doubt."

Aubrey said, "She will do a good job, and when she is finished, Spike will have his turn to argue. If he says what we think he is going to say, then when he is done, I will argue on the field of battle that Spike has chosen."

"What do you mean by that?" Dwane said.

"It would be a mistake for me to spend my time arguing what Stephanie will have already said. I think the jury will be looking for a way to let Cody go, and if I do not answer Spike's simple argument, they will seize on what he says as gospel. For that reason, I plan to deal head-on with the issue of our culture and how our local beliefs relate to the law. Then I will take on Spike's contention that the jury does not have to follow the law if they don't want to. That will be tricky, since it is true that they don't have to follow the law if they don't want to."

Dwane said, "Can you talk about such high-toned stuff without putting the jury to sleep?"

"I'll have to if we want this to come out right. It was wrong for Cody to kill Randy Trice. He should have just gotten out of the car and run home. If the jury acquits him, it will not stop our pursuit of Cletus and Artus and the Mysterion, but it will confuse what we hope to accomplish."

Lieutenant Smothers said, "What is that? What do you hope to accomplish, Mr. Prosecutor?"

"Justice is what I hope to accomplish. I'm still working on how I'm going to say it to the jury, but if you will come to court Monday, I'll have it together by then."

Annie Smothers said, "I'll be there Monday, but what you just said—'Justice'—sounds pretty good to me. It will be hard to do much better."

EIGHTY-THREE

Ruby Lou Jones was born and raised in Randolph County, and her best friend, growing up, was Josie McBride. By the time the girls got to the ninth grade, they were as wild as March hares. The boys who chased after them agreed that Ruby Lou and Josie were the prettiest girls in school, real knockouts. Josie, a brunette, was trim with the chiseled look of a New York model; Ruby Lou was a little on the fleshy side, always struggling to keep her weight down. She would never be a model, but her blond hair and cute baby face gave her a come-hither look that Josie could not imitate, no matter how hard she tried. The hot-blooded high school boys had their own way of describing the girls: "Ruby Lou's made for comfort, but Josie's made for speed."

Their frequent sexual escapades included several tag-team seductions of Josie's "kissing cousin," Cletus Bolton, a feat the girls repeated every time he came from Campbell County to visit his great-uncle. Actually, Cletus was a second cousin, but that did not matter to him, or to the girls.

After high school, Ruby Lou married a truck driver and moved to Campbell County. He threw her out three times after catching her with other men, but each time he got to feeling sorry for her and took her back. Finally, after five years and two more adulterous affairs, he had had enough. He divorced Ruby Lou, and she moved in with an old couple to serve as their caregiver. During that time, on her twenty-fifth birthday, an old-timey primitive preacher persuaded her to come forward during altar call. She did, and he baptized her the next week in Blackberry Creek. Ruby Lou joined his church and did very well for the first year. Then she struck up an illicit relationship with a long-time deacon, and the women in the congregation blew a gasket. They wanted to excommunicate Ruby Lou, but the old preacher came to her rescue once again. He got her to confess her sins and promise to give up her promiscuous ways. The congregation did not believe her, but the preacher persuaded the churchwomen to pull in their horns. They forgave Ruby Lou, or at least they said they did.

When she turned thirty, Ruby Lou met and married Tom Simms, a mousey little man who owned the general store in Draco as well as a quarter section of good grazing land that adjoined the lake. Set for life, Ruby Lou taught herself how to speak in tongues and handle snakes.

Snake handling was complicated for Ruby Lou because she hated the damn things, and they seemed to know it. She had to go to the doctor for treatment six times, but by the time she was forty, Ruby Lou had become the featured performer at the brush arbor gathering, an annual affair held on the second Sunday of August. People stopped calling her "Ruby Lou." Everybody in that neck-of-the wood began calling her "Sister."

She loved everything about the brush arbor meetings. Her church sponsored the event, and the deacons put up the arbor frame on a hillside overlooking Sycamore Lake. The churchwomen gathered magnolia cuttings for the roof and sent word throughout the community that the brush arbor gathering was open to the public. But they made it clear that the gathering was mainly for folks who liked the ways of the primitive church.

The organizers expected a big turnout for the 2007 meeting because a special guest, Apostle Artus MacArthur, was going to conduct the sunrise service. People liked to hear Artus preach because he always talked about the old ways of the hill country, and many—especially the Mysterions—believed he could divine the hidden mysteries of the Bible.

Sister did her usual good job with the snakes. Three people came forward to be saved while she was performing, her all-time high. When the gathering was over, Artus got into a conversation with her and the trio that had led the shape-note singing. It was not long before the singers started talking about the Cody Ransom trial, and the fact that the state police were looking for Cletus Bolton in connection with the 1968 lynching.

Sister said, "I remember Cletus from years ago. He had a mean streak in him, and he didn't like queers, but he wouldn't do anything like that."

Artus said, "I think you're right. I'd like to help Cletus if he's in trouble." He paused and then added, "Sheriff Odom thinks he is over in Randolph County."

Sister said, "I'll be danged. That's where I grew up. I bet my old high school girlfriend, Josie McBride, knows where ole Cletus is. He had some relatives over that way, and he and Josie are kissing cousins."

Artus' ears perked up. "She lives over there?"

"Yeah, she's got a place on the Eleven Point about five miles upriver from the little town of Dalton."

"Josie McBride, huh?"

"Well, she goes by Belford now. That's the name of the guy she married, but he got killed in a car wreck. You want me to call her and see if she knows where Cletus is?"

"No, you don't have to do that. Cletus knows how to get in touch with me if he needs me."

Artus patted Sister on the shoulder and walked over to where some of the men were smoking or having a chaw of tobacco. He spoke to two of the young men, and they left in a hurry.

—∾—

Josie and Cletus were sitting at the kitchen table in her house, drinking coffee, when the phone rang. "Who would be calling at 10 o'clock on a Sunday morning?" Josie said as she picked up the receiver.

"Hey, Josie, it's Ruby Lou. How you doing?"

"Hey, Ruby Lou. I'm doing fine. What's going on?"

"Same old stuff, but I was talking to some folks this morning at church meeting, and they got to talking about the state police looking for old Cletus. It made me think of the good times me and you and Cletus had."

Josie said, "Why's that?"

"Well, they said the sheriff here thinks Cletus is in Randolph County. I told them if anybody would know where to find Cletus, it would be you."

"Who were you talking to, Ruby Lou?"

"I was talking to Artus MacArthur. He remembers Cletus from the old days when Cletus was in his Mysterion outfit. Said he wanted to help him if he is in trouble."

Josie hesitated, trying to think up a way to change the subject. "Well, ain't that something? I thought they had a falling out."

Ruby Lou started to say something, but Josie cut her off. She had thought of a sure-fire way to stop the talk about Cletus. "How's your back, Ruby Lou? Still giving you fits?"

That prompted a five-minute tirade on the relative merits of chiropractor adjusting versus real doctoring, and it gave Josie the time she needed to gather her wits and tactfully end the telephone call.

As soon as Ruby Lou finished telling about her latest visit to "some quack doctor in Springfield," who had done her no good, Josie told her she had to hang up, but encouraged her to come and visit as soon as she felt better.

"I will. Good to talk to you, Josie."

Josie put the phone down. She looked at Cletus and told him, word for word, what Ruby Lou had just said about Artus.

—◦—

Cletus said, "They'll be coming. Probably on their way right now."

"Let's get out of here, Cletus. We can go stay with Curly over in Pocahontas, or we could drive to Jonesboro and stay with Raymond."

"You go, get out of here. I'm tired of running. I'm going to wait on them. I'll call you when it's over. Those bastards tried to dry-gulch me in Kentucky. Now it's my turn to dry-gulch them."

PART FOUR

ELEVEN POINT

EIGHTY-FOUR

As Josie was driving away, Cletus went directly into the family room and jimmied the lock on her dead husband's gun cabinet. Jimmy Belford was a deer hunter, and he had collected several high-priced long-range rifles, shotguns, and handguns. Cletus looked them over and pulled an old Remington Model 721 off the rack. It was identical to the rifle he learned to hunt with in the woods of Campbell County when he was a boy, but this one had a scope mounted. Cletus put it to his shoulder, turned toward the window, and sighted down the barrel to a woodpile.

Yep, this will do, but I'll need to snap off a round or two to be sure the scope is set right.

He opened the big drawer beneath the gun rack and found two boxes of .270 Winchester hollow-point cartridges. He loaded the shells into Jimmy's leather ammo belt, fastened it around his waist, and pulled the rifle sling over his shoulder.

Cletus was not sure how much time he had before the Mysterion boys would show up; it could be hours or it could be minutes. He hurried outside, heading to the open area between the house and a small outbuilding that doubled as a tool shed and storage place for yard and garden equipment.

Cletus found two empty cans in the shed and lined them up on a log at the edge of the woods. Then he backed off to the other side of the clearing, loaded the rifle, aimed and fired. The can on the left disappeared into the woods, and that brought a smile to Cletus' face. He racked the bolt action, aimed and fired at the second can and got the same result. *All right*—he thought to himself—*I could knock the ass off a gnat with this baby.*

He went back into the tool shed. In a few minutes, he came out, pulling a garden cart filled with tools and equipment that included a good-sized roll of rubber-covered wire and a few sticks of dynamite that Jimmy Belford had kept around to blow out tree stumps. Cletus was not sure how he might use the explosives, but he knew it would be impossible to come back to the shed or house once the Mysterion boys arrived.

He headed down the road that led to the cabin. The half-mile walk gave him time to think about his predicament and make a plan.

The bastards will come today. It won't take them long to find this place now that they have Josie's name, and know that we are on the Eleven Point upriver from the Dalton bridge. They will check out the house and then they will start looking around. This road ain't easy to see, grown over as it is, but they will find it, and then they will ease their truck on down to the cabin. I need to whack them then, right when they get to the clearing, before they scatter out.

—~—

At 7 o'clock, a white Dodge truck pulled up next to Josie's house, and two burly men went onto the porch. They knocked hard on the door, and when no one answered, they pushed it open and went in. Shortly, they came out and walked all around the house, not saying much, just looking. The heavier man had a pistol holstered and strapped to his waist. The other man, leaner and shorter, carried a rifle, and when he noticed the road to the cabin, he gave a military hand-signal to his partner, who immediately joined him. They talked quietly for a moment, and then they got into their truck and started down the road, going slow. When they were halfway to the cabin, the driver spotted something red in the woods. It was an old Ford truck parked well off the trail, almost hidden from view. The driver got out and made his way through the tangled woods, and when he got close to the red truck, he saw that it had a Kentucky license plate. He gave thumbs up to his partner. Then he returned to the Dodge truck, and they continued their slow roll down the road toward the cabin. The farther they got, the more grown-over the road got. Soon the engine noise of the Dodge gave way to the screeching of tree limbs and brush scraping against the truck.

—∾—

Cletus was not hiding in the cabin. He had positioned himself behind a big rock formation just inside the tree line, twenty yards from the cabin. He had a clear view of the exact spot where the little road opened to the cabin and a small yard that was empty except for two Walmart-quality yard chairs and a fishing-boat trailer. Cletus was pleased with his position. He thought of it as triangulating; he had heard that word somewhere, and it seemed to fit his setup.

—∾—

When the Dodge scraped its way into view, Cletus got a look at the two men, and said to himself: *I'll be damned. It's the same two monkeys who came to my place in Kentucky.*

He waited for the truck to come even with a large boulder that marked the entrance to the yard. Then Cletus cackled and squeezed the grip on a small handheld device, sending an electrical charge through a rubber-covered wire to the blasting cap and dynamite planted behind and beneath the boulder.

The boulder headed skyward on a low trajectory that took it into the right side of the truck, even with the front axle. The Dodge was airborne for a full second before it came to rest with a thud, crossways to the road. The sound was deafening. A cloud of dust and acrid odor quickly engulfed the scene.

Cletus waited, thinking he had killed the Mysterions. But the one who had carried the rifle stumbled out of the cloud, shaking his head and rubbing his eyes. The other man, the one with the sidearm, soon appeared. He was walking loppy-jawed, but he looked as if he might live. Cletus marveled, thinking aloud. *Them boys is tough—but they ain't as tough as ole Cletus.*

He raised the 721 and fired a warning shot into the ground between the Mysterions, who had given up walking in favor of rolling around on a grassy spot just outside ground zero. The man with the sidearm took it out of the holster and threw it deep into the woods. "Shit, Cletus, we just wanted to talk."

"Bullshit. I know what you came here to do. Next time I won't give you no break. I'll send you fuckers straight to hell."

—ʬ—

Cletus slung the 721 over his shoulder and walked down to the river. He stepped into the fishing boat, untied it from the sycamore tree, and pushed off into the Eleven Point River. He cackled at the top of his voice, mocking the Mysterion boys.

The old wooden boat found the current and began to drift. Cletus lay back and lit up an old-style Camel, his first cigarette since Josie got the call from Ruby Lou. He felt good and slightly proud of himself for dry-gulching the Mysterion boys. He figured he deserved a moment's rest, so he took his time, enjoying every puff. He tried to blow a few smoke rings, something he was good at, but the perfect circles busted up too fast to suit him, so he went back to plain smoking. When the butt got down to the nub, he tossed it over the side and picked up the paddle.

Cletus headed for a tiny sandbar two miles downriver from Josie's place. It was getting dark, and he knew better than to float the Eleven Point on a night when a new moon was still forming. The sliver of moonlight would not be enough to steer by, and he was in no hurry now that he had taken care of the Mysterion boys. They were lucky to be alive, their truck was now a piece of junk, and they had no boat. Cletus smiled as he thought about the explosion and the Mysterion boys staggering around, whining and claiming that they only wanted to talk.

Cletus beached the boat and stretched out on the warm sand. He needed to start thinking about Josie, Junior, and his predicament with the law, but he fell into a deep sleep. He did not stir until the sun began to light the river.

When he awoke Monday morning, Cletus saw a heron, standing sentinel, waiting for its breakfast in a quiet reach of still water near the sandbar. He was stiff and sore from sleeping on the ground in the night air, but he needed to get going. He was hungry and kept thinking about a ham-and-egg sandwich and a cup of hot coffee, all available at the old Dalton store, just a few miles farther downstream. He tried to brush the sand out of his hair, but the harder he brushed, the worse it seemed to get. He stripped off his clothes and waded out into the cool, clear water, and when he was up to his waist, he just stood there admiring the river and the fringe of trees and foliage that protects it. Cletus loved the Eleven Point, now more than ever. He had fished the river when he was a boy, but living at Josie's cabin gave him a new fondness and respect for the spring-fed river that begins in the Ozarks of Missouri, and runs south into Randolph County, Arkansas. Josie's place was one of the best on the river, and he wanted to stay there, with her, if he could figure out a way to do it.

Cletus finished his bath and dressed. Then he pushed the boat off the sandbar, climbed in, and paddled to the deeper part of the river. When he was drifting south, he started thinking about his options.

Junior and Josie are the onliest ones I trust. Junior says the new prosecutor is a good man, but I ain't one to trust cops or politicians. Junior says they want to talk to me about the 1968 thing, the queer that Artus killed. I don't know. Maybe I ought to talk to them, or maybe I ought to cut out and go back to Kentucky, or somewhere away from here. I'd miss Josie and the river. I'm not too far now from the bridge at Dalton. I'll figure something out, but first I've got to get a cup of coffee and some eats.

EIGHTY-FIVE

At first light on Monday, August 13, people began to gather at the entrance to the Campbell County Courthouse. A few of them were local regulars, courthouse groupies who never miss a criminal trial, but most of the early birds were outsiders who had come from all directions to get a seat for the closing arguments. The strange assortment, drawn to the drama, straggled toward the courthouse from their cars and trucks. As they neared the main walkway, they converged and shuffled past the silent, dew-covered TV trucks. They stepped over assorted cables and joined the line, a queue that would soon reach the street and curl around the corner to where the Confederate general stood guard.

Over the weekend, the mainline news networks and every major cable channel had run at least one hour-long feature, and countless promotions telling viewers all across the world about the trial of Cody Ransom, the 1968 lynching of Ike Swanson, and the history of Campbell County, Arkansas. Most were unflattering, paeans to notions inapposite to the conservative, traditional culture of North Arkansas.

By 8 o'clock, when the old bailiff Wes Caldwell made an appearance to say the doors would open in fifteen minutes, the crowd was getting noisy. The TV crews had come to life, as had their generators and other noisemakers. Protesters shouted at one another and waved an array of homemade signs for the TV cameras under the enthusiastic direction of the ever-present George Freemont and Jamie Kress. Two signs called for acquittal and one for conviction, but most of the signage promoted political causes that had nothing to do with the case on trial. Freemont, Kress, and their followers were like ships passing in the night on irreversible courses.

Aubrey had arranged seating for Dwane, Zach, and the Ball boys. They gained admittance to the courthouse through the door reserved for court officials, the jury, and the families of Cody Ransom and Randy Trice.

When Zach rolled Dwane's wheelchair to a stop in the aisle by the first row of seats behind the prosecution's table, the boys gathered around him, seeking answers to a host of questions.

—~—

Dwane loved these moments, rare in the modern world: youngsters eager to learn from old-timers instead of from the internet or from the pap being fed to them daily through television, magazines, and social media. Dwane had not studied law, but he knew a lot about it, and the boys knew that. He had served on four petit juries: one civil case, two murder cases, and one rape case. The boys begged him to tell them about the civil case, and he did. It was famous throughout North Arkansas because the jury, with Dwane as its foreman, awarded two million dollars to a widow-woman who sued her dead husband's rich mistress, claiming she slit his throat in a fit of jealousy.

"That would make a good book, Mr. Pollard. You ought to write it." Zach said.

Dwane bumped fists with the boys and realized from the way they were looking at him that this was a forever moment. It reminded him of his teenage years in the CCC when he, thirsty for knowledge, learned to read and write mainly because an old man cared enough to help him.

"Why do they call it a 'petit' jury?" Eight Ball, as usual, interrupted the lesson with a basic question.

"They call it 'petit' because it is smaller than a grand jury. Grand juries can make accusations, but the smaller, petit juries like the one in Cody's case are the ones that will decide whether there is enough proof to support the charge."

"That seems to me a bigger job than what the grand juries do. Looks like somebody got the naming backwards." Eight Ball had a puzzled look.

"Well, that's a good point, but all this—the judge, the jury, the rules we live by—goes way back, almost a thousand years." Dwane gave a satisfied look and gestured to the judge's bench and the jury box. "Sometimes a page of history tells us more than a volume of logic."

"That's pretty cool," Zach said. The Ball boys nodded in agreement, and as they did, the jurors filed into the courtroom from the jury room. They took their seats in the jury box and looked out over a standing-room-only crowd that shushed up to watch the show. The spectators scrutinized each juror, and when they tired of that, the crowd noise returned.

Within minutes, the lawyers made their appearance, and the noise died down again, this time for good. Spike took his seat by Cody Ransom, and Aubrey and Stephanie walked to their places. As they did, they nodded to Dwane and the boys, and that set off a teenage squirm, complete with little hand-waves and big smiles. A serious glance from Dwane settled the boys down just in time, because the door to the left of the judge's bench swung open, and the old bailiff came in singing yet another screechy version of his call to order.

Judge Oglethorpe burst through the door on cue, robe flowing. He called for order in the court and turned to the jury. "Ladies and gentlemen, the prosecution and defense have rested their cases. You have heard the evidence, so today I will instruct you on the law, and then we will hear the closing arguments of counsel."

The judge cleared his throat, fiddled with his half-eye glasses, and began to read. "The faithful performance of your duties as jurors is essential to the administration of justice. It is my duty as judge to inform you of the law applicable to this case by instructions, and it is your duty to accept and follow them as a whole, not singling out one instruction to the exclusion of others. You should not consider any rule of law with which you may be familiar unless it is included in my instructions."

The jurors focused intently on the judge, but the lawyers did not. They were watching the jury as if the jurors were twelve hungry bugs crawling around a vacated dinner table. The instinctive surveillance—a futile attempt to discern the thinking of individual jurors—never works, but lawyers cannot help themselves. They watch anyway.

When Judge Oglethorpe finished reading, he said, "We will now hear the closing arguments of counsel. The prosecution will speak first, followed by the defense. When the defense finishes its argument, the prosecution will have a chance to speak in rebuttal, and that will be the end of the arguments.

"After that, you will retire to deliberate about the case. Mr. Hatfield has informed the court that Deputy Prosecuting Attorney Stephanie Brooks will open for the prosecution, and he will close."

The judge looked at Stephanie. "You may proceed."

The noises that had ricocheted off the courtroom's plaster walls when the crowd first gathered were now in hiding, subdued by the grand entrances, the reading of the instructions, and the judge's invitation for Stephanie to proceed. The courtroom was as hushed as a graveyard, but the tension that caused the noise had gone nowhere. It was bottled up, raw energy waiting for a time to escape.

Dwane watched as Stephanie pushed back from the table and stood up. She was wearing her close-fitting navy blue suit, the one she had on the day Dwane first met her, and she had her shiny black hair done up in a sassy but professional chignon. Dwane imagined himself as a member of the jury, wondering. *She is a beautiful woman, and that is what first catches your eye. But she has done a good, professional job as the deputy prosecutor, and this is not an easy case. It involves two men, one young and one older who is now dead at the hands of the other. It will be good to hear a woman's perspective on all of this.*

As she approached the lectern, Dwane saw that Aubrey had the same goofy look on his face as he had that morning at Hatfield House, after his first night in bed with her. *Aubrey is obviously in love with Stephanie. But so am I.*

The next thing Dwane noticed was that Stephanie had no notes or papers with her. She was just standing there, studying the jurors, taking her time, giving them time to rearrange themselves and study her.

—∾—

They are truly undecided, perhaps leaning in Cody's favor. Stephanie could see it in their faces. I have to do my job and do it well. Spike is a gadfly, but he has more trial experience than the two of us put together. *I was going to start with a review of the proof, but I had better start with the main point we want to make, the one that will force Spike into a corner.*

"Ladies and gentlemen, we have all taken an oath to uphold the law, but the defense counsel has spent two weeks tempting you to ignore it. When it is his turn to speak, he will talk about the law, but he does not want you to follow it." Stephanie paused to let her words sink in. "Now, why would a lawyer, an officer of the court, encourage a jury to ignore the law?"

The jurors stirred, but the answer did not come. Stephanie walked a few steps from the lectern, scratching her head with one finger as if searching for the best way to deal with her own proposition.

Judge Oglethorpe cast an odd glance in her direction.

Good. The judge and jurors think I have frozen up or lost my train of thought.

Stephanie returned to the lectern looking the part of someone undergoing a brainstorm. "There is a simple explanation for what he is doing."

She used a stage whisper, and separated her words for emphasis. "He has no defense. No legal defense, that is."

The jurors stirred again. Some seemed relieved that Stephanie had solved her own puzzle, and that she was back on track. Some were grim-faced and tense. Others just settled back, ready to hear more.

All right, I have their attention. Now I have to make my case.

"Let me put it plainly. First, Cody Ransom is not crazy; everybody in this courtroom knows that. Second, this is not a case of self-defense: Cody, faced with a nonviolent homosexual advance, could have, and should have, gotten out of the car and gone on with his run. The same goes for the contention that Cody was provoked. The defense wraps all of these concepts in the guise of 'homosexual panic,' but the judge did not say a word about 'homosexual panic' in his instructions because it is not a legal defense to what Cody Ransom did.

"Nevertheless, the defense will argue that Cody panicked and that his upbringing and our local culture influenced him to react as he did. But, ladies and gentlemen, please understand, 'homosexual panic' is nothing more than an argument—it is not the law.

She pointed at Spike. "He has no defense, and he knows it."

Spike gave a toothy smile to the jury but said nothing.

Stephanie then told the jury it was her responsibility to go over the proof and the issues raised during the course of the trial. She asked the jury to bear with her, but then she captured them with a lawyerlike presentation. It had been a long two weeks, but she quoted witnesses perfectly and explained the law with precision. Most impressively, she did it without referring to a single note.

When she finished, she thanked the jurors and started to turn away, but an afterthought transformed her. The skilled prosecutor suddenly became a softhearted woman. Her voice mellowed, and she spoke to them as if confiding to close kin. "Cody Ransom was right to be upset when Randy Trice touched him, and asked him if he had ever had oral sex, but Cody should not have hit him with the dumbbell, much less five times. He should have said, 'No, I do not want to do that.' I wish he had gotten out of the car and gone on with his run. If he had done that, he would not be here, on trial for murder, and Randy Trice would not be dead."

—≈—

Tension stayed in its hiding place; the room was deathly quiet. Judge Oglethorpe announced a short recess, telling everyone to be back at 10 o'clock, and the crowd-noise returned in force as soon as his gavel hit the sound block. It started as a murmur but quickly became a raucous jumble of chatter.

The Ball boys headed for the restroom, but Zach stayed with Dwane because he was full of questions. "She did good, didn't she, Mr. Pollard? It looked to me like they were taking what she said: hook, line, and sinker."

"It's hard to tell about juries, Zach, particularly in a case like this."

"Meaning what?"

"Well, if we were to take the jurors one by one, we would say they are all good and reasonable people. The judge swore them in, and they all said they could be fair but there is no way to scrub them clean of their resentments, their biases. They take all that into the jury box with them, and it shows up when they start trying to reach a verdict." Dwane waited for Zach to find the meaning of what he just said.

"So, you are saying the jurors might agree with Stephanie, but turn Cody loose because they don't like gay people?"

"Yes."

"If that's how it works, then I'm not sure I like it."

"It's been working that way for a thousand years, Zach, mainly because no one can come up with a better idea."

Zach slumped down. "I thought there were rules to make sure that courtroom stuff would be on the up and up."

Dwane saw that the boy needed a ray of hope. "There are plenty of rules like that, but Aubrey and Stephanie decided a long time ago that Spike was going to use every trick in the book to get around the rules."

"So, that's what Stephanie was getting at when she said that Spike has no defense; that he will ask the jury to ignore the law?"

"Exactly. She was setting him up. If it works—if Spike overplays his hand and winds up asking this jury to ignore the law—Aubrey will be ready for him."

The Ball boys returned along with the rest of the spectators. It was almost 10 o'clock, and everyone was in place, ready for the judge to call on Spike to give his closing argument. Zach looked across the courtroom to the defense table. Spike was scribbling notes, and Cody was leaning over the railing that separated the crowd from the court officials. He was giving his mother a hug, and the sight of that sent an ache through Zach's heart. Cody was his longtime classmate. They were not especially close, but they were good athletes in a small town, and that meant they were teammates as well as classmates. Cody was an outstanding football player, but for some reason he did not play baseball, Zach's true love. Suddenly, Zach understood Dwane's point about juries taking their friendships, feelings, and beliefs into the jury box. He wondered how such things might affect his vote if he were on the jury.

EIGHTY-SIX

Judge Oglethorpe gaveled the trial to order and recognized Spike to make the closing argument for the defense.

Spike thanked the judge. He took a stack of papers from the counsel table and pranced across the room, arrogance in full bloom. He was wearing his trademark green suit and yellow tie, and for this very special occasion, Spike had pinned a big red carnation to his lapel. The colorful getup hinted of a traffic light, but he could not have cared less. For his entire career, he had been waiting for this moment.

As he neared the lectern, Spike took a moment to appreciate his good fortune.

Everything is in place. The whole world is watching. Trials don't get any bigger than this. I have a young, good-looking, sympathetic figure for a client, and I am fighting for a cause worth fighting for. People around here are on my side because they want to preserve their way of life.

"May it please the court?" Spike sought and got Judge Oglethorpe's nod of approval. He cleared his throat and began by accepting Stephanie's challenge.

"Ladies and gentlemen, I have the utmost respect for the prosecution, but let's get something straight. I do have a defense, and it is this: Cody Ransom is a good boy, raised in these hills and taught to believe in the Good Book. He never hurt anybody in his life. Then one day he goes jogging to keep himself in shape, and Randy Trice, a homosexual, pulls up alongside him and lies to get him in the car, telling him he wants to talk to him about his college scholarship. The next thing Cody knows, a queer is grabbing his privates and asking him if he ever had a blow-job. Cody panicked and hit him with a dumbbell to get him to stop, and then he got out of the car and ran home. When the police came to his house, he did not try to hide anything. He told them exactly what had happened. Now, if a middle-aged man had done that to an eighteen-year-old girl, and she had hit him with a dumbbell, we would be giving her an award.

"The deputy prosecutor, Stephanie Brooks, rattled off a bunch of legal mumbo-jumbo about insanity, self-defense, provocation, and stuff like that. She says the law requires you to convict, but you do not have to leave your common sense behind when you go into the jury box. This boy did what most boys around here would have done; he fought back when the queer went for his privates. You can call it 'gay panic' or 'homosexual panic' or whatever you want to. Cody Ransom does not deserve to go to jail for what he did.

"She says I'm going to ask you to ignore the law, but that is not true. I'm asking you to follow one of our oldest and best laws—the law that says you, the jury, can turn someone loose if you think it is the right thing to do."

The jurors were enthralled, listening to his every word. Spike had tapped into the hatred that hill people have for anything that tears down their culture, their way of life, by casting Randy Trice as a homosexual monster on the prowl for innocent young boys. Now Spike was telling them that the law was on his side, and his explanation of the law was much easier to understand: Just let Cody go if you think it is "the right thing to do." Spike had them fired up, and he could see that they were ready for a convincing story about the power of juries.

He went to the counsel table and picked up an old leather-covered book, and then he walked back toward the jury, thumbing through it. When he found what he was looking for, he gave the jury a theatrical wink and began telling a tale in his folksiest manner.

"Folks, in 1670, long before we got our independence from England, there was a famous trial. William Penn was on trial for preaching a sermon in a place other than the Church of England. Since that was against the law, the judge told the jurors they had to convict him if he had done it. The jury found that the meeting took place, but they refused to say that Penn was guilty of violating the law. The judge got mad and threatened to lock them up without food, water, heat, tobacco, or light until they returned a verdict of guilty."

Spike paused to let the story sink in, shaking his head to show disbelief. Then he continued.

"William Penn said the judge could not force the jury to find him guilty, so the judge locked him in a cage where he could be heard but not seen by the jury. Then the judge started browbeating the jury, and Penn shouted some famous words, 'Ye are Englishmen, mind your privilege, give not away your right.'"

Spike paused, pretending to choke up, and then he put his hand to his ear.

"The jurors heard what Penn said, and they shouted back. 'Nor will we ever do it.'"

Spike closed the old leather-covered book. "Well, folks, the judge kept them locked up for two days and two nights, but they never gave in, and that great case established the right for trial juries, like you, to decide cases according to your own convictions."

Stephanie hated to do it, but she admitted to herself that the gadfly was off to a very persuasive start. *Even so, he has taken the bait. He is openly telling the jury to substitute the conscience of the community for the instructions of law that Judge Oglethorpe has just given them.* She looked at Aubrey to see what he was thinking. He winked and whispered to her, "We've got him right where we want him." She gave him a little smile, but she was not so sure. She thought to herself, *Aubrey has his work cut out for him.*

Spike had mastered the art of cornball flamboyance. He was born with the raw ingredients, but it had taken years to perfect the slightly moronic demeanor that disguised his many skills as a trial lawyer, not the least of which was his uncanny ability to divine the innermost thoughts of jurors and opposing counsel.

He had been on his feet for less than twenty minutes, but already he had correctly sensed that Stephanie was nervous, on edge about the way he had dealt with her argument. That was important information, but it paled in comparison to his calculation that seven jurors were on his side—certain votes for a complete acquittal, no matter what Aubrey might say in his argument.

Spike was in clover, having a ball, basking, feasting, and occasionally gloating. His mind was working overtime, and he could not resist a prideful thought: *God help me, I love it. I've got them on the run. Now it's time to stick it up their ass.*

"Ladies and gentlemen, I don't know why the prosecution charged this boy with murder. The judge has told you that it cannot be murder if Cody was acting under the influence of extreme emotional disturbance. In other words, if you find that Cody had a reasonable excuse—looking at it from his viewpoint, the way he believed things to be—then it is not murder."

Aubrey objected. "Your Honor, that is not a complete statement of the law. Counsel failed to say that the language he read comes from your instruction on manslaughter. What he just said would require the jury to find Cody guilty of manslaughter."

The judge nodded in agreement. "Ladies and gentlemen, I have told you what the law is, and what it is not. You should take that into account during the arguments."

Spike, unruffled, carried on with his argument. "Thank you, Your Honor. I was about to say, as I said earlier, that Cody Ransom is not guilty of anything—manslaughter or murder. I was only making the point that the prosecution was way out of line in charging him with murder."

Spike did not want to dwell on the subject of manslaughter, because he knew Aubrey was right. But he was determined to stoke the fires of prejudice and willing to risk another objection. He returned to the language about "reasonable excuse" as if it had just occurred to him.

"Before I move to my next point, I ask you to bear in mind that you are supposed to look at the issue of emotional disturbance—'homosexual panic'—from Cody's point of view." He paused to see if Aubrey would say anything, and when he did not, Spike continued. "Here's a boy who was raised to believe that homosexuality is bad, wrong morally and scripturally. He knew Randy Trice was a car dealer, but when Randy lured Cody into his Cadillac, fondled his privates, and asked the boy for a blowjob, he was not a car dealer. No siree! Put yourself in this boy's position. He was shocked. How would you have seen it? Would you have seen Randy as a car dealer or would you have seen him as a monster—the personification of evil—someone who was trying to get you to do something that goes against everything you believe."

Spike watched the jury for reactions and decided to up his count of acquittals to eight. Then he scanned the courtroom and saw nods of approval amongst the spectators. One subtle but important gesture came from Sheriff Odom, who was leaning against the wall near the judge's bench. Spike reveled, thinking: *I do not know a single lawyer who can read people as well as I can.* His good feeling slipped a little when he looked to his client for a sign of approval. Cody was slouching and his head was down, in stark contrast to his father. Carl Ransom was sitting bolt upright, acting as if he were ready to jump up and start giving high-fives. Lillian, Cody's mother, showed no emotion, but that did not bother Spike. She seldom showed her true feelings.

—∞—

Aubrey was keeping a close eye on Sheriff Odom. He kept showing up in the courtroom, and nearly always stood in the same place, in clear view of the jury. He had a right to be there, but his body language was telling the jury that he agreed with Spike's view of the case. Aubrey chided himself for being paranoid, but Stephanie said she felt the same, particularly when Spike got into high dudgeon about the "monster" that had attacked Cody. The sheriff was witnessing for the defense, and they could do nothing about it.

—∞—

When the state police issued the APB for Cletus Bolton at the end of the first week of trial, Spike had blown up and made a scene in the judge's office. He suspected Aubrey was using the 1968 lynching case to shame the jurors into voting to convict Cody. He had thought about asking for a mistrial but decided against it, figuring news about the old case would blow over. But the search for Cletus Bolton was now generating headlines as big as the trial of Cody Ransom, and Spike had not planned for that. His suspicion turned to certainty.

The damned media frenzy is helping Aubrey. The stories are making the whole county look bad, and nobody likes to be called a bigot. I have to deal with this.

"Folks, I trust you understand that all references to the 1968 lynching case have been solely for the purpose of explaining the history and cultural development of Campbell County. That case has been in the news lately, but then everything is in the news these days. These modern newsreaders can stir up more trouble than a sack of snakes, but we are not trying that case here. It is something that everyone around here has heard about, but it has nothing to do with Cody, except as a bit of history."

There was one other thing to clear up. When Spike saw Carl Ransom in a state of readiness, looking as if he wanted to give high-fives, it reminded him that he needed to deal with Carl's outburst, the one that caused Judge Oglethorpe to get mad and break his gavel. "Ladies and gentlemen, I probably don't need to say anything about the time Cody's dad was testifying and flew off the handle, but I will. He is like a lot of us; he is worried about all the stuff that is going on in the country and how it is affecting our kids. Then, there he was on the witness stand, looking at his only son, a boy caught up in this mess. It just got to him, and I'm certain you won't hold that against the boy."

Spike reckoned that his acquittal commitments were holding tight, and he was beginning to think he might pick up a ninth vote if he finished with a whiz-bang peroration. And so he decided to add a little gasoline to the fire.

His closing theme was, of course, the culture and how Cody came to believe that homosexuality is a sin, wrong in every respect. It was a familiar argument that he had used throughout the trial, but Spike wanted to inflame the jury once more before Aubrey started his argument, and he knew just how to do it. "Ladies and gentlemen, this is a hard time to raise children. In the old days, we taught our children good, conservative Arkansas values, and we did not have to compete with the internet, television, magazines, and all the new gadgets that are coming out. Nowadays, all sorts of corrupting influences are coming in here, and messing up our way of life. Can we blame an eighteen-year-old kid for being confused and scared? Cody learned that homosexuality is wrong, but then he turns on the TV and sees pictures of weirdos marching in Gay Pride parades in San Francisco wearing drag, looking like something out of a nightmare. Can you blame Cody for panicking when a real-live queer suddenly attacked him?

"Folks, this is not a complicated case. Do the right thing. Use your common sense. Apply our community values and standards—our community conscience—to this situation. And let this boy go on with his life."

Spike thanked the jurors and returned to his table wearing a self-satisfied look.

—~—

Judge Oglethorpe said, "Ladies and gentlemen, it is a little after noon. Court will be in recess until 2 o'clock, at which time Prosecuting Attorney Aubrey Hatfield will give the final argument in this case."

EIGHTY-SEVEN

Aubrey did not go to lunch with Dwane, Stephanie, and the boys. He had planned to go, but he changed his mind when Spike raised the stakes with his scurrilous appeal to raw prejudice. Spike had cast the trial, and his plea for Cody's acquittal, as the last line of defense against evil outsiders intent on destroying the culture and the way of life in Campbell County, Arkansas.

Aubrey told Stephanie he needed some private time to rethink his closing argument. She offered to bring him a blue-plate special from Ma Phipps's, but he said he would eat later, when the jury retired to deliberate. He did not tell Stephanie or Dwane that he was worried, but he was. His mind was racing, replaying Spike's argument.

The outline of what he intended to say to the jury was on the table before him, but Aubrey was not looking at it, nor was he scribbling notes. He just sat there, staring out the window, thinking.

I have to change my style. My argument's OK, but my laid-back nature won't get the job done. I've got to show indignation; soft-pedaling won't do. I've got to fight fire with fire without stooping to Spike's level. He is coaxing the jury to let their prejudices run wild, urging them to ignore their duty. The same disease infected the sheriff and prosecutor back in 1968. They chose to be indifferent—turned a blind eye—to the lynching of Ike Swanson. Old Blacky Blackburn was right about me, too. I wasn't prejudiced, but I did sink into a spell of indifference because I didn't want to face the truth and fight. And that is worse than being prejudiced.

This is not going to be easy. People around here do not like homosexuality, and neither do I. But, if I do this right—if I can get the jurors to see this the way I see it—they will reject Spike's demagoguery. They will not turn a blind eye.

How's that, Prissy?

—~—

Zach and the boys rolled Dwane into the office, and Stephanie was close behind. Aubrey heard the commotion and came out of the conference room. "I brought you a sandwich just in case," Stephanie said.

"Good. I'm hungry, now."

Dwane said, "Does that mean you have figured out whatever it was that was bugging you?"

Aubrey, not given to cussing, said, "Damn straight. I'm fixing to give Spike Spivey a lesson in civility."

Stephanie saw fire in Aubrey's eyes. She smiled and gave him double-thumbs up.

Zach had his eye on the prosecutors. He saw mutual respect, but he also saw love, and it did not surprise him. He nodded his approval just as Eight Ball jammed his fist into the sky and said, "All right!"

—~—

Judge Oglethorpe, gaveled the court into session and recognized Aubrey to give the final argument for the prosecution.

Aubrey looked squarely at the jurors, one at a time, as he approached the lectern. Like Stephanie, he took no notes or documents with him. He paid his respects to the court, and then he began, his voice steady but soft.

"Ladies and gentlemen, I am not here to convict anyone. Oh yes, I filed the charges, and I believe that the evidence and law, so ably summarized by my deputy prosecutor, justifies a finding of guilty. But that decision is yours, not mine. My duty is to lay the evidence before you so that you, guided by the court's instructions, might reach a sensible and just verdict."

He pointed toward Spike. "Mr. Spivey and I are on opposite sides of the case, but this is not a contest. It is not a prizefight." Aubrey added a little volume and a touch of indignation. "This is a search for truth and justice. I know that sounds corny, perhaps melodramatic, but it is something I need to say, and soon you will see why." Aubrey knew that the jurors would hold him to that, but first he had to lay a foundation.

"Spike Spivey doesn't have a good case and he knows it, so he talked about something he calls 'homosexual panic,' although he sometimes calls it 'gay panic.' He also told you that you do not have to follow the instructions of law that the judge has given to you.

"If he had done that and nothing more, I wouldn't need to talk very long, because you have spent two weeks listening to the proof, and my deputy covered all that in her closing argument. Unfortunately, that is not the case. Mr. Spivey did not stop there. He has taken an approach that I must answer."

Aubrey stopped and heaved a sigh, as if he hated to go on. Then, with as much indignation as he could muster, he poked his thumb toward the defense table and said, "He doesn't want you to search for truth or justice. He has used every trick in the book to poison your minds. He is probing, agitating, and searching for the prejudice that may be hiding deep in your heart, so deep that you don't know it is there, much less how it got there. He does this to blind you—"

Spike jumped to his feet, "You Honor, I resent the insinuation—"

Aubrey said, "It is not an insinuation, Your Honor. I meant exactly what I said, nothing less. Spike made a direct appeal to prejudice in his closing argument. And I mean to deal with it, openly."

Judge Oglethorpe quickly addressed the jury. "Arguments of counsel are just that. As jurors, you are entitled to judge for yourself whether they are well founded." His cursory response signaled to Aubrey that the judge was not going to intervene.

Aubrey could feel his blood pulsing. He was tempted to stay on the issue of prejudice, but he decided to let it simmer.

"Ladies and gentlemen, I'm not finished with that issue. I'll come back to it shortly, but first I need to talk about Spike's attempt to get you to ignore the law."

—∾—

"Queer-lover! Aubrey Hatfield is a queer-lover!" One of George Freemont's anti-homosexual protesters could take no more. He was on his feet, shouting. Judge Oglethorpe demanded order and told the old bailiff and a deputy sheriff to remove the man from the courtroom. People in the front rows stood up to see the action, and that blocked Aubrey's view. By the time he got to where he could see what was going on, the protester was scuffling with the deputy sheriff, and the old bailiff was sitting on the floor in the center aisle, rubbing his head. The deputy managed to get a hammerlock on the man and started pushing him toward the exit, but he was still hollering. "Queer-lover! You should've stuck to running a hardware store. You are a disgrace."

At first, Aubrey thought the outburst might help Spike, but then he realized the man had done him a favor. The idiot protester was a living example of prejudice in action. Aubrey resolved to use the incident later on in his argument.

"As I was saying." Aubrey grinned, shrugged his shoulders, and paused long enough for the jurors to see that the verbal assault did not bother him. Half of the jurors smiled; the other half sat stone-faced.

"I love the old story Spike told about William Penn. It is a story about the power you have, as jurors, to perfect the law. Notice that I said 'perfect the law.' I did not say 'ignore the law.'" Aubrey pointed to the double doors leading out of the courtroom. "If we are going to ignore the law, then we do not have to be here. We could just go through those doors and head over to Gentry's Pharmacy. The coffee klatch meets there every morning, and it only takes a few minutes for them to decide cases like this. Heck, I was there one morning and we retried the entire O. J. Simpson case in less time than it took me to finish off my cinnamon roll."

Seven jurors laughed aloud, but the other five were still stone-faced. Aubrey took it as a sign of progress, but he had more to say on the subject of jury nullification.

"The law is not perfect, but it is pretty doggone good. Sometimes we need to tweak it to get it right, and that is a job for the legislature. Sometimes we need an interpretation of the law, and that is a job for the courts. Your job is to follow the law as written by the legislature and interpreted by the court, but there are times when people are fussing and disagreeing so much that we need a way to make sure that the law reflects the conscience of the community."

Aubrey looked at the stonefaces. "That's where you come in, and that's what the old William Penn case is about. That is what juries are for—to fix things that need fixing. Nobody is forcing you; we can thank William Penn for that. You are free to decide this case, and if you need to tweak the law to perfect it, then tweak it. But don't ignore it."

One of the stonefaces seemed to squirm. *I'm sure he did,* Aubrey thought. *Good—I'm making progress. But I had better say more about why they need to follow the law.*

"The judge read the instructions of law that apply in this case." Aubrey paused and rubbed his chin. "I know you recognize those laws. They have stood the test of time. The laws of murder and manslaughter, self-defense, insanity—these are laws we learned about as children. They have been around for centuries, and they have been thoroughly tweaked."

Aubrey motioned toward Spike. "The defense counsel knows what I have just said is the truth, so he has hung his hat on something he calls 'homosexual panic.' There is no law by that name. It is just an argument that Spike is making. Many prosecutors would have objected, saying there is no such thing as 'homosexual panic.' I thought about doing that, but then I came to my senses. Spike is a clever lawyer; if I had tried to blindfold you, he would have slipped his argument in, here and there, and I would have been jumping up and down asking the judge to tell you to ignore it. You and I know that it is impossible to unring a bell, so I decided to take a different approach. I decided we ought to talk openly about Spike's argument."

"Now, let me say something you wouldn't expect a prosecutor to say." Aubrey looked at Juror Number Two, a woman who seemed to be buying what Aubrey was selling. "In all honesty you all might find Spike's argument sufficient as a partial excuse. You might find that Cody was provoked and that he went into some sort of panic. That wouldn't set him free, but it could justify reducing the charge from second-degree murder to manslaughter."

Aubrey let his concession sink in, for effect. The stonefaces seemed to like it, but they returned to their default demeanor as soon as he said, "I would not agree with you on that, because Cody did not need to hit Randy. He should have just gotten out of the car and gone on with his run. If he had done that, we would not be here. But he did hit Randy—not once but five times, with a five-pound dumbbell.

"That is not a reasonable excuse for taking a man's life, and that is why I charged Cody with second-degree murder."

Aubrey stepped to the counsel table and took a sip of water, pausing long enough to get some sign of approval from Stephanie. He got a small wink, or was it a twinkle? He was not sure, but at least she did not roll her eyes.

"Ladies and gentlemen, I will now come back to what I said earlier. Spike is trying to blind you with prejudice. He is not looking for truth and justice, and he is not looking for you to reduce the charge to manslaughter. He wants you to ignore the law and turn Cody loose, a complete acquittal. That is the real reason for his argument about 'homosexual panic.' It is a contrivance—a way for him to tap into irrational fears, revulsion, and hatred towards homosexuals. The Bible tells us to love our fellow man, but Spike figures he can get you to forget that if he stirs up enough prejudice. Think about the man they had to drag out of this courtroom a few minutes ago. How do you think he would vote if he were sitting in that jury box with you? My guess is he would let Cody walk free even though he beat another human being to death with a five-pound dumbbell."

One stoneface got stonier, but Aubrey felt good about the other jurors, especially the ones who had laughed when he smiled and made a funny after the protester called him "a queer-lover." He felt so confident that he decided it was time to stop the occasional shows of indignity. He shifted to serious and soft-spoken, a style that came naturally to him.

"My wife, Prissy, who died in childbirth almost forty years ago, was fond of saying, 'We should not turn a blind eye to our prejudices.' She believed our differences are the root cause of prejudice. This case forces us to think about our differences, and as we do that, we reveal the greatest of all human failings—indifference.

"We all push things out of our consciousness from time to time, but in this court of law, we do not have that luxury. It is our duty to recognize prejudice and deal with it, for if we do not, we cannot do justice. Put simply: We cannot tolerate indifference in the courtroom."

Aubrey did not like the look he got from one of the stonefaces, but he was sure that Juror Number Two was with him.

"Speaking of differences and indifference, I know that our culture here in the hills does not approve of homosexuality. I do not agree with it myself. I would rather it not exist, but it does exist. It has existed throughout the ages. The challenge for us is to be fair when we are working on a case like this, one that repulses us and goes against our culture.

"Is it OK for a man to kill a homosexual man who tries to have homosexual sex with him?" He paused and added, "What if the attempt is nonviolent?

"Spike urges you to find that it is OK to kill the homosexual man even if it is nonviolent, but what would that say about the conscience of our community? What would such a verdict say to our young people, to all the good people in Campbell County? What would it say to the world? If we are indifferent, if we allow prejudice to twist and distort our conscience, how then shall we live?"

Aubrey knew he was getting a little preachy, but he carried on.

"Spike says you should use common sense, but that is just another not-so-clever way to ask you to forsake the law. To reject laws that we have used and trusted for hundreds of years, laws written by the legislature and carefully reviewed by our courts.

"I urge you to reject his ill-conceived notion and see his demagoguery for what it is."

Aubrey could see that the jurors were listening, but he did not want to make the mistake that speakers often make—repeating points already made or speaking too long. He considered stopping and took a step back, but then he changed his mind. He had one more thing he was determined to say. It was sensitive, but he was going to say it anyway.

"Now, you may be saying to yourself: 'Not to worry, Mr. Prosecutor—I am not biased.'" Aubrey took a step back and pointed to himself. "I wish I could say that, but I think of the scripture, 'Who can understand the error of his ways? Cleanse me from my secret faults.'"

"When Spike Spivey appeals to your emotions—for instance, when he tries to say Randy Trice was a monster, he is whispering to the devil in you. Those secret faults, the error of our ways.

"Our better angels tell us to overcome our greatest vice: the refusal to see wrong and do something about it.

"George Bernard Shaw said it well: 'Indifference is the essence of inhumanity.'"

It was time to stop. Aubrey took time to look into the eyes of each juror. Then he said, "I ask you to follow the law. I ask you to do justice."

When he turned and headed back to the counsel table, Stephanie gave him a look that he had not seen before. Dwane and the boys seemed satisfied, but Spike pursed his lips and, in a mocking gesture, made the sign of the cross.

Aubrey took his seat, and Judge Oglethorpe said, "Ladies and gentlemen of the jury, you have now heard all the evidence, the instructions of law, and the arguments of counsel. It is time for you to retire to the jury room to begin your deliberations." When they were gone, he said, "For the record, the jury retired to deliberate at 3:30 p.m., Monday, August 13th. The court is in recess, awaiting word from the jury."

Stephanie gave Aubrey a hug, not a lovey-dovey hug, just a professional hug. Dwane and the boys seemed happy, and the family of Randy Trice thanked Aubrey for the way he had handled the case. Timmy Harper, Randy's lover, said nothing, but he gave Aubrey a nod of appreciation. Then he slipped out of the courtroom, crying.

Aubrey glanced toward the defense table. The spectators were beginning to mill around, and the crowd noise was building. Spike was gathering his papers, but when he saw Aubrey looking his way, he said, in a voice loud enough to reach the last row of seats, "Hey, that was a good sermon, Hoss." He guffawed and made an even bigger sign of the cross. "Judge Oglethorpe should have given a benediction." Spike hollered it out, and then he put on an angry look, shook his head and headed for the exit. Carl Ransom followed close behind, trying to get Spike's attention.

Stephanie said, "What a jerk," but Aubrey did not hear her. When Spike marched off, Aubrey's attention shifted to Cody, who was consoling his mother. Lillian Ransom was crying on his shoulder, the first sign of public emotion she had shown. The sight of a boy hugging his loving mother—a mother in pain—sent a flurry of guilt through Aubrey's bones. He thought of his own mother, and the day she died while watching the launch of Apollo 11. And, he thought of Prissy and Bridgette, mother and child, buried together, body and soul.

His heart was sending a message, loud and clear. *I have to make this come out right. The father is no good, but Lillian Ransom is a fine woman. She does not deserve this, and Cody has a life to live.*

EIGHTY-EIGHT

It was just past 6 o'clock when the jurors sent a note to the judge saying they had not reached a verdict. They were tired and hungry, and they wanted to go home for the night. Judge Oglethorpe called the jurors into the courtroom and asked them to confirm what was in the note. They responded with such enthusiasm that the judge readily agreed. He told them to be back in the jury box at 9 the following morning, Tuesday.

—∞—

Funny little odd-shaped cartons with tiny wire handles, now empty, littered the kitchen table at Hatfield House. The Chinese food was all gone, and the sayings found in the fortune cookies had shed no light on what the jury might do. Aubrey, Stephanie, and Dwane were tired, but they could not resist the temptation to speculate about the likely verdict.

Dwane said it was a good sign that the jury had not reached an early verdict and that they wanted to go home for the night. Stephanie and Aubrey were not about to disagree. Neither of them had ever served on a jury, and Dwane had served on four. When Stephanie asked him to explain why he felt as he did, Dwane said, "I think you all have forced them to think, and thinking and talking make it hard for Spike's poison to work. The longer they stay out, the better your chances for a conviction or a hung jury."

Stephanie said, “I hope you are right, Dwane. An acquittal would– “

A loud knock on the kitchen door was followed by the strong voice of Lieutenant Smothers, “Mr. Prosecutor ... Stephanie.”

When Aubrey opened the door, the lieutenant’s first words were, “We’ve got him.”

The jury trial was on his mind, but something told Aubrey this was about Cletus. He said, “Cletus?”

“Yes sir, we picked him up in Randolph County. He got into it with the Mysterion boys, and then got away from them by floating down the Eleven Point River in a fishing boat. When he got to Dalton, he called Junior and said he was ready to come in.”

“Did Junior call us?”

“Yes, Junior called me. He said he tried to get you, but he couldn’t get through. He had my cellphone number from the time when Stephanie and I interviewed him.”

Stephanie said, “Junior is a Godsend. We have been hoping for a break, and this could be it. If Cletus will tell us what he told Junior about the killing of Ike Swanson, we will have enough to get a warrant for Artus.”

Aubrey said, “Where is Cletus now? And has he said anything about 1968 yet?”

“No, he hasn’t said much at all. After Junior called, I sent troopers to pick him up, and they put him up at a fishing cabin close to Dalton. I figured you would want to keep him out of this county until after we have talked to him.”

“Yes, we need to keep this to ourselves until we know exactly what Cletus is going to say about Artus.”

“He’s safe for now, and we will stay with him. I have asked the Randolph County sheriff to keep this confidential, and he agreed to do that. I’m getting ready to drive over there tonight, and I will start interviewing Cletus early tomorrow morning.”

“I want you to do the interview, but I think Stephanie should be there. She has studied the 1968 case and knows as much about it as I do.”

“Good, I can use the help.” The lieutenant nodded to Stephanie, and then he got a curious look on his face. “It should be an interesting interview." The curious look gave way to laughter, and that puzzled Aubrey and Stephanie. It was unlike the lieutenant to veer from professional mode.

When he had collected himself, Lieutenant Smothers continued, "There's one more thing. We had a call about 2 o'clock this afternoon from the police in Mammoth Spring." He started laughing again, but he took a deep breath and that allowed him to carry on. "A Randolph County farmer brought two men suffering from multiple cuts, burns, and bruises to a doctor's clinic in Mammoth. He had found them sitting on the side of the road, addled and talking nonsense. As best he could make out, the men claimed to be in the business of stump removal, and said they got hurt when some dynamite they were carrying in the back of their truck accidentally blew up. One of the men identified himself as Jimbo MacArthur of Campbell County."

Stephanie clapped her hands. "Yea! Sounds like Cletus got his revenge on the Mysterion boys. I can't wait to talk to this man. I'll be ready to go in five minutes, Lieutenant."

The lieutenant said, "By the way, our troopers found the truck, a white Dodge, on land belonging to a Josie Belford. It was a mess, and the troopers said from the look of things, the dynamite did not explode on its own."

Aubrey cracked up laughing. "I shouldn't laugh, but this reminds me of the Roadrunner and Coyote cartoons." He cracked up again.

During all of the conversation about Cletus, Dwane had said nothing. Now he was trying to get their attention. He was waving the little scrap of paper that had come out of Aubrey's fortune cookie. When they looked his way, Dwane was wearing a big smile. "Hey, we pooh-poohed the fortune cookie messages, but get this: 'Good news from afar may bring you a welcome visitor.'"

EIGHTY-NINE

The little community of Dalton, Arkansas, is perfectly situated to serve the canoeists and fishermen drawn to the Eleven Point River. They come from faraway places to this hidden treasure of the Ozark foothills.

Cletus spent Monday night in a three bedroom Jim Walter prefab that overlooked the river a few miles below the bridge. Most of the rentals in Dalton are smaller, typically two-room spartan cabins, but the state police needed a bigger place because Cletus had not come to Dalton to fish or canoe. He was there to talk about the 1968 lynching of Ike Swanson.

Stephanie and Lieutenant Smothers got to the cabin at 7 a.m. Trooper Albert Johnson, a Smothers protégé, came out to meet them. He said Cletus was awake, but he was demanding a cup of strong coffee and a good breakfast before talking to anyone.

Stephanie said, "Tell him we have country ham, redeye gravy, scrambled eggs, biscuits and coffee."

"You're kidding, right?" Trooper Johnson said.

"No, I'm serious. We stopped at a café, and the food is right there." She pointed to a paper sack in the back seat of the lieutenant's car.

"Well, that ought to get us off to a good start," the trooper said.

They went into the cabin. Stephanie opened the sack and spread the breakfast out on a table in the gathering room.

She and the lieutenant poured themselves a cup of coffee and sipped it as they stood looking through a big picture window to the river below.

Trooper Johnson joined them, and said, "This guy is a study. When I got here yesterday, he was working on an old Ford car, trying to help a tourist who had flooded the engine. They were laughing and carrying on, but when I drove up, Cletus turned hostile. He did not run or resist, but he made it plain that he did not like the police. He cooled off a little when I told him I wasn't there to arrest him, and that I was going to put him up in a cabin. But he hasn't said much of anything to me since then."

Stephanie said, "Junior said Cletus doesn't trust anyone in authority, but that's par for the course around here."

At that moment, Cletus came out of his bedroom. He was barefooted, wearing threadbare jeans and a T-shirt soiled from his encounter with the Mysterions and his night on the sandbar. He had combed his hair, but he needed a shave and a change of clothes.

Cletus did a classic double take when he saw Lieutenant Smothers, a big black man in uniform, and Stephanie, a good-looking woman. He rubbed his eyes and mumbled, "What the fuck?"

Stephanie quickly sized him up. *He has a fat ass that looks odd on his scrawny body, but I see a trace of handsomeness that has given way to old age. He was probably a ladies' man when he was younger. He looks like a bumpkin, but there must be a kernel of goodness in him. If there is, I have to find it, because we need him.*

She smiled, walked over to Cletus, and extended her hand. "Mr. Bolton, I am Stephanie Brooks, the deputy prosecuting attorney for Campbell County." She pointed to the lieutenant. "And this is Lieutenant Smothers of the Arkansas State Police."

Cletus seemed stunned, in shock, so Stephanie put her hand on his shoulder. "Don't be scared, Cletus. We are here because Junior Tucker told us you are his friend, and he said you might be willing to talk to us about what happened in 1968."

"What's in it for me?" Cletus said it with bluster and stepped back like a man intending to hang tough. But he did not fool Stephanie. She said nothing. She just stood there and let him give her the onceover. He studied her from head to toe, and when he cracked a little smile, she knew she had him.

Cletus was dumbstruck, and from that point on, Stephanie played him like a fiddle. "Well, it depends on what you say, but Junior Tucker told us you were present at the scene the night the homosexual, Ike Swanson, was killed. We are hoping you will help us figure out what happened."

"I was only there for the curing. I didn't have nothing to do with the killing of no queer, even though I ain't got no use for them. Artus done the killing."

Stephanie turned on the charm. "All right. Well, Cletus, why don't we sit down and eat breakfast, and then we can write down what you remember from back then."

Lieutenant Smothers admired the way Stephanie got Cletus to admit the guts of his testimony at the very beginning. Now they could take their time pulling the rest of it out of him.

Cletus sopped up the last of the redeye gravy and pushed back from the table. He watched Stephanie like a hawk as she set up a video camera and barked orders to the cops. She looked at him occasionally, and he got the feeling that she liked him, at least a little bit. She was a cut above the women he had known, and that got him to wondering what it would be like to take her to bed.

The big nigger ain't doing much. He's got on an officer uniform, but I'm betting the pretty lady will be asking the questions.

Stephanie said, "All right, we are ready. Cletus, you sit there at the end of the table, and the lieutenant and I will sit across from each other."

When they were in place, Lieutenant Smothers asked Cletus to give his full name, date of birth, and other identifying information, and Cletus did that. Then the lieutenant asked him to tell where he was living, and what he was doing in 1968. Cletus looked at Stephanie to see if that is how she wanted him to start. When she nodded her approval and smiled, Cletus opened up.

"I was doing shade-tree mechanic work out of a trailer on my maw's place up at Draco. It's all I've ever done, and it's what I did when I was in the Army."

The lieutenant said, "Did you know Artus MacArthur back then?"

"You know I did. I already said as much."

Stephanie said, "Cletus, we know what you told Junior, and what you told us, but we are videotaping this, so you need to start from scratch. It's important for us to get what you know on the record. Will you help me do that?"

Damn, this chickadee has got my number. Oh well, might as well make her happy. Who knows what will come of it?

"Yeah, OK. When I got home from the Army, I went to a little church one Sunday with a girl I was trying to get close to, and that's where I met Artus. He was the preacher. I ain't never been much of a church-goer, but some boys I met that morning said Artus was an apostle. Said he had special powers like a prophet. They said I ought to come to a meeting of the Mysterions, an outfit Artus started that was outside the church. They said it was different, that they liked it more than church. So I thought I would try it.

"I went to a meeting, and it was interesting. Artus had figured out all the things that were going wrong with the country. He had boiled it all down to the perverts and the commies. He said he knew he was right, because God had given him a gift. He said he could tell the secret meaning of scripture, that he understood the mysteries of the Bible. That is why he named it Mysterions."

Stephanie said, "So what did Artus want the Mysterions to do about it, the problems facing the country?"

"Artus had studied it out, and it sounded real good, back then. I joined up, and right after I started going to the meetings, Artus told us he had come up with a new way to stop the perverts from ruining our way of life."

"What did he mean by that?" Stephanie said.

"He said the scriptures were telling him that we ought to cure the queers. He said you can't cure Jews or nig–, uh, black people, but you could cure queers. He said it didn't do no good to preach against them, and bitch about perverts. He said there was a cure, and it was our duty as Mysterions to use it."

Cletus asked Trooper Johnson if he could get another cup of coffee. The trooper brought it to him, and Cletus continued.

"That's when Artus said he was going to start by curing the queer that had just moved to Woodville to run the grocery store. He told us we could see how it works if we would meet him at the old Spradlin Mule Farm that night."

Stephanie said, "Did you go? Who was there, and what happened?"

"I went with two other boys, James Stark and Sleepy Martin, just to see what it was all about. I guess I was curious about it. When we got there, we saw three trucks and a light coming from down by Muleshoe Creek. We headed down there, and when we got to where they could see us, Artus said, 'Here's some more of the boys. We can get started now.' They had the queer, Ike, all tied up and stripped down."

Cletus hesitated and looked at Stephanie. "This next part gets pretty rough. You sure you want me to go on? I ain't good with fancy words, so I'll have to tell it the only way I know how."

"Go ahead, Cletus. I have worked on lots of rough cases."

"I bet you ain't worked on one like this."

"Go ahead, Cletus. Tell what happened."

"Artus made a little speech about what the scripture was telling him to do. And then he told the queer—Ike Swanson—that he was going to cure him of his sinful ways. Artus took an old-timey telephone and ran wires from it to Ike's balls. Then he got out some pictures of queers doing it to each other, and when he showed that to Ike, he cranked the telephone real hard, and Ike jerked and twitched. When he quit crying and screaming, Artus showed him a picture of men and women screwing. He told him that was God's way or something like that, but he didn't crank the phone when he showed that picture. Then Artus showed Ike a different picture of three queers playing with each other, and gave him another shot of juice from the telephone. Ike came plumb off the ground that second time, and Artus said a prayer asking God to cure him. When Ike passed out, Artus woke him up and started the whole thing all over again.

"That's when me and the boys that came with me left. Artus and the two boys that was helping him work on Ike had started talking about cornholing him with a hoe handle. And we didn't want no part of that."

"Who were the two men that were with Artus, the ones who stayed behind with him?" The lieutenant said.

"It was Butch Porter and Nate Collins. I think they are dead now."

Stephanie said, "Is this the same story that you told Junior and Doughboy?"

"It ain't no story, ma'am. It is what happened."

"Why did you leave and go to Kentucky?"

"I quit Mysterion, and I told Artus I didn't want no part of his catch-'em-and-cure-'em program. He told me nobody quits Mysterion, and I better not say anything, because I had been heard calling Ike a queer a few days earlier at the Black Cat Café, and the cops would figure I was in on the killing. He also said he had it fixed with the sheriff, and I needed to get lost.

"I got scared and moved over to Kentucky, and the whole thing died down. I thought it was all over until this winter, when I heard about the boy who killed the queer with the dumbbells and saw on TV that someone was looking into the killing of Ike back in 1968. Right after that is when the Mysterion boys came to Kentucky and tried to dry-gulch me. Artus wanted me killed because he was afraid I would do what—by God—I'm doing right now."

Cletus leaned back in his chair and sighed. "I guess that's about it, except I need to tell you that I damn near killed them Mysterion boys Sunday when they came to get me at Josie's place."

The lieutenant said, "We know about that, Cletus. They had to go to the doctor in Mammoth Spring. Their truck was totaled in the explosion. But they will live."

Cletus smiled, and then he looked at Stephanie to see if he could get a friendly look, or at least a look of understanding. But he could not read the expression on her face.

"Am I in a mess of trouble, ma'am?"

"It's up to Aubrey Hatfield, Cletus. He is the prosecuting attorney, but you were not present when Ike was killed, and a lot of time has passed since you went out there just to see the curing."

"Junior says he is a good man, a fair man. I reckon that's all a man can ask. What about me blowing them Mysterion boys up? Will I go to jail for that?"

"Again, it's up to Aubrey, but that sounds like a case of self-defense to me."

"Wham bam—thank you, ma'am."

NINETY

The lieutenant and Stephanie packed up the video recorder and left the cabin at 10:30, headed for Woodville.

Trooper Johnson stayed with Cletus, and promised to keep him safe and happy now that he had come forward to tell the truth about the 1968 lynching.

When they were clear of Dalton and headed west on the main state highway, Stephanie placed a call on her cellphone. "Aubrey, the lieutenant is listening on the speakerphone. We are on our way back, and we have several good things to report."

"I need some good news. The jury is still out, and I don't have the slightest idea what they are going to do. Did Cletus cooperate?"

"He did, big time. He has nailed Artus MacArthur to the wall. We have his complete statement on video. We will be there in a couple of hours, and you can see for yourself that he will make a powerful witness."

"You said there were several good things. So there's more?"

"Aubrey, this is John Smothers. I had a call a half hour ago from our lab. The DNA report is back, and we have a cold hit. One of the semen stains from the Ike Swanson crime scene traces back to Butch Porter, who is deceased. He was an early entry on CODIS, the FBI's national database for DNA. He was born in Arkansas but was convicted as a sex offender in Maryland about ten years ago."

"How is that a cold hit for us?"

"Cletus named Butch Porter in his statement as one of the Mysterion boys who stayed at the crime scene with Artus the night Ike Swanson was killed."

"Bingo. That really ties it up," Aubrey said.

Stephanie said, "There's more, Aubrey. The state police say the Dodge truck that blew up at Josie McBride's place was registered to Jimbo MacArthur of Campbell County, Artus' son."

The lieutenant joined in. "We are still investigating the incident at Josie's place, Aubrey, but we did find a rifle in what was left of the truck, and Cletus told us one of the Mysterion boys threw a pistol into the woods. We have people out there right now looking for the pistol, but all of this proves that Artus was going after Cletus. And Cletus told us the boys he blew up are the same boys who tried to dry-gulch him in Kentucky. We are sending photos of them to the Kentucky State Police to see if we can get a positive identification from the people at the trailer park where Cletus lived."

Aubrey said, "Stephanie, we need to get ready to charge Artus with capital murder for the torture and killing of Ike Swanson."

"I'll get the paperwork done as soon as we get back."

"Good, but we will need to wait until the jury is finished with the Cody Ransom case before we go public with any of this. I don't want anyone saying we timed the arrest of Artus to influence the jury in a pending case."

"I agree," Stephanie said.

"What was Cletus like? Did you say he will be a powerful witness?"

Stephanie said, "He is a character, Aubrey. He is rough as a cob, but he comes across as honest. I think you will see that when you watch the video."

"He won't back out on us, will he?"

"Not a chance. I think he is relieved to get it off his chest, and I know he is happy right now."

"Why's that?"

"Trooper Johnson lined up a boat and some fishing gear. He and Cletus are out on the Eleven Point River as we speak."

NINETY-ONE

At 11 o'clock Tuesday morning, the jurors sent a message to Judge Oglethorpe saying they were deadlocked.

The judge called them into the courtroom and asked a few carefully worded questions to see if it made sense for them to continue their deliberations.

Aubrey could see frustration and touches of anger among the jurors when Judge Oglethorpe asked his questions, but he could not tell which way they were leaning. He learned long ago that no honest man would daresay which way a jury was leaning.

Aubrey looked across the room at Cody Ransom, who sat stoically beside Spike. Lillian Ransom was in her usual place directly behind her son, but Carl Ransom sat well apart from her, at the far end of the second row of seats. Aubrey had a passing thought: *That is odd. Why is he back there?*

The judge asked the jurors if they would like the bailiff to bring sandwiches and drinks to the jury room so they could work through lunch, if necessary, and they nodded yes. Judge Oglethorpe then read the Allen Charge, an instruction of law also known as the Dynamite Charge.

"Members of the jury, you have advised that you have been unable to agree upon a verdict in this case. I have decided to suggest a few thoughts to you.

"It is in the interest of the State of Arkansas and of the defendant for you to reach an agreement in this case, if at all possible. A hung jury means a continuation of the case and a delay in the administration of justice.

"You should consider that this case will have to be decided by some jury and, in all probability, upon the same testimony and evidence. It is unlikely that the case will ever be submitted to 12 people more intelligent, more impartial, or more competent to decide it.

"Under your oath as jurors, you have obligated yourselves to render verdicts in accordance with the law and the evidence. In your deliberations you should weigh and discuss the evidence and make every reasonable effort to harmonize your individual views on the merits of the case. Each of you should give due consideration to the views and opinions of other jurors who disagree with your views and opinions. No juror should surrender his sincere beliefs in order to reach a verdict; to the contrary, the verdict should be the result of each juror's free and voluntary opinion. By what I have said as to the importance of the jury reaching a verdict, I do not intend to suggest or require that you surrender your conscientious conviction, only that each of you make every sincere effort to reach a proper verdict.

"You may now retire and continue your deliberations."

At 11:20 a.m., the jurors went back to the jury room to see if they could break the deadlock. Stephanie was on her way back from Dalton, but Aubrey knew she would not be back to the courthouse for at least an hour.

As the courtroom cleared, Aubrey stayed at the counsel table, complicated thoughts tearing at his conscience.

I argued for justice and told the jury it was their duty to follow the law, but what if they convict Cody? I wish I could tell them what is in my heart right now—that a hung jury might be the best outcome. But at the time I spoke to them, I was not sure we could make a case on Artus MacArthur.

Now, it is too late. This case is out of my hands. Maybe I ought to say a prayer. Maybe God can help.

I should have—.

God, I'll be glad when Stephanie gets back.

NINETY-TWO

At 12:30 p.m. Stephanie and Lieutenant Smothers walked into a courtroom that was empty save for Aubrey. He was still at the counsel table.

"Aubrey, let's go to your office. I'll play the video for you, and while you are watching it, I will prepare the information that we will file charging Artus MacArthur with capital murder." Stephanie was talking faster than usual, and the lieutenant had a big smile on his face.

"You all filled the morning with good news, but now I'm worried that the jury may overreact to the strong pitch we made for them to follow the law." Aubrey was talking slowly. The trial had sapped his strength.

"You can't worry about that, Aubrey. Let's go to your office. We will know soon enough what the jury is going to do."

—∾—

At 3:30 p.m. the bailiff announced that the jury was ready to come back into the courtroom. The empty courtroom filled within minutes, and when the judge got the crowd quieted down, the jurors paraded in and took their seats in the jury box. The foreman announced that the jury was hopelessly deadlocked. He said they had tried as hard as they could, but they could not reach a unanimous verdict on anything.

There were a few sounds from the spectators. But an odd quiet took over as everyone looked to the judge, waiting for him to rule.

Judge Oglethorpe declared a mistrial. He thanked the jurors for their service and discharged them. It seemed for a minute that he was going to comment further, but he did not. "Court is adjourned." The judge banged his gavel, left the bench, and headed out the door leading to his office.

Aubrey slumped back in his chair and closed his eyes. *Thank you, Lord.*

He was tired and relieved by the verdict, but his day's work was just beginning. The crowd noise was back in full force, but hung juries seldom produce clear-cut reactions. The sharpest noise was from the gaggle of reporters and TV people who had worked their way to the railing behind Aubrey.

"Will you retry Cody Ransom, Mr. Prosecutor?"

Aubrey and Stephanie were ready; they stood and turned to face the reporters and the cameras. "I will decide that in the next few days, and when I do, I will make a public announcement of my intentions."

The reporters pounced, probing for something that would make a better story.

Aubrey said nothing until they stopped talking over each other. Then he hit them right between the eyes.

"As I said, I will let you know in a few days. Meanwhile, I am right now announcing that I have instructed Lieutenant Smothers and the Arkansas State Police to arrest Artus MacArthur for the torture, murder, and lynching of Ike Swanson, a horrendous capital offense that took place October 2, 1968, here in Campbell County."

The reporters were dumbfounded. They had prepped themselves to pick over Aubrey's bones if Cody had gotten off. They were ready to ask the usual questions about a hung jury or a conviction, but they were not ready for the bombshell about Artus MacArthur and the 1968 lynching.

Aubrey stared directly at George Maxwell, the stringer for the big Eastern newspapers, the man Aubrey had called a curmudgeon after he wrote ugly stories insinuating that Aubrey had turned a blind eye to the 1968 lynching when he was a deputy prosecutor. Though Maxwell was older and more experienced than the other reporters, he had the blankest stare of all.

Aubrey did not get to enjoy Maxwell's stupid look, because Carl Ransom muscled his way through the reporters and got right in his face. "You are ruining my boy's life, Hatfield. The jury would have let Cody go, but you kept bringing up all this crap about the 1968 case, a case that you screwed up." Aubrey backed up, but Carl was out of control. He continued his rant, staying close enough that Aubrey felt the spittle-spray coming from his mouth. The bailiff and the deputy sheriff finally pulled him off Aubrey and got him back to where Cody and Lillian Ransom were standing, beside the defense table.

Aubrey declined to take questions about Carl's flareup, so the reporters turned their attention to the news about Artus MacArthur. Stephanie was ready for them. She handed out copies of the information that Aubrey had signed and she had just filed. Then she handed out a news release that told as much as they could about the case, and how they had managed to solve the lynching thirty-eight years after the fact.

Meanwhile, Carl Ransom had taken his act across the room to the defense table. He was cussing at Cody and Lillian, browbeating them about something, and Spike was at his side.

Cody Ransom was almost in tears but Lillian was not. Her face was red and getting redder by the minute. The demure homemaker was close to boiling point. She let Carl wind down, and then she pushed him back and shook her finger in his face. "I don't care what you say, Carl. Cody wants to make a change, and I am sticking with my boy. You and Spike, the sheriff, and that no-good Artus MacArthur have caused more trouble than you are worth."

Lillian took a step toward Spike and raised her voice. "You, sir, are fired. Cody is done with you."

Carl went back to browbeating mode. "You can't do that, Lillian. I hired him and found a way to pay his fee. Besides, who in the hell do you think you are?"

"I'm his mother, that's who I am. I'm tired of Spike, and I'm tired of you and all the embarrassment you have brought to me and your son. You are a bully, Carl. I'm not going to take any more of it, and neither is Cody."

Carl shut up. She turned back to Spike and said, "Any questions?"

Spike said no. He picked up his briefcase and headed for the exit.

Carl said, "Lillian—."

"Hit the road, Carl, and don't come home until you get off your high-horse."

Cody put his arm around his mother and gave her a kiss. "She's right, Dad. Things need to change."

—~—

Stephanie had just finished her impromptu conversation with the reporters when Lillian Ransom came up to her.

"Miss Brooks, I haven't been able to talk to you during the trial, but can we talk now, woman to woman?"

"Certainly, Mrs. Ransom. I hope you understand that we are just doing our job; we have no hard feelings toward you or Cody. On the contrary, Aubrey Hatfield and I are very concerned about him. We do not want to ruin his life."

"I know that and so does Cody, but we have been struggling with his dad about how to handle all this."

"I saw the argument you all were having. I hope you got things straightened out."

"We have. Cody has fired Spike. His daddy didn't agree with that, but I did. And it is done. I fired Spike. He is off the case. I don't know where this is headed from here, but I'm wondering if you know another lawyer I can call to help us figure it out."

Stephanie saw a mother in pain, but she also saw a woman who was rising to the occasion—fighting for her son. Stephanie wanted to help on two levels, as a woman and as a lawyer. “Have you ever heard of Jake Blackburn? I grew up with him, and he is a good man. He is the grandson of a longtime lawyer who was famous in this neck of the woods, Blacky Blackburn.”

“No, but if you say he is honest, that’s good enough for me.”

Stephanie gave Lillian Ransom Jake Blackburn’s telephone number. Then she called Jake and told him to expect a call from Lillian Ransom.

NINETY-THREE

The Campbell County Jail, a nondescript two-story building made of native stone, opened and took in its first prisoner on May 7, 1915, the same day a German U-boat sank the British liner *Lusitania* with over a hundred Americans onboard. Two years later, Congress declared war on Germany, and the United States entered World War I.

Sheriff Odom bragged that he and his political allies knew how to get around the minimum standards for jails required by federal and state law. Consequently, a stay in the Campbell County Jail in 2007 was not much better than it was on the day the *Lusitania* went down.

When Aubrey ran for prosecuting attorney, he pledged to support a bond measure to fund a new jail, and the vote on it was set for November 2008. Sheriff Odom tried to use the issue against Aubrey, calling him a "bleeding heart," but then a prisoner hanged himself and left a note saying, "I can't take another day in this place."

When Lieutenant Smothers brought Artus MacArthur to the jail late Tuesday afternoon, Sheriff Odom met them and personally took charge of the prisoner. He logged him in and supervised the booking process. Then he told the lieutenant that Artus would get the same treatment as any other prisoner.

As soon as the lieutenant was gone, the sheriff took Artus to a small room on the first floor next to a tiny apartment where the jailkeeper lived. The room contained a comfortable single bed, an easy chair, and a reading lamp. Sheriff Odom's grandfather furnished the room when he was sheriff and used it on "special occasions" when it became necessary to lock up a big shot, usually a local dignitary caught driving while intoxicated. Sheriff Odom's "luxury suite" had another purpose: It insured a steady flow of campaign contributions.

That night, after Artus settled into his new quarters, Spike Spivey came to the jail to talk with his new client. Sheriff Odom showed them to his office in the building next to the jail, and left them so that they could talk privately.

—∞—

Artus MacArthur measured just five-foot-five when standing ramrod-straight, which is the way he carried himself most of the time. His facial features, sharply chiseled, did not give him the look of a prophet or an apostle, but his eyes did. They looked like cat eyes. He seldom blinked, and when he did, it was fast, not slow. He wore the look of someone listening to a mystical frequency, which is what he wanted people to think.

When he sat down by the sheriff's desk, Artus pointed to the grotesque lamp and gave Spike a puzzled look. Spike explained, "He made that himself. That's his grandfather's badge and pistol grips, there on the base."

Artus shrugged and then said the first words he had spoken since Lieutenant Smothers arrested him. "Aubrey Hatfield is the anti-Christ. If he wants to put me on trial for doing the Lord's work, I will fight him to my last breath. There's not a jury in this county that will say I have done wrong."

He went on for five minutes, explaining how he could divine the true meaning of the Bible. Then he told why God picked him to set up Mysterion.

When he wound down, Spike said, "I hear you, Artus, and show trials are my specialty. But Aubrey Hatfield ain't no pushover, and he has already said publicly that he intends to seek the death penalty for you."

Artus sat still for a while, and then he turned his cat eyes on Spike. "What do you think I ought to do?"

"I'll be blunt. They have a few legal problems to overcome, but there's a good chance you will end up on death row, waiting to die by chemical injection."

"I didn't ask you what might happen, Spike. I asked you to say what you think I ought to do."

"I'll talk to Aubrey and get back to you. My answer depends on what he might be willing to do."

NINETY-FOUR

The national print media carried a story Wednesday morning under the byline of Aubrey's curmudgeon, George Maxwell. A five-column banner stretched across the front page, above the fold: ARKANSAS SEEKS JUSTICE IN KILLINGS OF GAY MEN.

There were separate two-column stories beneath the banner. The one on the left was headlined JURORS DEADLOCKED IN RECENT CASE. The story on the right was headlined CULT LEADER CHARGED IN 1968 LYNCHING. Between those two headlines was a picture of Prosecuting Attorney Aubrey Hatfield.

"Thank goodness Cletus came in when he did. The arrest of Artus has turned the media around, even the curmudgeon. These stories are fair to you and the people of Campbell County." Stephanie handed the morning paper to Aubrey.

—ɷ—

The Cody Ransom story was a thorough recap of the two-week trial. It told about the hung jury and Judge Oglethorpe's declaration of a mistrial. Then it told how seven jurors had voted to convict Cody for manslaughter while five were holding out for acquittal. Aubrey said, "I don't know why they report such stuff as fact. I bet they talked to one or two jurors, if they talked to any at all."

There was one quote from Aubrey at the end of the story saying that he would decide within a few days whether he would retry Cody Ransom.

—∞—

Aubrey was particularly pleased with Maxwell's story about the Ike Swanson lynching. It said Artus MacArthur was in custody, charged with capital murder for the lynching of Ike Swanson in 1968. Maxwell depicted Mysterion as a fringe organization, not representative of the culture and thinking of people living in Campbell County. He also explained, early in the story, that Aubrey was a deputy prosecutor for only a few months beginning in 1968, and that he resigned the position when his wife, Prissy, died in childbirth.

Maxwell's story ended with a paragraph promising a followup article to explore why Sheriff Mark Odom and Prosecuting Attorney Fred Cooksey failed to investigate and prosecute Artus MacArthur for the lynching of Ike Swanson.

When he put the paper down, Aubrey told Stephanie, "I meant to talk to Maxwell after he wrote those negative stories that gave the people of this county a black eye, but I never got around to it. I think I will call him and tell him this is a fair story."

"I think you had better wait," Stephanie said, "until we decide what to do with Cody Ransom."

NINETY-FIVE

Jake Blackburn came to Aubrey's office in the courthouse late Wednesday afternoon. He had the morning paper in one hand and a gift-wrapped box in the other. He set the box on the conference table and pointed to George Maxwell's front-page story. "I never thought I would live to see the media apologize for trashing us hillbillies."

"It's a good story," Aubrey said, "but I don't think it is an apology. They never do that."

Stephanie said, "What's in the box, Jake?"

"It's a gift for Aubrey from my grandfather—Benjamin Blackstone Blackburn—the greatest trial lawyer ever to argue before a jury in North Arkansas."

"Hear, hear," Aubrey said, pounding the table with his knuckles.

"Open it, Aubrey," Stephanie said.

Aubrey removed the wrapping paper and lifted the top off the box. He saw right away that it was a set of books, so he took a volume out and looked it over. "My gosh, Jake, this is an early set of *Blackstone's Commentaries.*" He studied the Roman numerals imprinted at the bottom of the leather cover and made the conversion. "This four-volume set was printed in 1791 in Philadelphia. It must be worth a small fortune."

Jake said, "Grandpa Blacky would be very proud of you, Aubrey. He loved these books, and he would want you to have them. It would make him very happy. Don't fuss with me about it."

"Well, I am not going to fuss, but I think it would be best for you to put them on permanent display in the county library with a proper tribute to old Blacky. How about that?"

"I figured you would propose something like that," Jake said. "It's a good suggestion, and I agree. I'll donate them to the county. Now let's get down to the business at hand—Cody Ransom and Carl Ransom."

"You are representing Cody *and* his father?" Stephanie said.

"Yes, Carl Ransom came to his senses after Lillian Ransom dressed him down at court. He is already back home, a changed man. He asked me to tell you he is sorry for all the trouble he caused, and says he will apologize personally when he sees you."

Stephanie said, "That's good news, Jake, but Carl may have been involved in an attempt to bribe a witness, and he may have helped Sheriff Odom obstruct justice by funneling information to Artus. How do you propose to deal with that?"

Jake said, "I've been thinking about that, and here's what I propose—see what you think. How about deferring prosecution of Carl if he will tell you everything and agree to testify for the state, if needed?"

Aubrey said, "What about Cody?"

"I was hoping you would agree not to retry the case against Cody if Carl apologizes, and comes forward to help you deal with the sheriff and Artus."

"Let me think on it, Jake. I need to talk to the family of Randy Trice to see what they think. But they are good Christian people, and I imagine they would like for all this to be over and done with."

Stephanie said, "If we did that, Jake, would Cody and Carl be willing to make a public apology in open court?"

"Yes, of course."

Aubrey said, "Can you bring Carl in? We need to find out what he knows about the sheriff's activities."

"He's outside. I'll go get him."

—w—

Carl Ransom seemed oddly submissive when Jake led him into Aubrey's conference room. This muscular timber man, who had disrupted Cody's trial with a foul rant about homosexuals and sprayed venomous spittle in Aubrey's face, now wore an ill-fitting, out-of-fashion suit and a tie too narrow for the times. He was scrubbed up, his hair slicked and his nails manicured; he was a poisonous redneck transformed. He looked the part of a mild-mannered seed salesman, but an overly docile manner gave him away. The strong-willed man, once mean and overbearing, had gotten his comeuppance. He was in trouble with the law, but what had put him in his place was the tongue-lashing he took from his sweet wife the day before, when she fired Spike and told Carl to hit the road.

"Mr. Hatfield, ma'am, I want to apologize for my conduct at the trial, and for the things I have done. I got filled up with hate somewhere along the way, but I've been on my knees praying to be a better man."

Jake said, "Sit here, Carl." He tapped the top of a chair, and Carl took the seat directly across from Aubrey and Stephanie. Jake sat to his left. "Carl, I have told Aubrey that you want to make a clean breast of things, is that right?"

"Yes sir."

Aubrey said, "Before we get started, let me say—I accept your apology. We all make mistakes, and I'm glad you have patched things up at home."

Carl lowered his head to his chest and put the back of his hand to his face. He paused, and then answered in a hoarse whisper, "Thank you, Mr. Hatfield."

The interview lasted an hour and a half. Stephanie took notes and asked most of the questions. When it was over, Carl had implicated Artus and Sheriff Odom in the ill-starred attempt to bribe Louie Jenkins, a defense witness who would have portrayed Randy Trice as a monster if Stephanie had not forced him to back down and take the Fifth Amendment.

He also told the prosecutors that Sheriff Odom urged Artus to pay Spike's fee for representing Cody, and in exchange for that Carl had agreed to relay secret messages from the sheriff to Artus. The most recent of those messages was about Cletus Bolton hiding somewhere in the vicinity of Mammoth Spring.

During the interview, Carl gradually relaxed. He even managed to smile a time or two. Each disclosure of wrongdoing seemed to produce a happier Carl, and by the end of the interview, he was a new man—chastened, but feeling better about himself. Telling the truth—peeling back layers of guilt and shame—had worked a miracle of redemption. He was once again the Carl Ransom who won Lillian's heart years before.

Aubrey thanked Carl for coming in and said he would do his best to work something out with Jake.

As he neared the door, Carl turned back. "Cody's good at heart, like his mother. It is my fault, not his, that Randy Trice is dead. The hate in me is what killed Randy."

Aubrey said, "I know what you mean, Carl."

"Do you?"

The two men were connecting as if they were the only people on earth. Aubrey said, "I've seen what hate can do, how it takes root. But I've seen worse. I've seen good people look the other way and do nothing about hate."

"You're talking about the old lynching case?"

Aubrey hesitated and then said, "Yes. My friend Dwane says, 'Hate is bad and love is good, but the worst thing is indifference—it's the place where people go to hide from shame and guilt.'"

Carl gave him a puzzled look. Aubrey took it as a plea for him to say more. "This whole thing—Cody's trial and the arrest of Artus—gives all of us a chance to deal with hate and think about love. But to do any good, everyone has to come out of the hiding place. Do you see what I mean?"

"I ain't sure, but I know you mean to do good." Carl studied Aubrey's face and then looked at Stephanie. "Ma'am, I ain't said much to you, but Lillian told me to say thanks for sending us to Jake Blackburn. We're on the right track now."

Jake patted Carl on the shoulder. "Let's go home, Carl."

—w—

When they were alone, Stephanie said, "It is interesting, isn't it? Sometimes you learn more about a person in the-meeting-after-the-meeting."

Aubrey smiled. "Did we learn more about Carl, or did Carl learn more about us?"

"Both, but we also learned more about ourselves."

NINETY-SIX

Sheriff Odom told the jailer to bring Artus to his office. Minutes later, the small man took a seat by the sheriff's desk. "Spike tells me you are going to fight Aubrey tooth and nail. That's good. He's making a mess of things around here, and someone needs to take him down a notch."

Artus said, "I told Spike to tell Hatfield that no jury in this county will ever convict me. Am I right?"

"The best Hatfield could do on Cody Ransom was a hung jury. The Ike Swanson case is almost forty years old. I think a hung jury is the most he could hope for."

"Spike says Hatfield is going for the death penalty."

"Hatfield's a weenie—he ain't gonna do that. He's bluffing."

"That's easy for you to say, but I've got to think about it."

The sheriff was not satisfied with Artus' answer. *What is Artus thinking? Is he getting weak-kneed? What is Carl thinking?*

He scooted his chair closer to the desk, and straightened up. "Have you or Spike heard from Carl? I've been trying to reach him, but he won't return my calls."

"Spike thinks he is talking to Hatfield."

The sheriff said, "Shit. That's all I need, is for Carl to tell a bunch of crap on me." The sheriff looked closely at Artus. He was looking down, fiddling with the snaps on his orange jumpsuit, the one the jailer told him he had to wear. "You ain't going to cave in and spill your guts to Hatfield, are you, Artus?"

"I ain't planning to, but I've got to think about myself. Hatfield's trying to strap me on a table and shoot me full of poison."

Sheriff Odom shivered. Artus did not see it, but the sheriff felt it, and it bothered him. Something gnawed at him, deep inside—something he did not want to admit. Jack Odom, a proud and haughty sheriff, was scared, afraid of shame and embarrassment.

"Artus, you little shit, I've treated you like a king. If you want to stay in the luxury suite, you had better stay on the right team. If you go over to Aubrey, I'm going to put your skinny old ass upstairs with the rest of the no-goods."

He hollered for the jailer to come get the prisoner. When he was gone, Sheriff Odom slammed the door and returned to his swivel chair. He fingered the badge and pistol grips on the big lamp, wondering what his grandfather would do. He shivered again and hated himself for it, but he kept thinking: *What if Hatfield tries to run me out of office?* He took a deep breath and gave a sickly laugh, but the dreadful image would not go away. *Aubrey Hatfield, of all people. Aubrey Fucking Hatfield."*

NINETY-SEVEN

Spike Spivey got to the Campbell County Courthouse early Thursday afternoon. He strutted past some onlookers and entered the building, his overweening manner in full bloom. He was feeling good. He was back. The hung jury had been a disappointment, but Spike had no trouble spinning it as a great victory, "the next best thing to an acquittal."

Explaining why Lillian Ransom fired him had been a little trickier, but Spike told everyone the firing was commonplace. When the media tried to turn the firing into a bad thing, Spike responded to their questions with a phony laugh and a wave of dismissal. "We get fired all the time. If you don't have a thick skin and a high tolerance for rejection, you shouldn't be a criminal defense lawyer."

Now, forty-eight hours after the hung jury, Spike had a new high-visibility client, Artus MacArthur. And he was determined to show that he was eager and ready for another big trial, one that would outdo the publicity generated by the Cody Ransom case.

As he approached the entrance to the prosecutor's office, Spike took the unusual step of reminding himself how to act confident.

I need to be bold, slightly saucy. I'll tell Aubrey he will have a hell of a time proving the cause of death, which he will. The medical examiner that autopsied Ike Swanson is dead, long gone, and so is the coroner. There are always chain-of-custody problems with the evidence. And this Cletus

Bolton guy will be a lousy witness for the prosecution. He's trying to save his own skin, and that's how the jury will see him.

He burst into the office, and marched unannounced into the conference room where Aubrey was sorting through a stack of research that Stephanie had done. "What say, Hoss?"

Spike tossed his briefcase on the table and sat down.

Aubrey nodded but said nothing.

"How's it going, Hoss? You've been getting some pretty good press."

"It's not about the media, Spike. It's about taking care of business, some of which is long overdue."

"Well, you ain't convicted anybody yet, and that's why I'm here. I'm representing Artus, and I don't think you will convict him either."

"Why so?"

Spike went through his talking points, struggling to keep his impertinence at the slightly saucy level.

Aubrey let him talk.

When Spike came to the end of his spiel about the evidence and Cletus' credibility, he presented his best argument: "Artus is itching for a show trial. He sees it as a way to preach the message of Mysterion to the largest audience he's ever had."

Spike was feeling good. He told himself: *Aubrey is worried. I can see it in his eyes.*

Aubrey let some time go by before he spoke. "Are you done?"

Spike did not like Aubrey's cursory manner. It did not match the worry he thought he saw in his eyes. He decided he had better add another point. "If you aren't willing to reduce the charge to something we can live with, then we will have to go to trial."

—∾—

Aubrey had watched Spike carefully from the moment he issued his customary greeting. His demeanor was generally the same, but Aubrey sensed playacting. Spike's theatrical style made it hard to be certain, so Aubrey listened to his entire pitch before engaging.

He gave Spike high marks for cleverness until he made the overture for a reduced charge. It was then that Aubrey knew he had him. Spike was looking for a deal, something to keep Artus off death row.

Aubrey struck hard and fast. "I have a rock-solid case against Artus. Why should I back off?"

Spike said, "It's an old case. Something could go wrong."

"Nothing will go wrong, Spike. We have DNA evidence proving that a member of Mysterion was with Artus at the scene the night Ike Swanson was lynched." Aubrey paused for effect. "Butch Porter's semen was found on Ike's underwear."

Aubrey continued, "As you know, we can prove *corpus delicti*—the death, and the fact that Ike was murdered—by circumstantial evidence. Even so, we have the direct testimony of Cletus Bolton, who was at the scene, and he will tie it all together."

"They tell me that guy can't be believed." Spike said.

Aubrey stood up and motioned for Spike to follow him into the adjoining room where Stephanie was waiting, ready to show the video statement of Cletus Bolton. She said, "Have a seat, Spike. This video is a recording of Cletus Bolton giving a statement to me and Lieutenant Smothers last Tuesday morning."

Stephanie played the video. When it ended, Spike got up, walked to the window and looked out. "What are you looking for, Aubrey? What do you need to back off of the death penalty?"

"I would consider backing off if Artus will plead guilty and testify against Sheriff Jack Odom. He has obstructed justice and conspired to bribe a witness."

"I'll go talk to him and get back to you."

"Tell him if he would rather have a show trial, I am prepared to give it to him. But when we are done, we are going to strap him to a gurney and send him straight to hell."

Spike got up to leave and was almost out of the door when Aubrey had an afterthought. "Oh, by the way, tell Artus it might take a few months before we can schedule a show trial, and he will spend that time upstairs in the county jail. He will not be staying in Sheriff Odom's luxury suite."

—ↀ—

On Monday morning, Aubrey called Jake Blackburn to tell him what he had decided to do with Cody and Carl Ransom. "Jake, Stephanie and I have been working all weekend, but it was worth it. We are close to wrapping this thing up. It's hard to believe how quickly it has all come together."

"You sound tired, Aubrey."

"I am, but here's the deal. The Trice family is OK with what you and I discussed. In fact, they are relieved. If Carl agrees to testify against the sheriff, I will defer prosecution of Carl, and I will not retry the case against Cody."

"I'm curious, Aubrey. Do you have a good case against the sheriff?"

"Yes, Artus has also given us a statement. He is going to plead guilty, take a life sentence, and testify for the prosecution."

NINETY-EIGHT

At 1:15 p.m. Monday, August 20, Aubrey and Lieutenant Smothers walked from the Campbell County Courthouse to the sheriff's office for a meeting with Sheriff Jack Odom. He had agreed to answer what he called "trumped-up allegations of misconduct."

When they entered the office, the sheriff's receptionist greeted them. "He said for you all to come on in. The door is not locked."

The lieutenant pushed the door open, and they entered. Sheriff Odom did not get up to greet them. He was leaning back in his swivel chair, his feet propped on the desk with his trousers hiked up to show off his boots, a pair of roach-killing Tony Lama ostrich-skins with quill-holes that looked freshly plucked.

"Sit down, boys." The sheriff's words reeked of disdain, and he continued to work on his fingernails with the point of an eight-inch switch-blade knife.

Aubrey started to thank him for agreeing to meet, but the sheriff cut him off.

"Now, what's all this shit about me doing something wrong?"

Aubrey said, "You have been working against us."

"Bullshit, Hatfield. You are just looking for cover—some way to explain why you lost the case against Cody Ransom."

Lieutenant Smothers said. "That's not right, sheriff. You have been working against us, and you know it. For instance, I have spoken to Sergeant Nestor. He first denied it, but then he admitted he told you

Cletus Bolton was somewhere near Mammoth Spring. That was confidential law-enforcement information. And you gave it to Carl Ransom and told him to pass it on to Artus MacArthur so he could get to Cletus before we did."

Sheriff Odom glared but said nothing.

The lieutenant continued, "Carl Ransom and Artus MacArthur will testify to that and more, and that is why I need to advise you of your rights."

"Fuck you, I know my rights. We Odoms have been sheriffin' for fifty years, and I have forgotten more about law enforcement than the two of you will ever know."

Aubrey said, "Well, it seems you have forgotten the most important thing—your duty to the people. Go ahead and advise him of his rights, Lieutenant."

The sheriff took his feet off the desk and sat up straight in the chair, looking as he might shoot the two of them. But he sat still until the lieutenant had finished reading the Miranda warning.

"You assholes can't make a case on me and you know it. You are just trying to run me out of office."

Aubrey said, "For the life of me, Sheriff, I can't understand why you have taken up with Artus MacArthur. He forced your grandfather to back off and drop his investigation of the 1968 lynching."

"Bullshit. That's an outright lie, Hatfield."

"No, it's true. Here, I have something for you to read. Artus told us he used this statement that he got from Shirley Barden to threaten your grandfather." Aubrey handed the sheriff a copy of Sweet Pea's statement telling how the first Sheriff Odom stole money from the county and paid her off to keep her from telling.

He took several minutes to read the statement. "This is a trick." Sheriff Odom spoke with authority, but his facial expression gave him away; he was crestfallen.

Lieutenant Smothers said, "You've been had, Sheriff."

The sheriff paused and, for a second, Aubrey thought he had gotten to him. But then the sheriff exploded, hate oozing from every pore.

"You're still trying to blame my grandfather for your own failures, Hatfield. You were the deputy prosecutor back then, and you didn't do anything either."

The sheriff stood up and walked to the door.

"This meeting is over. I'm calling Red Carper. You can talk to him from here on out."

NINETY-NINE

Claude "Red" Carper, the man Aubrey beat in the 2006 campaign for prosecuting attorney, got to the prosecutor's office at 4 p.m. He had just spent an hour with Sheriff Odom. Stephanie led him into the conference room, and he took a seat across from Aubrey and the lieutenant. Stephanie sat at the end of the table by the video machine and a stack of documents.

There was no idle conversation to begin the meeting. Red Carper did not like Aubrey, and the feeling was mutual.

"The sheriff tells me you all are trying to run him out of office."

Aubrey said, "That is partially true. I am also fixing to lock him up for obstruction of justice and conspiring to bribe a witness."

"That's pretty big talk for someone who just lost a murder trial." Red Carper laughed, but the others did not.

"We can make this easy or hard, Red. Why don't I just show you what we have on him, and then we can talk."

Stephanie had started the video of Artus MacArthur. The screen lit up just as Aubrey stopped talking.

Red Carper made a few notes during the first few minutes, but then he put his pen down and watched as Artus crucified the sheriff. It all started, Artus said, when Sheriff Odom approached him to pay Spike Spivey's fee for representing Cody Ransom. He said the sheriff liked Carl Ransom and hated Aubrey, whom he called a "sorry-ass do-gooder." To help make Aubrey fail, Artus said, he would need something in exchange. He would pay Spike's fee if the sheriff would agree to funnel inside information to him and protect Mysterion from any further investigations. In the video, Artus gleefully told how he duped the current sheriff into thinking that he and the first Sheriff Odom had been friends and allies. He laughed aloud as he bragged that the sheriff's grandfather "would jump when I said frog." Then he explained how he had the grandfather "by the balls," thanks to the statement he got from Sweet Pea.

Stephanie paused the video. "Artus is megalomaniacal. The delusions of great power and importance led him to form Mysterion, and start his stupid 'catch and cure the queers' scheme. The man is sick, there is no doubt about that. But he is telling the truth about Sheriff Odom."

Red Carper did not say anything, so Stephanie restarted the video.

In the next segment, Artus told how he sent the Mysterion boys to find Cletus to "scare him up" so that he would not talk about the 1968 lynching. Then he explained how the sheriff's tip about Mammoth Spring helped him find Cletus. He said he mentioned it to Sister, and she put him on to Josie. The video showed Artus laughing about his good fortune to stumble onto Cletus' hiding place, but then he said, "He damn near killed my boy, Jimbo. Blew his truck sky high."

Aubrey signaled Stephanie to pause the video. "Artus' son, Jimbo MacArthur, and that other Mysterion boy are also in custody, and they have given statements confirming what Artus just said on camera."

The rest of the video told of the attempt to bribe Louie Jenkins. Artus said Sheriff Odom sent word through Carl Ransom that Jenkins was willing to testify that Randy Trice had attacked him sexually. Jenkins said he would get on the witness stand and make Randy into a monster if someone would pay him a thousand dollars. Artus said he agreed to pay the money, but "Louie never got on the stand—he chickened out when he was asked in front of the judge if he had been paid."

That ended the video. Red Carper was the first to speak. "The bribery charge would be hard to make. The other allegations make the sheriff look bad, but I doubt a Campbell County jury would convict him."

Aubrey said, "I am planning to give immunity to Louie Jenkins to get his testimony about the bribery attempt."

Red Carper said, "Look, Aubrey, I know you don't like the sheriff. But isn't there another way to settle this?"

"What are you suggesting?"

"I don't have authority to make deals, but I'm just fishing around to see where we stand. What if Jack Odom resigned? Would you forego prosecution, and not file charges?

"It's against my nature; I'd rather prosecute him. But several people I trust tell me that would be a good outcome."

"What about that written statement that tells about his grandfather stealing from the county? If he decides to resign, would you agree to keep that buried in the file and never release it?"

"Yes. The statement makes Sweet Pea look bad, and she does not deserve that."

ONE HUNDRED

The radio talk shows buzzed with talk about the resignation. The news broke at noon on Tuesday, August 21, when Sheriff Jack Odom issued a short statement saying he was quitting for family reasons and moving to Texas to take a better-paying job on an offshore oilrig.

The talk show hosts and callers did not buy it. They excoriated the former sheriff for being hardheaded, saying he was unwilling to work with the new prosecuting attorney and the state police. Several said the old Odom-Cooksey political machine had outlived its usefulness and the county would be better off without it.

Dwane spent the afternoon at Aubrey's office, listening to the radio. Stephanie had never seen the old Marine so demonstrative. He was working himself into a lather, using every expression and all the signs that a one-armed octogenarian in a wheelchair could perform. He gave thumbs up. He did fist pumps. He saluted callers with the classic OK sign. And he did it all with gusto.

Stephanie could not resist. "Dwane, did you set this up?"

He grinned mischievously. "I would never do that." Just as he said it, a new caller said something nice about Sheriff Odom. Dwane stretched his good arm toward the radio, scowled, and gave the caller the finger. Then he settled back in his wheelchair and gave Stephanie a sheepish wink.

ONE HUNDRED-ONE

Two days after Labor Day, snaky lines of people inched their way along, converging in clusters on the grounds around the Campbell County Courthouse, waiting to enter. It was a perfect day. August was gone, and the colors of autumn would soon come.

The media had thinned out. Half-crews of reporters and one TV truck were on hand to record the final steps in the saga that had gripped the nation for the last month. Judge Oglethorpe had set the hearing for 10:30. The doors to the courtroom would open at 10:15.

The activists George Freemont and Jamie Kress had moved on to organize elsewhere. One reporter said they were planning to disrupt a new case in Little Rock.

The freelance writer George Maxwell was there, but this time the big Eastern newspapers were not paying him. This day would bring closure to the people of Campbell County, but the media cares not about closures but about open wounds, especially ugly ones that bleed and ooze pus. Maxwell, now upset by that attitude, had decided to write a book about the Campbell County lynching and the Cody Ransom trial. He hoped to find his storyline on this day. Closure, he thought, was the time when people learn lessons and make resolutions.

At 10:30 the old bailiff screeched his announcement. Judge Oglethorpe swooshed into the courtroom, climbed up on the bench, and called the court to order.

The door to the right of the bench opened, and Harold Espy, a retired state police officer chosen to serve as interim sheriff, led the orange-clad Artus MacArthur and the two Mysterion boys into the courtroom.

When Aubrey saw the new sheriff, he thought about his decision to let Jack Odom resign and leave the state. It was the right thing to do. It would have been a difficult case to prosecute, and it would have kept the county stirred up for months. It was better to end the mess now.

Artus MacArthur stood before the judge, and Spike announced that Artus was entering a plea of guilty to the charge of capital murder. The judge asked Artus a series of questions to prove, for the record, the factual basis for the plea of guilty. It was in the course of that conversation that Artus admitted killing Ike Swanson after he tried to "cure him of the sin of homosexuality." He also admitted to sending the two Mysterions after Cletus but said it was only to "scare him up a little." He confirmed that Cletus had been on the scene of the lynching only to watch the curing, and that he left before he and two Mysterion members, who were now dead, "cornholed and stabbed" Ike.

Judge Oglethorpe interrupted Artus. "That's enough. The court accepts your plea of guilty and finds that there is a factual basis for the plea."

He looked at Spike and asked if there was any reason to delay sentencing. Spike said there was not.

The judge sentenced Artus to life in prison. In the course of his remarks, he told him, "You are a disgrace to humanity. You brought shame to the good people of this county and to the state of Arkansas, shame that we have suffered for almost forty years."

The judge told the sheriff, "Get him out of my courtroom."

The sheriff took Artus out of the room and then led the two Mysterions to the bench. The men, bruised and scarred from the explosion at Josie's place, stood before the judge. The heavier man, Artus' son, had lost his hearing in the blast, which explained why his attorney, Red Carper, was shouting into his ear.

The judge read the charge. Red Carper entered pleas of guilty for the two men to the crime of terroristic threatening in the second degree, a misdemeanor.

Stephanie spoke for the prosecution. "Your Honor, we recommend that these defendants be sentenced to six months in the county jail."

The judge satisfied himself that the pleas were voluntary. He then imposed the sentence Stephanie recommended.

Aubrey said, "Your Honor, there is more to be done—here in open court."

"Proceed, Mr. Prosecutor."

Aubrey motioned for Carl Ransom to come forward.

Carl was in the first row of seats behind the railing. He stood up and slowly made his way to the judge's bench. He looked at Aubrey, who nodded for him to begin. "Your Honor, I want to apologize for disrupting your court and making a fool of myself when my boy was on trial. I know you all were trying to be fair, and I should have kept my mouth shut. I'm ashamed of myself. I ain't looking for forgiveness or anything like that. I just wanted to say I'm sorry and tell everyone that I'm going to do everything I can to be a better father to my boy, who—thank God—takes after his mother."

Aubrey said, "Your Honor, the state was concerned with what Mr. Ransom did during the course of Cody Ransom's trial, but I am deferring prosecution so long as Carl Ransom practices what he has just promised to do."

Judge Oglethorpe said, "Very well, Mr. Prosecutor. Is that all?"

"Your Honor, I have already announced that I do not intend to retry Cody Ransom for the death of Randy Trice, but Cody wants to make a statement."

Cody and his mother Lillian approached the bench, and Carl Ransom followed two steps behind. Cody turned and took his father's hand, encouraging him to come forward. When they turned to face the judge, Cody was standing between his mother and father.

The Trice family then came forward to stand behind the Ransoms.

Cody spoke. "Your Honor, I made a terrible mistake, and I will pay for it the rest of my life. I cannot explain why I hit Randy Trice. He was a good man, and I know he did not mean to hurt me. I should have just gotten out of the car, but I did not. I lashed out, and I see now that it was because of hate. Nothing good comes from hate. Randy Trice should be alive, but he is gone and his family misses him. That is what I've got to live with. I just hope God will forgive me for what I did."

There was a pause, and then Randy's mother put her hand on Cody's shoulder. "Your Honor, I'm speaking for the Trice family. We agree with Aubrey Hatfield's decision to drop the case against Cody. We can never forget, but we can forgive, and we do not want two lives to be lost to this tragedy. We want Cody to go to college, play football, and go on with his life." She choked up but managed to finish. "We all believe that is what Randy would say if he could be here today."

There was not a sound in the courtroom. Judge Oglethorpe seemed to be enjoying what was taking place, fixing it in his mind.

Then, as the crowd noise began to grow, he stood up and said, "Court is adjourned."

He struck the sound plate with one blow of the gavel and stepped down from the bench. He peeled off his robe and joined the citizens of Campbell County.

Sister came up to Aubrey and introduced herself. "Cletus told me to tell you he is going to stay at Josie's place for as long as the Eleven Point River has got catfish in it that need catching."

Aubrey grinned. "Sister, what happened today came about because Cletus turned himself in, and told the truth. You tell him he is home free."

Sister shook Aubrey's hand. "I'll tell him, but I doubt if Cletus is worried about any of that. I'm guessing he's on the river right now, waiting for a mudcat to bite." She giggled and returned to the crowd.

Spike Spivey was roostering around, but no one was paying any attention.

—w—

As Aubrey watched the others, he was thinking and sorting through the pages of his life.

Zach and the Ball boys are huddling around Cody, smiling and jabbering.

Is that a smile on Cody's face? I'm not sure.

The Ransoms are watching the boys too. Carl is smiling and has his arm around Lillian. Good.

Ha! Lillian is laughing and crying. Well, that is a mother's right. Isn't that so, Prissy?

Look at Eight Ball, working his magic, waving his arms, talking loud and fast to his buddies. Zach and Seven Ball are losing it. They are bellylaughing. But so is Cody.

Good.

I'm out of Dante's hell, Mother. No more chasing the banner, or waving away the swarms of insects.

Everything is going to be all right.

Life is good. This is home.

Stephanie wheeled Dwane to a spot by Aubrey's side and slipped her arm around his waist. Dwane looked up at them and said, "Praise God."

Aubrey smiled. He ruffled the old man's hair and pulled Stephanie close.